Lavish Praise for
THE RAVEN AND THE NIGHTINGALE
featuring Professor Karen Pelletier

"As usual, Dobson delightfully skewers the pretensions and politics of academic life while respecting the importance of education." —*Booklist*

"College politics and savvy plotting make this new series a contender for the Amanda Cross chair which, sadly, appears vacant."
—*Booknews* from The Poisoned Pen

"As Pelletier's life continues to expand, so does the possibility of this series being around for a long time."
—*Chicago Tribune*

"Will definitely be a favorite among those readers who love academic mysteries." —*The Snooper*

THE NORTHBURY PAPERS

"Dobson has created an attractive heroine with the courage and wit to take on the toughest adversaries." —*The Dallas Morning News*

"Dobson moves easily between impassioned evocations of forgotten women writers and catty contemporary shafts at familiar ivory-tower targets."
—*Kirkus Reviews*

"Few are better than Dobson at recording the minutiae of academic committee-speak, power plays in body language and jargon, and what ignites a classroom."
—*Booklist*

"An intriguing mystery with excellent secondary characters." —*Rendezvous*

**And Joanne Dobson's Agatha Award–
nominated debut mystery**

QUIETER THAN SLEEP

"A white-knuckle ride through the hallowed halls of
higher learning and through the dangerous rapids of
personal conflicts with a delightfully funny heroine who
gives as good as she gets." —*Rendezvous*

"A genuinely good read." —*Time Out New York*

"A literate and absorbing novel with an ingratiating
main character and intriguing setting . . . a smashing
debut. Don't miss this one."
—*I Love a Mystery*

"A superior academic mystery that reminds me of early
Amanda Cross."
—*Booknews* from The Poisoned Pen

"Deftly balancing its literary and mystery elements,
Dobson's debut sparkles with wit and insight into
college politics. Readers academic and otherwise will
look forward to the next adventure of the smart and
scrappy Karen Pelletier." —*Publishers Weekly*

"A truly stunning academic mystery . . . You'll be all
the richer for this nineteenth-century view of a very
modern murder. A literary and intricate mystery with
connotative power. Watch this one."
—*Mystery Lovers Bookshop News*

"Emily Dickinson scholar Dobson's first novel has an appealing heroine, a nifty payoff, and a beguiling way with the extracurricular entanglements of her teaching stiffs." —*Kirkus Reviews*

"Anyone who thinks the word 'academic' is synonymous with 'detached' needs to read Professor Dobson's tale of seething passions and deadly animosities within the English department of Enfield College. It's a cutthroat world, academia, polished and elegant though the blades may be, and the author captures all the nuances of jealousy and fear that lie beneath the foundations of the ivory tower. Emily Dickinson, shall we say, with a stiletto in her hand."
—Laurie R. King, Edgar Award winner

"A witty and fast-paced adademic mystery. Joanne Dobson has a light touch."
—Joan Hedrick, Pulitzer Prize–winning author of *Harriet Beecher Stowe: A Life*

"An intriguing plot with a motive for murder that's as old as human nature. Good characterizations and fast-paced action make *Quieter than Sleep* an entertaining novel." —*The Chattanooga Times*

"An engaging story . . . a tense confrontation . . . will have readers rapidly skimming pages to see how it ends. An entertaining read."
—*Colorado Springs Gazette Telegraph*

ALSO BY JOANNE DOBSON

The Northbury Papers

Quieter than Sleep

Dickinson and the Strategies of Reticence:

The Woman Writer in Nineteenth-Century America

AND COMING SOON IN HARDCOVER

FROM DOUBLEDAY:

Cold & Pure & Very Dead

The Raven

AND THE

Nightingale

A Modern Mystery of
Edgar Allan Poe

Joanne Dobson

BANTAM BOOKS

New York   Toronto   London   Sydney   Auckland

THE RAVEN AND THE NIGHTINGALE

A Bantam Book

PUBLISHING HISTORY
Doubleday hardcover edition / 1999
Bantam mass market edition / September 2000

ISBN 0-553-57999-1

Bantam Books are published by Bantam Books, a division of Random
House, Inc. Its trademark, consisting of the words "Bantam Books" and
the portrayal of a rooster, is Registered in U.S. Patent and Trademark
Office and in other countries. Marca Registrada. Bantam Books, 1540
Broadway, New York, New York 10036.

Acknowledgments

Colleagues, friends, and family have assisted in making the writing of this book possible. My thanks to Frank Boyle for his pursuit of a manageable teaching schedule, and to Connie Hassett for her always-savvy professional advice. To Phyllis Spiegel and Vicki Saunders I owe much, including good health. Sandy Zagarell and Eve Sandberg read *The Raven and the Nightingale* in manuscript and provided that most invaluable of reader response, confirmation of the writer's own instincts. Frank Couvares gave me one of Piotrowski's best lines. Kate Miciak has been a dream of an editor, and Deborah Schneider a model agent.

I wish to acknowledge scholarly debts: to Cheryl Walker for her groundbreaking study *The Nightingale's Burden: Women Poets and American Culture before 1900*, which, along with Perry Miller's classic *The Raven and the Whale: Poe, Melville, and the New York Literary Scene*, inspired my title; to Dwight Thomas and David K. Jackson for their exhaustive historical-biographical compilation *The Poe Log: A Documentary Life of Edgar Allan Poe, 1809–1849;* to Kenneth Silverman for his biography *Edgar A. Poe: Mournful and Never-ending Remembrance;* but most of all to Edgar Allan Poe himself for a life so bizarre and fascinating he made it effortless for my imagination to take that one further, fatal, leap.

Dave Dobson knows how much he has brought to this

novel—and to my life and writing career—time, energy, endless encouragement, and absolutely vital contributions to the plot. Other members of my family—Lisa Dobson Kohomban, David McKinley Dobson, Rebecca Dobson, Jeremy Kohomban, Myriam Denoncourt Dobson, Bill Cosgrove, Nicky, Serena, and Shea—provide love and laughter and continual interesting developments.

Thank you all.

No man had ever heard a nightingale,
When once a keen-eyed naturalist was stirred
To study and define—what is a bird,
To classify by rote and book, nor fail
To mark its structure and to note the scale
Whereupon its song might possibly be heard.
Thus far, no farther;—so he spake the word,
When of a sudden,—hark, the nightingale! . . .

EMMA LAZARUS, "CRITIC AND POET"

1.

Deep into that darkness peering,
long I stood there
wondering, fearing . . .

—EDGAR ALLAN POE

S HE WHO HAD BEEN DEAD *once again stirred . . . ,*
I read to the freshmen slumped at their desks in standard eight A.M. curved-spine classroom posture. *The corpse, I repeat, stirred, and now more vigorously than before. The hues of life flushed up with unwonted energy into the countenance—the limbs relaxed. . . .* It was the perfect day for studying the horror tales of Edgar Allan Poe: November, cold and damp, with an ominous threat of snow. My mood matched the weather: cold and dismal with an ominous threat of—whatever; I didn't want to think about it. I read on, adjusting my voice to the desolate rhythms of the story: . . . *arising from the bed, tottering with feeble steps—*

"The guy was a necrophiliac!" Mike Vitale called from the back of the room. I glanced up, startled. The other students in my Freshman Humanities class tittered. As an English professor at Enfield College, an elite institution of higher education tucked away in the green hills of western New England, I wasn't used to Mike's type of classroom irreverence—most of my students were all-too-serious about their thirty-thousand-dollar-a-year educations.

"Sorry, Professor Pelletier." Mike apologized, paused, then blurted, "It's just that I *do* think he preferred his women dead." His gold hoop earring and crisp, dark curls springing from a tightly pulled-back ponytail gave my student a street-smart appearance. "You know what I mean? He gives these really detailed . . . you know . . . *erotic* . . . portraits of their corpses. And even when the women are still alive, they look like they have *rigor mortis!* Listen to this." He glanced down at the page and read, " 'She placed her marble hand upon my shoulder.' I mean, *marble hand, yeeech!''* He glanced around at his classmates, grandstanding, "I don't know about the rest of you guys, but this does *not* turn me on."

I laughed. In twenty pairs of dutiful eyes I could see the question: Was it really okay for Mike to make fun of Great Literature? They stared at me, and I could well imagine what they saw: A woman, if not yet exactly *dead*, at least on the cusp of old age—thirty-five, maybe—tall, with straight dark hair caught up in a wide silver barrette, dressed in the height of what was probably last year's style, a long cobalt-blue sweater over black leggings and polished black lace-up boots. A woman long past her sell-by date and feeling, this gloomy November morning, every second of it.

"Well," I said, "maybe it turned *him* on. Poe wasn't the most emotionally balanced of men. In one of his essays, he says that the death of a beautiful woman is 'the most poetical topic in the world.' But, you know, he deliberately intended the weird effect. Melancholy—that's what Poe was after—at least in his poems. He believed that melancholy was, what he called, 'the most legitimate of all the poetical tones.' " I related Poe's account of having chosen the word *nevermore* as the refrain for his famous "The Raven" based on what he presented as a near-scientific analysis of the emotional impact of its vowel and consonant sounds.

"I think he was melancholy because his *heart* was *broken,*" supplied a pudgy eighteen-year-old with lank blond hair and a fair complexion, far more loudly than he seemed to have intended. Still, if Tom Lundgren hadn't been sitting in the front row, practically under my feet, I wouldn't have caught the words—he'd practically whispered them. Sharp-eared little Frederica Whitby heard him, though—Freddie always sat front and center.

As Tom blushed fiercely upon hearing his words repeated, Freddie informed the class; "Tom says Poe's heart was broken. And he's right. Edgar Poe had lost Ligeia, his one true love," she bemoaned, "and all the happiness had leaked out of his life. Nevermore would he find joy. Nevermore—"

Leaked out of his life? Jeez!

"Ligeia," I said, "was *not* Poe's wife. His wife was named Virginia." For some unfathomable reason this morning I really couldn't handle a classroom discussion about the loss of love. "Ligeia was merely a character in one of his short stories. In fact, in creating this tale of a dead woman who takes over the body of another dead woman, Poe was working in the well-established Gothic literary tradition of the Doppelganger—"

"What's a Doppelganger?" Freddie demanded, predictably.

"It's a *double*, of course," Mike responded, as if this piece of arcane information was something every literate person ought to know.

"Yes," I elaborated. "Mike's right. The Doppelganger is a sinister double—a mythic creature who assumes the physical or spiritual likeness of his doomed victim. Along with other literary conventions—the dark, brooding hero, the entombed maiden, the decrepit mansion—Poe borrowed the Doppelganger from the Gothic horror tales of Europe."

Tom raised his plump hand and waited for me to acknowledge him. "But didn't his wife really die?" He gestured toward his anthology. "It says here in the headnote—"

"Virginia did die," I replied, "very young, of tuberculosis. And there were other dead women in his life as well—real ones, not simply fictional ones." My students listened intently as I recounted the tale of Poe's beautiful actress mother, who died when he was only two years old. "And it's been rumored that Emmeline Foster, a 'poetess,' as women poets were often called in those days, committed suicide out of love for Poe. There's no hard evidence to prove either that it was suicide, or that it had anything to do with Poe, but Foster's death by drowning in the Hudson not far from Poe's New York home has become a powerful element of his dark mythology. After Foster's body was found near the docks on a cold February morning, one Manhattan newspaper even called Poe 'The Demon Lover.' But," I concluded, "the truth is much more mundane: Poe was depressed and alcoholic, and he was overly susceptible to women. Women, much to their disadvantage, were also susceptible to him." I thought briefly about Poe's romantic involvements with such women poets as Frances Osgood and Sarah Helen Whitman, but didn't mention them; I wanted to get back to discussing the literature. "But nothing worked out for him. His life was as unhappy a story as any of his tales. Now, turn in your books to—"

The slap, slap, slap of notebooks closing alerted me to the time. I glanced at my watch: 8:50 A.M.; FroshHum, the required freshman seminar in Literature and Humanities, was over for the day. I held up a hand to keep my students in their seats. "Remember, class, your papers on 'The Raven' are due Monday morning. For anyone who wants help or advice, I'll be available during office hours this afternoon. If you haven't found your way over there yet, the English Department's in Dickinson Hall, and my office is on the first floor, catty-corner from the main office. Any questions?" Twenty blank faces: No one wanted to stay in the classroom an instant longer than absolutely required—especially on a Friday. "No? Okay, then. I'll expect you all to have thoughtful things to say about the poem in class on Monday. See you then."

"Professor Pelletier?" I glanced up from attempting to stuff too many books into an already overloaded canvas book bag. The classroom, with its high ceilings and dark oak wainscoting, was now empty except for Mike Vitale, who stood before my desk clutching a sheet of cantaloupe-hued paper. "Can I talk to you about my paper?"

"Would office hours be okay?" I had an urgent need for coffee; I'd gone cold turkey too long this morning. "I'll be available from two to four this afternoon."

"Well . . ." Mike seemed oddly tentative for a young man who was so outspoken in the classroom. "It's just that I . . . I would rather stay out of Dickinson Hall."

"Oh?" Stay out of Dickinson Hall? How odd. "Why?" I looked at him more closely. His usually animated brown eyes had taken on a guarded expression.

"I . . . I'd rather not say." He'd placed his sheet of paper on the desk, and now he nudged it toward me. "I just want to show you my essay outline. It's real short. Does this look okay to you?"

I gave Mike's outline a quick once-over. "This looks fine, Mike—as I would expect." Then I smiled at him—the poor kid looked so earnest. "You're doing terrific in this course, you know. Have you ever thought about becoming an English major? You're a natural-born writer."

Mike broke out in a grin so resplendent with sudden joy, you might have thought I'd just awarded him a Pulitzer prize. "You think so?" he replied.

He accompanied me down the path from Emerson Hall, eagerly outlining in meticulous detail his proposed career path as the pre-eminent American novelist of the first half of the new century. I nodded and smiled; if I were the type of professor who went in for having a teacher's pet, this smart, lively kid would have been it. But, as I walked with him, I noticed for the first time something behind Mike's infectious enthusiasm that hadn't been apparent in the classroom, a darkness like a psychic bruise shadowing the brown eyes. Was this young man more complex, more pained, than one would assume from the naive schoolboy manner? *But—no*—I assured myself, *you're probably just imagining it, Pelletier; you're not in such high spirits yourself these days.*

Then, as I turned down the walkway toward Dickinson Hall and the English Department, Mike suddenly stopped dead in his tracks—you could almost hear his Converse One Stars skid on the asphalt. He went silent, stared blank-eyed at the sober brick siding of the old building. Then, on the intake of his breath, he gasped "Gotta go," and peeled abruptly away from me, heading in the direction of the student residences. *Whattheheck?* I watched him slouch away, a lanky, slightly disheveled figure in a tattered army-green fatigue jacket, cutting through the crowds of neat, mall-clad students and across the brown-edged winter lawns. From this distance I had a different perspective on Mike's appearance, which suddenly seemed oddly altered to me, as if I'd seen the young man somewhere before I'd met him in my classroom. As if I'd known him in an entirely different context, sometime before he'd arrived at Enfield College as a freshman in September. I kept my eyes on him until he turned the corner between the library and the dining commons and vanished. *Who*, I wondered, *did he remind me of?* Then, noting a student from my Honors seminar heading in my direction, I geared my thoughts into grammatical auto-check: *Of whom did Mike remind me?*

2.

"Infection in the sentence breeds."

—EMILY DICKINSON

IN MY SPACIOUS, BOOK-LINED OFFICE in Dickinson Hall a few hours later, I was reviewing an essay outline with another student from the freshman class when we were startled almost out of our seats by a furious bellow emanating from the adjoining office. *"Why, you double-crossing, scheming, careerist bitch!"* my neighbor Professor Elliot Corbin roared. *"You're going to WHAT?"* Even on a quiet day, given Elliot's normally booming orator's tones, it was difficult to avoid eavesdropping on almost every word my colleague uttered in the supposed privacy of his sanctum sanctorum: Today the thick lath-and-plaster walls of this old building did absolutely nothing to mute the raw rage in every bellowed syllable. Much in demand on the academic lecture circuit, the eminent Professor Corbin did not spend a great deal of time in his office, and I had trained myself to filter out his orotund tones when he was in residence. But this particular outburst was impossible to ignore.

"Bitch!" he bawled again. In the comfortable green vinyl chair I reserve for students, Penelope Richards flinched nervously. Penny and I had been discussing thesis development in essay writing, and the crude word tore through the bland subject matter like the jagged edge of a grapefruit knife. *"We had an agreement, and you damn well know it!"* Elliot blared. An unintelligible female voice mumbled in response, and I could hear Elliot choke in muffled rage. Then a chair scraped back, smashed against a wall, and a heavy silence was broken by the abrupt slam of a door. Footsteps tripped off down the hallway— unfortunately in the opposite direction from my open door, so I couldn't tell whose they were—and then all was silent.

Jittery little Penny gaped at me: What was the decorum for dealing with this shocking lapse of professorial dignity? I swallowed—hard—and continued determinedly with my interrupted sentence: "—the single most important cohesive element of a short essay. . . ." Her hand almost steady, Penny inscribed my deathless insights on her yellow lined pad.

This was my third year as an assistant professor of English at Enfield College, snug in both the bosom of academic privilege and the encircling arms of the western New England mountains. How I, Karen Pelletier from Lowell, Massachusetts, ended up at Enfield is a mystery to me; I don't really belong at such a cushy place. Nobody else seems to realize it, but I never forget it. I grew up in a gritty mill town, in a gritty house, on a gritty street, in a pretty damn gritty neighborhood, and became a mother at about the age of this student currently ensconced in my green vinyl chair. An elite academic position wouldn't have seemed to be in the cards for me, but somehow I'd managed to beat the odds.

My French-Canadian father had immigrated to Lowell just as the New England manufacturing economy began to skid downhill, and he swiftly discovered how sour the Great American Dream could turn for people with eighth-grade educations and not a hell of a lot of drive. But I'd had my ticket out of Lowell. Mr. Spiegel, my senior-year high-school English teacher, had insisted I apply to the University of Massachusetts and to every one of the elite women's colleges known as the Seven Sisters. When Smith College offered me a full scholarship, my father went on a weeklong drinking binge that drove me out of the house and into the family of my girlfriend Linda. And while I was at Linda's, her older brother Fred took it on himself to initiate me into the hazardous mysteries of sex. I was nineteen when my Amanda was born, twenty years ago—six months after I'd graduated from high school. Six months after I'd declined the Smith scholarship. Six months after the last shotgun wedding in the history of the modern world.

After four disastrous years with Fred, I walked out, went to work waitressing at the local truck stop, and Amanda and I grew up together. When I signed up for night courses at the state college, I learned that my agile little brain could still be the passport to a life different from those lived in the narrow row houses of Lowell and North Adams. It was just going to be a whole lot harder now. Scholarships, more waitressing, teaching fellowships, and bone-wearying, single-minded determination got me through college and graduate school and into the ranks of the professoriat. And now Amanda was at Georgetown, and I was teaching at Enfield College. The American Dream still works, but it's got a hell of a lot of rough edges. Still, no complaints: I have Amanda, and she's great; I have my job, and—most of the time—I love it.

Today, however, didn't seem to be one of those times. I was exhausted. Nature's days were getting shorter, but my workdays were growing exponentially longer. November is the armpit of the fall semester: classes, papers, committee meetings, frenzied students. Now this disturbing verbal eruption from Elliot's office, which didn't help at all. In addition, I should never read Edgar Allan Poe in any month when there are fewer than twelve solid hours of sunlight in the day; melancholia is contagious.

I'd often puzzled over how any reader could take in a sentence such as "The Raven"'s *"leave my loneliness unbroken"* without a massive infusion of gloom. Especially if that reader's former boyfriend Tony is now married to someone else and happily expecting the child he wanted so long with that reader—okay, me—and that reader—I —had placed her career above home and family and accepted a job at Enfield College, necessitating a move so far away from Manhattan where Tony and she—I—had lived, and now she thinks maybe—

"Karen." Monica Cassale, the department secretary, interrupted my musings, shouldering past slender, insubstantial Penny as the latter left my office, and standing foursquare in my doorway. "Karen, you've got a delivery."

"A delivery?" I rose from the black captain's chair by the desk, and met Monica at the door. "What kind of delivery? I wasn't expecting anything." Flexing my shoulders, I rolled my head to relieve the stressed muscles. I'd been talking to students all afternoon, and I wanted to go home.

"How would *I* know?" Monica had been with the department for less than three months, but her lack of deference to the faculty was fast becoming legend. "It's a humongous box, in the main office. The UPS guy said you had to sign for it personally."

Outside my door, Frederica Whitby groaned ostentatiously, leaned back against the wall and slid down until her skinny butt rested on the carpet. If there's one thing more than any other that seems to characterize students at elite little Enfield College, it's a heartfelt sense of entitlement to the utterly undivided attention of their professors.

Entitlement is something I, personally, know very little about. I don't take anything for granted, including the tenured professorship at Enfield I would be eligible for in a couple of years if everything went as I expected it to. But even the promised tenured position wasn't enough of an incentive to make me kowtow to this rude student.

"Excuse me, Freddie," I said, and frowned.

Frederica Whitby huffed like a skittish mare. She'd probably learned the eloquent snort from one of her stable of thoroughbred riding horses back home in Bucks County. Monica, a chunky presence in the doorway, shuffled impatiently, hurrumphed, and jerked her head meaningfully toward the main office. *The UPS man awaits.* I stepped over Freddie's short, jodhpur-clad legs. No matter how privileged they were, most Enfield students were not spoiled brats, but so far this semester Freddie Whitby had given the term texture and dimension.

"I shoulda been outta here an hour ago," Monica grumbled as I followed her stocky figure in its khaki pants and white shirt into the department office, "but Miles wants the Palaver Chair applications on his desk first thing Monday, and it's just been one interruption after another."

The Palaver Chair. The Enfield College English Department is habitually fraught with factionalism and professorial self-interest. This semester, the hiring for the Palaver Chair of Literary Studies was added to the contention caused by curriculum reform, course scheduling, and tenure decisions. A loyal alum had eons ago bequeathed a considerable sum to the department to endow a distinguished chair named after the donor: Paul Palaver, Class of '29. The previous occupant of the Palaver Chair had died two years previously, and Miles Jewell, English Department Chair, had last month sent out discreet, and floridly flattering, letters of invitation to well-known scholars, soliciting applications for the position.

It was no secret that my office neighbor, Elliot Corbin, wanted the Palaver Chair for himself. It comes with all sorts of perks, even beyond the distinction of a named chair: reduced course load, personal secretary, huge salary. The majority of my colleagues wanted to use the Chair to bring someone new into the department, but Elliot was lobbying zealously for his own appointment and had one or two influential department members in his pocket.

Elliot's furious words were still echoing in my mind: *you double-crossing, scheming, careerist bitch!* Could they possibly have something to do with the Palaver Chair?

"Karen? Karen? Are you with us?" Once again Monica prodded me out of my abstraction. Monica Cassale was an enigma to me. She'd replaced a secretary whose retirement was long overdue, and there was no question but that she was well qualified for the position. But her rudeness was unprecedented in the department—except for certain members of the faculty, of course—and I couldn't understand how she kept her job, much less, how she'd gotten it in the first place.

"Sorry, Monica," I said. I was annoyed by her attitude, but hadn't intended the words to come out quite so curtly. Our new secretary cast me an evil look.

Shit! The worst possible thing a professor can do is to get off on the wrong foot with the office staff: Letters get delayed, phone calls misdirected, memos garbled. I backpedaled: "I didn't mean—" But Monica jerked her freckled hand toward a cart holding a cardboard box the size of a dorm-room refrigerator and thrust a pen at me.

"You sure this is for me?"

The dark-skinned deliveryman glanced down at the sheet on his clipboard. "You Professor K. Pelletier, Department of English, Enfield College?" The question was delivered with a Jamaican lilt.

"Yes, but—"

"Then it's for you, mon. Sign here."

I signed, squinting in a futile attempt to decipher the scrawled return address, then nodded my thanks to Monica and directed the handcart toward my office. I had the deliveryman unload the big box next to my desk. It was securely strapped with shiny reinforced packing tape; I could tell I wasn't going to get into this surprise package without some kind of cutting tool. But, what? Someone had borrowed my scissors, and they'd disappeared into the same black hole as the rest of the department's lost equipment. Nail clippers weren't going to do the job on that tough strapping tape. I slid my desk drawer open: the letter opener? But that was a fragile-looking piece of balsa wood. I was itching to get into this carton, but the shuffle of impatient feet from the doorway recalled me to my waiting students.

"Basically," Frederica Whitby said, "I want to know what I have to do to get an A on this paper."

I was still pondering the illegible return address on the box. "An *A?*" I queried, turning my distracted gaze back to Freddie. Glancing down at my grade book, I noted the marks next to Whitby, Frederica L. Along with the D her first paper had earned were three C's, and numerous x's to indicate her numerous absences. "An *A?*" I repeated.

"Yeah. I always got A's on my English papers in high school."

"Really?" I recalled Freddie's last essay. It began: *Literature is alot like life.* After that it got vague and unfocused.

Frederica tossed her blond-streaked mane. "We never had to do poetry in high school, and I'm not very good at it, so I need some help. I just don't get what you mean by *metaphor.* . . ."

Ten minutes later, mind numb from repeated collisions with the impervious mass of Freddie's intellect, I reminded her that someone else was waiting to see me and ushered her to the door.

"You can do it," I exhorted Frederica's departing back as she pushed past Tom Lundgren and sulked down the hallway. "Remember what I told you," I called after her, *"focus, focus, focus."* She turned and treated me to a petulant frown. In spite of all my advice about concrete, coherent, to-the-point essays, I knew that come Monday morning I was going to be reading at least one paper that began, *Poems are alot like life.*

When I turned back from ushering Freddie out, Elliot Corbin had materialized behind me and my one remaining student. Elliot was an attractive man in his early fifties, tall and slender, with very broad shoulders, clipped dark hair that would have curled if he'd let it grow more than a half-inch long, a high forehead, and well-shaped ears tight to a nicely contoured head. Small glasses with thin gold frames and a carefully trimmed goatee completed the mien of European Intellectual. "Karen," he said, with some asperity, "could you please lower your voice."

My voice! Who'd been screaming at his lungs' full capacity not fifteen minutes earlier?

"I can't have you chattering with students and disturbing me," he continued. "I've got important work to do, and I need to concentrate."

"*Chattering* with students?" I was so pissed, I almost choked. "I was simply doing my job—"

But he had headed back to his office without waiting for a reply. I turned to my waiting student.

"Tom," I said, swallowing hard. "Come in, please. How can I help you?" This was the pudgy, pink-cheeked, blond kid who had made the comment in class that morning about Poe's broken heart. I glanced surreptitiously at my watch. *Six-twelve.*

"Uhh." Tom Lundgren stopped abruptly in the doorway; he'd seen me grab that peek at the time. "Uh, it's really late, isn't it. Umm, maybe I'd better come back another day."

I sighed. This was a conscientious young man who wrote dutiful papers. I hadn't intended to hurt his feelings. "Don't be silly," I said, mustering my last reserves of professional dignity for a welcoming smile. "You've been waiting *hours;* come on in." I gestured toward the green chair.

Tom took one step into the office, balked again, and went pale. "Uhh-h," he stuttered nervously. "It's mu-mu-much later than I thought." His eyes roved around my office, settled on the desk, the computer, the coatrack, the unopened box, anywhere but on me. Then his gaze fixed on the green, nubby carpet at a spot just beyond the toes of his grubby Reeboks. "I sh-should go. You're pr-pr-probably really bu-bu-busy."

"No, not at all," I replied. I was exhausted. I was starving. I was livid over Elliot's petty reprimand. I wanted nothing more right then than to drive the twenty minutes home, flop in front of CNN in my ratty old plaid bathrobe, and forget all about Elliot Corbin—and the entire Enfield College English Department. *Supper?* I wondered vaguely. *Do I have enough milk for a bowl of Cheerios?*

"No, really, Tom," I said. "Come on in." The poor kid seemed to need a great deal of reassurance. "What can I do for you?" I touched him encouragingly on the arm. "Name it."

He glanced at me sharply, blinked, then blushed. It was a full-faced, crimson-to-the-hairline, complete-and-utter-giveaway, infatuated-student blush. *Oh, God,* I thought, recalling his lovelorn commentary on "The Raven." "Oh God," Tom Lundgren said, and spun around on a huge besneakered foot. Face half-hidden in his hands, he crashed out through my office door, then blundered away down the hall.

"Tom?" I called after him. "Tom?" But the heavy outer door thudded shut, and he was gone.

The mysterious box resisted all efforts to be opened. By the time I'd finished with Freddie and Tom, Monica must have gotten the Palaver applications sorted, because the main office was dark. Darn! That meant the scissors and other sharp instruments belonging to the English Department were unattainable behind a locked door. As predicted, my balsa-wood letter opener cracked in half as soon as I applied it to the carton's strapping tape, and I broke two pencils and the tail of a comb before I gave up. The box would still be there on Monday morning. I was never the type to let curiosity overwhelm me; after all, look what happened to the proverbial cat. A ludicrous image of a black cat, stiff and belly up, plunked into my mind. I shuddered. To tell the truth, I *often* was the type to let curiosity overwhelm me.

3.

Come, get for me some supper,—
A good and regular meal,
That shall soothe this restless feeling,
And banish the pain I feel.

—PHOEBE CARY

T HAT WOMAN IS A WITCH,'' Jane Birdwort hissed
in my ear. The night was dark and cold as I left my
office, and I couldn't understand why Jane, this year's
visiting poet, was lurking outside Dickinson Hall, nearly
hidden behind a marble column. Except for Ms. Birdwort,
the campus common seemed entirely deserted, and both
Jane and her odd greeting startled the hell out of me.

"Wh-who?" I stuttered, as I regained my equilib-
rium.

"That one." The small woman in the drab quilted
jacket pointed at a bulky figure just disappearing around
the corner of the college library. The short, stocky shape
was easily recognizable as that of Monica Cassale. Funny,
the English Department office had been unlit and

locked for at least an hour; I'd assumed she'd left campus long ago.

"Monica? Well, she's not the *friendliest* person in the world," I replied, "but I wouldn't exactly call her a *witch*."

"She's a *witch*," Jane asserted, nodding sagaciously. "She—"

The massive Dickinson Hall door creaked open. As Elliot Corbin advanced down the granite steps, Jane put her finger to her lips, as if to vow me to silence, and scurried away into the darkness. I stared after her, until she vanished in the same general direction as Monica. Had Jane been standing there waiting for that one brief glimpse of Elliot? But why?

Lights flickered on in dormitory windows as students returned from dinner and prepared for Friday-night dissipations. The library, just to the left of me, was lit up like the *Titanic*, but the academic departmental buildings clustered around the oval campus common were dark. Not many Enfield professors had as little to do on a Friday evening as I did. A chill wind whistled around the corner of Dickinson Hall and blustered through my wool jacket. Winter was lurking somewhere behind the placid facades of this tidy New England campus, and I was in no way prepared. I followed Elliot in the general direction of the parking lot. Thoughts of the lonely bed awaiting me did nothing to take the bone-numbing chill out of the walk. He got into a red BMW. I got into my ten-year-old gray Jetta. The Jetta's failing heater gave off about as much warmth as a mouse panting on my ankle. I'm certain my colleague was as toasty as his distinguished career could make him.

The phone began ringing the second I inserted my key in the deadbolt keyhole. I counted one ring as I turned the bolt, then two more as I fumbled with my key-ring in an effort to find the other doorkey. On some evenings the moon and stars would have provided key-light, but not tonight, and at seven-fifteen that morning, rushing to get to class on time, I hadn't found it essential to turn on the outside light. I was operating in the Stygian darkness of a narrow porch attached to a small house on a country road with no visible neighbors. On the fourth ring of the phone I found the key. *Five. Six.* I found the keyhole. *Seven. Eight.* The door slammed behind me as I dropped my book bag on the floor and sprinted toward the kitchen. On the ninth ring I knocked my shin on an end table in the unlit living room. Just as the tenth ring began, I grabbed the phone. "Karen? Help!" choked a distraught voice on the other end of the line.

"Jill? My God! What's the matter?" The overhead light flared on as I flicked the wall switch.

"You've gotta help me," she sobbed, "before I do something violent."

"Whaa?" I was used to Jill Greenberg's hyperbole, but my young friend had never threatened violence before.

"Oh, Karen, she's been screaming all day, and I can't make her stop! I've tried everything, and nothing works. Now I've started screaming back. Who knows what I'll do *next!*"

"Oh, you mean *Eloise!*" I relaxed. Jill's baby was four weeks old. The infant had inherited not only her mother's red hair, but, obviously, her relentless determination as well.

"Yeah. *Eloise!* Nothing's *wrong* with her, but she won't listen to reason; she just keeps on screaming. I never heard anything like it. I don't know *what* to do. Oh, I'm such a *terrible* mother!"

Listen to reason? A new-born baby? "Jill, you're not a

terrible mother. You're just overwhelmed—it's all so new to you. What can I do to help?"

"Kenny says if I want to go out for a while, he'll watch her. He says I've just got to relax. So I thought maybe you and I could get a bite somewhere." Kenny Halvorsen was Jill's neighbor. He lived in the other first-floor apartment in the sprawling college-owned Victorian that housed half a dozen faculty members. Big blond Kenny, the soccer coach, had taken on the role of Jill's friendly protector, but I'd suspected for some time that his feelings for her had become a bit more complicated than that.

In the month since Eloise's birth, Kenny had become a surrogate uncle and I'd become a surrogate aunt. Jill needed all the help she could get; the father of her child was five-months dead—and probably wouldn't have been on the scene had he been living. Jill seemed to prefer that kind of guy—the irresponsible kind, *not* the deceased kind.

A half hour later, having changed my teaching duds for jeans and an acid-green sweater, I was back in Enfield, at the Blue Dolphin diner. When Jill rushed in fifteen minutes after the appointed time, she threw her arms around me. "I can't believe it," she cried. "A night out! Just like a grown-up person!" I hugged her back, then held her at arms' length to get a good look at her.

I couldn't get over the change in Jill. A week before Eloise's birth, she'd had her wild red-gold curls radically clipped—a "mommy cut," she'd called it—and, if it weren't for the newly zaftig nursing-mother bod, she'd have resembled nothing so much as an eight-year-old boy from Norman Rockwell Land.

"What're you looking at?" she demanded. Then she gave a little shriek. "Oh, my God! Are my boobs leaking?"

I laughed. "No, your boobs are fine. It's just that . . . that . . . well . . . there's so *much* of them!"

"Yeah? Well . . . every cloud must have a silver lining, they say. I just hope some of it sticks to my boobs. Now, listen, Karen," she said, beckoning to the waitress, "I don't want to talk about boobs or babies; I'm starved for food and I'm really starved for gossip. What's going on at school? Tell me everything." Jill was on maternity leave from the Sociology Department.

I filled her in on all the gossip, then told her about that afternoon's altercation in Elliot Corbin's office. "Wow!" Jill responded. "He actually said *you double-crossing bitch?* Who do you think he was talking to? And what do you think it was all about?"

"I've been pondering that . . ." I paused to order the Blue Dolphin's famous Friday-night beef stew. Jill requested a bacon cheeseburger, extra-large fries, and a salad with blue-cheese dressing. ". . . and Monday is the deadline for the Palaver Chair application—"

"What's the Palaver Chair?" As I began to answer, she held up a slim hand. "Oh," she said, looking solemn, "I remember. That was Randy Astin-Berger's position, wasn't it?" My colleague Randy had been mysteriously murdered two years earlier, and I'd had a hand in assisting the police investigation.

"By the way"—without giving me a chance to respond, Jill veered abruptly off the topic—"do you ever see that homicide cop? The lieutenant? You know, the one that you—"

"Piotrowski? No. Why would I see *him?*"

"It's just . . . you know . . . that I thought he was kind of *cute*, in a very *large* way. And, you, you're all alone—"

"Jill! Give me a break! I do *not* need another cop in my life. One was enough!" Tony, my ex-boyfriend, was a state police captain in Manhattan, in charge of a drug investigation unit.

"Yeah, but you really *loved* Tony, and I don't think you've ever gotten over—"

"I have *so!*" I sounded more petulant than I'd meant to. The waitress delivering the tall, sweating glasses of Diet Coke shot me a sympathetic look. *Men: Ain't they the pits?*

I smiled at her meekly, and stripped the wrapper off my straw. "And besides," I told Jill, lowering my voice, "Piotrowski has no interest in me. He thinks I'm a pain in the neck. *And,* I don't even know if he's married or not."

"He doesn't have that married look." Jill smiled knowingly. "Methinks the lady—"

"Give me a break!" I repeated. "Let's get back to Elliot. . . . That nasty quarrel I overheard probably had something to do with one of his political machinations." I told her about how my colleague had been lobbying for the Palaver position.

"What's his research field?" Jill asked.

"He's an Edgar Allan Poe scholar. A couple of years ago he came out with a book called *The Transvestite Poe.*"

"I saw that on the Enfield authors display shelf in the library. It's got a really hunky picture of Elliot on the back."

"Yeah." I laughed. "The picture's even more famous than the book: the scholar as postmodernist pinup boy." The black-and-white photograph was a dramatic shot of Elliot casually dressed—in black, of course—smiling ambiguously at the camera, with a semi-industrial wasteland in the near background. The book, a cutting-edge investigation of gender fluidity in Poe's poems and stories, had made Elliott's current reputation. It had deviated sharply from his earlier, more traditional, work, ending a scholarly dry spell of over a decade, and establishing him on the contemporary map of the American intelligentsia as a fearless avant-garde literary critic. Thus, the plethora of speaking engagements after Elliot's long academic silence.

"About Elliot's book," I said, cattily, still affronted by his earlier rudeness, "I, personally, thought it was trendy and shallow."

"You think *that* counts for anything? What you, a lowly-worm assistant professor, *personally* thought?" Jill teased. "Face it, Karen, you're not the one globe-hopping on the expense accounts of prestigious international institutions of higher learning."

"You're right, of course. But I'm also not the only member of the Enfield English Department who finds Professor Corbin's reputation just the teensiest bit inflated. Miles Jewell—"

"Oh, I've heard about *that*. Your chairman has a blow-up of Elliot's picture taped up in his garage, right? And after department meetings he hurls tournament darts at it."

"So they say," I replied. The beef stew had arrived, and I speared a potato with my fork. "But that's enough about Elliot Corbin. Let's talk about you and why you're feeling so frazzled. And by the way, there's this little damp circle right in the center of your left breast—"

Jill gave another little shriek, dropped her burger without taking a bite, and scurried to the ladies' room.

4.

In the swamp in secluded recesses,
A shy and hidden bird is warbling a song.

—WALT WHITMAN

S UNDAY AFTERNOON, ELLIOT CORBIN WAS the
first person I noticed as I walked into the Stevens
Memorial Community Room at the Enfield Public Library. The decor of the Community Room was muted,
blues and grays accented with the warm tones of cherry-
red chairs set up in rows before a spare charcoal podium.
Dressed in a black turtleneck sweater and off-black jeans,
my colleague had placed himself directly in the long, thin
strip of wan November light admitted by the room's one
narrow, floor-to-ceiling window. The effect was dramatic.
As intended.

At two o'clock, Jane Birdwort was scheduled to read
from her forthcoming book of poems. I was curious about
Jane and her work, especially since our odd encounter
outside Dickinson Hall Friday evening. And besides, I'd

been alone at home grading seminar papers all weekend:
Anything was sufficient excuse to get out of the house.
One more dangling modifier informing me that *Bloom-
ing like roses, Emily Dickinson thought of her poems as
flowers,* and I'd be tempted to proceed directly back to
truck-stop waitressing. On an impulse, I'd put the papers
aside and changed from my jeans and sweatshirt into a
better pair of jeans, a black turtleneck jersey, and a
cardigan my daughter Amanda had given me for my
birthday, a frivolous thing I would never have purchased
for myself, bright persimmon wool knit cropped just at
the waist. I donned the brown leather bomber jacket
Amanda had not yet taken off to college and checked
myself out in the mirror by the front door. Not bad for
almost forty.

The lecture room was not crowded. A few Enfield students—probably members of Jane's poetry-writing work-
shop—filled the front row. Several faculty members and a
scattering of town residents had taken seats a little farther from the action. Amber Nichols and Ned Hilton sat
side by side without speaking. Ned, tall and weedy, was a
recently tenured colleague whose office was on the other
side of mine from Elliot's. Amber, honey-hued from her
long smooth hair to her slightly tanned skin and beige
pantsuit, was an adjunct teacher in the English department. A doctoral candidate at the state university in
nearby Amherst, she'd had the supposed good fortune to
land a part-time job at Enfield teaching one section of
FroshHum. Neither Ned, chronically depressed since a
nasty tenure battle, nor Amber, habitually taciturn,
tempted me to make any social moves.

Dressed as usual in tweeds and tie, Miles Jewell stood
by the podium, conversing in soft tones with Harriet Person, a senior member of the English Department and
Director of the Women's Studies program. Harriet had

forgone her customary severe jacket and pants for jeans and a purple silk shirt. She had also forgone any hint of makeup, but her thin face with its large dark eyes was striking nonetheless, especially given the dramatic streak of white at the left temple of her otherwise dark hair. I was surprised to see this often antagonistic pair so deep in what seemed to be congenial discussion. Harriet's intent expression and the chairman's air of fervid agreement intrigued me. Without making a conscious decision to eavesdrop, I found myself wandering toward them. A tall display stand offered an oversized folio of local-history photographs through which to leaf. Thoroughly ashamed of myself, of course, I managed to overhear one enigmatic phrase as Harriet hissed to Miles: "I'm not about to let that s.o.b. screw up all my hard work—"

"Karen?" A hesitant voice startled me, and I spun around. Sophia Warzek. Sophia was my daughter Amanda's friend and my former student—and a talented young poet. I abandoned departmental espionage and welcomed her with a hug. Sophia, blond and far too slender, wore the requisite Enfield cold-weather costume of bulky jacket, jeans, and lace-up leather boots. The heavy winter-weight fabrics overpowered her pale beauty. I briefly imagined a makeover for Sophia. Her almost emaciated frame would fit in nicely in lower Manhattan, I thought; with dark lipstick, eyeliner, and clinging layers of Greenwich Village microfiber, she would look every inch the part of the hot young poet. When she smiled tremulously in response to my greeting, the vision vanished. Sophia Warzek had a hard enough time negotiating the relatively uncomplicated social and economic life of Enfield: Manhattan would eat her alive.

"I wondered," she faltered, "if I could ask your advice on something?" She clutched a manila file folder to her chest as if she were attempting to keep its contents warm.

"Sure. I've always got time for *you*." I sat, and pulled her into the chair next to me. "What's up?"

"Well . . . Professor Birdwort asked a couple of us in her Creative Writing seminar to read one poem each when she's finished with hers. I wondered if you could help me choose. That is, if you have time. . . . I mean, I wondered . . . I mean . . ."

After much urging, I'd finally gotten Sophia to drop the *Professor Pelletier* and simply call me Karen. But her general insecurity and habitual deference to authority weren't quite so easy to eradicate. Every claim to individual attention, every assertion of her singularity, took an enormous psychic effort. But at least she was finally venturing those claims, no matter how timidly. Her father was in prison, but the effects of his brutal domestic tyranny would always imprint Sophia's personality. Like me, Sophia had grown up desperately poor. Like mine, her restless mind refused to accept the limitations poverty attempted to impose.

"Hand 'em over," I replied cheerily, then opened the folder. The first poem was entitled "Birdsong," and began: *Lonely, the pond keeps its silence* . . . I glanced up at Sophia, smiled, then turned back to the page: *lonely, indeed.* After two delicate verses on the separation of nature and humanity, the poem concluded:

> *I am not tempted by the cry of feathers;*
> *wings flash ebony and red in vain.*
> *Only one urgent bird pierces my solitude;*
> *his shrill remonstrance cannot be called a song.*
> *Incessant, he tenders his three harsh notes,*
> *cries, "come away, come away, come away."*

"This is very nice," I said sincerely, "this one's a *good* possibility," but before I could read any further, Miles Jewell tapped on the microphone.

"Ladies and gentlemen," he said, gender- and class-traditional as always, "it is my distinct pleasure to present to you this afternoon Enfield College's eminent visiting poet, Jane Birdwort. Jane will read to us from her long-awaited forthcoming volume of poems." The fickle beam of light had deserted Elliot Corbin and now illuminated Miles's shock of white hair, his round cheeks with their high color.

Miles led the small audience in applause, and Jane Birdwort stepped primly to the lectern. She wore a pink suit, and her graying hair was curled as if she'd had it cut and permed in her youth—sometime in the late fifties—and had never seen the need to change her style. The vagrant shaft of afternoon sun turned the outdated hairdo to a radiant silver halo. "So very nice to be here," Jane twittered, then opened her slim book. I settled into my chair, anticipating adept, sensitive poems about birds and flowers. " 'Doing Violence,' " Jane announced unexpectedly, and the first words jerked me to attention.

Night and day to cruise
the streets in my high red boots
screwing all the sullen gang,
cigarette hanging from my lip
like another fang, this is the silent me.
This one knows death,
reads the paper, thrives on rape.
But she is apocryphal. . . .

"Wow!" I said, under my breath. "Wow! Who would have thought it!" Jane Birdwort's demure facade obvi-

ously concealed a passionate, and fiercely angry, consciousness.

"Isn't she amazing?" Sophia whispered, her pale blue
eyes aglow with adulation.

Amazing didn't begin to cover it. I sat riveted as Jane
continued with her startling verses. After the third poem,
as Jane paused for a sip of water, I glanced around, wondering how the audience was responding. Harriet Person
sat catty-corner in front of me, beaming in approbation.
Miles Jewell, next to her, as their seeming new-found alli-
ance dictated, frowned in puzzlement. Both responses
were predictable: Harriet was a feminist scholar of modern poetry and had written a number of articles on the
poems of Sylvia Plath; Miles was most comfortable with
the Puritans. Then my eyes lighted on another listener.
Elliot Corbin had focused on Jane Birdwort a curiously
contemptuous glare, one that seemed genuinely out of
sync with the powerful poems she was reading. It wasn't
likely that any informed literary critic—and Elliot was
certainly that—could despise these poems, I thought.
But, if it wasn't Jane's poetry that elicited such a hostile
reaction from Elliot, what could it be? The inoffensive-
seeming Jane herself?

As Jane Birdwort neared the end of her reading, Sophia began rustling restlessly through the sheaf of poems
on her lap, anxiously scanning first one, then another. I
sympathized. Jane would be a hard act for any poet to
follow. The sweet melancholy of Sophia's bird poem
would surely be swamped in the wake of Jane's passionate voice. But, when the applause had died down, and
Jane called Sophia to the lectern, she went. For a few
long seconds, she stood silent at the podium, clutching
the chosen poem, and I feared she'd been struck mute by
anxiety. Then she breathed in deeply, released the breath,
and began. This was not the birdsong poem I'd seen ear-

lier. This one was called "A Dream of Statues." In a clear, high voice, Sophia read:

> I know this place, this tangle of old night, this
>   clutch of dark.
> Rose trees sprung into a wilderness of withered
>   hands.
> (What strength our ancients grip, our briers.)
> But, no matter. I float along this garden path
> more like a ghost, more like a whimsy, than a
>   woman. . . .

Sophia had chosen well. This was a strong poem, almost in dialogue with Jane's startling work, and the applause was appreciative. My student remained at the podium for a moment after she'd finished reading, appearing overwhelmed by the approval. Then she nodded in thanks, and hurried back to her seat.

Following the reading, I left Sophia to her well-wishers and headed for the Brie and chardonnay at the long table by the window; I hadn't bothered with lunch, and my stomach was clamoring. As I spread a crusty slice of French bread with soft cheese, Amber Nichols sidled up to me. "Karen," she said, "we never get a chance to talk." That was true—mostly because I made it my business to stay out of Amber's way. Something about Amber really put me off, something in her faint, sidelong smile that was annoyingly suggestive of secret knowledge. *Don't be judgmental,* I admonished myself, *you don't really know this woman. Maybe she's merely extremely shy.*

"Amber," I replied, popping a fat green grape into my mouth, "how's FroshHum going?"

"Fine," she replied, much too hastily. "Just fine." Given Amber's golden appearance, she should rightfully have been gifted with a rich, butterscotch voice, but instead she enunciated her words in a thin, pedantic tone that rendered everything she said just a little bit more academic than it needed to be.

"Uh huh," I said. FroshHum, with its semiweekly papers, was a killer to teach, and everyone knew it. But Amber was probably terrified she'd lose the job if she admitted to a full-time faculty member how difficult she found the labor-intensive course. And, for someone in her situation, not yet quite finished with her dissertation, good jobs were difficult to find. In the current academic job market, neophyte English teachers were caught up in a merciless round of exploitation, often teaching four or five courses a semester at two or three different colleges for salaries that could most generously be described as exploitative. My own graduate-school career was recent enough that I was deeply sympathetic to doctoral candidates, but every time I tried to empathize with Amber, she said something so obnoxious she put me totally off.

Like right now, tossing back her silky hair. "Of course, bourgeois ideology in the neocanonical curriculum lends itself with particular immediacy to the deconstruction afforded by postmodernist pedagogy." Amber flashed her supercilious smile.

"Well, *that's* good." I responded, inanely. "As for me, I'm totally swamped. All those papers to grade!"

The honey-colored hair fell in smooth waves along Amber's cheek. If it weren't for the faint, dark semicircles under her eyes, I would have assumed she had the key to all serenity safely tucked away in the pocket of her beige wool pants. There was a long pause. Then she asked, "Are you coming to the study-group meeting?" The nineteenth-century American Literature study group met monthly to share research and discuss developments in the field. Composed of scholars from several colleges in the area, meetings rotated from campus to campus, and often from home to home.

"Sure. Tuesday evening, right? At Elliot's."

Another long pause, then Amber replied, enigmatically, "Elliot's. Yes, that's right. Elliot's."

And speaking of Elliot, I could see him over the adjunct teacher's shoulder, refilling his glass with the fairly decent chardonnay I'd only gotten to take one sip of. "Elliot," I called out, anything—even a chat with Elliot Corbin—to get me out of this awkward conversation. Amber's countenance altered from enigma to chill blankness, an instantaneous negation of all expression. But, when Elliot appeared at her side, sipping his newly replenished wine, Amber turned to him with her customary knowing smile.

"Professor Corbin," she said, "how nice. We were just discussing you."

"Oh," he replied, and his tone seemed hedged.

"Yes. The meeting Tuesday? The study group?" Amber's mask of civility slipped, and her voice abruptly took on so hard an edge that several nearby conversations ceased. "Karen reminds me that it's to be held at your house, Professor. And I do expect it might be an occasion of genuine . . ." She paused. ". . . genuine *revelation*. Don't you think *revelation* is an appropriate word, Professor?"

Elliot's olive complexion blanched. He opened his mouth as if to reply, closed it, stood frozen for a long wordless moment, then spun on his heel and strode from the room. With each step chardonnay sloshed from his plastic glass onto the pale blue carpet, as if he were a Hansel leaving a trail of wine puddles instead of bread crumbs. Her odd smile firmly back in place, Amber excused herself and followed after him.

"What the hell was that all about?" Harriet Person demanded, abrasive as only a full professor can afford to be.

I shrugged. "For once," I replied, "Elliot seems to have found himself at a loss for words."

"Would that the loss were permanent," Elliot's longtime colleague replied, and reached for the cheese knife.

At Amazing Chinese I picked up a carton of General Tso's chicken and headed for home and class preparations. In the car, I kept remembering lines from Jane Birdwort's haunting verses. I'd misjudged Jane, I mused. I'd thought of her as a chirpy little woman of the type Betty Friedan had killed off with the publication of *The Feminine Mystique*. But Jane's poems were genuinely passionate—vivid and immediate—if a trifle raw. Then I realized I probably hadn't read anything other than nineteenth-century poetry since I'd come to Enfield. That was the downside of being a scholar; I was living the most meaningful part of my intellectual life in the long ago and far away. The twentieth century had happened without me.

Once again, the phone started ringing the minute I entered the house. I hastily twisted the thermostat to a temperature that would support human life, and grabbed the receiver.

"Hi, Mom!" caroled Amanda. Although she was hundreds of miles away at Georgetown University, I could envision my daughter's plucky grin. All by myself, in that chilly, half-lit house, I grinned in response. I was *not* a total, abysmal failure with young people; Amanda had turned out pretty damn well. And in four—no, three—days, she was coming home for Thanksgiving break.

"Can't wait to see you, kid! You eating meat this month? We doing tofu for Thanksgiving?" Amanda's vegetarian commitment vacillated, and I never knew where I stood with holiday preparations. "Or should I get a turkey?"

"Sure," she said, with resignation, "get a turkey. I seem to be into chomping flesh again. Just can't free myself from my carnivorous instincts. And, besides, the stuffing's never any good if it's not cooked in the bird. And, Mom? . . ."

"Yeah?"

"Could Sophia and her mother come for Thanksgiving? I was talking to her last night, and things seem pretty grim at her house. She hasn't been able to get her mom to go out by herself since they put Mr. Warzek in jail, and now Mrs. Warzek spends most of her time in front of the soaps."

"Of course they can come. I should have thought of that myself. I saw her this afternoon."

"Great! It'll be good for Sophia to get out, and Thanksgiving Day might be the only possible time for me to see her. On the weekend, I want to—" She broke off mid-sentence.

"What? You want to *what?*"

"Oh—nothing. I'll tell you when I see you."

Probably none of my business. Probably something to do with a guy. "Tell me *now*," I demanded.

"Mother!"

When I'd finished talking to Amanda, I shucked off my clothes, donned my bathrobe, gobbled the pungent Chinese chicken, and called Sophia. She answered with a thick, waterlogged sound in her voice that suggested she'd been crying, but eagerly accepted my Thanksgiving invitation. She even offered to bring the pies. Sophia had been a full-time student on scholarship at Enfield when I'd first met her. Now she worked full-time as a pastry chef at the Bread and Roses Bakery and Café to support herself and her mother. She'd been taking a course a semester, and was just about to complete her B.A. in English. With an ineffectual, emotionally fragile mother—an immigrant from Poland—totally dependent on her, Sophia was limited in her career options. As far as I knew, she intended to stay in Enfield and continue baking her delectable dainties at Bread and Roses. But I meant to keep an eye out for other possibilities. After today's reading, I knew Sophia could make a name for herself in poetry even without leaving town. If she wanted to, that is.

On impulse, I picked up the phone again and issued invitations. By the end of the evening I had more guests lined up for Thanksgiving dinner. My good friends Greg and Irena Samoorian had begged off. New parents, they were dying to get the family holiday train on track, and Greg had already laid in the groceries for a complete soup-to-nuts feast. I hoped their twin daughters Jane and Sally, now a whopping, toothless, two months old, were feeling especially hungry. But Earlene Johnson, Enfield's Dean of Students, and Jill were only too happy to sign on for turkey day. It had been a while since I'd had a chance to cook a big meal, and I found myself looking forward to it. This was going to be a good time.

5.

Quoth the raven,
"Nevermore."

—EDGAR ALLAN POE

AT 7:51 MONDAY MORNING, AS I pushed open the
heavy front door of Dickinson Hall, a shadow detached itself from the general darkness in the corridor as
if in response to the intrusive wedge of misty daylight. I
peered down the hallway and fumbled for the light
switch. The shadow seemed to falter, then gathered mo-
mentum and slipped around the corner. I flicked the
switch and illuminated the hallway. Nothing there. Hal-
lucinating again. That'll happen when you stay up half
the night reading Poe in preparation for an early-morning
class.

An eight o'clock session with my freshmen was a
challenge. Everyone was still groggy. Because I was all
too often tempted to indulge in a few extra moments of
sleep, I usually trotted directly from the parking lot to

my classroom in Emerson Hall, the large administrative building in the center of campus. But this morning I'd stopped at my office first, to retrieve a photograph of Poe I'd filed away with other literary miscellanea. I was moving fast, because I hate to be late for class. Certain other professors, naming no names—certainly not naming powerful, full-professor names such as *Elliot Corbin*—will, without apology, stroll into the classroom five, ten minutes late, open their briefcases, open their mouths, and, without looking up from their notes, pontificate without ceasing until the bell rings.

I don't teach that way. The literature classroom is a seldom-again-to-be-encountered-in-one's-lifetime opportunity for students to engage in thoughtful, informed dialogue about crucial human dilemmas. *Dialogue* is the operative word—not professorial *monologue*—at least, as far as I'm concerned. In later years, a student can always go back to a reference book and recover facts and scholarly opinions, but in my classes we *talk*. How often will a student have the occasion to figure out for herself that, when Walt Whitman refers to his poetry as a *barbaric yawp*, the image has something to do with snatching American poetry from the hands of the educated and privileged? Or, when Emily Dickinson refers to herself as *Nobody*, she seems to think that's a good thing? Or, when Charlotte Perkins Gilman has her narrator peel away the yellow wallpaper, maybe, just maybe, that narrator is deconstructing centuries of male texts that oppress and imprison women? I like to leave my comfortable Enfield College students just a little bit less comfortable when they finish a course than they were when they began it.

The big UPS box stood in the middle of my office, directly between me and the filing cabinet where I kept the

Poe photograph. The *box!* If I'd been thinking a little more coherently when I'd gone to the town library yesterday, I could have brought a knife or something, proceeded to campus, and opened it then. But—there was no time now: four minutes to class time, and it would take me that long to get across campus.

That morning I taught "The Raven." *Once upon a midnight dreary, while I pondered, weak and weary, / Over many a quaint and curious volume of forgotten lore . . . ,* I read to my dreary—weary, bleary-eyed—students. In spite of my admonition at our previous meeting, nobody had come to class with anything particularly thoughtful to say about the poem. Including me. So I read aloud some more: *Eagerly I wished the morrow;—vainly I had sought to borrow / From my books surcease of sorrow—*

"Why didn't he try Prozac?" Today Mike Vitale looked like himself again, rather than like the ghost of someone I couldn't quite identify. The bristling ponytail and gold earring gave a sardonic edge to the long jaw, intellectual forehead, close-set ears.

I laughed. "What is it with you and Poe, Mike?" I teased him. "You haven't been this unrelentingly critical of any other writer."

He slapped his hand down hard against the open pages of his poetry anthology, startling Tom Lundgren, who jumped almost as ludicrously as I did. "I think 'The Raven' is the stupidest poem I've ever read. I mean— *Take thy beak from out my heart, and take thy form from off my door!* Give me a break! That's like a line from some kind of a third-rate computer game—something with a name like, oh, *Avian Raptor!*" And Mike went on to wax even more sarcastic about this poem than he had about Poe's stories, almost as if he had some personal agenda in deflating the poetic reputation of America's Poet of the Terminally Weird.

Most of the other students, however, liked the poem —although they were relentlessly biographical in their discussion of it. I urged the kids to re-examine their direct equation of life and poem. "Edgar Allan Poe is such a compellingly bizarre figure that I know it seems impossible to separate his personal history from the art of his poetry," I said. "Now, Whitman's poems, and Dickinson's, too, would doubtless survive on their own merits, even if we knew nothing about the authors. But would Poe's?" I asked. "Without the legends of drinking, fighting, illicit romance, charges of forgery, Emmeline Foster's purported suicide—not to mention his marriage to a thirteen-year-old cousin—would you still be interested in this poem?"

They gaped at me: Was I kidding? Drinking? Fighting? Suicide? Teenage sex? Who *needed* poetry? And besides, it was the final day of class before the Thanksgiving break; nobody wanted to think about *poetry*.

After class, I stood in the doorway and collected essays. As Freddie Whitby handed me hers, Elliot Corbin pushed through the double doors that lead from the administrative offices. I nodded at him as he passed by in the hall, and slipped Freddie's paper to the bottom of the stack; the sight of Freddie Whitby's prose wasn't bearable quite so early in the morning. As my colleague disappeared down the corridor, I couldn't help wondering what Poe expert, Professor Corbin, would have made of my class's discussion of "The Raven." There had been nary a mention of transvestism; Elliot probably would have thought the discussion was hopelessly banal. With difficulty I jammed the freshman essays into my book bag. I really had to take a few minutes and go through this bag;

it was so overloaded I hardly knew what was in it any more. One of these days I was going to lose something— probably a student's paper; then I would really be in trouble.

"Here, let me help you carry that." For some reason Mike Vitale had again lingered in the classroom after the others had trooped out for their breakfasts. "It looks heavy."

"Thanks, Mike, but I can manage. Did you want to see me about something?"

"No," he replied. "Not really." Cautiously he poked his head out into the corridor and looked around. Then, giving me a breezy goodbye, he departed.

The campus seemed soaked in a clammy late-fall miasma as I headed for the coffee shop after class. Brick and stone buildings wavered in the mist as if they were emanations of the air itself. Students and colleagues wafted by, as indistinguishable from one another as if they were phantoms. I shivered in my heavy wool jacket and pushed open the door of the coffee shop. The pungent scent of dark-roast Colombian roused me from my own personal fog. Dumping my heavy book bag on a table in a sequestered window nook, I slid my tray along the stainless-steel counter, reached behind the bagels to retrieve a pumpkin muffin, then poured coffee into a white ceramic mug and sipped it as I waited in line to pay. Round tables hosted a mix of students and between-classes professors. Wan light slanted through the mullioned windows and illuminated the white stuccoed walls and ceiling, casting faint, narrow shadows next to faux half-timbered beams. A good place for a few moments of quiet reflection before the FroshHum staff meeting later that morning.

I'd scarcely had a chance to take a bite of my muffin when Elliot Corbin plunked his mug of black coffee and

plate of unbuttered whole-wheat toast down on my secluded table and plopped his gym bag on the floor next to
my feet. "What are you doing way back here in the corner, Karen?" he asked, sliding into a chair. "Hiding from
students?"

And colleagues, I thought, but I laughed at his sally,
nonetheless. Being untenured weasels an assistant professor into all sorts of petty hypocrisies.

"That's not a very healthy breakfast," Elliot com-
mented, gesturing toward my muffin with a virtuous tri-
angle of dry toast.

I smiled noncommittally, broke off a big muffin
chunk, and stuffed it in my mouth. *None of your business,
big boy,* I thought.

"So," my companion continued, munching his toast,
"you're teaching Poe, are you? I was walking by your
classroom this morning and heard a few snatches of the
discussion."

"Oh, really?" *Damn.* Why hadn't I remembered to
close the classroom door?

"I suppose it's none of my business," Elliot said,
"but I do think biographical analysis is a markedly
wrongheaded approach."

I sighed, and tried to hide it in a gulp of coffee. What
the hell was Professor Elliot Corbin doing lurking outside
my classroom long enough to get the drift of a class discussion?

"But, then, of course, it's understandable that I
would have developed a far more sophisticated pedagogical approach than you, Karen, immersed as I am in Fou-
cauldian theory. . . ." I nodded, swallowing my sudden
hot irritation along with my coffee. *Tenure,* I consoled
myself. *Tenure.* "And also seeing as I have some not in-
consequential experience with graduate teaching." He
paused. I was supposed to be impressed.

"Really?" It was all I could manage.

"Oh, yes. I've taught several graduate seminars at the state university over the past few semesters. They're only too happy to avail themselves of a scholar of my reputation."

"How nice." I got the words out, but the admiring smile died somewhere between my servile untenured status and my integrity.

Elliot was off, in full lecture-hall mode. "As I advise my grad students, when we literary critics speak of an *author*, we have an obligation to address, not some putative human being, but, rather, the *author function*. When *I* say *Poe*, for instance, my reference elides the man as an independent historical or biographical entity, and contemplates *Poe*, the discursive function, the 'author' as a body of language operating within a social and cultural field, a published, circulated, and commented-upon compilation of *words* and *works* generated by and functioning within cultural discursive formations. And thus . . ."

I stopped listening; I'd heard it all before. I've read Foucault; I am, after all, a late-twentieth-century literary critic and my thinking has been indelibly impacted by postmodernist theorizing. But I wouldn't want to imagine the response in a freshman classroom to the bloodless suggestion that we discuss the badly behaved and deliciously fascinating Edgar Allan Poe as a *discursive function*. I'd rather talk about anything else, even the ways in which *all the love was leaking out of his life*—or whatever it was Freddie Whitby had claimed. In spite of my impatience with the emotional hyperbole of eighteen-year-olds, I do understand a little bit about the loss of love.

I banished the thought of Tony immediately; he was married now, and gone, gone, gone. Another image flitted by: Avery Mitchell, Enfield College's president. Since an evening last spring when he'd kissed me on a lovely New

England mountainside, we'd had only fleeting, and awkward, encounters—mostly over the establishment of a research center recently donated to the college. I bit my lip to subdue my wayward imagination. My elegant and handsome boss was reconciled with his wife and living an exemplary college-presidential life.

"The positionality of authorship within a systemics of race, class, and gender . . . ," Elliot droned. I think he was boring even himself; we both started as his watch beeped. "My God, handball," he exclaimed, jumping up from the table. Elliot's daily handball game was a big deal. He designed elaborate computerized handball schedules around his classes and the classes of the colleagues he bullied into playing him, then posted them on the bulletin board in the department hallway and on the department's Internet website. Elliot allowed nothing to come between himself and handball. Without saying goodbye, he grabbed his gym bag and pivoted toward the door, bulldozing between Earlene Johnson and the student with whom she was in earnest deanly conversation. Earlene glared after Elliot, then turned, curious, to investigate his trajectory. When she saw me in my corner, she raised her eyebrows: *What now? Handball,* I mouthed. Earlene slumped her shoulders dramatically—*Jeez*—and turned back to the student.

I sipped at my cold coffee, and brooded. Guys like Elliot, arrogant, with super-organized lives—and super-organized intellects—get to me. I didn't know Elliot Corbin very well; he was too busy being an academic celebrity to have much time for the junior faculty. But he seemed to be a man who had it made: full professorship, hefty salary, clearly theorized intellectual life, no personal encumbrances—at least I'd never heard of any wife or children. I wasn't looking forward to the meeting at his place tomorrow evening. I could picture the house a man like that would live in: white walls, blond wood furniture, leather and chrome chairs, cool, light, uncluttered space. Just like his mind: fashionably furnished uncluttered space. *The author function,* I thought, sarcastically. How *disinterested.* No need for Professor Corbin to consider messy human lives and messy human needs: All he had to do was deconstruct a body of language constituted within a cultural field.

But surely there was something just a little bit smarmy in Elliot's need to eavesdrop outside a colleague's classroom?

"What're you doing back here in the corner, Karen?" Earlene slid into the seat Elliot had just vacated. "Hiding from students?"

I laughed, with genuine humor this time. "Earlene, I'm not going to tell you who else just asked me that very same question."

"If it was Saint Elliot of the handball court, *don't* tell me. I don't even want to share the same *language* as that man. I can't begin to tell you how many students have— Well, Karen, you know I can't talk about the problems students bring to me. But, you can imagine. . . ."

An icy drizzle rendered the campus walkways slippery and treacherous. When something slammed into me from behind, I went down hard, my overloaded bag flying, books, pens, and class notes scattering. I hit the ground with a thud and an *uffff* as all the air in my lungs was forcefully expelled; then I lay dazed on the ice-slick concrete.

Sprawled near me on the frosted grass, a young boy, a kid of about ten with a cap of tight black curls, lay pale and frighteningly motionless. Five yards away, an overturned skateboard spun its lethal little wheels. I scrabbled to my knees and knelt over the inert child. Open eyes stared blindly at an empty sky. My indignant rebuke died on my lips. "Ohmigod, kid," I gasped, "are you okay?" No response. "Ohmigod!" I shook him. The small body was limp; arms and legs wobbled bonelessly; the open eyes snapped shut.

"Professor Pelletier," Tom Lundgren cried, rushing up frantically, "what happened? Are you okay? Oh, my God, are you okay?" He grabbed me by the arms and tried to lug me to my feet. I pushed him away. The last thing I needed at this moment of crisis was a white knight smitten with a terminal case of puppy love.

"I'm okay, Tom. Don't worry about me. But this poor kid—I think he's . . . unconscious." I bent more closely over the boy. Not a notion of a breath emerged from between his parted lips. "Or, Ohmigod, maybe, he's . . ." I couldn't bring myself to say the word. In my oblivious haste to get to my FroshHum faculty meeting on time, I'd become an unknowing obstacle to this child's innocent play, and now he lay sprawled lifeless at my feet.

"Don't move," Tom cried, not even glancing at the boy. "You're probably concussed. I'll get the EMS! I'll get an ambulance! I'll get the cops!" Attracted by the eruption of misadventure into an otherwise routine day, a small crowd of students was beginning to gather. They hovered, buzzing with excitement. Amber Nichols, on her way to the same meeting I'd been heading for, joined them, but, in her usual disengaged manner, she lingered at the edge of the swarm.

"Hurry," I exclaimed to Tom, and he leapt to his feet. From the corner of my eye, I thought I saw the child's eyelids flutter. Then he gasped involuntarily, as if his lungs were starved for breath.

"Wait," I yelled at Tom's departing back. I bent over the child again. One eye opened, then the other. They were brown and sly. They closed again. *Why, you little faker!* I thought. *You . . . you little phony! I'll teach you . . .*

"Tom," I commanded, "there's no time for an ambulance. He's . . . he's not breathing! I'm going to have to do a . . . a . . . an emergency . . . ah . . . *tracheotomy!*" I didn't even know how to pronounce the word. I winked at the gaping crowd. "Does anyone have a sharp knife?"

The little fraud's eyes popped open like chestnuts on hot coals. "I'm okay, lady!" He jumped hastily to his feet. "Really, really, I'm fine! Just . . ." He paled for real this time. "Just don't tell my mother. She'll . . . she'll *kill* me if she finds out I ran into you!"

I tried not to laugh. His consternation was so comical my irritation with his rotten little play for attention had instantly vanished. "I'm not hurt," I reassured him.

"I mean—she'll kill me if the skateboard's broken," the boy clarified, examining the painted board minutely. "I just got it last week, and if it's wrecked, I'm dead meat."

"Oh," I murmured, chastened. My throbbing wrist and scraped knees were obviously of no concern in a world where skateboards were so highly prized.

"Oh, crumb. Look at this! It's got a humongous scratch!" The words were accusatory. As I struggled to my feet, I studied the boy, but not as closely as he examined his precious board. This kid looked familiar—the close set of the eyes, the pugnacious jut to the chin, the dark curly hair—quite familiar. Had I seen this child—or someone very much like him—recently? Was he maybe a faculty kid or the brother of one of my students?

By the time I collected my belongings and turned

toward Dickinson Hall and the FroshHum meeting for which I was now very late, the small crowd had dispersed, Tom Lundgren had retreated once again into mumbles and blushes, and the curly-haired little kid and his skateboard had vanished.

6.

Clasp, Angel of the backward look
And folded wings of ashen gray
And voice of echoes far away,
The brazen covers of thy book. . . .

—JOHN GREENLEAF WHITTIER

MONICA, DO YOU HAVE A KNIFE?'' I asked.
After the FroshHum planning meeting, my colleagues and I exited the departmental conference room into the central office. Monica was sorting mail into the professors' pigeonhole mailboxes. Harriet Person strolled over to the secretary's desk and began to shuffle through an uneven stack of correspondence.

"The meeting was that bad?" Monica's expression remained deadpan. I checked for a glint of humor in her dark brown eyes. Nope. She was her usual crabby self. Today she wore an acid-yellow cotton shirt with her khaki pants. The color didn't work at all well with her sallow complexion.

"Almost," I replied, and inspected my mail: two letters, a memo, and a publisher's catalog. "It's for that big

package, you know, the one UPS delivered Friday afternoon. I need something sharp to open it." I slipped the
letters into my book bag. The memo and catalog, like
eighty percent of my professional mail, went directly into
the trash. Monica turned from her sorting, noted Harriet
at her desk, and stiffened. "Excuse me, Professor Person," she snapped. "Excuse *me*. That material is confidential."

Harriet jumped, as if Monica had jabbed her with one
of the lethally sharp number-two pencils poking out of
her pencil cup. "These are applications for the Palaver
Chair, aren't they?" Monica had just snatched one from
her hand.

"Yes. And like I said, they're confidential."

Harriet's expression hardened. "But—"

"You are not on that committee, Professor." Monica
shoved the pile of applications into a desk drawer and
twisted a key purposefully in the lock. Then, snubbing
Harriet, she turned to me. "Karen, you haven't opened
that box yet? Jeez, you were so hot to get into it when it
came, I thought you'da ripped it open with your *teeth* if
you had to." She pulled a brown canvas bag from a desk
drawer and rooted through it, came up with a large Swiss
Army knife, and flicked out an efficient-looking blade.
"This oughta do the trick."

"Thanks." I took the open knife carefully. "I'll bring
it right back."

"What box is that?" Harriet asked, withdrawing her
furious gaze from Monica for a moment. At a small college, everyone wants to know everyone else's business—
as evidenced by my senior colleague's unauthorized pe-
rusal of the job applications.

"Just some big package that came the other day." I
shrugged. "I don't know what's in it."

"A mysterious package? How exciting," Jane Birdwort said, trailing out of the central office behind me. *Damn, is there no privacy on this campus? A person can't even get a package! What do they think I'm expecting? A male stripper in a birthday cake?*

The big box stood exactly where I'd left it, halfway between my desk and the captain's chair. I removed the key from the door lock and dumped my book bag on the green vinyl chair. I had attracted a retinue. Along with Harriet and Jane, Amber Nichols and Monica had followed me into my office.

"You really don't know who sent it?" Harriet admonished. "Then, for God's sake, Karen, don't open it! You remember we got that memo from the security office?"

I did remember. Professors had received a "security alert" memo warning us to be on the lookout for suspicious packages in the wake of exploding parcel bombs at several colleges. The idea of a parcel bomb on a bucolic little campus like Enfield's had seemed ludicrous to me, and that memo, too, had gone into the trash.

"Harriet," I replied, "they've *caught* the Unabomber. He's in prison."

"Yeah, but who knows what other crazies are out there—"

"Can't be many more than there are on this campus," Monica muttered.

"Karen, I'm serious," Harriet persisted, scowling. She ran a hand distractedly through her short, white-streaked hair. "You can't be too careful. Right-wing conspirators will do anything to derail the feminist project—"

"Fuck that! I'm curious. Let me at it!" Jane grabbed the open Swiss Army knife from my hand and plunged it into the box. Along with everyone else in the room, I jumped back at least three feet. No explosion ensued.

"What are you all up to in there?"

The abrupt male voice startled us, and Jane's blade tore a long, jagged zigzag through the cardboard. I knew just how she felt; the gruff query just at the moment of penetration had set my heart racing. Elliot Corbin loomed in the doorway, an officious expression on his face. Handball was done for the day, and Elliot was showered and groomed, and once again ready to stick his nose into his colleagues' business. It occurred to me that this was the second time today this man had surveyed me from a doorway.

"You might as well come in, Elliot. Everyone else is here." Along with my rather cool regard, four other sets of female eyes watched Elliot enter the room. *Odd*, I thought, *when he's such an attractive man, that these women should all look so . . . so, unwelcoming.* Jane's eyes held a spooked expression. Amber's mien could only be described as calculating, eyes narrowed, facial muscles immobile. Harriet's countenance had taken on a stony aspect, like marble chiseled in sharp planes. And Monica—Monica's expression was perhaps the least complicated of the group: Monica was furious, plain and simple furious. Puzzling, all this ill will. But it wasn't Elliot who interested me at the moment: It was my box.

I plucked Monica's knife from Jane's suddenly limp hand. Slitting the packaging tape, I ripped open the top of the carton. Thick bubble wrap obscured the contents, but an envelope addressed *Professor Pelletier* was taped to the top layer, the handwriting the same almost illegible scrawl as that on the box's label. I held the envelope up to the light and squinted at it.

"Open it, Karen," Monica grumbled. I did. Gingerly. No explosion.

Professor Pelletier, the enclosed typed letter read, *Recently, in clearing out the attic of my late uncle's home in*

Greenwich, I came across the old books and letters I've enclosed here. They are signed with the name Emmeline Foster— Behind me Amber exclaimed, "Emmeline Foster? Really?"

Harriet, too, peered over my shoulder. "Who's Emmeline Foster?" she asked.

"She was a poet," I replied distractedly. "About a hundred and fifty years ago." Emmeline Foster? Hadn't her name just come up in class? She was the New York poet who'd drowned herself in the Hudson—or North River, as it was then called—when Poe was living in lower Manhattan.

I continued aloud: *"Since inquiries at the New York Public Library have disclosed that Miss Foster was a New York poetess whose writing had a brief vogue during the middle of the nineteenth century—"*

"Is that *Poe's* Emmeline Foster?" Elliot interjected. I had forgotten he was in the room.

I glanced up from the letter. "Well, I think she belonged to *herself,* not to Poe, but, yes, I imagine it's the same Emmeline Foster."

". . . I have decided to forward this substantial body of papers to you. Having read in the Enfield alumni magazine about the bequest to the college of a Center for the Study of Women Writers to be instituted under your direction—"

"The Northbury Center," Harriet said, on a meditatively calculating note.

"Ten million dollars," Elliott said, running his tongue over his teeth.

The previous year, the great-granddaughter of the nineteenth-century novelist Serena Northbury had left Enfield College her ancestral home and a goodly chunk of her fortune to endow a research center and library dedicated to the study of American women writers. Her sole stipulation was that I must serve as director of the Cen-

ter. Ever since the announcement of the bequest, my colleagues had been trying to horn in on running the
research institute that was to be established at the
Northbury mansion.

"Well, yes. The will is likely to be tied up in court for
a while, but the college is already soliciting donations of
authors' papers for the research library. These are the
first we've received."

"Hmm," Amber Nichols said. It was one of those
*hmm*s that resonate with unspecified significance.

I glanced at her. I understood only too well my senior
colleagues' self-interested focus on anything pertaining to
the Northbury Center, but I was puzzled by Amber's interest in such an obscure poet as Foster. She raised her
eyebrows, and spoke in her high, precise voice. "I'm interested in the destabilization of established constructs of
authorship afforded by the disruptive intrusion into the
epistemological field of previously marginalized authorial
modes and venues."

I stared at her for the three or four seconds it took to
translate. "Yeah, me too," I said, and turned back to the
letter: ". . . *I feel certain that this is the best disposition of
this material. My late uncle, Christopher Cummins, was heir
to the family estate of Edward Cummins of the nineteenth-
century Manhattan publishing house, Cummins and Sons,
and Miss Foster seems to have been one of their authors. At
least, I assume so from her letters to Edward, and from the
enclosed books and personal memorabilia that somehow
ended up in his possession.*

*I am certain that you will know far better than I what to
do with this material. Feel free to call on me if there is anything more I can tell you.*"

The letter closed with a Manhattan address and
phone number, and was signed "Alex Warren."

"Wow!" I was delighted. "I don't know much at all

about Emmeline Foster—I don't think anyone does—but it looks like we're about to learn. Let's see what we've got here."

I rummaged through the layers of bubble wrap and seized the first object that came to hand, a small blue leather-bound notebook with page after page of close handwriting. Leafing through the book, I saw that from beginning to end its pages were covered with lines of poetry. I read a verse at random.

The tumult in the shadowed woods,
The babble in the tree,
The clamor in the scudding clouds,
Speak silently of thee. . . .

Nothing new or startling there, I thought. A poem about love, in conventional verse form. Pretty typical for nineteenth-century women's poetry. Monica and Harriet had begun pulling books and manuscripts helter-skelter out of the box. I laid the little notebook on the table and moved to forestall them: This was not a professional way to go about receiving a donation to our new research library. Out of the corner of my eye I saw Amber pick up the blue notebook and riffle through it, then pause to read a poem. I turned back to retrieve it, and as I did so, Elliot plucked it from her hand. She glared at him, and seemed about to protest, when Jane, who'd been silent since Elliot's arrival, distracted us all with an abrupt exclamation.

"Karen, look at this picture! Is this Emmeline Foster?"

A hinged brass portrait case opened to reveal an astonishingly clear daguerreotype image, a head-and-shoulders portrait of a delicate-looking young woman with bunches of dark ringlets framing her thin face. Amazing!

Fifteen decades ago, a photographer had manipulated io-
dine, mercury vapors, and common table salt to affix a
woman's image to this copper plate, and here that image
remained. I took the daguerreotype case by its edges and
studied the portrait closely.

"I've never seen this picture before," I said, thinking
back to my research on the popular poets. "As far as I
recall, there's only one known portrait of Emmeline Foster, and it's an engraving, not a daguerreotype." Pluck-
ing the thick, well-worn *Encyclopedia of American Women
Authors* from one of the floor-to-ceiling bookcases, I
turned pages rapidly until I came to the F's. "Fergusson,
Fern, Fields—*Foster*. Here we are: Look, there's the engraving." The sketch was typical of the period, a black-
and-white line drawing with its subject captured in a demure pose.

"This is the same woman—Emmeline," Amber exclaimed. She had taken the daguerreotype from Jane, and
now she placed it next to the picture in the reference
book. Her voice held an unmistakable note of excitement.
"Look, the same curly hair, the broad forehead—"

"The *button nose*, the *rosebud mouth*, the *porcelain
complexion*," Elliot interjected, sarcastically. "Dearest
Emmeline was a walking compendium of hackneyed poetic conventions."

I shot him a nasty look. "Maybe that's why Poe was
so interested in her."

Behind me, Amber Nichols emitted a sharp, instantly
suppressed bark of laughter.

Monica was reading through the encyclopedia entry.
"Unlike most of what goes on around here," she re-
marked, "this is actually sort of interesting."

"What does it say?" Harriet asked. "I don't have my
glasses."

Monica plopped herself down at my desk and read

aloud from the open encyclopedia. *"FOSTER, Emmeline Charlotte (1811–1845). Little is known of this poet's early life, as she refused to disclose personal details to the editors and anthologists who clamored for her verse in the early 1840's. She arrived in New York City in late 1839 after having had poems published in* Ladies' Magazine *and in* Godey's Lady's Book. *Some reports suggest she was the daughter of a prominent Hudson River family, but, although she was established comfortably in the elite society of the New York literary and cultural scene, she never mentioned the source of her income to her Manhattan friends. Foster published widely in the periodicals of the day, and her one book,* The Nightingale *(1842), was produced by Cummins and Sons, and well received by contemporary reviewers. Nonetheless, after Foster's early death, her work slipped into obscurity. Emmeline Foster is perhaps best remembered as one of Edgar Allan Poe's lady loves, and it is rumored that her death by drowning in the Hudson River near the house occupied by Edgar and Virginia Poe, was no accident, but rather, as one contemporaneous newspaper said, 'the desperate act of a woman scorned.'"*

"That's fascinating," Monica said. *"The desperate act of a woman scorned.* Just like a romance novel." These were the only words of approbation I had ever heard from our cranky secretary.

When everyone had finally tired of the new toy and left, I began to repack the box, not quite knowing what to do with this unexpected bonus. Its contents had certainly cluttered up my office. Books and papers were piled on the desk, the floor, the chairs, wherever a bare surface had been found. A stack of composition books on the floor caught my eye. The thin books were tied together with a length of maroon grosgrain ribbon. I sat cross-legged, pulled the stack toward me, untied the careful bow with a tug on the ribbon, and spread ten identical black-covered school notebooks around me. Feeling eerily like a voyeur, I opened the first. A young person's round, unformed handwriting filled the blue-ruled page from top to bottom, side to side, leaving no margins.

> *19 November 1824*
> *my thirteenth birthday*
>
> *Dear Friend, for I shall call you my friend for now and ever, today Papa gave you to me, to practice my penmanship he said for it needs much to be improved. A Lady's hand he said must always be decorative, and my scrawl as it is would never grace any epistle of Love. Fond, foolish Papa, as if any beau would wish a letter from such a scapegrace as I! Instead of my copybook, you shall become my confidant, for it is lonely here. Papa is much away and Mama lies long days in bed with the sick headache. I read today in the Ladies Magazine a verse by Mrs. Sigourney that I like very much. I wonder how a young lady gets to be a poet??? Must ask Papa.*
>
> *My name is Emmeline Foster and I am thirteen today. I presume I should think Important Thoughts on such an auspicious date but have none on hand. There will be roasted goose for dinner and Annie promised a raisin cake with sugar icing. I think Papa has a story by Miss Austen for me—he has been hinting about it forever!!! Mama says I should be a very grateful girl and I am sure I am. Miss Ross is calling for me to come down to lessons. I will write more tomorrow, and I vow everyday hereafter.*

I raised my eyes from the page. *Emmeline Foster's journal! And ten volumes long! Had the poet kept it up throughout her entire life? If she had, I might be able to uncover the truth about her death. Surely if she had been as desperately in love with Poe as was rumored, she would have written copiously about her feelings.* Greedily I opened the final notebook somewhere close to the end. A more mature handwriting met my eye, prim, rounded little letters.

3 October 1844

Dear Friend:
Today I walked down Broadway as far as the Astor Hotel. Am beginning to recover strength and flesh and trust that if the weather holds fine I will sit in the sun one full hour a day and write again.

The large Maple in the square displays a single branch of scarlet foliage even this early in the season and the leaves dance. I read in the book of Miss Barrett's poems dear Fanny gave me. Otherwise I am idle, but content—although it is hard to be alone in this big City. Mr. Poe has written, requesting another poem, but I declined. When I am ready to publish the new verses I will offer them to Mrs. Hale. Though I would not admit it to a living soul, I know they will be my Triumph!—

"Professor Pelletier?"

The voice yanked me far too abruptly from the past to the present. Shamega Gilfoyle, a senior English major, stood in the doorway regarding me curiously. Dark eyebrows furrowed quizzically in her slender face. "We're waiting for you?" she informed me, with the interrogatory lilt of the truly puzzled.

"Waiting?" I rubbed my right eye with the heel of a grimy hand.

"Yes. Some people thought we should leave, but I said I'd check and see if you were coming. I knew you were on campus 'cause I saw you this morning in the coffee shop."

I stared at Shamega blankly, then slapped my forehead. "The seminar! I'm supposed to be in class! What time is it?"

"Two forty-five," Shamega responded. "Should I tell them you're coming?"

"Yes!" I jumped up from my cross-legged position on the floor, brushing myriad paper specks from my trousers. "Give me five minutes," I said, then hastily gathered up Emmeline Foster's notebooks, retied the ribbon, and placed the stacked journals in the box. As I gathered up my own textbook and class notes, I noticed that I had overlooked one of the old copybooks, so I scooped it up, crammed it in my book bag with everything else, and hurried out the door, twisting the knob to make certain the lock was engaged.

I was hustling across campus when it hit me that Emmeline Foster's little blue book of verses had not been among the artifacts I'd repacked with the other Foster materials.

7.

. . . and all our proudest lore
Is but the alphabet of ignorance.

—LYDIA HUNTLEY SIGOURNEY

K AREN, THANK GOD YOU'RE HERE! This time I
think she's really dying!" Jill had her apartment
door wide open before I'd even set a foot on the bottom
step of the wide, wraparound porch. Eloise was screaming
bloody murder. I'd heard the shrieks the second I opened
my car door. I'd groaned, then scooted around the Jetta
to retrieve the sausage-and-eggplant pizza, still blistering
hot in its flat white box.

It was five o'clock Tuesday, and I'd dropped by to
lend Jill a hand. Eloise was braced against her mother's
shoulder, body stiff, face red and scrunched, mouth a
wide orifice of fury. Any human being who could expend
that much energy on making noise was nowhere in the
same universe with death.

"It's just colic, Jill. She'll live." I set the pizza box on the kitchen table, shifting aside bright pacifiers, plastic baby bottles, and an electric breast pump to make room. "The question is—will you?" I took the baby from Jill and held her facing outward with both my arms around her midsection. Then I strolled around the room, jiggling her gently up and down. Her howls subsided to sobs, then ceased. She craned her little head like a turtle, trying to get a fix on the lights, the colors.

"How'd you do that?" Jill queried, wide-eyed. She appeared exhausted; the shadows of sleep deprivation were imprinted under her green eyes like etiolated bruises. "She's been screaming half the afternoon. I was about to go out of my mind."

I shrugged, looked wise. Truth is, I was lucky. With colic, it's a crapshoot—so to speak—sometimes a simple change of scene will help, sometimes you're doomed to hours of perdition.

Jill showered while I changed Eloise and snuggled her down in her crib. Then Jill and I sat at the kitchen table dispatching pizza. "I'm soooo tired, Karen. And I'm getting to be soooo boring," she confided. "All I want to talk about is Eloise. All I think about is Eloise. All I dream about is Eloise. I eat, sleep, walk, talk baby. Me! I can't believe it! And now I'm turning into a *cow;* every time she makes a peep, I spurt at least a gallon of milk. Nobody ever comes to see me anymore, except for you, of course—and Kenny. And I don't *blame* them; I *am* a cow. Does it ever get any better? Am I going to be a cow for the rest of my *life?*" Jill actually had tears in her eyes.

"Don't be silly," I said, and gave her hand a squeeze. "By the time you go back to teaching next semester, you'll be your old sexy self."

"Ha!" she exclaimed. "I'll never be sexy again!" Despondent, she dropped her head into her hands, rested her elbows on her knees. Then she peeked up at me. "Really?"

"Just ask Kenny," I replied. "We'll see what *he* thinks." I slid the last slice of pizza across the table to her and pushed back my chair. "I've got to go now, or I'll be late for the study group. I'm so beat, I'd skip the damn meeting, except I'm scheduled to give a presentation on the plans for the Center." I sighed, thinking about the hassle that was bound to ensue. "It's at Elliot Corbin's house, and I'm not looking forward to *that*. You know he's a guy who really pisses me off."

"I think Elliot's cute," Jill said. "For an *old* guy." Jill is twenty-six. Elliot is, oh, maybe fifty. That didn't seem so old to me anymore.

"Handsome is as handsome does," I replied with a prissy little twist, then laughed. I couldn't believe such uptight words had actually come out of my mouth. "I don't know what it is about him, Jill. Maybe I'm just envious. My life is so—*messy*—" Jill sighed in agreement. "And Elliot seems to have it all together. Neat little boxes—that's what his *mind* is like, anyhow: row upon row of neat little analytical categories that theorize the hell out of everything. And I'll bet anything his life is exactly the same way: row upon row of neat little personal relationships, secure little tenured job, comfy little balance in the bank account, witty little postmodernist house. I'll bet his *brain cells* are lined up in neat little rows—"

"Life *is* messy," Jill said with the hard-won wisdom of the new mother, dabbing at a milky stain on the left side of her green sweater. "It's the nature of the beast. Don't let anyone theorize you out of *that*."

• • •

I was wrong: There was nothing either neat or postmodernist about Elliot's place. The house was large, a mustard-colored, three-story mid-Victorian, with tall windows and a mansard roof. On the outskirts of town, it was set back from the street behind a wilderness of overgrown cedar and rosebushes. When no one answered my knock on the dark green door, I tried the ornate brass knob, and it turned in my hand. The hall was two stories high, featuring a massive mahogany staircase and a huge wrought-iron chandelier with only a third of its two dozen or so flame-shaped bulbs functioning. Although the hallway was dimly lit, I had the distinct impression of sparse furnishings and extremely dusty corners. *This is a house that needs a woman's touch,* I thought, then automatically ran my thinking through the feminist p.c. machine: *This is a house that needs the administration of a unionized, equitably reimbursed, affirmative-action-sensitive, domestic-maintenance service.*

I was late for the meeting—I'd had trouble finding the house—and from a room to the right of the entry hall, I could hear voices. To the left was a formal dining room whose mahogany table was cluttered with books. Following the increasingly louder tones, I wove my way through a stuffy formal living room, then came to a large chamber which appeared to run the full width of the house. My colleagues were gathered there, in a room with floor-to-ceiling bookcases that had obviously been built as a library. At the moment, though, it seemed to serve as a combination office and recreation room, exercise equipment in the front of the room, and at the back a wide oak desk, surrounded by a conglomeration of mismatched couches and chairs in a ragged seating arrangement.

"Ah, Karen. Finally!" Elliot exclaimed when he saw

me in the doorway. "Now we can begin. Please bring us up to date on the status of the Northbury Center."

I glanced around. I was acquainted with everyone in the room, a scattering of scholars from the state university, Amherst College, Williams, Enfield, and other schools in the area. We gathered monthly to share research and ideas. At the last meeting, Miles had brought in a copy of a newly discovered sermon by Henry Ward Beecher. The month before that, Harriet had shared an essay on hegemonic masculinities in nineteenth-century literary culture. Tonight was my turn, and I had the biggest show-and-tell of all.

"Karen?" Elliot wanted to get this over with. I looked for a seat. There were none available. "How about a chair, Elliot? I'm too tired to do this standing."

"Oh, right." Elliot scurried into the dining room, as Miles Jewell, always the gentleman, jumped up from his armchair. I waved him back into it, and accepted the straight chair Elliot ungraciously plunked down next to me. Elliot returned to his seat on a black-and-white-striped couch and ostentatiously took up the pen and the lined yellow notepad he'd had to abandon in order to play host. Miles poured a glass of red wine and handed it to me.

"As most of you know," I said to the small group, "a recent bequest to the college of ten million dollars and the Meadowbrook estate in Eastfield—" I sipped my wine and told the group about Edith Hart's will.

I've always thought of myself as a teacher first and foremost, so I'd initially been reluctant to take on the administration of the Northbury Center. Eventually, however, I'd become enthusiastic about setting up an archival center where women writers would receive the same kind of loving attention that the major libraries have always paid to the canonical men. Because Edith's will had been contested, no one had any idea when Meadowbrook and the money would become available so the center could get under way. It could take years, but that didn't abate my zeal.

"A reading room," I told my colleagues, "a conference room, book stacks, archives of personal papers, classrooms, bedrooms for visiting scholars, perhaps even a fully restored nineteenth-century kitchen," I said, really getting into it now, "so that researchers can reproduce material conditions of early-industrial domestic life."

"Poppycock." Miles shook his head. "Great minds transcend mere household concerns. Literature has nothing to do with kitchens." *Translation: Men's literature is the only real literature.* He popped a cube of stale-looking Swiss cheese into his mouth.

"It certainly does," Harriet retorted, knitting needles clacking irritably, "if you're an exploited woman trapped in domestic discourses—" *Translation: You men don't have a clue about the real world.*

"No, no, no," Elliot interjected, jabbing his pen into his notepad. "A postmodernist theoretics demands the elision of such irrelevant biographical trivia as domestic life—" *Translation: There is no real world. It's all just language.*

"Ahem, Elliot, I was speaking!" Harriet asserted. *Translation: You neosexist trend slave!* Her needles clattered faster. "Unpaid domestic labor is an integral factor of hard and fast economic reality. Nineteenth-century marketplace conditions excluded most women from literary production. What we need here is not so much a center for the study of literature, as an Institute of Material Feminism. Karen, do you think—?"

"That's the problem with you feminists!" Elliot jabbed at the yellow pad again, and the rickety table on which it rested tilted to one side. "A slavish adherence to outmoded cultural materialism. What this money should be used for is an International Library of Epistemological Studies. Karen, when I become Palaver Chair—"

"Palaver Chair!" Harriet croaked, and Miles jumped in hotly.

"Epistemology be damned, Corbin! Puritan Spiritual Narrative is the wellspring of American Literature. For an Institute on Puritan Studies, ten million dollars would purchase numerous—"

"But . . . but . . . but—" I interposed. "What about women's literature? It's supposed to be a center for the study of *women's* literature."

In the next hour the battle raged. I left the meeting as soon as I could. Classes were suspended for the Thanksgiving vacation, and after the heated debate of the evening, I was more ready than ever for a few days away from colleagues. On my way out of the house, I glanced around once again at the shadowy, sparsely furnished hallway, bemused by the grimness of the place. Once again I thought, *This is a house that needs a woman's touch.* Then, curiously, I noticed Amber Nichols, in the dining room, pawing through the collation of volumes on a table that looked as if it hadn't hosted an actual meal in decades.

"Oh, Karen!" she blurted, startled by my presence. Then, after an almost infinitesimal pause, "What a feast of books. I never *can* resist books." Uncharacteristically, she was babbling. "How about you?"

"No," I replied, "I can't." But I didn't find this bland-looking collection of what appeared to be scholarly tomes at all appetizing. In addition, I was suddenly struck by Amber's docility so far this evening; I'd forgotten until that very moment her implied threat to Elliot at Sunday's poetry reading. What was it she had said?

Something about a *revelation* at the Tuesday night meeting? But she'd remained totally silent during my talk, her tight little smile stitched ineradicably in place, no shocking disclosures forthcoming at all. And thank God! After all the tongues hanging out and teeth bared for a bite of the Northbury Center, I don't think I could have tolerated any further skirmishes at knife point.

I went right from Elliot's to the supermarket. Turkey, cranberries for sauce, bread for stuffing, potatoes for mashing, onions, yams, parsnips, peas, pickles: I was ravenous just thinking about it. I'd filled my cart and was rounding the dairy aisle, hustling toward the checkout counter, when I ran into a familiar-looking kid. I mean, *literally* ran smack-dab into him. It was the dark-haired little curly-head who had knocked me down with the skateboard on campus the day before. Now here he was, pawing through a sales display of sugared cereals. Unable to slow down fast enough, I bumped him hard with my grocery cart.

"Ufff," he said as we collided, and he staggered, sending a pyramid of Sugar Pops and Froot Loops boxes crashing to the ground.

"Watch where you're going, lady!" an irate mother-type voice commanded. A heavyset woman descended on me. "What d'ya think? Ya own the place?"

I pivoted toward her, automatically defensive. "He shouldn't have been—" Then I did a double take. "Monica?"

"Karen?" Our department secretary seemed flabbergasted to see me, as if I had no right to a life off campus. Monica was dressed in gray sweatpants and a dark blue quilted jacket open over a gray sweatshirt. Around her neck she wore an odd pendant, a star enclosed in a circle, dangling from a black leather cord. Her short brown hair was rumpled, as if she hadn't taken a comb to it all day. Her cart was piled with the same holiday fare as mine— turkey, stuffing, cranberries—only a great deal more of it, as if she were cooking for two or three dozen instead of the measly six I was expecting.

"This is *your* kid?" I picked up a box of Sugar Pops and set it back on the display, bent over to snag another. The boy followed suit, glancing skittishly at his mother.

Monica recovered her usual irascible aplomb. "Yeah, this is Joey." She paused, and a complicated set of expressions flitted across her round face: pride, exasperation, wariness. The latter won. "Ya got a problem with that?"

"No, it's just that—" I was about to tell her how I'd met him on campus. But, behind her, Joey was frantically signaling to me, jumping up and down, shaking his head, desperately mouthing, *Don't tell her don't tell her don't tell her.* I remembered how upset he'd been about his skateboard.

"—that I didn't know you had any children," I finished. It was a smooth save. I could easily imagine what it must be like to have someone as overbearing as Monica for a parent. Behind his mother's back, Joey took a histrionic breath of relief and mimed wiping the sweat off his brow. It was clear to me that a significant part of this child's life was going to take place behind his mother's back.

I could see now that the boy did indeed look a great deal like Monica. He shared the close set of her dark brown eyes, the pugnacious jut of her jaw. That must be why he'd seemed so familiar to me when I'd first met him. But still, there was something else. . . .

The three of us, Monica, Joey, and I, picked up cereal boxes and restacked them in an approximation of their original formation. A store manager bustled toward us, officiously ready to chastise these careless shoppers, but one glare from Monica was enough to send him on his way. As I was the tallest of the three, I replaced the final box of Froot Loops at the apex of the pyramid.

"Looks like you're cooking for a crowd." I gestured at Monica's overflowing cart.

She shrugged. "Just the usual," she grumbled, and I realized that, whereas the secretaries were privy to all sorts of information about the professors—from phone calls and personnel files—I knew absolutely nothing about this woman's life. I hadn't even known she had a child. Was Monica a local woman, I wondered? Did she come from a large family? Did she have children other than Joey? Why was she buying all that food?

As I pushed my bag-laden cart through the super-market's automatic front doors, Monica and Joey were loading their groceries into the back of a rust-eaten white Ford Bronco parked as close to the door as you could get and not be in a handicapped-parking zone. The car's bumper was plastered with tattered slogans: SONIA JOHNSON FOR PRESIDENT; GODDESS RULES; I'M PRO-CHOICE AND I VOTE; WILD WOMEN DON'T GET THE BLUES.

"Enjoy your holiday," I called inanely as I passed them.

Monica rolled her eyes. Enjoyment obviously had nothing to do with it. Enjoyment was for people like me—privileged people. For Monica, it looked like, Thanksgiving was just another day of work.

8.

Over the river and through the woods

—LYDIA MARIA CHILD

T HANKSGIVING TURNED OUT TO BE a turkey—
emotionally as well as gastronomically. It started at
supper on Wednesday night with Amanda, as she sat
down at our kitchen table. "Remember on the phone the
other day I told you I had plans for the holiday weekend?" she asked. Tall and slim, with cropped brown hair
and dark-lashed hazel eyes, Amanda was garbed in her
usual jeans and sweater. I hadn't seen her in weeks, and
she looked wonderful but exhausted, having just fifteen
minutes earlier pulled her little red Volkswagen Rabbit
into the driveway after an exam in the morning, and then
a seven-hour drive home from school. She also looked nervous. This was not at all characteristic of my usually fearless daughter.

"Yeah?" I set a pasta-and-bean casserole on a cast-iron trivet and plunged a serving spoon into the cheddary topping. "What's going on?"

"Well, I've been thinking about something for a long time." She twisted the spoon in the steaming casserole. "And I'm afraid you're gonna hate it—what I want to do, I mean. I've been terrified to mention it to you. . . ." I had just slathered a cheese biscuit with butter when Amanda dropped this daughterly bombshell.

I let the biscuit fall back onto my plate untasted. "What?"

"Because I'm afraid you'll be devastated. . . ." She dug out an oversize spoonful of pasta and beans, plopped it on her plate, went back for more. This seemed to require an enormous amount of concentration, so much that she was unable to look at me.

"What!" I demanded. *Ohmigod—she's going to become a Hare Krishna. Or—Ohmigod—she's going to have transsexual surgery. Or—Ohmigod—she's going to take a job as a U.N. weapons inspector in Iraq.* "Tell me!" *Or—Ohmigod—even worse—she's decided to go into law enforcement, like Tony.*

"And if I go ahead and do it, that doesn't mean I don't love you—" Her eyes remained focused on the gooey mess on her plate.

Oh! My! God! "Amanda! What *is* it? Tell me! *Now!*"

Amanda dropped her fork with a clatter, sat back in her chair, took a deep breath, and looked directly at me for the first time in what seemed like millennia. "Okay, I'll tell you. Now don't freak out, Mom, okay? It's just that . . . I'm going to try to find my father."

If she'd socked me in the gut, she couldn't have hurt me more. I'd raised Amanda completely on my own from the time she was three years old. We hadn't heard from Fred in seventeen years. Neither of us. Not a word. Never a birthday card for Amanda. Not a single phone call or check. And now my daughter was going to search for this man who'd resented her from the moment of her conception and who had completely disavowed her since I'd walked out on him after three-and-a-half years of calamitous marriage.

"Sweetie," I said to her, "Honey. Don't do it. You knew your father was bad news when you were a tot. Don't set yourself up for heartbreak."

Immediately after our hasty wedding, Fred and I had moved from the factory town of Lowell to the factory town of North Adams, clear on the other end of the state. Then he'd taken his truck back on the road, driving long-distance hauls for Eaton Paper. Fred's occasional layovers quickly convinced me that his extended road trips were the best part of our marriage. At first I took abuse passively; given my family background, I thought that's what marriage was. I stayed with Fred, because what else was I going to do? I was nineteen; I had no job skills; I had no education; I had no place else to go. But, on Amanda's third birthday, when her father called her a "smart-mouthed brat who was gonna get hers," I grabbed my daughter and my nearly empty wallet, and slammed out of the house. And that was it.

"If my father is 'bad news,' what does that say about me?" twenty-year-old Amanda said now. "I want to find him, talk to him, because I have to know." For the first time I allowed myself to notice that her long, delicate jaw could take on the same truculent line as her father's. "First thing Friday, I'm going to Lowell, and I—"

"Lowell?" The very name of the town made me queasy. "What's taking you there? Is your fa— Is Fred back in Lowell? Have you heard from him?"

"No." She sounded impatient. "At least, I don't know if he's there or not. And you don't have to sound so freaked out. I know you think he's a creep. You've made that clear enough. But I've got to meet him—at least once. I've got to know where I come from."

"Oh, *Amanda*."

"I know you don't like it, Mom, but you can't stop me."

"I know that, Sweetie. I just can't bear to see you get hurt."

That was the end of the discussion, but her father's stubborn jaw remained in evidence for the rest of the evening.

And this announcement was only the beginning of the holiday stresses.

Thanksgiving afternoon, Earlene started in on me. The kitchen was redolent with the scent of roasting turkey, and the table was heaped with pies, towel-covered pans of rising dinner rolls, and a pile of yams, scrubbed and ready for the oven. Our appetites were whetted by the holiday aromas, the irresistible intimacy of kitchen talk had overcome discretion, and Earlene had decided I needed a man in my life. She didn't realize how bad her timing was. The threat of Amanda's reunion with Fred polluted my holiday like a noxious cloud; the last thing I wanted to think about was a man—any man. But I keep the disasters of my early life to myself, so, even though it was nagging at me like an abscessed tooth, I wasn't about to tell Earlene about Amanda's determination to search for her father.

Earlene is a slender woman, dark-skinned, with close-cropped hair, a long, thin, arched nose and high cheekbones. I don't know how old she is. Mid-fifties, maybe, and gorgeous in that world-weary been-there-done-that-loved-every-minute-of-it way of certain mature women. She has two grown children and is long-divorced from their father, but never seems to suffer any dearth of male company. We are good friends. We share similar impover-

ished backgrounds, out of which has sprung a knee-jerk
intolerance of pretension and wacky iconoclastic senses of
humor understood by very few others at our prestigious
institution. I know Earlene as well as anyone at Enfield
does. With most faculty members she is pleasant, but re-
served. I can understand that; she's black at a white college—a college that waffled on abolition in the nineteenth
century and jumped on the Civil Rights bandwagon only
when it became imperative to do so in the 1960's. Of
course there are black professors now, and a carefully re-
cruited population of minority students. Earlene is in an
awkward position, however, as liaison between the students, faculty, and administration, but our joint concern
for Sophia Warzek brought us together a couple of years
earlier, and a friendship has grown.

"You ever hear from that big cop?" Earlene asked, as
we peeled Idaho potatoes for mashing.

"Tony?" I replied, absently. "No. He's married
now." I plucked the last remaining spud from the plastic
five-pound bag, held it under running water, applied the
peeler.

From the living room I could hear cheers and groans
as Amanda, Sophia, and Jill won huge fortunes at Monop-
oly, then squandered them recklessly. Agata Warzek,
Sophia's mother, had perched herself in front of the tele-
vision upon arrival, and hadn't been heard from since.
Eloise slept soundly in her infant seat, oblivious to the
pungent scent of a feast in the air.

"I don't mean Tony. I know that's over." Earlene
plopped her potato in the huge green-and-white-striped
plastic bowl. Salted water splashed over the side onto the
Formica countertop. "I'm talking about that homicide
guy. You know? That lieutenant who hung around so
much last summer?" She ripped a wad of paper towels off
the roll and mopped up the water.

"Piotrowski?" I was paying only minimal attention: Amanda's ill-advised wild-goose chase still preoccupied my thoughts. "Why would I hear from him? The Hart case is now in the hands of the lawyers." I dropped the final potato in the big bowl, causing another tidal wave. "And besides, he didn't *hang around.* He was working."

Earlene secured more paper towels. "Well," she replied, drawing the word out coyly. "I always thought that big dude had a bit of a thing for you."

"For *me?*" Then I narrowed my eyes, remembering. "Earlene, are you and Jill up to something?"

"Up to something? Uh, uhh." Her dark eyes were so innocent you could have bathed a cherub in them. I wasn't convinced, and concentrated on wiping the paring knife. "And besides, Piotrowski thinks I'm a pain in the ass."

"That's the first step, isn't it?" Earlene took a large pot from the cupboard next to the stove, placed it in the sink, and began filling it with water.

"Earlene, you are so wrong." Fragmented images of the lieutenant's broad shoulders, his shapely lips, flickered through my consciousness. He was a man, all right. I stuck the knife ruthlessly in its block. I didn't know why I was protesting so vigorously. "And, besides, I don't want to have anything to do with cops, ever again. Living with a cop is hell: You never know when they're coming home. You never know *if* they're coming home. I can't take any more of that."

"Who said you had to *live* with him?" Earlene grinned at me slyly. "How about just a teensy-weensy little fling? It's not natural for a woman your age to live like a nun."

"Who says I'm living like a nun?" I ripped open the bag of parsnips, thrust a fat one in her hand, plucked the paring knife from the block again, slapped it in front of her. "You don't know everything about me!"

This time I got the age-old, infinitely wise, African-American-woman-understands-the-blues look. The trouble was, although I hadn't ever told her about my daughter's father, Earlene really did know a hell of a lot about me. I *was* living like a nun.

Earlene proved to be a lively dinner companion, relating hilarious accounts of Thanksgivings with nutsy relatives in her large family in the Cleveland projects. She even got Agata Warzek to reminisce haltingly about holiday traditions when she was a child in Poland. And I did my part, with holiday-cooking disaster tales. Having lived with a cop for years, I had all too many of those to tell; *so, there, Earlene,* I longed to say.

Surprisingly, the younger women at the table were no fun. I knew exactly what was on Amanda's mind, and Jill was preoccupied with Eloise, who, after sleeping like a hibernating bear cub all afternoon, had begun to whimper the instant I finally got everyone gathered around the laden table. But I didn't know what was keeping Sophia so quiet, and that bothered me. Even though she was habitually reticent, my former student usually allowed herself to be drawn out in congenial company. But to-day—flat monosyllables greeted any query. And when I complimented her on the poems she'd read at the library on Sunday, Sophia went bone-pale and practically choked on her mashed potatoes. After that she didn't eat much of anything, just pushed food around on her plate, and I realized I'd better leave her alone with her distress— whatever it was. I realized this particularly strongly when Amanda kicked me under the table. A Doc Marten is a big boot, and it makes an impression.

So I resorted to gossip. That never fails to liven

things up. "Earlene, you know Elliot Corbin, of course. What's the buzz about him? I was at his house for a meeting the other night, and he was going on and on about the Palaver Chair—you know, that prestigious position we're hiring for in the English Department—and what he's going to do when he gets it. Not *if* he gets it, but *when* he gets it—"

"Is that a sure thing? That he'll get it?" Earlene looked troubled.

"*He* seems to think so."

"Too bad. I think I mentioned to you how many students have—" Earlene glanced over at Sophia, who was, after all, still an Enfield student. She let her words trail off. As Dean of Students, Earlene was privy to all sorts of information about both faculty and students, but much of it was confidential.

"Isn't Harriet Person expecting to get that job?" Jill had silenced Eloise by opening her loose-fitting pumpkin-orange blouse and popping a nipple in the baby's mouth. That was good for about five minutes of peace. "At the last Women's Studies meeting, she seemed really confident. She was promising great advances for feminism on the Enfield campus—a new 'wimmin's' center, a sexual diversity initiative, safe rooms in every dorm."

"I was kind of hoping we'd hire a poet." Sophia said the word *poet* reverently, as another person might say *saint*. This was her first voluntary contribution to the conversation, and I immediately turned to her. She had dressed up for the day, wearing the sky-blue sweater I had given her the previous Christmas and a long navy-blue wool skirt. Her blue-gray eyes shone briefly, like a spring sky between showers.

"Who'd you have in mind?" I asked. As if I didn't know. I loaded more stuffing on my plate, pulled the gravy boat in my direction.

"Well, Professor Birdwort, of course. She's so accomplished. . . ." Sophia actually took a bite of cranberry sauce—to celebrate the thought, I assumed: *Saint Jane.* Then I noted the snideness. Was I just a little jealous? *I'd* always been Sophia's hero.

"Doesn't Jane Birdwort have some connection to Corbin?" Earlene asked, loading her fork with peas. "It seems to me I heard something. . . . What *was* it?" She slapped her head with the heel of her hand, but didn't knock any information loose. She shrugged, and said, "Old age! It's pretty bad when you can't even recall the juicier bits of scandal."

"Scandal?" I replied. "Oh Earlene, do *try* to remember."

Amanda laughed, for a moment her usual lively self. "Mom, Enfield College must be the scandal center of the universe. I've never heard so much downright salacious gossip as you've passed on to me since you've been on this quiet little campus."

"*Salacious!*" I exclaimed.

"Good Lord, girl!" Earlene joked. "What kind of education are they giving you there at Georgetown? What's the next tidbit of expanded vocabulary you're gonna run by us: *concupiscent?*"

"No," Amanda replied. "But try this one on for size: There's a woman in one of my classes called *Chastity.*"

"Oh," said Earlene, grinning at me wickedly. "Your mother knows all about *that.*"

Just as Sophia was about to set the pumpkin pie in the center of the table, between the apple crumb pie and the vanilla Häagen-Dazs, the doorbell rang. Sophia jumped and let the pie plop onto the table. "Who on earth? . . ." I said, mystified, and hefted myself up off the suddenly gravity-intensive chair. I reached the door as the bell

THE RAVEN AND THE NIGHTINGALE | 81

gave a second peremptory jangle. Who could it be? On
Thanksgiving Day? An image of Tony's battered Irish
face came immediately to mind. We'd been together so
long that no holiday seemed complete without him. As I
threw the door open, I saw immediately, of course, that
my former boyfriend was nowhere in sight. But I stared
in astonishment at the bulky figure who was framed there
in the doorway. Broad shoulders, nicely contoured lips,
just as I'd recalled. As horrified as I should have been
about the presence of this particular man on my doorstep
at—let's see—6:47 Thanksgiving evening, Earlene's speculations momentarily blocked out all other conjectures,
and I simply gaped at him, like an adolescent with a pre-
cipitous crush.

"Doctor Pelletier." Lieutenant Piotrowski cleared his
throat twice. He looked extremely solemn. "I am terribly
sorry to interrupt your holiday meal." He peered over my
shoulder at the guests gathered around the table, and I
knew each one would be indelibly registered in his memory. "And I wouldn't do it unless it was absolutely necessary. But something real nasty has just come up, and I
gotta talk to you. I believe you know a man named Elliot
Corbin."

9.

So fallen! so lost! the light withdrawn
Which once he wore!

—JOHN GREENLEAF WHITTIER

ELLIOT CORBIN WAS DEAD—an apparent homicide, Lieutenant Piotrowski said, but wouldn't elaborate. Next to his body, police had found a lined yellow pad, with my name scribbled on it, heavily underlined.

I focused only on the initial information. "Dead? Elliot *dead?* But he can't be! I just saw him two nights ago!" The second the words tumbled out of my mouth, I realized how stupid that sounded.

"Nonetheless, Doctor, he *is* dead. And in case you didn't hear me, I'll say it again: Your name was found at the scene.

"At first glance, it looks like the name was there before the blood spatters," the lieutenant continued carefully, as I dropped like a stone into the nearest chair,

THE RAVEN AND THE NIGHTINGALE | 83

suddenly light-headed with shock—*blood spatters!*—"so
we don't necessarily read it as a dying accusation—"

"What do you mean, *necessarily?*" my Amanda exploded, instantly ready to do battle for her mother. "Of
course it's not an accusation! Mom had nothing to do
with—"

"I would assume not," the lieutenant interrupted,
with a faint smile. He liked Amanda, had told me the
previous summer that he thought she had the kind of
smarts that would make her a great cop. Not that I
wanted to hear that: *No daughter of mine* . . .

Now Piotrowski turned to me. "But, I gotta admit,
Doctor Pelletier, it gave me a hell of a jolt to find your
name at a crime scene—so prominent-like. So . . .
well . . . I need to talk to you. Is there somewhere you
and me could have a little privacy," he held up a meaty
hand to forestall Amanda's protest, "so I could ask you a
few questions confidential-like?"

I led Piotrowski into the kitchen and closed the door
on my gaping family and friends. As I cleared a spot for
the lieutenant at a table littered with cold potatoes, con-
gealed gravy, and a mutilated turkey carcass, I noted him
eyeing the food with what appeared to be more than investigative interest.

"Have you eaten, Lieutenant?" Even though, as far
as I knew, my scrawled name seemed to constitute the
sole clue so far in this homicide—or, maybe *because* of
that—I couldn't let this man go hungry.

"Nope. Call came late afternoon. Haven't had a minute to think about food." Piotrowski didn't look particularly malnourished. In fact, he looked no different than
last time I'd seen him: tall and broad, with medium-
brown hair cut short, wearing a conventional gray tweed
sport jacket and gray pants spiffed up a bit with a char-

coal-gray turtleneck jersey, as if for a holiday. Was there a wife waiting with dinner for the lieutenant somewhere? I knew he had grown sons, but he'd never said anything about a wife. "So, yeah," he continued, "I could eat. If you're offering. The minute I walked in here I got hungrier than a bear."

"Tsk. On Thanksgiving!" I loaded a plate, covered it loosely with plastic wrap, and placed it in the microwave. To live with death on a daily basis as the lieutenant did seemed only to give him a heightened appetite for life. I liked and respected this big cop. I'd first met Piotrowski two years earlier, when a colleague and a student had been murdered on campus, and then had come across him again when the death of a friend had proven to be a murder. On each occasion my scholarly expertise had assisted the detective in identifying the killer. But I hadn't thought about Piotrowski since the Hart case had been resolved—at least, not until my friends' foolishness had brought him so vividly back to mind: broad shoulders, surprisingly shapely lips. Yeah, yeah. But surely my matchmaking pals were mistaken in their speculations that the lieutenant had a "thing" for me.

"Listen," he said, in a business-like manner, "what I need to know right off is, how well d'ya know this guy Corbin?"

The microwave beeped. I removed Piotrowski's plate, placed it in front of him, found napkins, butter, salt and pepper shakers. "Well, he's my colleague of course." The glass of white wine I placed by his plate got a nod of thanks.

"Yeah, so I assumed. He was a professor in your department, huh?" I noted the change in tense: *was*.

"Yes, but I don't . . . didn't . . . know him at all well." I shifted the turkey carcass to the counter—suddenly the debris of the holiday table revolted me—poured wine for myself, a generous glass, and sat down across from the lieutenant. "Do you have any idea yet what happened? I know you can't tell me much, but—"

"Believe me, Doctor, this case is *fresh*. I mean, listen, I get the call, I show up, and *your* name's at the scene. I got myself over here quick as I could. So tell me what's what with you and Corbin. Just get me clear on that up front." He forked down a heap of potatoes with gravy.

"What do you mean *what's what?* He's my colleague." I paused. *"Was* my colleague." Piotrowski's graphic description of the crime scene—*blood spatters!*—made Elliot's death all too real. "God, it's just beginning to sink in. Elliot is *dead!"* I searched for words of grief—or at least, shock—but what came to my lips was something far more mundane. "Jeez, all hell is going to break loose at work!"

"Yeah? Tell me about that." The lieutenant was seriously engrossed in the turkey and stuffing. I shuddered. I was still thinking about the blood.

"Well . . ." I sighed profoundly, and related everything I knew about Elliot Corbin, which wasn't much: the recent work on Poe that had finally brought him the scholarly acclaim he'd yearned for, his ambitions for the Palaver Chair, even the handball. "And, aside from his being generally obnoxious," I concluded, "he didn't seem to have any particular enemies. Oh . . . wait a minute. . . ." I told Piotrowski about the altercation in Elliot's office I'd overheard a week earlier.

"A *woman's* voice?" He relinquished his fork for a notebook and pen, made chicken-track marks on the pad. "And, you're saying you didn't recognize the other speaker?"

"I have no idea who it was. She was speaking very quietly."

"As I recall, anybody has access to that building. . . ."

"Students, faculty, staff, prospective students,
alumni, even casual visitors."

"Great! Female, huh? That gives us, let's see, exactly
fifty-one percent of the world's population to investigate."

"You don't have to get sarcastic, Lieutenant."

The hinges on the kitchen door creaked. Amanda
poked her head into the room. Earlier she had moussed
her chestnut hair in trendy spikes, but now it lay flat on
the right side, as if she'd been nervously running her fingers through it. "Mom? You okay?"

"She's *fine*," Piotrowski replied, grinning at her. "Did
I see pie out there on that table?"

"Monica Cassale found him," I told my dinner guests,
after the lieutenant had scarfed down two slabs of pumpkin pie and hurried back to the crime scene.

"Monica? You mean the English Department secretary?" Sophia queried, appearing as mystified as I was.
"What was *she* doing at Professor Corbin's place?"

We sat around the dinner table, sobered by Piotrowski's news.

"I don't know." I stared at the pies, then rejected the
thought. Who could eat with such appalling news on her
plate? Almost immediately, I relented and cut a sliver
from the pumpkin, placed a teaspoonful of ice cream on it.
Jill opted for a slice each of pumpkin and apple; after
all, she was eating for Eloise. "For some reason, she
stopped by his house—with a serving of Thanksgiving
dinner, I think he said. I have no idea why she would
be taking dinner to Elliot. And she found him there.
Dead." I examined the dessert on my plate. Did I really
want that?

"Poor Monica," Sophia said, unexpectedly. "She

never gets a break. No thanks," she demurred, when I slid the pie in her direction. "I don't touch that stuff."

"You know Monica?" I asked, surprised.

"*I* know her," Sophia's mother said. We all started. It was as if the dead had spoken. Agata Warzek probably wasn't much older than me—maybe five or six years. But I still thought of myself as young. I *was* young. Life—and a brutal husband—had defeated Agata. She was a rag of a woman, with Sophia's fine features and delicate coloring, but wrinkled and threadbare and washed out.

"You *do?*"

"Yes." And that was it, nothing further forthcoming from Agata Warzek.

"She's our neighbor, has been for years," Sophia clarified. "She moved in down the street when Joey was a baby. She works all the time—I mean, *all* the time—and her mother takes care of Joey."

"Really?" I finished the sliver of pie, cut another, dipped into the now-soppy ice cream.

"I was happy for her when she got such a good job at the college. She quit cleaning houses then, and cut back to just weekends at the Stop N' Shop. I thought maybe she'd be able to take it a little easier, but she still seems to work around the clock."

"Huh. I didn't know all that about her."

Sophia and her mother exchanged meaningful glances. Then Sophia spoke. "Well, you wouldn't, would you, being a professor and all?"

That was a complex assessment, and I let it rumble around in my mind before I attempted to respond. Had my life taken a different turn I could easily have been Monica, but it hadn't, and I wasn't.

"Is she married?"

Again the exchange of glances. "Not that I know of. But my mother thinks she goes to see some guy. . . ."

"What do you mean, goes to see some guy?" I asked, as I finished my second sliver of pumpkin, eyed the apple pie.

Sophia glanced at her mother. Agata shrugged. Then Sophia shrugged. That was clearly as much as I was going to get from them.

"Mom," Amanda commanded, "just cut yourself a decent size slice and get it over with." I did. Earlene and Amanda followed suit. Then Agata. We ate slowly and solemnly, as if in the shared ritual we might somehow discover the key to a great mystery.

"Why are we talking about Monica, anyhow?" Jill asked, as she pushed her plate away. Eloise was spread out across her mother's knees, face down and blissfully asleep.

"It's just so intriguing that she would be there," I replied. "I can't conceive of any possible reason for her to be at Elliot's house—taking him Thanksgiving dinner, for God's sake!"

"What's really intriguing," Earlene countered, "is that Elliot Corbin is *dead*—and someone seems to have killed him." She began stacking empty cups in front of her. "And it might very well be someone we know."

First thing the next morning, Lieutenant Piotrowski called. Amanda answered the phone; after the lieutenant's startling announcement about finding my name at a homicide scene, my daughter hadn't said another word about going to Lowell, and I hadn't asked. In her mismatched sweats—green pants, orange top—with her short hair still mussed from sleep, she looked about fourteen years old. She handed me the phone without comment, and I gave her a quick hug as I grabbed it. We may have our misunderstandings, but I do love that kid.

"Doctor." The way Piotrowski enunciated the word —in two quick syllables—you would have thought it was my first name. "It looks like I'm gonna have to call on you again for some help. What you told me last night was real useful, and I've got something here at the station—a piece of evidence—I wanna run by you. Would you be able to stop in?"

Stopping in meant going way the hell out of my way, clear down to Springfield, but I did it. A person whose name appears to be the final written word of a murdered man gets real cooperative with the police.

The car radio blared as I turned the ignition: *—homicide of the eminent Professor Corbin! More details at ten!* WENF, Enfield Public Radio, was as electrified by Elliot's death as public radio could possibly be.

At the station, the lieutenant met me at the door of a grungy green evidence room. He shook my hand solemnly. "Thanks, Dr. Pelletier. It's good of you to come by so prompt." He led me to the battered table and pulled out a chair. Then he sat and regarded me solemnly. I took it for several long seconds.

"You have something to show me, Lieutenant?" I prompted.

"Yeah. I do. But first—since earlier, when I talked to you on the phone, Sergeant Schultz . . . you remember Sergeant Schultz? . . ."

Schultz was Piotrowski's partner, and until the magic moment last summer when I'd helped her apprehend a killer, she'd made very obvious her contempt for someone in my wimpy profession. I nodded.

"Well, as you can imagine, Schultz has been talking to a few people at the college today, and she's just brought in a fresh piece of information." He gave me another enigmatic look.

I nodded, again. It seemed the best response: I had no idea what he was getting at, and I didn't want to risk incriminating myself in any way.

"I understand that you and the victim had a bit of an altercation the other day. . . ."

"We did?"

"And what I don't understand is why you didn't inform me of that fact."

"*What* altercation? There *was* no altercation. I've never had an altercation with Elliot Corbin."

"In front of your office? Last Friday? Something about you disturbing him?"

"Huh? Oh, you mean when he accused me of talking too loudly? No . . . *chattering*. *Chattering* was what he said. Lieutenant, that was nothing. He was just being his usual obnoxious self."

"Umm," Piotrowski replied.

"And who told you about that anyhow? No one was around."

"Can't reveal sources, Doctor. You know that."

"Monica!" I exclaimed. "It must have been Monica! Of all the—"

"Okay, Doctor, calm down. So you say it was nothing?"

"Damn right, it was nothing!"

"Okay, then, relax. See, I'm writing it down: *nothing*. Look, here it is: *nothing*. See?" He turned his notebook toward me. An entire page was scrawled over with the single word, *nothing*.

I gave him fish eyes.

"Now, can we get on with why you're here?" Piotrowski slid a plastic-sheathed notepad in my direction. "Okay, Doctor, have you seen this tablet before?" The yellow pad looked familiar only because all yellow lined pads look exactly the same. Except for the blood spat-

ters. I must admit, with all the faculty battles I'd been
involved in, I'd never seen a blood-speckled notepad before. The facing page of this pad, as the lieutenant had
told me, featured my name, underlined with three bold
scores of a black ballpoint pen. The final stroke of the
underscoring had been inscribed with such force that the
pen had ripped a hole through the paper. I glanced up at
Piotrowski, mystified. He motioned me back to the page.
Including my name, the jottings read as follows:

Karen Pelletier

Northbury Center
$10,000,000!
Int. Lib. Epistem. St!!!
Harriet P   Mat Fem
Jewell   Pur Inst

and, way down at the bottom of the page, in smaller,
fainter letters: *Emmeline Foster $$$——???* Rust-colored
droplets spattered the page lightly.

"Well," I mused, looking up at the lieutenant again,
"I haven't actually seen this page before—especially not
the blood!—but I'm quite certain I know what it is."

"What's that?"

"Notes from a meeting." I studied the jottings again.
"Yes, it must be. Tuesday evening a study group I'm in
met at Elliot's house, and I gave a report on Edith Hart's
bequest to the college—"

The big cop grunted. He knew all about that bequest.
"That explains some of what's here: the Northbury Cen-
ter, the ten million dollars. But what is this *Int. Lib. Epis-
tem. St?*"

"Elliot was interested in epistemology."

"Epistem—?"

"It's a term from philosophy, having to do with the nature of knowledge, its instability and relativity. Very central to postmodernist thinking—"

"What knowledge?"

"All knowledge. But, in literary studies, especially issues such as authority, evaluation, methodology, interpretation . . ." My eyes fixed on the spatters. The pad had not been soaked in blood but, rather, sprinkled, so that the droplets formed an enigmatic free-flung design. *If you were to take a pen,* I thought, *and connect the dots of gore, you might come up with some meaningful pattern.* I tilted my head first one way, then the next, attempting to decipher the figure, but just as I thought I began to perceive some sort of configuration, Piotrowski spoke.

"There's only one kind of knowledge I'm interested in right now, Dr. Pelletier, and that's who killed your colleague."

"Well, yes . . . that does . . . er . . . seem to take precedence over philosophical problems. So, then—I think I understand why everything on this sheet is here. I even remember Elliot taking the notes. As I told you yesterday, Elliot was very ambitious. At the meeting I began to sense that he was scheming to take over the Northbury Center and its funds for some kind of a prestigious institute he himself could direct. That would bring him power, money, acclaim, *and*—he'd never have to enter a classroom again if he didn't want to." I glanced back at Elliot's notes—and the dried spatters. Could those connect-a-dot bloodstains possibly form the outline of a bird—a *crow,* maybe? But surely I was being fanciful. Piotrowski was waiting for solid information from me, not Rorschach-test hallucinations. "The other names on the sheet are Harriet Person and Miles Jewell, and it seemed to me at the meeting that both Harriet and Miles also had self-interested ambitions for the Institute, so it makes sense that their names should be there. But I don't understand why Emmeline Foster's name is here—or why it's followed by dollar signs."

"Who's Emmeline Foster?"

"She's nobody—now. But a hundred and fifty years ago she committed suicide because of unrequited love for Edgar Allan Poe." I paused, and the urge for scholarly accuracy overcame the urge to tell a dramatic story. "Well, that's the myth, anyhow. I don't know how true it is."

Piotrowski slumped back with an exasperated little crash. His chair shuddered. "Shit!"

I said nothing. The lieutenant was usually extremely careful about not using crude language around "ladies."

He sat up again, folded his hands in front of him. "Excuse my French, Doctor, but don't tell me this homicide is going to turn into another one of your literary mysteries."

"*My* literary mysteries, Lieutenant?" I turned the pad in its plastic sheath so that it faced him and shoved it back across the table. "You're the one who brings these complicated conundrums to me. I'm beginning to think the state police should put me on the payroll!" From this new upside-down perspective, the blood-spatter pattern on the lined yellow page looked nothing like a crow.

I'd reached the exit when the lieutenant caught up with me. Since I'd left him two minutes earlier, he'd pulled on a gray down jacket.

"Sorry I had to ruin your holiday yesterday, but I needed to get some things straight. And, everything checks out—just like I knew it would." He paused, looked cautiously around, moved closer to me, lowered his voice. "Forget about that fight with Corbin, Doctor. You got nothing to worry about. I want you to know you're gonna be totally in the clear here."

"Gonna be?" That obviously sounded better to the detective than it did to me, but then I was in a profession where I was hypersensitized to the tense of verbs. I'd much rather he had phrased that assurance solidly in the present—You *are* totally in the clear here—than in some kind of shaky colloquial adaptation of the future tense. *Gonna* be? *Gonna* be? There was no secure grammatical underpinning for *gonna* be. "God, Lieutenant, couldn't you have just said *will?* As in, You *will* be totally in the clear here?"

Piotrowski made a circle of his thumb and forefinger, surreptitiously flashed it at me. "And thanks for the meal last night, Doctor. It was real good. Made me think of the old days. . . ." He let the words trail off, pushed the door open, nodded goodbye, and headed determinedly down the sidewalk toward the center of town. Earlene was dead wrong, I thought. This man had no interest in me as a woman. And for a brief second, before rational thought came flooding back, I felt inexplicably bereft.

When I got home, Amanda's car was gone. A note on the kitchen table said, *"Mom, I know you can take care of yourself with the Lt. I'm heading for Lowell. I'll call when I can. Don't worry. Love and kisses, always, Amanda.*

"P.S. You've had at least *a dozen calls—and all before noon! Wanna bet they're all about Professor Corbin's death? What* are *you, anyhow? Gossip Central?"*

10.

"The poet has a lonely soul."

—ROSE TERRY COOKE

I T WAS 10:07 P.M. THE same evening, and I was curled up on the living room sofa, with a yellow-and-green wool afghan over my legs and the woodstove burning full blast. A frigid wind assaulted the little country house, and windows bumped and rattled in their wooden frames. *Poems are alot like life,* I read, and sighed. In spite of holidays, homicide, and ill-advised daughterly hegiras, the grading of freshman papers must go on. The stack of essays on the coffee table had diminished only slightly since I'd begun on them after dinner, but I was too tired to do justice to even one more. Once again, I shuffled Freddie Whitby's paper to the bottom of the pile. I'd deal with her when I was fully conscious. Right now it was time for thermal long johns, flannel pj's, two pairs of heavy socks, and my cozy bed. Amanda had called earlier to let me know she'd gotten to Lowell, was fine, just fine, and was looking for a motel. I didn't know why I worried: Amanda was savvy and tough—and she had my credit card.

I was wandering through a maze of dimly lit basement passageways in Dickinson Hall, the long-time home of the English Department and one of the oldest buildings on campus. The walls of the corridor were rough stone and I could feel a chill dampness emanating from them. Suddenly I noticed that the fluorescent light strips spaced widely along the wall had vanished, and smoky hanging lanterns had taken their place. I turned to Amanda and said, "Look at that! That must be whale oil they're burning there!" But Amanda had inexplicably become Jane Birdwort. "Follow me," Jane commanded, and we passed through an arched doorway into a beautifully furnished parlor where a woman in a long lavender dress sat alone at a spinet piano. I leafed through books on a small table, ornate, gilt-edged, beautiful nineteenth-century books—and brand-new! Jane attempted to talk to the melancholy woman at the piano, but Jane was no longer flesh and blood; she was merely a transparent shadow. "Can she hear you?" I questioned, urgently. All at once, I understood that Jane and I had traversed a threshold into the past—we had somehow actually penetrated directly into the solid, material past—and neither of us had any more substance there than that of a shifting shade. "She hears me," Jane replied, "but not my words. She thinks it's birds chirping." I took a closer look at the woman and gasped. "That's the poet Emmeline Foster," I told Jane, and I was thrilled to be there with her, in her room, in her time! "Talk to her! Talk to her!" I urged Jane. And at the sound of my heartfelt tones, Emmeline Foster raised her head and looked vaguely in my direction, puzzled. Then Elliot Corbin threw open the door to my classroom. But Elliot's dead, I thought.

My eyes opened. I lay immobile, my heart pounding, for what seemed like an eternity. But no matter how hard I tried, I could not get myself back inside that dream.

Saturday morning I vacuumed, dusted, folded laundry, repotted an ivy plant that had outgrown its clay pot months before—anything to avoid having to sit down again with those damn freshman papers. At noon, CNN informed me that Professor Elliot Corbin's murder was symptomatic of a disturbing trend toward violence on our campuses nationwide. That his death did not occur on campus was evidently beside the point.

Finally, fortified by my thick turkey-and-cranberry sandwich and strong coffee, I picked up the stack of essays, trudged over to the desk. *Poems are alot like life,* I read, and groaned. Not Freddie Whitby again! I always turn back the title pages of students' essays to hide the names, so I can read each paper without knowing who wrote it. Otherwise, after the first assignment of the semester, it's almost impossible to grade without preconceived expectations. But I knew immediately who'd written this paper; I would have had to be comatose not to. "Okay, Freddie," I muttered, "Let's just get it over with." I picked up the green pen I was using for this batch of essays, scrawled a bright green *Focus!* in the margin—and, mercifully, the phone rang.

Hugo Domato, a stocky, white-haired man in the navy blue parka of the Enfield College Security division, met me at my office door. "I know it's Saturday, Professor, but I thought you'd want to check this out." Hugo pushed the door open, and I gasped. He'd informed me that my office had been ransacked, and I'd come speeding to campus through a gray late-autumn drizzle the moment I'd gotten the call, but I'd had no idea of the extent of the devastation. Books had been pulled off their shelves. Every drawer in my filing cabinet was gaping open, and manila file folders had been flung all over the floor. The intruder had plundered the desk drawers, stacking piles of course notes, syllabi, department newsletters, and research notes chaotically on the desktop. My first thought was: *Thank God I took my grade book home with me.* Then I noticed that the Emmeline Foster box had been overturned, and books and papers were spread all around it on the wide oak floorboards like some kind of paper island.

"Jesus Christ, Hugo! What happened here?"

The security guard spread his hands wide. "George found it this way when he came in to clean this morning. The custodians were off for the holiday since Wednesday. George says your office was fine then."

"Yeah, it was." I'd last been on campus Wednesday around noon, when I'd come in to pick up my mail and photocopy a book review I'd written for *Signs*. This break-in could have happened anytime since then. My gaze fell again on the box of Emmeline Foster's papers. I'd been in a rush on Wednesday and hadn't had time to unpack the box in search of the misplaced little book of verses—or to do any further reading in the journals. I looked around the chaos for the maroon-ribbon-bound copybooks and saw no sign of them. But the room was such a mess, I reassured myself, the journals could be anywhere.

"You have any idea who woulda done this?" Hugo asked.

I shrugged. "Did Security see anyone hanging around?" I sat down at the desk, switched on the computer, scrolled through the files listing. Everything looked fine there, thank God.

"I dunno. I been on vacation too. Ask them in the

office. You're gonna have to stop by there and fill out a report, anyhow."

Great. "Was this a real break-in, do you think, Hugo?" I walked back to the door, checked out the lock. "I don't see any damage here."

"No sign of forcible entry. Looks like the intruder musta had a key. Keys can be pretty easy to come by around here."

"Yeah, anyone who wants it can get the cookie key in this department. At least during office hours."

"Cookie key?"

"The passkey; it's on a ring with a giant plastic chocolate-chip cookie. Hangs right by Monica's desk." *Monica? Here was Monica, again. At the scene of Elliot Corbin's death. And with easy access to my office; Monica had keys to everything. But why would Monica—?*

Stop it, Pelletier! I admonished myself. *If you start suspecting everyone, you'll drive yourself crazy!* I wondered if perhaps I shouldn't call Piotrowski about the break-in. But, no, I didn't want to overreact. How could this incident have anything to do with Elliot's death? The intruder was probably a disgruntled student. It had happened before. *Damn* good thing I hadn't left my grade book behind.

I filled out the report at Security, returned to my office, sat in my desk chair, surveyed the debacle, and groaned aloud. Cleaning this up was going to take the rest of the day. I righted the UPS box so I could repack it before I tackled the file cabinets and bookshelves. Then I looked again for the stack of Emmeline's copybooks; I'd better take them home for safekeeping. They were probably behind—or under—the heaps of books that had been yanked helter-skelter from the bookcase. I'd begun reshelving books, in no particular order—off the floor and onto any shelf—when I heard Jane Birdwort's voice in the hall.

"What in heaven's name happened here?" Jane stood in my doorway, wearing loose-fitting khaki pants, her beige quilted jacket, and brown leather lace-up boots. A battered leather book bag hung by a wide strap from her shoulder.

"You tell me, Jane." I wiped my sweaty hands on my jeans, and tried to steady my breath. She'd startled me. Obviously, I was more shaken by this ugly incident than I'd thought. "Hurricane? Tornado? Pissed-off student?"

"You think it was a student?" She stepped inside and let her bag fall to the floor. "How appalling!" She picked up a sheaf of papers from the green chair, glanced at it casually, then immediately began to study the pages more thoughtfully. Peering over her shoulder, I saw that she held a grouping of poem manuscripts in the careful, small writing with which I was fast becoming familiar.

"That's Emmeline Foster's," I said. "You remember, don't you? She's the poet whose papers were just donated to the Northbury Center."

"Interesting," Jane replied, and sank into the nearest chair, still studying the poems. She leafed through the pages in a contemplative silence. Then she looked up at me. "These appear to be early drafts. See all the cross-outs and substitutions? Not too different from the way I work." She read further, immersed in the verse. When she'd gone through several pages, she placed Foster's manuscripts carefully on the edge of my desk, gave them a last, lingering look, then turned to me. "If you like, I could help you clean up this . . ." She gestured uncertainly around the room.

"Would you?" My efforts had barely made a dent. "I could really use some help. But I'm a little unnerved right now—as you can probably tell. How about a trip to

Bread and Roses first for coffee?" I didn't know how much help Jane would be, but hers was the only offer I'd had, and I'd be a fool to turn it down.

The drizzle had ended and a wan sun shone fitfully as we crossed campus heading for Field Street. I nodded to Avery Mitchell on the walkway outside Emerson Hall. Enfield's president was in dress-down mode today: jeans, navy blue pea jacket, Rockports. In spite of the nasty weather, he was hatless, gloveless, and scarfless. Tall, lean, and sandy-haired, with the angular facial planes of the true WASP, Avery looked as good to me—damn it!— as he always had.

"Karen? . . ." Avery said, when he saw me, as if he intended to speak about something that genuinely concerned him. Then he noticed my companion and instantaneously altered his tone. ". . . *and* Jane," he added smoothly. "How are you?" It was a collective *you*—a phatic interrogative, as the linguists have it—no longer the kind of question to which either Jane or I was expected to reply. "I do hope you are both enjoying your Thanksgiving break." He smiled, nodded, and passed us without slowing down for a response.

"He seems like a nice man," Jane said, turning briefly to gaze after him.

"He is," I replied, and repressed any urge to comment further. Avery disappeared down Field Street in the direction of the President's House. Probably on his way home for a spot of afternoon tea. Or, for a spot of something a bit more stimulating, I thought enviously. Avery's wife Liz had returned to him a few months earlier after several years of separation; they were probably still in the second-honeymoon stage.

In the center of town, a crew with a cherry-picker lift was affixing giant non-sectarian electric candles to the faux-Victorian lightposts. Otherwise, the streets were almost empty as Jane and I waited for the traffic light to change at the wide intersection. Next to us at the curb, a slender young woman in jeans and a hand-knit Peruvian sweater fussed anxiously with the plastic stroller shield that protected her infant from the cutting wind. Across Field Street, two elderly women I recognized as faculty wives—faculty wives emeriti, if such a title is possible—descended the steps of the public library, each laden with a stack of brightly colored books. Suddenly, standing there, waiting for the green light, I had the uncanny feeling that someone was watching me. I spun around. A few students were scattered singly and in pairs on the sidewalk, but none of them was looking at me. Jane glanced at me quizzically. I shrugged: *Just paranoid, I guess.*

Bread and Roses smelled of chocolate and coffee. With most students gone for the holiday, things were slow, and only a half-dozen shoppers occupied the round marble tables. Bread and Roses was a sixties counterculture coffee shop that had matured and flourished over the decades without going upscale in any way but price. Its coffee came in only two permutations—caffeine and decaf—leaving anything more ambitious to the new Starbucks down the street. Baked goods were Bread and Roses' real claim to fame, and I secured a couple of sherried raisin scones as I ordered coffee for myself and Jane. Sophia Warzek, wrapped in an enormous white apron, emerged from the kitchen carrying a lemon meringue pie. I widened my eyes histrionically at the sight of the gorgeous pie, and Sophia grinned.

"So," I said to Jane, as I joined her at the table, "I assume you've heard about Elliot."

"Elliot?" she echoed, and her small face with its country-girl cheeks assumed a hedged expression. "What about Elliot?"

I stared at her, amazed. The Enfield College gossip network prides itself on one-hundred-percent saturation, and I'd been on the phone all yesterday afternoon with people wanting to talk about poor Elliot's horrid death. Plus, the *Enfield Enquirer* had gone for megasize headlines in both the Friday and Saturday issues. How was it possible the news hadn't gotten to Jane? But, then, our visiting poet had been on campus only three months, and she wasn't a particularly sociable woman. Maybe she didn't read the local paper; maybe nobody had called her.

"Oh," I said, "I thought for sure you would have heard. Elliot Corbin is dead."

"Dead!" Jane's hand jerked, and her milky coffee sloshed over onto the table. She concentrated on mopping it up with a Bread and Roses recycled-paper napkin. "Was it his heart?" she asked, her eyes still on the soggy napkin.

"No—"

"Well, then, what?" She looked up at me suddenly. Her lips had gone pale. "Was it an accident? He always did drive too fast."

"No, not an accident." How would Jane be familiar with Elliot Corbin's driving habits? Why would she seem so upset about his death? "Elliot was . . . murdered," I said.

"Murdered?" Jane slumped back in her chair, as if all her muscles had failed at once.

"I know—it's inconceivable." I took a sip of coffee, and the caffeine went straight to the necessary brain cells. "He was killed at home," I told her, "on Thanksgiving Day. Stabbed with a knife." My report was factual, but, as I related the details, they sounded like elements of some nineteenth-century melodrama. "It's simply incomprehensible," I concluded. "I just can't get my mind around it."

"Elliot?" Jane whispered. "Dead?" She sat motionless for a few seconds, then dropped the coffee-sopped napkin onto her untasted scone and abruptly pushed her chair back. "Karen, I'm very sorry, but I'm not going to be able to . . . I've just remembered . . . I . . . I have to leave." She zipped up her bulky quilted jacket and slipped the strap of her book bag over her shoulder. "Sorry," she said again, vaguely, and headed for the door.

Sophia, setting out a tray of the infamous Bread and Roses fudge-frosted brownies, watched Jane's exit from behind the glass-topped display case. When the door closed behind her poetry mentor, Sophia glanced over at me with a frown. I gave her a reassuring smile. Truth was, Jane Birdwort was the last person I would ever have expected to express any concern for anything that happened outside what some scholars call *the life of the poem*—in other words, in the real world. But obviously Elliot's death meant something more to Jane than just another college scandal. But what?

Emmeline Foster's journal was gone. There was no longer any denying it, and I wanted to cry. George the janitor had come by toward the end of his shift and had helped me get the books back on my office shelves. My file folders and desk contents were back in an approximation of their original places, and I was once again packing the Emmeline Foster materials. But the stack of copybooks in which Foster had so conscientiously inscribed the happenings of her days and years had vanished. I stood by the repacked box and surveyed the office one last time. No ribbon-tied stack of journals to be seen anywhere. And no sign, either, of the little blue notebook that had inexplicably disappeared the day I'd first opened the Emmeline Foster box. Someone on this campus seemed to have sufficient interest in this virtually unknown nineteenth-century poet not only to filch an easily pocketable little book, but also to undertake a search of my office. But who? I thought back to the people who'd been present when the box had been opened: Jane Birdwort, who, that very afternoon, had shown herself to be fascinated with Foster's poem manuscripts; Monica Cassale (again!); Harriet Person, who had her own ambitions for the Northbury Center; Amber Nichols, who, in her characteristically enigmatic manner had expressed an interest in the acquisition of the Foster papers; and—of course— Elliot Corbin. Who was now the *late* Elliot Corbin.

I hesitated—was I simply conforming to the hoary stereotype of the hysterical woman? Well, didn't I have good reason to be paranoid? I shuddered, and carefully closed and locked my office door; even in this deserted campus building, you could never tell what curious ears might be attending to your phone calls. Then I pulled a dog-eared business card from my wallet, studied the name and number written thereon, picked up the phone, took a deep breath, dialed the number . . . and asked for Lieutenant Piotrowski.

11.

To show the laboring bosom's deep intent,
And thought in living characters to paint

—PHYLLIS WHEATLEY

ON SUNDAY MORNING, AS I cracked the turkey carcass apart at the joints and shredded the remaining meat from the bones, I planned the soup. It would be a simple turkey-and-rice soup, with plenty of julienned vegetables: ribs of celery, strips of carrots, a small potato grated into the broth for body, onions, garlic—a welcome-back-Amanda-no-one-else-loves-you-the-way-I-do kind of soup. Once I had the turkey bones simmering in my largest pot, I began grading papers, anxious to get them completed before my daughter returned with whatever disturbing news she had for me. I'd slipped Freddie Whitby's essay to the bottom of the pile again, and this time it had stayed put. Finally, I placed the next-to-the-last paper in the stack of graded essays, and again contemplated Freddie's opening salvo: "Poems are alot like

life." With the green pen, I underlined the *Focus* I'd written in the margin earlier, circled *alot*, scrawled *Spelling!*
"Many people write poems when they want to know
about life," Freddie continued. *Ditto*, I wrote under the
Focus. "I think Edger Allen Poe . . ." *Spelling!*, I wrote
under the *Ditto*. ". . . wanted to know about life alot so
he wrote poems." My pen hovered over the margin as I
decided what to address here: *Get to the point!* "I think
Edger was really, really, really upset," she went on,
"about the vast and empty caverns of existential ignorance that underlie our common life." *Whaaa?* "As a case
in point, the infamous bird in Poe's 'The Raven' functions as surreal trope for a pre-modernist unknowing, as
emblem of an existentialist angst prescient of post-
Freudian, post-Christian poesis, as enigmatic metaphor
for a poetics of the abyss." *Surreal? Trope? Poesis? Poetics
of the abyss? Shit! This was the language of professional
literary criticism. Freddie Whitby could not possibly have
written this analysis herself.*

I finished reading the essay, which went on in the
same vein for four and a half pages, scrawled *your own
language?* in the margin, deliberated for two seconds
about whether or not it would be inconsiderate to call
Earlene at home on a weekend, then called Earlene. At
home. On the weekend.

"As the Dean of Students," I told her without preamble, "you should know about the blatant plagiarism I've
just stumbled across."

"Hello, Karen," Earlene replied. "How are you? Nice
to hear from you. Thanks for the wonderful meal on
Thanksgiving."

"Hi, Earlene. I'm sorry. I'm really sorry. I know this
could wait until tomorrow, but I'm just so upset. Listen."
I read Freddie's opening paragraph.

"*Post-Freudian, post-Christian poesis,*" Earlene said,

and laughed. "My, but we do recruit a knowledgeable class of eighteen-year-olds these days."

"What do I do about this?" I was angry. How stupid did this student think I was?

"Can you identify the source? I mean, we can make a charge of plagiarism based on the fact that the essay is written in a specialized vocabulary available to a college freshman only in the unlikely instance that she has graduate training in literature. But the college policy on academic honesty asks the professor to attempt to find the source from which the material was taken before making a formal accusation."

I groaned. "Earlene, do you know how many millions of words of litcrit have been written about Poe? Do you know how busy I am at this time of year?"

"Just make an attempt," she said soothingly. "Go to the library. Look at some books. You might be surprised, Karen. Sometimes the source just leaps into your hands. If you can't find it, we'll handle Ms. Whitby some other way."

I slipped the offending paper, ungraded, in a folder separate from the others and jammed it into my briefcase, then turned on the CD player with its resident Emmylou Harris albums. I was in desperate need of Emmylou's good honest voice. To the background of "Goin' Back to Harlan," I piled carrots, celery, onions, and garlic on the chopping block, and filled a pan with water for the brown rice. Thank God for my own wonderful daughter. Amanda was such a good kid; I was going to make her the very best turkey-rice soup in the entire world.

Amanda got home about two that afternoon, tired, hungry—and glum.

"Did you find your father?" I asked, tentatively, setting a bowl in front of her.

"No," she replied, and, without further comment, began scarfing down the world's best turkey soup.

"Oh." I slipped into a chair across from her. "Was anyone able to tell you where he is?" With a serrated knife, I sliced two crusty whole wheat rolls and placed them on Amanda's plate.

"No." She continued to spoon up soup.

"Oh. Well, did you—" Amanda's deliberate refusal to meet my gaze jolted me into a realization that I was asking too many questions. She'd tell me all about it when she was good and ready. Absently I buttered one of her rolls and ate it.

"Mom?" Amanda asked, when she'd finished her second helping of soup. She set the bowl to one side, and, over a cup of tea with honey, finally looked directly at me. "Mom? I've got something to ask you. Why don't you ever talk about your family?"

The light from the hanging frosted-glass globe over the table illuminated the angular bone structure of Amanda's face, cast the shadow of long lashes over cheeks blushed only by her own high coloring. Her short brown hair shone with red highlights. Her eyes challenged me.

My family? I hadn't seen my family in years. The last time had been at my father's funeral, when Amanda was only five. She and I had gone to the funeral, but I'd panicked and left before the coffin was carried out. My sisters never spoke to me again.

"What's to tell?" I replied. I toyed with the ceramic rooster and hen salt and pepper shakers, dancing them back and forth between my hands. The rooster and the hen did a frantic little jig, stopped dead, faced each other, beaks touching. "My family never wanted anything to do with me after I left your father, you know. When Fred started hitting you"—Amanda paled, flinched—"and I walked out, my father was deathly afraid he'd have to support me—and you. The last time I phoned my family, honey, my father called me a slut and told me not to come back home. I've never told you about that because you didn't need to know. But, since you've asked . . . And we've gotten along without them, haven't we? We've done okay for ourselves."

"Yeah." Her voice had lost its tone of challenge. "But he's dead now. He's been dead for a long time. And Aunt Connie says . . ."

Aunt Connie! My heart sank at the sound of my sister's name. Amanda had looked up my family.

". . . she says you didn't talk to anybody at the funeral. She says that now that you're a big-time college professor you've got a swelled head. She says you think you're too good for the rest of the family—"

"That's bullshit! When you and I were in North Adams, my family wouldn't even send me the bus fare home. For all they cared, we could have starved in the streets. I had to go to the Salvation Army for housing." My face burned at the memory.

Amanda was staring at me, appalled. "I didn't know any of this stuff. Why didn't you tell me?"

I took a deep breath. "Why would I tell you? Total strangers at the Salvation Army were kinder to us than our own family. I'm not proud of that. The Sallies found us an apartment, got you into a day-care program, even made me an appointment with an admissions counselor at the state college. I think they saved our lives. Then I got a job waitressing and started going to school at night."

"I remember when you worked at the truck stop. That was in North Adams, wasn't it?"

"You remember that? You were just a tyke."

"You used to bring home pie."

"Yeah—we lived on stale truck-stop food, pie and muffins and stuff. I can't believe you remember."

She shrugged, granted me a disarming smile, and gestured toward her empty bowl. "That was great soup,
Mom." I took another deep breath, let it out slowly. This
wasn't the end of it, I knew, but I had my daughter back;
maybe the soup had helped. But Amanda wasn't done
yet. "Listen, Mom, I don't know what's going on with
me, but I really need to know who I am. I don't feel like
I'll be satisfied until I know my . . . my . . . origins."
She was being delicate with me. Amanda and I had been
a family forever, stale-pie dinners and all. Now she
wanted to explore beyond that bond. I held my hands
tightly together in my lap so I wouldn't give in to the
impulse to reach across the table and clutch her to me. On
the CD player, Emmylou moved into "Orphan Girl."

Amanda left for Georgetown at dawn on Monday, loaded
down with turkey sandwiches, a plastic container of soup,
and fresh molasses cookies, and I'd been up extra early to
pack it all and say goodbye. I wanted to make certain I
had time to photocopy Freddie Whitby's plagiarized essay before I questioned her about it, so I got to campus a
good half-hour early. As usual when I arrived in Dickinson Hall before the first class of the day, the corridors
were dark and deserted. At least I assumed they were
deserted, until a flick of the light switch caught a furtive
shadow slipping around the corner in the general direction of the side door. I had the most extraordinary sense
of déjà vu: Hadn't this happened the last time I'd come
into the office early? College campuses are heavily popu-
lated places, but I was hard put to think of a legitimate
reason why anyone would lurk in the English Department hallways in the dark at seven-thirty A.M. on two
Mondays in a row. When I got my office door open, I
turned on all the lights in the room, including the little
desk lamp. The fugitive shadow in the hallway was prob-

ably nothing but an anxiety phantom, a figment of my all-too-active imagination, but suddenly I had a yen for as much illumination as possible.

Pulling my department photocopy card from my wallet, I retrieved the folder with Freddie's paper and carried it to the little copy room at the end of the first-floor hallway, flicking on each light switch I passed. Three copies of this plagiarized essay ought to do the trick: one for my records, one for the Department's records, one for my report to the Dean. With a little persuasion and a chipped fingernail, the staple came loose from the pages. Then I slipped the essay into the multiple-pages slot of the multifunction photocopy machine and pressed the start button. The machine went through its various initial groanings, swallowed the first page of the essay as it was programmed to do, then, without warning, ground to a halt. The little display window read REMOVE JAMMED PAGES, FOLLOW INSTRUCTIONS, BEGIN OVER. I groaned, more dramatically than the machine, and dutifully followed instructions. The machine jammed again. *Shit!* I removed the one page that the machine had gobbled, followed instructions, began over. The machine jammed. *Double shit!* After all my precautions, I was going to be late for class. I yanked open the front door of the machine for the third time, pressed down one green lever after another, probed all the photocopier's secret inner compartments. Nothing. Began over. The machine jammed. It was now seven minutes of eight; I'd give it one more try. I pulled open the front door, pressed levers, opened compartments. Nothing. *Wait!* Was that infinitesimal scrap of white in the machine's innermost bowels the corner of a sheet of paper? I yanked, and the offending sheet emerged. Good. Just enough time to copy Freddie's masterpiece and get to class. As I crumpled up the retrieved sheet preliminary to tossing it in the wastebasket, a line of familiar handwriting caught my eye. Precise, print-like handwriting. Emmeline Foster's handwriting. Suddenly alert, I laid the wrinkled page on the machine's cover and carefully smoothed it out. My God! The last person to use this copy machine between the final day of class before Thanksgiving break and this very moment had photocopied Emmeline Foster's purloined book of poems.

12.

I like these plants that you call weeds,—
Sedge, hardhack, mullein, yarrow,—

—LUCY LARCOM

CLASS THAT MORNING WAS FAIRLY lackluster,
overshadowed, I was certain, by the ominous awareness that violent death had hit the Enfield College community. Also, Mike Vitale hadn't shown up, and that
made a real difference in the class dynamics. I hadn't
realized until this—his first—absence how much I de-
pended on Mike, always present, always responsive, always reliable. After class, I returned papers to my
freshmen. "Freddie," I said to the sole remaining student,
when I'd finished handing the other essays back, "I have
a few questions to ask you about your paper. Could you
please come see me during office hours?"

"What kind of questions?" Freddie's plucked eyebrows furrowed, her pale blue eyes grew very still. Today
she wore black jeans and a fitted jacket reminiscent of an

English riding coat. "How can there be any questions? I worked hard on that paper."

"Please stop by this morning, Freddie. Sometime between ten and noon."

"But . . . but—"

"I'll see you later, Freddie. We'll talk then."

As I pushed through the double doors into Dickinson Hall on my way back from class, Monica emerged from her lair. "Karen, there's someone here to see you." Her usual abrasive manner was overshadowed by a wary apprehensiveness. She seemed exhausted and stressed. She surveyed me evaluatively, with her head tilted. Oddly enough, it was the kind of look one woman gives another only under certain circumstances, the kind of look that has something to do with a man. "I put him in your office."

I found Lieutenant Piotrowski seated in the green chair, leafing through a copy of my recently published book on American writers and the constraints of social class. He must have taken it down from the bookcase where I hoard my complimentary copies.

I plopped my heavy book bag on the desk, hung my black storm coat on the rack, checked my appearance—stupidly—in the nonreflective pebbled-glass panel of the door and blindly smoothed my hair. "Hard up for reading material, Lieutenant?" I asked.

He glanced up from the book. "This isn't bad, you know. Interesting, the way the American class system works. Ya live in it every day, but ya never think about it. And who woulda thought those really brilliant writers bought into class prejudice like that—Emerson and Miss Dickinson and them." He chewed his upper lip thoughtfully. Then he nodded, as if he'd reached some conclusion.

"Interesting stuff. And—I can actually understand what you're saying." He closed the book and placed it on the small table next to the chair.

"Thank you, Lieutenant. Unlike many of my colleagues, I actually write to *be* understood. But I know you didn't come here to talk about American literature."

When I'd called Piotrowski on Saturday, he'd listened in silence to my speculations about the break-in at my office. "So," he'd said when I'd finished, "you're telling me you handled all the evidence?"

"Evidence? For God's sake, Lieutenant, I wasn't thinking of my office as a *crime scene*."

"Well, no. I'm just thinking, ya understand—if the evidence has all been tampered with already, I don't need to come running up there tonight."

"I didn't *tamper!*" The man was infuriating.

"—and any connection to the Corbin homicide is really . . . ah . . . tenuous. Look, Doctor, when are you free on Monday?"

So here he was, at 9:07 Monday morning, in my office, sitting back in the comfortable chair, looking for all the world like an exceedingly amiable Great Dane. The large chair accepted his bulk as if it were delighted to have a fitting occupant. As I sat in the black captain's chair opposite Piotrowski and centered the pleats of my olive-green wool pants over my knees, Monica walked by in the hallway, craning her neck for a glimpse of the lieutenant.

He watched her pass, his eyes like slits. "Can we close that door, Doctor?"

I jumped up and pushed the door. It closed with an emphatic snick.

"Thanks. This definitely should not be overheard. Now, listen, I really don't think there's anything to be learned here by investigating this break-in—" At my protest, he held up a hand. "I know, I know. Look, maybe it's linked to the homicide, I dunno. Could be. Have the security people look around. Maybe they'll find something, but . . . Dr. Pelletier, I'll be frank with you. Here's the real reason I came by. As you can imagine"— he gestured wryly at himself, the unmistakably official police-officer bulk—"I'm at a serious disadvantage asking questions around this campus. In my line of work, the people I'm used to dealing with are not exactly rocket scientists, if you get my drift. Them I know how to handle. Pull a little here, nudge a little there: Presto, they spill the beans. And I know how to listen when they talk. But here . . . here there's a whole kind of different . . ." He paused—at a loss for words. Translation: I was the expert in language. I should help him out.

"You mean *culture?* An academic *culture?*" Then I wanted to bite my tongue. I knew how the lieutenant worked. For some reason, today, he was intent on buttering me up.

"Yeah, that's it. An academic *culture.*" His brown eyes widened, expressing admiration for a superior intellect; he all but slapped his knee. *Give me a break,* I thought. He continued, "People think different here than they do in the kinds of places where I know how to lean on—ah, converse with—people. You know, bars, motels, public housing. . . ."

I sat forward in the captain's chair, and looked him straight in his innocent brown eyes. "Lieutenant Piotrowski, what is it you want?"

"You *know* what I want, Doctor." He was suddenly absolutely serious. "I want—I *need*—some help. You been real useful to me in the past, and you could be real useful now. You know this place. You know these people. You could nose around at Enfield without arousing suspicion. People will tell you things they'd never dream of letting slip if I'm around. And listen, those books that were taken? Right? If they've got anything to do with Professor Corbin's death, you'd be the one to make the connection. Right? What the hell do I know about *lit-er-ah-choor?*" He grinned at me. We both knew he liked to play the rube. "You help me out, and I'll share info with you. Maybe that way you'd have a better chance of getting those old books back. I know I'd catch hell for talking about an open investigation, but sometimes I gotta follow my gut. And my gut tells me you could be . . . real useful." He nodded his head judiciously. There was no resisting his level gaze; at some point in his police training he'd had those brown eyes magnetized.

I gazed back at him, long and hard. Any decision I made, I wanted him to realize, was my own conscious choice; he hadn't manipulated me into it. But, really, what harm would there be in asking a few questions? I was good at asking questions; that was the way I taught. The right question asked at the right moment carried more pedagogical weight than a ton of arcane information given in a lecture. "Just tell me what you want me to do, Lieutenant."

"Well," he said, sitting back and smiling again. "*That* was easy." He had a beautiful smile—full lips, a wide flash of straight white teeth. Damn that Earlene; she'd got me thinking about this perfectly efficient police officer as a *man*. A man with *lips*. "So, when would you have some time for a good long chat?"

"How about right now?" I didn't have another class until two-thirty, when my Dickinson seminar met.

"Now's good for me. Got coffee anywhere around here?"

I checked my two office mugs, one a burnt red with a crazed glazing, the other a spherical white ceramic with a schmaltzy rendering of a bluebird. I had no idea where these ugly cups had come from; even in my most poverty-stricken days, I wouldn't have allowed either of them in my home. Maybe I'd inherited them with the office. At the moment, each mug was half-filled with cold, black, scummy coffee, necessitating a trip to the bathroom for a sanitary scrub. Monica gave me a slant-eyed look when I entered the department office with the two clean cups. *None of your business, Monica,* I thought, as I decanted coffee from the department machine. It was good coffee, I'd say that for Monica, and she kept it fresh all day.

Piotrowski was again reading *The Constraints of Class* when I returned with our coffee.

"Lieutenant," I said, as I set the bluebird mug next to him—it was the less disgusting cup of the two—"I'm curious. You told me Monica Cassale found Elliot's . . . er . . . body when she was delivering him some dinner? Tell me, why on earth would Monica take food to Elliot Corbin?"

Piotrowski finished the paragraph he was reading before he closed the book and took up his mug. Obviously he was buying himself time to think about how he would answer my question.

When he spoke, the regulation disclaimer emerged mechanically from his lips. "Now, Doctor, you know I can't divulge—"

Exasperated, I plopped back down into my chair. "Well, Lieutenant, it was my understanding that any exchange of information was going to be reciprocal, but now I'm beginning to wonder. How's this divulgence thing going to work, huh? I divulge, you keep silence? How am I supposed to know what kinds of questions to ask? And whom to ask them of? Forget it, Piotrowski! Nothing doing! Deal's off." I wiped my palms together, cleansing them of our agreement.

Halfway into my tirade the big cop began to grin,

and as I ranted on, the grin got wider and wider. When I slammed to a halt, he raised a hand. "Okay. Okay. But you gotta understand, Doctor, everything I tell you here is in the deepest—and I do mean *deepest*—confidence." Since the investigation the previous summer, the lieutenant had taken to wearing roundish brown-rimmed glasses, and now he lowered his chin, raised his eyebrows, and looked at me owlishly over the lenses.

"Of course."

"There's more to Ms. Cassale than meets the eye."

Monica? "Really?"

"For one thing, she and the victim had a long-term . . . er . . . relationship—"

"Monica and *Elliot?*"

"Yeah. For a number of years she was Professor Corbin's housekeeper—at least it started out that way. He's got a huge house, ya know. Lotta stuff in it."

"I've been there."

"That's right; you have." He paused. His brown eyes suddenly became introspective—as if he'd just been struck by a possibility. "So—Ms. Cassale kept house for the professor starting . . . oh, maybe ten, eleven years ago. But it looks like she took on other . . . er, duties . . . in addition to the cleaning and cooking."

When he paused, as if that was all he intended to tell me, I prompted him. *"Sexual* duties?"

"Seems that way."

"I'm interested in the way you phrased that, Lieutenant: *duties.* It seems we're not talking about a love affair here."

"No. Not at all." The direction this conversation was taking seemed to make Piotrowski uncomfortable. "Strictly a business arrangement, as I understand it."

My God! And right here in staid little Enfield. We sat in silence for ten seconds or so. "So—that's why she was taking Thanksgiving dinner to him. She still *cooked* for him."

"So she says."

"But nothing . . . more?"

The shrug of the muscular shoulders was eloquent. "I think he was the one got her the job here."

"Re-e-e-ally!" Then, after a pause, "So that means . . ."

"What?"

"That means Monica's not out of the picture as a suspect in Elliot's death?"

"Nobody's out of the picture."

"Except *me?*"

He pulled out his notebook. "Seems I've decided that," he said, noncommittally. "So, enough about Ms. Cassale. Let's get on with business. The other day we talked about Professor Corbin. Right now, why don't you tell me more about these missing diaries, and . . ." He glanced down at his notebook. ". . . this Emmeline Foster. She was a poet, you said, but I didn't see any mention of her in the index of your book here."

"In that book I was just looking at the . . . er . . . famous writers."

"So, this Foster woman, you're saying she's not famous. That's what I thought. So what does that mean about the value of those lost diaries?"

"The journals weren't lost, Lieutenant—they were stolen. And it means their 'value' is solely scholarly, not *monetary*, which is what I assume you're getting at."

"So you don't think they were . . . stolen . . . so someone could hawk them and make a bundle, like with that Northbury novel?"

"I don't see how—"

"What about reputation? Would it advance someone's career to come up with this old stuff?"

"Jeez, Piotrowski, I can't imagine why. Emmeline Foster's only claim to the 'big time' was her relationship with Edgar Allan Poe."

"Poe, huh? Now *that's* the big time. Even *I* know that. So—anything of Poe's would sell for big bucks, huh?"

"Probably."

"Tell me about him and Miss Foster."

"There's not a lot to tell. Poe had this *thing* about women poets. He sort of collected them as admirers and semi-sweethearts, even carrying on public flirtations with them in the newspapers." I told the lieutenant about the poet Fanny Osgood and the teasing poems she and Poe wrote back and forth to each other in the pages of the *Broadway Journal* when he was editor—and when both of them were married to other people. "And, if I'm not mistaken, there were one or two poems in the *Journal* from Emmeline Foster, as well. I could check on that the next time I go to the American Antiquarian Society."

"I suppose I don't need to ask if you saw anything of Edgar Poe's in this here box of her stuff?"

"If I had, Lieutenant, believe me, I'd have told you—and I would have taken it someplace safer than my office. Probably to the Special Collections section of the college library. But, really, I haven't had time to go through the box carefully. And, Piotrowski, other than the Poe connection, I can't conceive of any monetary value Foster's manuscript poems or journals would possess. Only a very specialized library—or collector—would want them. Oh—" I jumped up from my chair. "I almost forgot. This morning . . ." I began digging hastily through my bulging briefcase, and tugged out the crumpled photocopy I'd rescued from the copier. ". . . I found this in the copy machine." I glanced down at the sheet with Emmeline Foster's handwriting on it. It was a copy of the verse I'd read when I'd looked through the little blue book. I held it out to Piotrowski.

The lieutenant took the poem, scrutinized it, looked up at me. "That's . . . pretty," he said, with the guarded response of the poetry-impaired.

"It's a page from the little notebook Emmeline Foster wrote her poems in—not her drafts, I imagine, but the finished poems. Don't you see? After somebody ripped off the book from my office the day I opened the box, he or she made copies—not right away, but sometime after the close of school on Wednesday. The machine was jammed when I tried to use it first thing this morning, and I'm certain Monica would never have left it that way Wednesday afternoon. Anyone who tried to copy something after the . . . the *thief* . . . jammed the machine would have had to clear the jam."

"Which confirms *what?* That your thief is someone who has access to this building—"

"*And* a copy card. The photocopier won't work without a department card."

"So, we're talking about someone associated with the English Department."

"Obviously—"

A tentative knock on my office door startled me. I glanced at my watch: ten-thirty. *Shit;* this unenlightening little chat with Piotrowski had slopped over into my office hours. I opened the door—and found Freddie Whitby waiting for me with a put-upon expression on her clever little face. Freddie stepped into the room with the confident tread of the entitled, but faltered, then stopped dead when she noted the enormous man occupying my big green chair. She stared at Piotrowski and her expression altered slowly. I made an attempt to see the lieutenant through Freddie's eyes; there was no way this man was anything but a cop. Freddie made a little noise, a squeak, an *eeek* that came from somewhere at the very back of her throat. Then, edging her way sideways out of the office with her eyes fixed on the lieutenant, she pivoted and took off at a trot down the hall.

I broke into an uncontrollable—and utterly unprofessional—fit of giggles.

"What was that all about, Doctor?" Piotrowski rose from the green chair and began donning his overcoat.

Still snickering, unable to speak, I waggled a hand at him helplessly. He gazed at me with a bemused smile on his broad face as he pulled buttons through their holes. When I'd composed myself, I wiped my eyes with a tissue from a pack the lieutenant held out to me. "What was that all about? I couldn't begin to explain it, Lieutenant. Just think of yourself as an agent of intellectual justice."

Tom Lundgren was lurking outside as I opened my door again. Yep. It was office hours all right. "I'll be with you in a minute, Tom," I told him. He blushed. *Jeez.* I escorted Piotrowski to the photocopier so he could make a copy of the Emmeline Foster poem. When the lieutenant followed me out of the copy room, he nodded at Monica, who gaped at him from the doorway of the English Department office across the hall.

A memo from the President's Office was waiting in my mailbox as I headed toward the college pool late that afternoon. Avery was every bit as smooth and reassuring as his job demanded that he be:

As I am certain all members of the Enfield College community are aware, the tragic death of Professor Elliot James Corbin of the Enfield English Department on Thanksgiving Day at his home has been ruled a homicide. Professor Corbin was a distinguished member of the Enfield faculty for well over two decades, and his scholarly expertise, his collegiality, and his pedagogical presence will be sorely missed by all. A memorial service is being planned for a later date.

The President's Office wishes to assure students, faculty, and staff that the College is cooperating in every possible way with law enforcement officials to identify the perpetrator of this heinous crime. Although the assault on Professor Corbin did not take place on the Enfield campus, I feel it incumbent upon me as President to assure all members of our community that customary security measures have been reviewed and enhanced, and that the Enfield College campus is, as usual, a safe environment for study and residential life.

13.

Earth is raw with this one note,
This tattered making of a song
Narrowed down to a crow's throat,
Above the willow-trees . . .

—LIZETTE WOODWORTH REESE

JANE BIRDWORT PADDED AROUND the locker room naked. I dropped my gym bag by the end of a bench, shrugged out of my heavy jacket, sat down to remove my boots. Since my early-morning encounter with the jammed photocopier, I'd had a long, exhausting day—a freshman class, the session with Piotrowski, office hours, an intense three-hour senior seminar, and, in between, all sorts of prurient gossip on the part of my colleagues about Elliot's murder. I desperately needed a swim. Jane had just showered; her usually tightly curled hair was wet and sleek, and she was gazing intently into the long mirror, rubbing moisturizer into her rosy face. Seeing my reflection in the mirror, she turned. "Karen," she said, "I have a question for you." She grabbed a towel from the chrome hook by the mirror, wrapped it around her wet hair and walked toward the lockers.

The women's locker room is a place of green walls, cream-painted metal lockers, long battered benches, and a heady aroma of chlorine. At 6:03 P.M.—dinnertime for students and domesticated faculty—the place was, as I'd expected, deserted, and I looked forward to a long, unobstructed swim. When I was a little girl, I'd had a childish notion of heaven—angels, harps, fluffy white clouds. Now, as a grown woman, I knew exactly what heaven was: eighteen laps in an unshared lane of Enfield College's heated, Olympic-size pool.

I pulled off a boot and looked up at Jane inquiringly. Naked, she was standing right in front of me and her breasts were practically in my face. From a perch just above her left nipple a tiny tattoo of a blue-black crow regarded me with raptor insolence. For a woman in her fifties—as I assumed she was—Jane was in splendid shape, hardly an ounce of fat or a ripple of flab on her compact, slender frame. I was close enough to notice. Aside from the faint striation of stretchmarks on her abdomen, Jane could easily have posed for the bikini edition of *Modern Maturity*. Maybe even—given that crow tattoo—she could have posed topless.

I really didn't know how to read Jane Birdwort. She seemed to be two different people: the frump of the pink suits and outdated hairdo and the surprisingly sexy woman of the carnal poems and the almost perfect body. Sitting down on a bench opposite me, she opened a locker, rooted through it for a faded pink Mount Holyoke sweatshirt, retrieved a package of Camel cigarettes and a Bic lighter from the pocket, dropped the sweatshirt on the bench. "We're the only ones in here, aren't we?" she asked. Then without waiting for a response, she tipped out a cigarette and lit up.

"You know you're not supposed to—" The "good girl" in me pays attention to house rules.

"Yes, yes, I know: no smoking in college buildings." She inhaled luxuriously, held it for a few seconds, breathed out a long, thin stream of smoke. "But who's going to tell?" Her gaze was cool and straight and challenging.

Not me, obviously. And I wanted to talk to Jane, so I wasn't about to antagonize her by objecting to the carcinogens she was at that very moment blowing in my face. Jane's stunned reaction when I'd informed her of Elliot's death intrigued me. In the interests of "nosing around" for Piotrowski, I'd try to follow up on that. "So," I reminded her, "you had a question for me?"

"Yes, I do. Monica told me the very large man I saw coming out of your office this morning was a police detective?"

"Yes. Yes, he was." I removed my suit pants, carefully avoiding puddles on the tile floor. Then I hung them on a wire hanger with the coordinated blouse and jacket. I'm much more comfortable in a sweatshirt and jeans, but try to dress like an adult when I spend the day in the classroom.

"I assume he was here about . . . ah . . . Elliot Corbin's . . . ah . . . death. Why was he talking to you? Nobody came by to ask me any questions."

"No? Well, consider yourself lucky, Jane." I stripped off my bra and panties and stepped into my black tank suit.

"Well, it's not that I'm fond of the police, you understand, but when I heard they were in the building, I was surprised not to be interviewed." Another greedy drag on the cigarette.

"I'm sure they'll get to you sooner or later. I got the impression they will be talking to all of Elliot's colleagues. Maybe they began with me because my office is next door to Elliot's." *Yeah, right. They began with me because I'm a police snitch.* "Umm . . . they probably thought I'd seen or heard something that would be useful to them."

Jane breathed out another volley of smoke. "Had you?" she asked impassively.

"Not in the least." I said it quickly, remembering the nasty argument in Elliot's office.

She took a short puff: in, out. "Just tell me—did they ask any questions about me?"

"About *you?*" What an intriguing inquiry—an absolutely ideal entree for some sleuthing. "No. No, they didn't. Why do you ask, Jane? Did you know Elliot well?" I suffered a qualm about this covert interrogation of a colleague, but fought it back by reminding myself that another colleague was dead, and that Jane, all unbeknownst to herself, might let drop a piece of information that could help the police identify the killer.

"Not really. I only met him in September, when I arrived at Enfield." She held her cigarette very still in a steady hand.

"You seemed so . . . disturbed when I told you he was dead."

She gave a nervous little trill of laughter. "It's just that we poets tend to be very . . . ah . . . emotional . . . people. The . . . ah . . . membranes are very thin."

"Membranes?" I stuffed my gym bag in the locker and slammed the door. I had to slam it twice before the lock would catch.

"Between other people's pain and our own. The shrinks would say we have boundary problems."

"Really?" *Membranes!*

"Yes," she responded, "all that psychic navel-gaz-

ing. I don't like poets much, you know. Including myself." She jumped up from the bench, strode over to the
sink, stubbed out her half-smoked cigarette. Then she
sauntered back to her locker and plucked out a pair of
khakis. I watched in fascination as she stepped into
them, then pulled on the faded Holyoke sweatshirt. No
panties. No bra. I had a decade or so to go before I
reached my fifties, but maybe it wasn't going to be the
stodgy time of life I'd been led to believe.

The coffee shop was moderately busy when I stopped by
for a quick supper after my swim. At the tables, students hunkered over dried-out pizza slices on paper
plates and foil-wrapped cheeseburgers with soggy to-
mato slices, as if they had no other option but to use
their meal cards on the fast food available here. Perhaps
the limited selections of the coffee-shop menu were easier to manage than the stress of having to choose among
the profusion of healthy entrees available in the cafete-
ria. As I proceeded along the food line, a burger, fries, a
brownie with thick, gooey icing, and a container of coffee somehow got onto my tray, instead of the chef's
salad and two-percent milk I could have sworn I'd
reached for. Well, no problem: I had a twenty-minute
drive home; I'd burn up the calories. My lovelorn student Tom Lundgren was seated by himself at a four-
person table. When I walked past with my tray and said
the most unprovocative thing I could think of—"Hi,
Tom"—he choked on a bite of his meatball wedge. But I
didn't pause to assist him; it would simply have made
things worse.

I spotted Harriet Person, half-hidden from sight at
a table in a far corner of the room. Harriet sat alone,
a tray full of empty dishes pushed to one side of the
table, and scribbled furiously on a yellow pad centered

squarely in front of her. As I was already in sleuth mode—although I'd learned nothing much from Jane other than that she had a great body and thin membranes—I decided I might as well take advantage of Harriet's presence to ask a few more questions about Elliot Corbin. She was as much a suspect as anyone else in the department.

"May I?" I queried, gesturing to the chair across from her.

"Of course." She hustled the tray of dirty dishes onto the next table just as two freshmen I recognized as new advisees of mine were about to sit at it. The girl with the buzz cut and the nose stud gave Harriet an indignant glower, but her friend sagely counseled discretion, and both veered toward a cleared-off table across the room.

"Listen, Karen," Harriet said, "I wanted to ask you: Are you on the hiring committee for the Palaver? I know the committee intended to include at least one member of the junior faculty." Academic departments are fond of the appearance of democracy, but in reality they are as hierarchical and class-bound as any medieval fiefdom: Full professors make all the important decisions, associate professors do all the work, assistant professors curtsy whenever the lords of the manor pass by.

"Miles asked me, Harriet, but I turned him down. I just couldn't do it; I'm on overload, what with the Curriculum Revision Committee, the Library Acquisitions Committee, the plans for the Northbury Center." *Not to mention, yet another homicide investigation.* "Are you? On the Palaver committee, I mean," I asked, and immediately remembered that she wasn't. Hadn't Jill told me that Harriet, herself, was a candidate for the position?

My tablemate ignored the question. "Damn. I'm desperate to know who's applied for the job. Now that

Elliot's . . . gone—and to be truthful with you, I really can't say, God Rest the Dear Man's Soul—the playing field has changed. Dramatically. I keep trying to get a peek at the applications we've received, but Monica's got them under lock and key. Miles doesn't want anyone looking at them until the committee has had a chance to sort through the dossiers, she says, and she's being a real witch about it."

"Don't take it out on Monica, Harriet. She's just doing her job. Miles is the one who made the policy. You ought to discuss it with him."

"Miles! Humph! For a while I thought I could depend on Miles to be reasonable about this hire, but I was wrong. That man is so reactionary! You know what his agenda is, don't you, Karen? He intends to weed out all the feminist applicants before the committee gets a chance to even look at their dossiers!"

A ludicrous image invaded my imagination: Miles, locked in his office, hunkering over his desk, muttering hideously into his beard, sorting out all the applications from women—and running them through the department shredder. "Miles wouldn't do a thing like that, Harriet!" I protested. "Not only would it be shoddy, it would also be illegal."

"Hah! Don't count on Miles's ethics, Karen. You haven't been around this retrograde, sexist department as long as I have. But, God damn it, I'm determined that if the hiring committee blackballs *my* application, we're going to get another nationally known Women's Studies scholar in the Palaver Chair, no matter what it takes to get her there!"

"Really?" *No matter what it takes?* And now Elliot Corbin, male, rumored to be the lead contender for the position, was dead. Hmm.

And, me, I couldn't keep my mouth shut. "So tell

me, Harriet, did you know for sure that Elliot had applied for the Palaver?"

"If he hadn't, he was about to. Elliot was so damn unscrupulous, he'd have gotten himself the Chair by hook or by crook." Then she seemed to hear herself. *No matter what it takes. By hook or by crook.* Not much ethical difference there. Harriet straightened the lapels on her navy-blue suit jacket, and cleared her throat. "What I mean is, Elliot wanted the Chair merely for reasons of personal aggrandizement. I want it for *political* reasons, to help ameliorate the stranglehold of white hegemonic masculinities on the academy—and I intend to do that through a series of organized disruptions of institutionalized sexist, heterosexist, and racist binaries—"

"You forgot *classist.*"

"And classist." She gave me a sidelong glance: Was I being a wiseass? I donned my most earnest non-tenured-professor expression, tugged at my metaphorical forelock—and got away with it. This time. I'm as much a feminist as any scholar who's thought seriously about the historical—and contemporary—imbalance of power between men and women—and whites and blacks, and gays and straights, and the rich and the poor—in all areas of society. What I can't stomach, however, is the knee-jerk ideological jargon, the rigid partisan thinking, that passes for serious reflection on the subject.

"You see this list here?" Harriet asked, carried by her fervor past any momentary doubts about my response. She turned the scribbled-on yellow pad toward me. "On this page, I've noted every feminist literary scholar of any repute, and I intend to go back to my office and begin making phone calls. I'll show Miles Jewell! He'll be so deluged by applications from Women's Studies scholars he won't know whether he's coming or going!"

• • •

It was peaceful at my house that evening. I put Emmylou on the CD player, ran a long, steamy bath, poured a jelly glass full of red wine, selected a paperback mystery novel from my pleasure-reading pile, and soaked for half an hour. When I emerged from the bathroom wrapped in a white bathsheet, a message from my student Mike Vitale waited on my answering machine. *"Professor Pelletier, I want to let you know why I wasn't in class this morning. Over the holiday I had a . . . a death in my family, but I'm back on campus now. I'll see you on Wednesday."* It was truly extraordinary, I thought, as the machine rewound, the number of grandmothers who chose the most stressful part of the academic semester to drop dead. One student I'd heard of had *three* grandmothers die—all in the same semester. Then I chastised myself for my cynicism. After all, Mike hadn't given me the grandmother line. He was a good kid, and he wasn't trying to bullshit me. I'd offer him sincere condolences when I next saw him.

14.

Though skilled in Latin and in Greek,

And earning fifty cents a week,

Such knowledge, and the income, too,

Should teach you better what to do:

The meanest drudges, kept in pay,

Can pocket fifty cents a day.

—PHILIP FRENEAU,
"TO A NEW ENGLAND POET"

TUESDAY MORNING I SLEPT LATE. I had no classes, and, blessedly, no meetings. At 9:23 by the luminescent numbers on my bedside clock, I stumbled out of bed and into the kitchen to retrieve a New York City bagel from the freezer. Then I showered leisurely, watched CNN in my old plaid bathrobe, munched my buttery toasted bagel. As I finished my second coffee, the phone rang.

"Karen? It's Earlene. You going to be on campus today?"

"Yep. Sure am. Gotta go to the library, hunt down Freddie Whitby's source—among other things."

She paused for a second, then said, "Good. So 'how about lunch?"

"I'd love it. I need to spend some time with a friend. You have a place in mind?"

"Rudolph's? One o'clock?"

"Sure. See you there." I moved to hang up.

"Karen, wait a minute. How'd Freddie respond when you confronted her with the paper?"

"I haven't. She didn't show up for our appointment. Well—she did, but I couldn't see her right then, and she didn't come back." At the memory of my student's reaction to Piotrowski's substantial presence in my green vinyl chair, I chortled. Earlene laughed when I told her the story. "Integrity cop," she said. "That's supposed to be my job. Maybe I should get myself a badge and a uniform."

"You'll have to bulk up a bit first."

The college library was bustling. In the main reading room with its Gothic arched windows, students cluttered the long tables with stacks of books, laptop computers, photocopies, notebooks, and illicit bags of corn chips squirreled away in bulging backpacks. Late November is a grueling time for anyone connected with an institution of higher learning, whether student or faculty: final papers to research, write, and grade; final exams to put together, study for, take, grade. Because the fall semester is tight, crammed between Labor Day and the Christmas holidays, the pace is brutal. More than one face poring over some obscure reference tome was tight with anxiety.

I had two compelling reasons to be here: There was, of course, the vexing problem of Freddie Whitby. I reviewed in my mind some of the language of her essay—*surreal trope, existentialist angst, post-Freudian poesis*—it should be fairly easy to identify such a source. It was just as well that the young plagiarist hadn't returned to my office yesterday: By Wednesday's class, I might actually have solid evidence with which to confront her. In addition to dealing with Freddie, I also needed to read up on Poe. Piotrowski's reminder that Edgar Allan Poe was "big time," even in the "real" world outside academe, and his speculation that there could be a profit motive involved in the disappearance of Emmeline Foster's journals and poems had booted me into action. I didn't know as much about Poe as I should—his melodramatic stories and agitated poems had never appealed to me—but a good browse through the scholarship should enlighten me about the relationship between him and Foster. Conceivably her journal held some previously unknown information about Poe that might render it valuable. If there was a connection to be made, I was the one to make it.

I glanced around the reading room one last time before I headed up the worn stone steps to the American Literature section on the third floor. The college desperately needed a new library. For a top-notch school in the final decade of the twentieth century, this was a surprisingly crowded and gloomy building. For over a decade, sentimental alumni had been battling the administration's plans to replace this beloved but outmoded building with a state-of-the-art, twenty-first-century computerized information center. At the most recent faculty meeting, Avery Mitchell had heatedly informed assembled professors that the current building was an embarrassing anachronism. Administrators and faculty should work together, he'd argued, to convince influential opponents that a nineteenth-century building and twenty-first-century information technology were incompatible. I could see, just by glancing around me, that fluorescent strip lighting placed high on vaulted ceilings did little to illuminate either dark nineteenth-century corners or twenty-first-century computer screens in this cathedral-like room. At a table by a pillar, Mike Vitale squinted at the screen of his laptop. He must be back in the swing of things after his family bereavement. I knew from experience that if he stayed in the reading room for more than an hour, he'd come out with severe eyestrain and a raging headache.

On the third floor, at a small out-of-the-way desk in the American Literature stacks, Amber Nichols sat hunched over a pile of books, her smooth, caramel-colored hair falling across her face. The lighting in this area was so bad, I was amazed she could see to read. Amber glanced up at me irritably as I brushed past her to get to the Poe section. Then, when she saw who I was, she deliberately closed her book, without marking the place, and set it down in front of her. "Karen," she said, "I've been wanting to talk to you, but you're always so busy. Do you have a few minutes now?"

I repressed a sigh; I was increasingly anxious to get to my research. "Sure, Amber," I replied, and lowered myself into the chair across from her. Automatically, my eyes slid over the titles of the volumes on the table. I'm a book person; print attracts my gaze the way Hester attracted Dimmesdale, the way Rochester attracted Jane, the way Poe's lovesick scholar attracted his fateful raven. *Complete Tales and Poems of Edgar Allan Poe,* I read; *The Poe Log: A Documentary Life; Edgar A. Poe: A Biography.* Of course . . . FroshHum worked off a common syllabus; Amber was teaching Poe too. Damn, these were the books I needed, and Amber had already laid claim to them. Casually, I picked up the heavy *Poe Log* from the table and leafed through it. Yes! The log listed in chronological order every extant contemporaneous document that had anything to do with Edgar Allan

Poe, from before his birth in 1809 until just after his death in 1849; this was exactly what I needed. I noted that Amber was watching me page through the book, so I closed it nonchalantly and placed it next to my brief-case. With any luck, she'd forget about it and I could scoop it up and check it out on my own card. To distract her attention from the book, I gave her a conversational nudge. "What's up?"

She wriggled in her hard chair until she found the most comfortable position, then, with a conspiratorial smile, asked levelly: "Karen, what did you have to do to get here?"

Huh? "Well, I walked up the stairs from the reading room, but I assume that's not what you're asking."

"Of course not." She looked around, warily, and when she'd ascertained that we were alone in the stacks, she leaned toward me cozily—just us girls together—and continued: "No aspersions on your ability, Karen, but you must have pulled some strings, or—ah, you know— made some, ah, *connections*, to get a tenure-track teach-ing position at a prestigious institution like Enfield. I mean, let's face it, with the academic market as bad as it is, nobody, but *nobody*, gets a job like yours without— you know—some . . . some *associations*. And you're young, and attractive—" Her pedantic tone belied the offensive implications of her words.

Nevertheless, I sputtered. "I didn't *sleep* my way into this job, Amber, if that's what you're suggesting." I glared at her, sorely tempted to stalk righteously away. Then, once again, I recalled the lieutenant's request. Who knew what casual piece of information Amber might be in possession of? Might she know some little factual iota that could unlock the mysteries of Elliot's violent death and the disappearance of the Foster jour-nals? Reluctantly, I swallowed my outrage and smiled.

"Well," Amber said, oblivious to my inner conflict, "there *have* been rumors about you and Avery Mitchell. . . ." Her enigmatic smirk was still in place.

I longed to slap her face. *God damn this nosy, meddlesome, gossipy little hellhole of a place!* But I continued to play Amber's game. "Don't I wish!" I wasn't sure how convincing my lascivious little snigger was, but she seemed to buy it.

"I'm asking," Amber elaborated, "because my dissertation is just about finished, and I'm on the job market. This adjunct work is killing me. Along with the course I'm teaching here, I've got two at the university, and two at Holyoke Community College."

I winced in very real sympathy.

"I'm working sixty hours a week and making peanuts. And aside from the exhaustion and the poverty, there's the humiliation. No office, no benefits, no respect: I'm treated like a second-class citizen." She paused, and narrowed her eyes. "I *resent* having to scavenge for a professional career like this."

I commiserated: "Of course you do."

"I've *got* to land a tenure-track job, Karen. I can't keep this up." She studied me from under carefully shaped honey-colored brows. "And, you"—she appraised me, head to toe, or as much of me as she could see above the table—"you've got yourself this . . . this *enviable* position. How'd you make it happen?"

"Connections," I said, and looked discreet. *And brains, and talent, and a hell of a lot of damned hard work!*

"I thought so," she replied, smugly. "Some people have things handed to them on a silver platter. But some of us have to do, well, whatever it is we have to do, for everything we get. Know what I mean?"

"Oh, yeah." Hand me a martini and a cigarette, and

I might pass for a worldly woman. An awkward silence ensued. Obviously the conversation was terminating. If I was going to do any sleuthing, now was the moment.

"I imagine you've heard about Elliot Corbin?" I asked it casually, as I hefted my book bag and rose from my chair.

"Yes?" Amber's uncharacteristic garrulousness ceased.

"A terrible thing," I said. "But, then, I didn't know him at all well. Did you?"

Amber considered her response. "I took a course with him."

"Really? At the university?"

"Yeah. Three or four years ago."

"Elliot told me he'd taught there. Was he a good teacher?"

"He was okay." Something wasn't being said, but Amber's abruptly shuttered countenance let me know I wasn't about to find out what it was.

The Poe Log was tucked casually under my arm when I'd finished searching the shelves—with no success—for Freddie's source. I murmured a goodbye to Amber and moseyed toward the east staircase. Amber suspected me of much worse dishonesty than the uncollegial appropriation of a library book; might as well be hung for a sheep as a lamb. Or vice versa.

"Don't get me wrong, Karen," Earlene said, over Caesar salad, foccaccia, and bubbly water, "and not that it makes any difference, but it has come to my attention that Freddie Whitby is the daughter of a major donor to the college."

Ah. "So she informed me on the first day of class. Whitby Field House, I believe."

"She did?"

"Oh, yes. In front of several other students, she let me know that the Whitbys had a century-long affiliation with the college, and that the new field house was the 'typically generous' donation of her father and uncles."

"Oh, God."

"Yes. Enfield College, she went on to say, had *always deeply appreciated the beneficence of her family.* The italics were there in her voice, and I was meant to hear them. Her first essay got a D anyhow. A well-deserved D."

Earlene shook her head. "That kid is some piece of work. All the more reason to have evidence in hand when you make an accusation of plagiarism, Karen. You could have a fight on your hands here."

"You telling me to back off?"

"No!" Earlene reached over and briefly squeezed my hand. "Don't even *think* about it. I'll say this for the administration: Never in my ten years at this school has there been pressure to provide special consideration for a well-connected student. But I'm just letting you know— also out of my long experience—it can become nasty. Some parents will sue. Get the source in your hands, if you can. Of course, Freddie may have gone to one of those mail-order term-paper mills that advertise all over the place, and that would make it harder."

"Yeah, I know. One of them slapped stickers on the insides of the bathroom stalls in Dickinson Hall. I scraped the damn things off. At least I did in the women's room. I imagine Miles took care of the men's room."

"You know, if she hired someone to custom-write the essay, it'll be virtually impossible to pin down the source."

I sighed. "Yeah, but I don't think the paper was written recently. Its language is outdated in such a particular way, as if it had been written, oh, say, thirty years ago, when psychoanalytic criticism was all the rage."

"You can date it that closely? Just by the language?"

"Oh, sure. Literary criticism does have its trends. But I leafed through every Poe critic on the shelves this morning and couldn't find the source. Of course, Freddie may have the book checked out of our library. Tomorrow I'll take a jaunt over to the university; maybe I'll run across something there. Or in one of the older scholarly journals. Until I find it, I'll just ask questions; I won't make any accusations." Then it hit me, what this kid had gotten me into. I dropped my head into my hands. "Oh, God. I . . . *don't . . . need . . . this!*"

"Sorry, Karen." Earlene patted me on the arm. "Just thought you should be forewarned." She beckoned to the waiter for coffee, then turned back to me. "So . . . that big cop . . . he turned up again, huh?"

I jerked my head up and glared at her. "Earlene!"

Back in the department office, Shirley, Monica's part-time assistant, informed me Monica had taken a sick day. Leaning toward me confidentially, Shirley whispered, "She's been under a lot of pressure lately, you know."

I nodded. *Honey, you don't know the half of it.*

Piotrowski's request for help had co-opted my time and energies at a time when I was already overworked. Among other things, I realized I could no longer allow the remaining Foster papers to languish unexamined in my office. What if there *was* a connection between Emmeline Foster's life and Elliot Corbin's death? That afternoon I made an inventory of the contents of the Foster box. I'd grown fond of Emmeline Foster merely from what I'd read in my brief glimpse of her journals: the excited little girl looking forward to reading her first Jane Austen novel; the meditative woman, focused on her poetry. I was beginning to fear that her carefully kept handwritten books might have vanished forever, and that possibility made me angry. It was bad enough that women poets like Foster had been ridiculed and ignored, to the point that they virtually had disappeared from the awareness of modern readers. Now this one poet's life had miraculously been resurrected, only to vanish again. But my sympathy had been aroused and my curiosity had been whetted. Emmeline Foster had cared enough about her world to record it meticulously in poems and in journal entries, and I owed it to her to bring those glimpses of a long-vanished woman's spirit back to life again.

I found the letter tucked between the pages of Foster's volume of Elizabeth Barrett Browning's poems. It was addressed in the handwriting with which I was now very familiar: *Mr. Edward Cummins, Cummins and Sons, Publishers, Broadway, New York City.* But here the prim hand was sloppy, as if the missive had been scrawled in a hurry. I removed the letter from its envelope. Dated January 31, 1845, it read: *My Dear Mr. Cummins, the language of my Soul means more to me than the Soul itself. I enclose herewith My Own Poem, which you have previously seen. You will have noticed certain Verses in this week's* Mirror. *May I trust you to prove yourself a more Faithful Custodian of my words?* The signature was clear: *In haste, Emmeline Charlotte Foster.* Other than that little note, the envelope was empty. Mr. Cummins had proven himself faithful to a certain degree, but Karen Pelletier had carelessly allowed Emmeline Foster's words to vanish once again from sight.

• • •

The knock on the office door brought me out of my funk. "Hello, Professor," Mike Vitale said. A dozen or so snow-flakes on my student's crisp, dark curls informed me that it was snowing out. Mike had wound a black, hand-knit scarf around the collar of his army-green military-surplus jacket, obscuring his chin and emphasizing well-shaped ears tight to a nicely contoured head. "I saw you in the library," he said in a flat tone. Then a fat tear rolled over his dark eyelashes and down his cheek.

"Mike," I exclaimed, "whatever is the matter?" I pulled my student into the office by his army-green elbow and deposited him in the vinyl armchair. Then I cleared the textbooks off my Enfield-crested captain's chair and positioned it so we were sitting practically knee-to-knee. Mike slumped into the chair, offering only monosyllabic responses to my concerned questions.

I usually avoid pressing students to tell me about their emotional problems: It ends up involving me far-too-deeply in their far-too-messy lives. But this young man's distress was getting to me. "Mike, is this about the death in your family?"

He choked on a half-articulated word, then shook his head—unconvincingly.

"Mike, this isn't like you. I'm worried. You have to tell me. What's going on?"

"Nothing," he croaked, and immediately began to bawl.

I suppressed a groan. I hate this stuff. If I'd wanted to become a psychotherapist, I'd have gone to psycho-therapist school. I jumped up, pushed the door nearly shut for privacy—all the way shut could invite a sexual-harassment lawsuit—then patted Mike on the shoulder, and provided tissues. Amazingly, when he'd finished crying, wiped his eyes and blown his nose—and looked me in the eyes for the first time that afternoon—Mike rose from his chair without saying a single word about what was upsetting him.

"Thanks, Professor," he said, and squeezed my hand firmly, "I really appreciate you being so understanding. Now I know what I have to do." Then he squared his shoulders, took a deep breath, let it out in a huff, and marched manfully into the hall.

I stood by his empty chair with my mouth hanging open: I hadn't *understood* a thing. If Mike Vitale had been one of my female students, I'd have known by now all the painful intimate details of his—or, rather, her—personal problems. But he was a guy, and at Enfield College, guys suck up the pain. It's part of the WASP ethos —even if your name is Vitale.

Maybe the opportunity to cry had in itself been relief enough for Mike. I could identify with that. When I was little more than a girl, my tears had been driven permanently underground. As an adult, the once or twice a decade I let that underground river flood over, I didn't need to add insult to humiliation by babbling on and on about it.

It was mailtime, and I trudged to the department office. My box yielded the usual uninspiring collection of memos and publishers' catalogs. The one handwritten—hand-printed, really—envelope disclosed a folded sheet of good-quality letter paper. In extremely neat, if immature, letters—also hand-printed—a love poem awaited me. A *stolen* love poem.

To Karen

Karen, thy beauty is to me

Like those Nicean barks of yore.
That gently, o'er a perfumed sea,
   The weary, way-worn wanderer bore
To his own native shore. . . .

The verse was unsigned. My involuntary snort was part laugh, part groan. *Tom Lundgren! Oh, no!* But I knew how to handle this; this wasn't the first time I'd been the object of communications from a lovelorn eighteen-year-old. Ignoring them was the best strategy. Any acknowledgment, no matter how discouraging, seemed only to seal the attachment. I folded the purloined Poe lyrics and the envelope, intending to rip them in pieces and throw them in the trash. Then, with an irrational fear that Tom might somehow learn that I'd coldheartedly discarded his poem, I slipped it in my book bag; I'd throw it out when I got home.

Before I left campus late that afternoon, I arranged for the box of Emmeline Foster's books to be temporarily stored in the Special Collections section of the library. Aside from the one letter I'd just read, a few poem drafts, and the daguerreotype in the brass case, books were about all that remained of Foster's possessions. Increasingly anxious about their safety, I'd accompanied the custodian with the handcart to the library and had waited for the box to be locked securely away. Then I headed for my car. As usual in the November twilight, the crows that make their winter home in the roosts of Enfield's rooftops were swooping and cawing before their nighttime slumber. I stood on the top step of the Enfield College library transfixed by the eerie beauty of the birds in motion—the discordant music of their calls—*awkah, awkah, awkah*—the gleam of the glossy black wings against the deep striated rose of the horizon. Then, as I strolled past Dickinson Hall on my way to the parking lot, a young boy fell in step with me. "Lady," Joey Cassale queried solemnly, "did you know that crows are carnivores?"

15.

Nor would I be a Poet——
It's finer——own the Ear——
Enamored——impotent——content——

—EMILY DICKINSON

THURSDAY MORNING FOUND ME PULLING into Elliot Corbin's unpaved driveway. The previous evening I'd gotten another unexpected call from Lieutenant
Piotrowski. Somehow the lieutenant had come up with
the notion that it would be useful to his investigation if I
did a sustained search through Elliot's books and papers
for, as he phrased it, "any little literary clue" that might
possibly lead to the identity of my colleague's killer. "I
put in a request for approval to hire an expert consul-
tant," Piotrowski told me, "and the suits approved it
right away. This is a visible case, and they want it resolved. So, I got you the same fee as last time—five hundred a day. That okay?"

"Lieutenant," I'd replied, "I don't have time. I'm
still teaching, and the semester's at its craziest. I can't

afford to take whole days away from my work." Wednesday's FroshHum class had clearly suffered from inadequate preparation on my part. We'd finished up our Poe unit, but nobody took much interest in the discussion of "The City in the Sea." Once again, Mike Vitale hadn't shown up for class, and I thought I could understand why: We would be discussing a poem about death, and Mike was a little too close to an actual death in his own family. I wondered just who it was who'd died. Must have been someone a little closer than the customary November grandmother. Freddie Whitby hadn't been in class either, so I didn't have to deal with her; when would I have time to locate the source of her pilfered essay?

"Yeah, Doctor. But you're in the classroom, what?—eight, ten hours a week?"

"Six. I'm teaching two courses. But you forget about class preparation, thesis supervision, office hours, advisee counseling, paper grading, department service—not to mention literary scholarship, which is what got me this job in the first place. And which is what will get me tenure someday. Maybe. If I ever get a chance to do any more of it. In between your investigations."

A chuckle on the other end of the line. Then, "I know you weren't crazy about Professor Corbin, Doctor. But there's no two ways of looking at it. He was your colleague, and now he's croaked. We don't have any idea why. I figured if you could spend one day going through evidentiary documents at the victim's house, one day at his office—on the weekend, so's no one knows you're there—and a third day down here at headquarters with his computer files, you could maybe help us determine a motive."

"Evidentiary documents?"

"Well, you know, we always look over stuff like

datebooks, diaries, letters ourselves. But here we also got books—hundreds of them—and file cabinets full of scholarly manuscripts, letters to and from other professors, student papers. No one in the department's got a clue what any of it means."

Oh, *documentary evidence*. "In the literary profession, Lieutenant, we call those things *texts*, not documents. Five hundred a day, huh?"

"Yep."

Hmm. Christmas was near. Even one day working for the B.C.I. and I could get Amanda something great without driving my MasterCard balance sky-high. Not that I didn't have disinterested civic-minded motivations as well, of course. "Could you get me seven-fifty?"

Not a second's hesitation. "Probably."

"Really?" For me, seven-fifty was not much less than a full week's salary. I did some quick math. *Really?* Well, okay, Lieutenant. Okay. I'll do it." So, who would it kill if my grades were maybe a little late?

Sergeant Felicity Schultz was waiting for me in front of Elliot's house. As I bumped the Jetta over the ruts in the overgrown driveway, the driver's door opened on the nondescript dark blue Ford by the curb. Like me, the sergeant wore heavy-weather gear: quilted parka, knit hat, snow boots. And with good reason: the sky was gray and sagging, stitched precariously to the summits of the encircling hills, ready at any moment to dump its load of snow.

"Doctor Pelletier," Schultz said, without wasting time on such frivolities as "Hello" or "Nice to see you again," "the lieutenant gave me instructions to let you in and show you what we want you to look at. There's really no need for you to go through the entire house, just the rooms where Corbin kept books and papers."

"His library?" The lieutenant's vivid description of the murder scene and the sight of Elliot's blood-spattered notepad had combined in my imagination to form a nightmare vision—an entire chamber awash in blood.

"That's where most of the papers are. I know it won't be nice for you. . . ." She let it trail off, a hardened professional speaking to a lily-livered amateur—as if the visual traces of violent death were "nice" for anyone. "But we've finished the forensic investigation and released the crime scene. And that's where we need you."

Oh, goody. A crime scene. My stomach clenched as we passed over the threshold into the big, unkempt house.

As it turned out, the crime scene was surprisingly mundane. The same book-lined combination recreation-room/library with the same mismatched furniture. Only now the room smelled . . . well, rusty . . . and it was hard to ignore the dark stains on the blotter and the floor around the massive oak desk. Outside the tall French doors, snowflakes slanted across the dead grass of the lawn. Local radio had forecast the first storm of the year, six to eight inches. I wasn't looking forward to the drive home.

"Can we lose the blotter, Sergeant?" Elliot's desk chair was missing. I didn't want to speculate about its condition. I hefted a yellow chrome-and-plastic side chair over to the desk as Schultz removed the large, rectangular pad. Not much of an improvement: the desktop now featured a clearly delineated rectangle of dusty, finger-print-powdered oak partially surrounded by an irregular stain where blood had soaked into the wood. In a chipped ceramic vase placed precariously at the edge, rested a half-dozen ballpoint pens and an ornate Victorian-style brass letter opener. The whole room seemed soaked in death and gloom. I took a deep, sustaining breath and pulled out the bottom desk drawer to reveal a rank of obscurely labeled hanging file folders stuffed with papers. The drawers of the shoulder-high filing cabinet in the corner were most likely similarly crammed. The first folder had no label. I opened it. It contained cryptic teaching notes, seemingly for the course in modern poetry Elliot had been teaching. I stared at the notes for maybe a minute and a half, then closed the folder, and glanced up at Schultz.

"Sergeant, what the hell am I supposed to be looking for?"

"If we knew that, Dr. Pelletier, we could find it ourselves. Listen, the lieutenant told me to fill you in on some major points of our investigation, so's you'll have some context for your research. Let's see if we can scare up some coffee in the kitchen. The less time we spend in this room, the better, far's I'm concerned." So much for the tough-guy act.

Elliot's kitchen had last been updated in the sixties: avocado appliances, green-speckled Formica-top table, brass and frosted-glass light fixture, cutesy matching maple spice rack and paper towel holder. By the avocado Princess wall phone, a black-cat cork bulletin board was layered over with what looked like years'-worth of grocery coupons, movie schedules, old postcards, departmental memos. Schultz located a can of store-brand coffee and an electric percolator. As she fussed with cups and spoons at the counter, I watched the random flakes outside become a steady swirl of snow. Maybe if I hustled through the files, I thought, I could get out of this place and on the road before dark. Fat chance.

While the coffee was brewing, Schultz brought me up to speed on the police investigation. I knew that Monica Cassale had discovered Elliot's body. According to Monica, no one else had been on the premises, and, because of the secluded location of the house, no neighbors had seen anyone arrive or depart anywhere near the time of the murder. The murder weapon had not yet been located, but, as Piotrowski had told me earlier, it was presumed, from the size and trajectory of the wound, to be a knife with a four-inch-long blade. Elliot had been seated and only a minor struggle seemed to have preceded the stabbing, so it was assumed Elliot knew his assailant and had no fear of him.

"Or her," I said.

"Or her," Schultz amended, without rancor. "No reason it couldn't of been a woman. And as per SOP—standard operating procedure," she translated, "we're looking at the victim's sexual relationships. Nobody has a . . . a perfect life, and Elliot Corbin, believe me, is living proof—well, was living proof—of that. Most recently, as far as we were able to determine, he had an . . . er . . . business arrangement with Ms. Cassale—"

"Lieutenant Piotrowski told me about that."

"Yeah, well . . . And we're looking into other relationships. Corbin was married briefly in the eighties, to a former student, and they had a kid. You know anything about that?" She gave me a peculiarly intent look.

I shrugged.

"No, huh?" She pulled out a notepad, scribbled something on it. "Okay, what else have we got? As for prior records, back in the sixties, Corbin had numerous arrests, possession of marijuana, disorderly conduct, resisting arrest—"

I laughed. "In *those* days, Sergeant, that kind of record was practically *de rigueur* for a young intellectual. It doesn't mean Elliot had criminal propensities."

"I guess." Schultz's sour expression demonstrated her contempt for trendy infractions of the law. "Other than that, we got nothing on him. Let's see, no living family—except for this kid he had with his ex-wife. His associates seem to be limited to other profs. His interests seemed kinda narrow, too. No clubs or hobbies, other than academic organizations. He taught, wrote, lectured—all literary stuff."

I chose not to comment on her assessment of a colleague's life. Instead, I took a second coffee into the library and got to work, pulling out folders, sifting through their contents. Financial records. Teaching notes. Research notes. Copy-edited manuscripts of a few essays and page proofs of his Poe book. Elliot Corbin, it seemed, was a pack rat. He even kept xeroxes of student essays. I leafed through a few. No student names I recognized. Then Amber Nichols' name flashed by on a paper, and I realized this must be graduate student work. Everything seemed to be as expected; absolutely nothing here seemed to relate to his murder. I skimmed it all. To read each document thoroughly would've taken days.

One letter did claim my full attention, however. But only because I'm nosy. Reading through a folder labeled Current Professional Correspondence, I came across an exchange of letters with a superstar literary theorist from Duke. One paragraph in particular intrigued me, probably because of my situation with Freddie Whitby. *There can be no such phenomenon as "plagiarism,"* Elliot wrote. *That which is denoted "plagiarism" is merely a naive concept based upon the notion of "originality," also illusory. "Originality" is in itself a fairly recent development within the historical continuum of authorship and is, it would seem evident, an inevitable consequence of the rise of commercialized print culture. All texts circulate within a prior textual matrix, and aside from meretricious capitalist claims of "ownership" of "intellectual property," no such act as "plagiarism" can be seen to exist, for, plainly, who can "own" ideas or hold "property" in language—*

"Jeez," I exclaimed, halfway through the dense paragraph.

"You got something there?" Schultz asked. She'd been wandering around the library, pacing restlessly from window to window, staring out at the ever-thickening bluster of snow.

"No, no. It's just that my colleague had some really . . . ah . . . unthought-through ideas about literature." And I explained how Elliot had bought into the poststructuralist idea that all reality is nothing other than a series of "texts." Elliot's personal twist, I told Schultz, was that all writing is then nothing but a constant recycling of texts. Therefore no author "owns" a text, and therefore there can be no such thing as literary theft—or plagiarism. "Unbelievable! As if his own comfortable tenure and salary—not to mention *royalties*—weren't based on the concept of 'intellectual property.' But that was Elliot for you, always following the most trendy ideas to their most untenable conclusions."

Felicity Schultz had remained expressionless throughout my somewhat heated explanation. Now she gave me a fishy look. "I'm sure all that intellectual stuff is real interesting to you, Professor Pelletier. But it's snowing like hell out there. Could you get on with the investigation so we can get the heck out of here? Please?" It was a mark of Schultz's somewhat improved opinion of me that she thought to add the *please*.

Two hours later, the slamming of the front door and stamping of feet in the entrance hall caused the sergeant and me to exchange startled glances. The pervasive silence of this old house, so recently the scene of a vicious death, had obviously spooked us both. "Who's there?" Schultz demanded, and Lieutenant Piotrowski tramped into the room toting a bulging plastic grocery bag. The

wind had become so loud and the snow so deep that neither of us had heard the lieutenant's car pull up in front
of the house.

"Jeez, Lieutenant, you could of let us know you were
coming. I practically went for my gun."

"Yeah? Well, Sergeant, no wonder you're jumpy, the
way it's coming down out there." Schultz threw him an
offended look: *jumpy?* Was the boss implying she wasn't
as macho as the best of them? Piotrowski seemed un-
aware of her pique. "I thought I'd relieve you so you
could get back to headquarters before the roads get any
worse. I've got the Jeep, so I'll be okay. And I'll see that
Dr. Pelletier gets home safe." As Schultz left in a miffed
silence, the lieutenant turned to me. "Ya have any luck
here?"

"Not yet," I answered. "But I'm working on it.
What's in the bag?" It was getting to be lunchtime, and
I was interested.

Piotrowski had brought sandwiches, roast beef with
horseradish on marbled rye. As we ate—in the kitchen,
not the library, thank you—I gave him an update on my
progress. "I'll finish the file folders in another hour—I'm
just speeding through them, which is about all I can do
here since I only have one day. Then I'll start on the
books."

"Thanks, Doctor. I really appreciate it. You look
wiped out. Here, have a cookie." He'd brought huge gin-
ger cookies about six inches in diameter and two twenty-
ounce cups of coffee. Mine was black, no sugar; he'd remembered how I liked it. I sat back in my chair and
opened the coffee. The wind had sculpted snow ghosts on
the sash bars of the windows, obscuring what little natural light existed. Even with the overhead fixture glaring,
the kitchen was about as cavernous and gloomy as it was
possible for a kitchen to be. We drank our coffee in si-

lence. I was indeed wiped out, and Piotrowski seemed
fixated on the steady snowfall outside the windows. He
must not be as consummately intrepid a human being as
I'd assumed.

"Piotrowski," I said impulsively, "tell me about your
life."

"My life?" His expression instantly became guarded.

"Yes, your life. Presumably you have one. Outside of
being a homicide investigator, that is."

He gave a short, dry laugh. "What do you want to
know, Doctor?"

"You're cagey, aren't you?"

"It's a professional liability."

"Yeah. I know. Believe me." My years with Tony
had taught me that. "Well, for starters, are you married?"

"That's your very first question, huh?"

"For God's sake, Piotrowski, this isn't an interrogation. Forget it! I thought we could have a conversation
while we're finishing our coffee, like normal people. But
maybe you'd rather talk about the weather? Hmm. Look
at that. Seems to be snowing out."

"Yeah it does. Hard. But the answer to your question
is, not anymore."

"Not anymore?" What was the question? "Oh—married—Not anymore?"

"I used to be married. Now I'm not." He didn't
seem very comfortable with this conversation.

"Like me."

"Yeah. Sort of."

"The thing is, Piotrowski, we're going to be spending
some time together for a while, until this investigation is
over. You know so much about me—that investigation
and all—and I know diddly-squat about you. It's awkward."

"Yeah, well, there's not a lot to know. My ex-wife and I, we had two kids—"

"Boys, you told me once."

"Boys. One's at Fordham Law. One's . . . in a band."

"Law school? You must have gotten married young." I'd figured the lieutenant was in his mid- to late-forties.

"*Oh* yeah. You could say that." He eyed a cookie I hadn't touched. I pushed it toward him. He took a bite, then laid it on the table, and ignored it. He wasn't hungry; he just wanted a momentary diversion. "So . . . So we got divorced a while back. That's about it."

"You live alone?" Why was I pushing this? But I knew the lieutenant was a feeling man, and that a whole complex history of pain and loss must underlie the dry recital he was offering me.

"My father lives with me. He's . . . uh . . . not capable of living alone. He's got Alzheimer's."

"God, Piotrowski, that's rough!"

"Yeah, he . . . he . . . used to be a great guy." His brown eyes fixed on something outside the window. I knew from bitter experience that he was seeing nothing but the past.

"But I mean—that's gotta be rough on *you.*"

The big cop shrugged, then threw back the last of his coffee as if he were slugging a shot of whiskey. He shoved his chair back from the table and jumped up, business-like once more. "Okay, Doctor. We both got work to do. I was gonna leave a trooper here with you, but there's so many accidents out there I got no one available. As for me, I got someplace I hafta be."

"You're going to leave me here *alone?*" The thought was not appealing, but, really, did I expect a state police lieutenant to babysit me for an entire afternoon?

The library had darkened with the worsening storm, and I switched on all available lights. This room was even more dismal than the kitchen. How could anyone have lived in such a lifeless house? I kept my eyes studiously averted from the dried stains on the desktop as I finished looking through Elliot's file cabinets. No one lived here anymore.

Having found nothing but the driest of academic trivia in the seemingly endless ranks of manila folders, I was only too happy to shift my search to the marginally more cheerful dining room. The books stacked in haphazard piles on the table there were mostly studies in literary theory—Derrida, Foucault, Jameson. After an hour of paging through one torturous treatise after another, I concluded they contained nothing of any relevance to a homicide investigation. I trekked reluctantly back to the library with its floor-to-ceiling bookshelves. Climbing the sliding library ladder, I went methodically through the books, pulling each one out, checking titles, inscriptions, marginalia, shaking each to dislodge any contents, returning each one to its place. Nothing.

Piotrowski stomped into the house again about a quarter to four, epaulets of snow decorating his broad shoulders. In his leather-gloved hands he carried two paper coffee containers. "Thank God. I'm dry as dust," I said, clambering down the ladder, prying off the plastic lid. The unanticipated, scrumptious aroma of hot chocolate engulfed me. "Oh, yum!"

"I thought we could use a bit of a lift," he replied. "Now listen. I really think it's time to get outta here. There's at least eight inches out there and it's still coming down."

"But I'm not finished—" I hate driving in snow, but once I get into a job, I'm like a pit bull.

"Yeah, but it's *bad* out. And if you're not finding anything anyhow . . ."

"Let me at least finish this shelf," I said, climbing back up the ladder, pulling out a copy of Foucault's *The Archaeology of Knowledge*. As I did so, I dislodged a slim paperback with a psychedelically flowered cover. It fell to the floor, and Piotrowski retrieved it, handing it up to me.

I turned the book in my hand. "That's odd."

"Odd is good. Odd means some kind of a . . . a telling incongruity. So, what's odd about this particular book?"

"Well, the book itself is incongruous. Elliot mostly has big books, substantial hardcover editions for the most part, on abstract philosophical and literary subjects, and here's this"—I examined the book more closely—"cheap volume of what look like . . . flower-power poems. You know? From the sixties? What on earth was Elliot doing with a frivolous book like this?"

I descended the ladder and showed the book to the lieutenant. *"Wings of the Mind,"* I said, "by Skye Larrk."

"Hey, wait a minute," Piotrowski exclaimed. "Ya know? I think I've seen this book before."

"Really?" I opened the volume to the title page. It had been published in 1968 by Far Out Press, obviously a shoestring publishing house, and one I'd never heard of. I'd bet anything that press hadn't outlasted Woodstock.

"Yeah. Wasn't it some kind of a hippie best-seller?"

I shouldn't have laughed. "How would you know about that, Lieutenant?"

"Oh, I did my share of undercover work, you know. This state . . . ya know, all the colleges . . . was a hot-bed of . . ."

"The counterculture?"

"Yeah."

I looked at the man with new eyes. Piotrowski as an undercover hippie? And he thought he didn't have any interesting stories to tell?

The lieutenant took *Wings of the Mind* from my hand and opened it purposefully to the inside back cover: on the dust jacket was a full-length photograph of Skye Larrk, the author, a pretty, daisy-crowned, wild-haired, bare-breasted flower child, with a smile as amiable and as dopey—in the narcotic sense—as that of the bandana-wearing yellow Labrador retriever reclining at her feet. Piotrowski grinned at me sheepishly, and tapped the photo. *"This* is what I remember."

I retrieved the book from the lieutenant to study the photo more closely. Something about Skye Larrk seemed familiar. Not the sun-streaked mass of flyaway curly hair. Not the dreamy smile. Not the drug-addled eyes. Was it the . . . the breasts? My eyes zoomed in on the small tattoo just above the left nipple: an image of an insolent blue-black crow! "My God, Piotrowski, this . . . this . . . this hippie *poet* . . . is Jane Birdwort."

"Birdwort? Jane Birdwort? Isn't she a prof?"

"Yes. Did you guys ever talk to her?"

"Hmm," he said, "by now we've interviewed everyone in the English Department, so someone must of questioned her. Musta been Schultz. As I recall, Ms. Birdwort said she didn't really know Corbin."

I turned to the opening pages of the volume, looking for inscriptions, and the book's dedication caught my eye: *To el, with eternal luv.* "She knew him all right, Lieutenant. Looky here." I handed the book over, open to the dedication page. "Who else could 'el' possibly be?" Then a faded color Polaroid worked its way loose from between the pages, and I caught it as it fluttered toward the floor. Together, Piotrowski and I stared at the idyllic pastel scene. A wedding, a hippie wedding, in a pasture. The bride wore a daisy-crowned veil, a gauzy peasant blouse and bell-bottom jeans. She carried a bouquet of pale green oats and wildflowers. She was barefoot. The groom wore jeans, an elaborately embroidered denim vest, and sandals. She was Skye Larrk. He was Elliot Corbin. Not only had *Wings of the Mind* been dedicated to my late colleague; he had at some time in the dim, departed past been married to the poet Jane Birdwort.

16.

"What is a man anyhow?
what am I? what are you?"

—WALT WHITMAN

Twin cones of swirling snow were all that was
visible of the narrow, winding road in the Jeep's
headlights. I peered intently through the windshield. It
didn't matter that Piotrowski was at the wheel, I knew
that only my hypervigilance kept the vehicle on the increasingly treacherous road.

While Piotrowski made calls from Elliot Corbin's
kitchen phone, I'd stared anxiously out the library window. Nothing was moving out there except the weather.
At the far end of Elliot's driveway, my Jetta was buried
up to its fenders in snow. It was the first day of December and an hour before sunset and it was already impene-
trably dark.

"Listen," the lieutenant told me, tucking his notepad into a jacket pocket as he returned to the library,

"there's no sense even trying to get your car out. I put in a call for a tow truck, but—the state of the roads out there—it could take hours. I'll give you a lift home in the Jeep."

"Lieutenant," I wailed, "if you drive me home, I'll be stuck out there in the boonies with no car. And I've got an eight o'clock class tomorrow."

"You really think there's gonna be school, the way this is coming down?" He gestured toward the window and, by extension, to the deadly white scene beyond. "We get your car out, and the roads get a little clearer, I'll have someone drop the Jetta off. Okay? Now, get your coat and I'll warm up the Jeep. That is, unless you want to hang around here in Professor Corbin's house till the storm's over? They're predicting it's gonna take all night."

I shuddered and headed meekly for the hall closet.

We'd left the town of Enfield—and its street-lights—behind, and had embarked on the long, feature-less stretch of wooded road that leads to my isolated little home just outside Greenfield. In the headlights, only the faint parallel tracks of a ghostly vehicle that had preceded us at some never-never hour in the past were visible. I kept a deathwatch on those tracks. "Re-lax, Doctor," the lieutenant said, glancing over at me, "we'll get there. We just have to take it slow, is all." The Jeep swerved. I gave a little screech. He laughed, eyes front again. "Looks like I better pay attention."

It was a long, slow trip. Snow beat relentlessly against the windshield, accumulating faster than the wipers could clear it. At first, neither of us had anything to say. Piotrowski was concentrating on the road. I was brooding about Jane Birdwort and the revelation that she'd once—in another life, I was certain she'd say—been

married to Elliot Corbin. I knew one of Piotrowski's
phone calls must have imparted that information to his
investigative team, and I felt guilty—and anxious about
Jane. Obviously she'd wanted to keep her relationship
with Elliot hidden, and if I hadn't recognized that tattoo
in the picture on the flyleaf, her link with the murdered
man might never have been uncovered. Now Jane was in
for some intensive police questioning. Police investigation, I realized—not for the first time—was a wee bit different than scholarly research. The stakes were infinitely
higher. Who was I, I wondered, to meddle around in
someone else's life, playing God?

"What?" Piotrowski asked.

"Huh?" I replied.

"You just let loose one hell of a sigh. What were you
thinking about?"

"Jane Birdwort."

"Yeah? What about her?"

I tried to make up for some of the trouble I'd caused
Jane. "Somehow, I just can't imagine Jane being involved in Elliot's death; she's so . . . narcissistic. I
don't think the usual motives for murder could possibly
pierce her psychic armor."

"The usual motives?" In the green glow from the
dash lights, I saw the lieutenant's thick eyebrows rise.

"Well, you know—greed, ambition, revenge—
ah . . . sexual obsession . . ."

"And? . . ."

I thought for a minute. "I'm tired. I can't come up
with any more."

"I can." He shifted down, and the Jeep eased out of
a fishtail.

"I'll bet you can," I said, far more crisply than I
intended, "but I don't think I want to know about
them."

We lapsed into silence again. I had no idea where we were, the headlight cones here—wherever *here* was—were identical to the cones we'd left behind in Enfield, half an hour back—blinding white swirls in the blackness. Then a green sign flashed ephemerally into view: GREENFIELD, 4 mi. Almost home. "Piotrowski," I said, "you know, this . . . job, this . . . whatever it is I'm doing for you . . . research? . . . investigation? . . . it's turning out to be a lot more than I ever intended to take on. I mean, for God's sake, I've just let a colleague in for a hell of a lot of trouble."

"Ms. Birdwort?"

"Yeah."

He shrugged. "The woman musta lied to us. She'd of been a good deal better off in the long run if she'd told us right away about her involvement with the victim."

"She probably has her reasons."

"Yeah, like maybe she offed Professor Corbin." He shifted up again, and the car picked up speed.

"No! Jeez, Piotrowski, that's just what I was afraid of!"

"What? Afraid of what?" He took his eyes off the road just long enough to cast me a challenging glance.

I bit back another hasty reply. "Piotrowski, just what the heck am I supposed to be *doing?* All I know about research methodology is this: First, *identify the problem.* Okay, here's the problem: Who killed Elliot Corbin? Then, second, *break down the tasks.* Okay, so I network friends and associates—which, as you can tell, makes me feel like a creep; I do scholarly research—with about a snowball's chance in hell of making any connections to the murder; I search Elliot's house and office—and find out dirty little secrets about people they've kept hidden for decades. So, okay, I'm doing all that. Then what's the third step? *Interpret data* and *draw conclu-*

sions. So, the only real data I've come up with is that Jane was once married to Elliot, and now *you* leap to the conclusion that Jane killed Elliot!"

"You know me better than that, Dr. Pelletier." The lieutenant's tone was one of infinite patience. "The only conclusion I'm gonna *leap to*, Doctor, is that Ms. Birdwort might *possibly* have had a motive to kill Professor Corbin. Nothing more. Nothing less. And . . ." Piotrowski said, as he swerved around a corner and pulled cautiously into what I hoped was my driveway, "that's a real orderly methodology you've developed for yourself, Doctor, as far as it goes, but you've left out one real important factor."

"What's that, Lieutenant?"

"You've forgotten the wild card."

"The wild card?"

"Yeah. Irrational human need. You always got to factor in the possibility of something totally off the wall. Something that doesn't make any sense to anyone but the killer. Something the killer wants or needs so bad he's willing to risk everything for it, even his eternal soul."

"His eternal soul?" We'd come to a stop just a few feet into my driveway, and I placed my hand on the Jeep's door handle.

"Or whatever," Piotrowski said. "I been reading some of Edgar Allan Poe's stories."

"You have?" Why was I surprised? I didn't know many people more intelligent than this big cop.

"And the thing that he gets right is all that stuff about damned souls."

"Damned souls?"

"He doesn't call them that, but that's what they are. Oh, yeah, I know: sociopaths, psychopaths, whatever. But all that clinical stuff doesn't begin to get at the

twisted darkness of some a these creeps the way Poe
does. I mean, whoever was desperate enough to stab Professor Corbin with such force that it only took one blow
with a knife. . . ." In the preternatural glow from the
dashboard, I could see Piotrowski's lips twist. He must
have had an entire gallery of graphic horror pictures imprinted in his brain. How did he get through his days
with those images of death always present?

"Ya know that story of Poe's where the brother
buries his sister alive? Then she comes back from that
burial vault under the house and she attacks him, and
the house collapses in on them?"

" 'The Fall of the House of Usher.' *'We have put her
living in the tomb!'* " I intoned in a sepulchral voice.
"That's one of my all-time favorite over-the-top literary
lines. And then just before the mansion collapses, a huge
crack appears down the front and the moon glows luridly
through the fissure. I'm not crazy about Poe's work,
Lieutenant, but he was always great with the creepy details. Did you read 'The Black Cat'?"

"That's where the perp bricks this cat up with the
corpse of his murdered wife, and the thing yowls and
yowls till the investigators find the victim."

"Weird." I shook my head.

"Yeah, but believable. The perp musta had an unconscious wish to be caught. I've seen that happen. The
killer hasta keep talking, hasta leave some little piece of
evidence. Hasta let us *know*. He doesn't really wanna get
caught, but this is the biggest event of his scuzzy little
life, and he's just gotta let someone know about it. Ya
can practically smell it on him—the urge to spill the
beans. All ya gotta do is keep him talking—gotta form a
bond. These creeps, they want someone—need someone—to understand them. Even more pathetic, they
want someone to like and respect them."

"God, you have a hideous job."

But he wasn't looking for sympathy; he wanted to talk about literature. "Poe wasn't so hot on the police stories, though. I mean—you know, that one about the *billet doux* that got stolen? . . ."

" 'The Purloined Letter.' "

"That's the one. Well . . . no criminal investigator with the right stuff wouldn't have gone through everything on that mantelpiece at least once. I mean, give me a break . . . that French police officer . . . Monsieur G—, was it? . . . he was specifically looking for a letter. No way he wouldn't have had everything off that cardrack. Sloppy."

Then the police radio crackled—something about a five-car accident on I-91—and Piotrowski abruptly terminated the conversation.

"So—you figure you can get to your house okay from here by yourself, Doctor?"

After his gruesome little meditation on the nature of the criminal mind, I didn't want to go anywhere by myself. Ever again. But Piotrowski was already looking over his shoulder, assessing his chances of backing out onto the road again without getting stuck in the ditch, and I opened the door like a big girl. It suddenly hit me that he was now going to have to make a return trip to—where? Wherever it was he lived; I had no idea. I stepped out of the Jeep, and promptly sank knee-deep into the snow. It had to be at least two feet deep in the drifts. "It's going to be a slog, Lieutenant. Can you keep your lights on me until I get to the door?"

"Of course. I'd a done that anyway."

"I know. Thanks. And, Lieutenant? . . ."

"Yeah?"

"Drive safely, will you? You've really gone out of your way for me. I appreciate it."

In the shadows, his wide smile flashed. "It's okay, Doctor. This oughta get me out of decades of Purgatory."

Even though the snow had ceased falling sometime before dawn, morning classes were canceled. When I got to school at noon—having found the Jetta safe and sound in my driveway when I awoke at eight A.M.—not much was moving on campus. Snowplows and snowblowers roared through the parking lots as I pulled my car in off the still-slick street, and snow shovelers scraped away diligently at the walkways. As I entered the quad from the path that runs between the library and Emerson Hall, I paused, awestruck by the sight in front of me. Boxy Victorian buildings were sunk to their windows in feathery drifts and further softened by pillows of snow drowsing on roof, cornice, and ledge. Branches of winter-stark trees curtsied gracefully, flaunting white velvet gloves. And here everything was hushed; even the shouts of the student snowballers behind the dorms seemed muted. I was momentarily entranced; the pastoral perfection, the mythic Currier and Ives fantasy of an ideal time, place, and purpose belied the Enfield College I had come to know. Backbiting, scheming, plagiarism, theft, even homicide: How could these horrors have contaminated the idyllic, almost sacral, scene now spread before me?

17.

"From childhood's hour I have not been
As others were—"

—EDGAR ALLAN POE

H ARRIET PERSON WAS LOOKING FOR a knife. I'd come into campus specifically for my afternoon office hours, but the holiday aura of the snow day seemed to have distracted students from anything and everything academic. After an hour at my desk without a visitor, I'd finished up some paperwork, and had impulsively decided it was a perfect time to clean out and organize my book bag, which was more choked than ever with the semester's odds and ends. I'd just dumped the contents of the bag on my desktop, when Harriet stopped in my open door holding a sturdy book-size cardboard package.

"Karen? I need something to pry these staples out with. Do you still have that big knife Monica lent you?"

"Knife? No. Didn't she take it back?"

"She says you have it."

As I entered the department office to acquit myself, Monica was sorting what looked like Palaver Chair application folders into three separate piles. She placed the final folder, thick with letters, dossier, and writing samples, on the top of the shortest stack, then noticed us standing in the door. Instantly she hustled the piles off her desktop and into a drawer. "You've got my knife, right?" she asked me.

"No. Are you sure you didn't take it back, Monica? I don't remember seeing it after we opened that box."

Monica sighed. "Let me look again." She pulled out her canvas tote bag and began fishing through it. When a search of maybe a minute and a half didn't locate the Swiss Army knife, the secretary abruptly dumped the entire contents of the bag. A battered leather wallet, clumps of used tissues, a pink plastic tampon holder, an address book, a half-dozen appointment cards, a dog-eared paperback book entitled *Xena: Warrior Princess,* a pendant—a five-pointed star in a circle—on a black leather cord, a half-eaten Snickers bar, an emery board, a large bottle of Advil, a dozen pennies. No knife. "I told you I didn't have it," Monica said. "It must still be in your office."

I tried to recall the details of the morning we'd opened the Foster box. "Well, I don't actually remember returning it to you. I just assumed you'd taken it back when you left. I'll look through my office, but I honestly don't think the knife is there."

"Oh, for God's sake, forget it." Harriet tucked the package under her arm. "Maybe my scissors would work." She grumbled her way out of the office: *God damn inefficient staff, how was anyone supposed to get any work done?*

I ransacked all the logical places—desk drawers, bookcase shelves, coat pockets—with no luck. And, really, if I'd had Monica's knife anywhere in my office, wouldn't I have come across it when I was cleaning up after the break-in last weekend? "Monica," I reported back, "it simply isn't there. Maybe someone picked it up by mistake."

The secretary scowled. "I'll be really pissed if somebody walked off with that knife. It was expensive—a gift from . . . a friend."

"Who was in my office that day—I mean, besides you and me?"

"Harriet was," Monica said, with a vituperative twist, "—Professor Pain-in-the-ass. And, let's see, Jane Birdwort, and that Amber person who's teaching Frosh-Hum, and, oh, yeah—Elliot." Her voice quavered on the final word, then gained strength as a new thought struck her. "Joey! Jeez, I wonder if Joey swiped the knife." Suddenly she got very busy with the stack of applications that had materialized back on her desktop as soon as Harriet had exited the office. "If I've told that damn kid once, I've told him a million times . . ."

The pile of folders in front of her was the thinnest of the three she'd hustled away earlier, and I assumed it contained the applications of those who'd made the first cut. On the pretense of checking my mail, I walked by the desk and peered at the name on the top file folder—*Professor Harriet Natalie Person, Enfield College.* Hmm, looked like the Palaver Chair hiring committee had indeed placed Harriet on the short list.

It was nearly dark by the time I left my office, and I bundled up the books, notebooks, file folders, and papers spread over the desk and jammed them back into my book bag without looking at them. Maybe I'd finally have a chance to go through the semester's detritus over the weekend.

• • •

Instead, I spent the weekend going through the detritus of Elliot Corbin's abruptly abbreviated life: Saturday in his office with the company of a uniformed state trooper, and Sunday with his computer files in an evidence room at state police headquarters. Aside from confirming my earlier sense that Elliot was a hardworking, but not particularly creative, scholar, who'd hit it big with the one book on Poe and who'd been riding the wave ever since, my search found nothing useful. I was dying to know about his marriage to Jane Birdwort and what the police had learned from her, but neither Piotrowski nor Schultz showed up, and the wiry little trooper who baby-sat me both days was deep in paperwork and had nothing to say.

Monday was the final day of fall-semester classes. Tom Lundgren was in his seat front and center when I arrived in the classroom five minutes before the hour, but neither Freddie Whitby nor Mike Vitale showed up for the eight A.M. FroshHum session. I wasn't worried about Freddie—the no-show was consistent with the rest of her semester—but Mike's absence concerned me. He'd missed Wednesday's class too, even though he had an otherwise perfect attendance record. I decided to speak to Earlene; maybe she knew what was going on with the boy.

That afternoon I wound up my Emily Dickinson seminar by discussing a group of poems famous in Dickinson's era: Longfellow's "Hiawatha," Lucy Larcom's "Hannah Binding Shoes," Whittier's "Snowbound," and Poe's "The Raven." Dickinson hadn't published her poems in her lifetime, and I wanted the class to think about her decision not to publish in the context of what she and her contemporaries would have been reading. This class met in a plush nineteenth-century seminar room with oak paneling and leaded windowpanes, and I asked my students to imagine themselves original inhabitants of the room, back when these four poems were first in print.

"But Professor Pelletier," Shamega Gilfoyle piped up, her dark, intelligent eyes bright with mischief, "I can't possibly imagine myself here in 1850: Enfield didn't accept black students then—or women, for that matter. And they certainly didn't have any female professors—"

"All right, Shamega, point taken. Forget the time-travel exercise; it was a bad idea."

"The Raven," in particular, elicited a good deal of discussion from my seminar students, a savvy group of junior and senior English majors. "Poe wants the reader to think this is a poem about love," Shamega said. "That he's like this really sensitive New Age kinda guy whose heart has been pulverized by the loss of this woman—this Lenore. But, you know, I don't think that's it at all. Something else is going on here. Listen." And she read a verse from the poem:

> Deep into that darkness peering, long I stood there
> wondering, fearing,
> Doubting, dreaming dreams no mortals ever dared
> to dream before;
> But the silence was unbroken, and the stillness
> gave no token,
> And the only word there spoken was the whispered
> word,
> "Lenore!"
> This I whispered, and an echo murmured back the
> word.
> "Lenore!"
> Merely this and nothing more.

Then Shamega went on, "The guy is terrified. I mean, think about it, he hears a scary sound in the night, and the first thing he thinks of is that the ghost of his lost girlfriend is coming back to haunt him? Is that supposed to suggest *love?* No way! The brooding atmosphere, the bizarre imagery, the haunting repetition of the refrain: That's not love at all, that's *guilt!* I mean, don't you think?"

"Well," I responded, "Poe had a lot to feel guilty about. He was a destructive—and self-destructive—man." Then I repeated what I'd told my freshmen about the poet's drinking and fighting, his marriage to his thirteen-year-old cousin, the accusations of forgery. "And at times," I told the class, "he even seems to have been willing to claim other poets' work as his own." Sitting on the edge of my desk, I prepared myself for some juicy literary gossip.

"Poe was the sole support of his young wife Virginia and her mother, his aunt Maria Poe Clemm, and he was desperate for money. When the prestigious Boston Lyceum invited him—and paid him—to compose an original poem to read to a large Boston audience, he accepted immediately, but then suffered a serious bout of writer's block. The rumor at the time was that Poe asked Fanny Osgood—a popular poet with whom he'd carried on a very public flirtation—to write a poem he could read as his own. I've actually seen the manuscript she produced. It's in the archives of the Boston Public Library." My students were rapt. I continued, warming to the tale.

"But for some reason, when push came to shove, Poe didn't read Osgood's poem in Boston. Instead, he showed up soused, read one of his own poems, then boasted at a reception following the performance that it wasn't really a new work at all, but something he'd written before he was twelve. He later claimed his choice of that juvenile poem had been a hoax to 'quiz' the stodgy Boston audience, but it seems clear he'd hit a dry spell after the publication of 'The Raven' made him famous early in 1845, and really couldn't come up with anything new. This performance, of course, made him extremely unpopular in Boston. Poor Poe," I concluded, "wherever he went, scandal dogged his steps like a dark demonic twin."

That night I had a difficult time getting to sleep. Sometime around midnight I gave up thrashing around, and turned to my latest time-wasting diversion: the Internet. I collected a few e-mail messages, read through the accumulated Emily Dickinson list messages, then began surfing the net. Having Edgar Allan Poe on my mind, I idly typed his name into the search box. When thousands of matches surfaced, I scrolled bemused through the various topics. Then I came across a website called *Raven,* and clicked on the link. There in my dark study, at midnight, alone in my little house miles from civilization, I was practically knocked out of my chair by a portentous burst of organ chords and the black flapping wings of an ominous bird zooming toward me at a zillion miles an hour from somewhere deep within my monitor. A sonorous voice intoned the familiar word: *"Nevermore . . ."* Edgar Allan Poe had come to cyberspace.

18.

"All day, like some sweet bird, content to sing
In its small cage, she moveth to and fro—"

—ELIZABETH OAKES SMITH

JANE BIRDWORT, IN PINK AS USUAL, looked nothing like a grieving widow on Tuesday morning as I tried hard not to gape at her across the conference table. Had the police spoken to her yet, I wondered, about her long-ago marriage to Elliot? If they had, she showed no particular signs of anxiety, spreading a hand of solitaire in front of her, then slapping cards on the appropriate piles as she waited for the FroshHum exam-preparation meeting to begin. I sighed in relief: My uncovering of her marriage to Elliot didn't seem to have caused Jane any problems. One more worry off my mind.

Miles Jewell had scheduled the meeting for ten. By 10:12 the fifteen professors who taught this collaborative course were seated around the gleaming mahogany table in the English Department conference room just off the main department office. We were attempting—with difficulty—to thrash out a common final exam that would satisfy everyone. All Enfield students began their college years studying the same literary texts, and we paid lip-service to the myth that all FroshHum professors taught exactly the same poems and stories in exactly the same way. In actuality, we each had taught the texts according to our individual literary and political interests. This made planning the final exam contentious. If the alphabet had been an assigned FroshHum text, we'd have disagreed over whether p really did come before q. Or, to put it in the current academic lingo, if alphabetic order was nothing less than the social construct of a patriarchal hegemony determined to maintain sole dominance over the medium of written expression.

An atmosphere of unease—even distrust—had hung over the department in the eleven days since Elliot's murder. Not only had our colleague's brutal death broken the routine of academic life—piling extra work on everyone in the department as we took over his courses, his advisees, his thesis students—but a certain moral anxiety now pervaded all our interactions. Was there among us someone who had no respect for that essential human contract, Live and Let Live? Would the killer ever be identified and the violation of that crucial contract be redressed? And could we live with the horrific knowledge of man's inhumanity to man when it was no longer a mere abstraction or poetic metaphor to be tossed around in the classroom, but rather an all-too-present reality in our daily lives? Among the hypereducated human beings gathered around this table, had Elliot Corbin's death elicited any higher sympathy for our fellows, any heightened empathy or compassion? Not so far as I could see. The exam-preparation meeting was proceeding as all our meetings did: long stretches of mind-numbing litcrit assertion, followed by short spurts of red-faced rage.

"Claptrap!" Miles Jewell exploded in response to Ned Hilton's insistence that our collaborative FroshHum exam question on T. S. Eliot's "The Love Song of J. Alfred Prufrock" should focus on questions of Eurocentric cultural imperialism. "Any idiot can see that the poem is about the loss of heroism in the modern world!" As Miles slammed his hand on the table, Amber Nichols glanced up briefly from the design of interlocking daggers she was penciling on the yellow lined pad in front of her. Her customary smile grew even more enigmatic as she gazed around, slit-eyed, at her colleagues.

Struck by the knowing superiority in Amber's smile, I, too, surveyed my associates, covertly attempting to assess just exactly what this adjunct professor saw in the oak-wainscoted room that caused her so much secret amusement. Sitting directly opposite me in the gloomy light that sifted through the wooden slats of ancient venetian blinds was Miles, our eternal department chairman, his normally rosy complexion watermelon-hued in indignation. Three fiercely sharpened yellow pencils lay catty-corner across his unmarked white Enfield memo pad. Under Ned Hilton's thinning, dead-grass-colored hair, his strained features had taken on the flat white of a discarded computer printout. With infinite attention he bent and rebent a large paper clasp until its twin trapezoids became a single lethal-looking needle of wire.

Harriet Person, with her white-streaked hair and jet-black eyes, wore a military-looking navy pantsuit with a white silk tee. *"Pru. Frock,"* Harriet said, enunciating each syllable separately. "The poem is best read in terms of the tyranny of female body image." Size-ten knitting needles clicked ominously as she purled a new row of scarlet worsted.

Jane Birdwort threw her a look of disgust. "You're so wrong, Harriet. Eliot was no feminist. 'Prufrock' is about The Poet and his plight in a world devoid of passion. . . ." Jane dipped swiftly into her large brocaded bag, then applied a thin steel file ruthlessly to the broken nail of her right forefinger.

The wrangling over the "Prufrock" question was winding down without me getting my licks in. "I've always liked to talk about the use of metaphor in 'Prufrock,' " I said, striking right to the heart of the matter. "The kids just love the stuff about being skewered to the wall." Why couldn't I stop thinking about sharp objects?

When I opened the door that leads from the conference room directly into the main office after the meeting, the first thing I saw was Monica, sitting ramrod-straight and pale-visaged behind her desk. She seemed to be staring through me at someone partially obscured by my presence. I glanced over my shoulder. Except for the inoffensive Jane Birdwort, there was no one immediately behind me. I turned back to Monica, puzzled by her uncharacteristic edginess. Then I saw the police officers and took a deep, involuntary breath.

As Jane entered the main office behind me, Schultz nodded abruptly to Piotrowski. The lieutenant stepped forward smoothly and took Jane by the arm. "Ms. Birdwort," he said, in a flat, controlled voice, "would you come with us, please? We'd like to ask you a few questions down at headquarters."

"Questions? About what?" Her round cheeks were very pink.

THE RAVEN AND THE NIGHTINGALE | 183

"About the death of Elliot Corbin." It had been a long time since I realized just how intimidating a figure the lieutenant could be, six foot three, an eighth of a ton, a face sculpted of New Hampshire granite.

"Me? But I—" Then Jane abruptly went bone-white and ran out of words. Behind us, Harriet Person gasped, and Amber drew in a long whistling breath. I turned quickly to Piotrowski, but my knee-jerk objection died on my lips—this stone-faced individual didn't seem to be the compassionate man I thought I knew. In fact, as far as the lieutenant was concerned, I wasn't in the room; his attention was totally fixed on Jane.

Miles Jewell bulldozed his way through the professors clustered by the conference room door and exclaimed, "What the hell is going on here?" Given his imperious expression, I half expected him to sputter, *unhand that woman!*

At his words, Sergeant Schultz, the good cop here, turned to our outraged chairman. "We understand, Professor Jewell, that this must be unpleasant for you. But we have a number of questions we need to ask Ms. Birdwort." *Based on a faded thirty-year-old photograph of a hippie wedding?* I opened my mouth to protest, but Schultz shot me a hard-eyed stare, the kind of hard-eyed stare that says quite emphatically: *I know exactly what you're going to say, Professor, but if you say it now you will immediately find yourself up to your eyeballs in duck excrement.* I closed my mouth. Schultz had the law on her side.

As a tall female trooper with a blond crewcut led the still speechless Jane to the patrol car idling by the front steps, the appalled silence that had fallen on my colleagues turned instantly to a babble of horrified speculation. Schultz took advantage of the distraction to address me *sotto voce.* "Professor Pelletier, the lieutenant is going to want to talk to you sometime this afternoon, when we're finished questioning Ms. Birdwort. Where will he find you?"

"Tell him to call me at home." As upset as I was about Jane's apprehension, I was also profoundly puzzled. This whole scenario didn't sit right with me. I needed to think about it away from the buzz and hum of the Enfield College scandal machine.

The sun was shining in a bright blue sky, but it was exceedingly cold. Walking down the Dickinson Hall steps, I tied the soft chenille scarf Amanda had given me last Christmas. As I flipped the ends of the long scarf over my shoulder, I caught a furtive movement out of the corner of my eye. Whirling, I saw nothing but movement: the campus was alive with movement. A group of lanky basketball players passed me, analyzing with fluid gestures the specifics of Enfield's most recent loss. I caught the words, *afraid to take the pressure shot.* Two young women in jeans and pastel ski jackets paused and eyed the players. One whispered in the other's ear, and both snickered, pivoted, and followed the players. A college groundskeeper in a dark blue work jacket chopped rhythmically at the frozen snow edging the walkway with his shovel. My colleague Ned Hilton muttered to himself as he crunched past me, bent under a bulging backpack. It sounded to me as if he were saying: *emerging pattern of heterosexist erotic predation.*

What furtive movement? I pondered. There are students all over the place. No one's trying to hide anything. But, nonetheless, I felt uneasy—as if someone had been waiting specifically for me to emerge from the heavy double doors. I thought of Jane Birdwort lurking in the darkness, waiting for Elliot Corbin to exit through these very same doors. In spite of the sun and the brilliant blue sky, a shadow seemed to overhang the glittering campus.

When I opened the door to Lieutenant Piotrowski at three-fifteen that afternoon, Emmylou was singing about looking for the water from a deeper well, and my home was redolent of cinnamon and cloves. I was baking molasses cookies. The anxiety kindling in my overburdened mind demanded the kind of psychopharmaceutical relief that could be obtained only in the kitchen, and I'd stopped at the supermarket on the way home to stock up on illegal substances: butter, sugar, molasses, eggs. The orderly steps of cookie baking had freed my mind to meander. Then—suddenly—I was struck by just exactly what had so puzzled me about the scene enacted in the English Department office that morning. It was the *performance* aspect of it, the oh-so-very-subtle theatricality—uniformed officers, patrol cars—the fact that Jane had been taken into custody in such a public arena in front of such a large and enthralled audience. What was Piotrowski up to? After all, the police could just as easily have waited until Jane returned to her own office and picked her up there with far less fuss and feathers. That they hadn't nagged at me. In six years with my New York state trooper ex-boyfriend Tony, I'd picked up a bit about criminal investigation, and maybe some of it had stuck.

In his near-twenty years on the force, Tony had engaged in very few gun battles or lights-and-sirens chases. For him, a good part of the energy of police work went into the mind games he and his partners played with suspects in order to get at the truths it was in the suspects' best interests to conceal from the police. His daily adventures consisted of improvisational scenarios played out with the "bad guys"—as he persisted in calling them in

spite of my horrified PC protests. Little impromptu
dramas—fragmented, ephemeral, quasi-fictive perfor-
mances—designed to pull a suspect in, mislead him if necessary, and seduce him into being indiscreet. Maybe the
little drama in the English Department office this morning had been staged along those lines. Maybe Piotrowski
had been attempting to dupe someone into complacency.

Piotrowski wiped his slushy boots thoroughly on the
worn doormat. His expression was part standard-issue
cop deadpan and part anticipation—he'd obviously
smelled the cookies. I relieved him of his jacket and hung
it over the back of a straight chair. "I'm going to do us
both a big favor, Lieutenant, and not rush to the outraged conclusion that you've brought in Jane Birdwort
simply on the basis of one ancient photograph." I fussed
with coffee and milk, then handed him the steaming cup.

"Of course not." He sank into the black recliner,
right at home in my tag sale–furnished living room. But
he watched me as cautiously over the rim of the mug as if
I were a suspicious package abandoned on an airport seat.

I slid a plate of still-warm cookies over the coffee
table in his direction. "Why the look, Piotrowski?"

"What look?"

"That look on your face, the one that says, *What's
this woman up to?*"

He smiled ruefully. "It's just that I know your feelings about this case, Doctor: You don't figure Ms.
Birdwort committed this homicide. So—I don't get it. I
don't understand why you're not going ballistic about us
holding her for questioning. You're usually, ah, up-front
with your feelings."

"You're right, I don't think Jane Birdwort murdered
Elliot. I *know* she didn't do it. I was with her when she
found out about Elliot's death. I'm the one who *told* her.

She couldn't possibly have feigned that reaction. No one could."

"Oh, so now you're a forensic psychologist?"

That wasn't worth a response. "So, yeah, you're right: I have a couple of questions for you, Lieutenant. First, what are you doing here?"

He bit into a cookie and munched it. "What's your second question?"

It was like grappling with an eel, the man was so slippery. "What I don't understand, Piotrowski—really don't understand—is why you chose to apprehend Jane in a public place, at a time when such a large number of faculty members were present."

He didn't even blink. "Dr Pelletier, you're too smart."

"Am I?" I countered.

"Okay. Okay. I'll answer your first question. I'm here because you been working with us on this case, and I figured it would be only courteous to let you know what transpired to lead us to take Ms. Birdwort in."

Transpired? Courteous? "Right."

He gave me his trademark slit-eyed look—he knew damn well I wasn't buying it—and then went on. "First, having found evidence of the suspect's marriage to Professor Corbin, we placed her in the category of persons who might of had a motive to harm him."

"Uh huh."

"But, that in itself wasn't enough for us to pick her up. Another thing that interested us was how well she fit the killer profile."

"Killer profile?"

"Personal involvement. Furious strength." He ticked them off on his fingers. "Not only had she once been married to the victim, she also had a long history of emotional instability and a grudge against Corbin—he ended their relationship in 1973 by having her committed, against her will, to a psychiatric hospital. She was there for eight months."

"Jeez!"

"In addition to which, the . . . ah . . . bizarre images in many of her poems suggest a propensity toward violence—"

"Piotrowski, they're *metaphors!* A metaphor is not meant to be taken literally. It's a figurative—" I flashed on a powerful image from one of the poems I'd heard Jane read: a woman cruising the streets in high red boots. Hadn't the poem said something about a stiletto?

"I know what a metaphor is, Dr. Pelletier. Let me finish. All of these things together, plus the fact that Ms. Birdwort has no alibi for the day in question, led us to request a warrant to search her home—"

"Oh—"

"So—we found the murder weapon. It's a very substantial knife—with traces of blood still on it; it is *not* a metaphor."

"The *murder weapon!* At Jane's house? My God! Are you sure?" I bit my tongue to keep from asking whether the knife was a stiletto. *That* was a metaphor.

"Of course we're sure. What d'ya think? I want to look like a fool in court?"

"Sorry. Where was it—the . . . the murder weapon?"

"Behind a row of books on the top shelf in her study. The knife is congruent with the victim's wound; the blood is human. So far the evidence leads in the direction of Ms. Birdwort's guilt."

It certainly seemed like a solid case. Was I wrong about Jane? But I couldn't forget her stupefied expression when I'd informed her of Elliot's murder: The gray eyes that had gone so flat with shock could not possibly have been the eyes of a killer. Could they? And why would she have *kept* the knife she'd used to kill someone? She was not a stupid woman. I thought for a moment before I responded. "The knife could have been planted there, you know." His brown gaze remained impenetrable. "Lieutenant, I am not convinced that Jane killed Elliot." Then I paused, chewing my upper lip. "And you know what? I don't think you are either."

"Like I said, Doctor, sometimes you're just too smart." He fell silent for a half-minute, as if he were considering his words. "Look, here's what I wanta say—just between us, right?—you might wanta keep your eyes open around that English Department. See if Ms. Birdwort's . . . ah . . . apprehension jogs anything loose, if ya get my drift, shakes anyone's tree. Don't take any risks, but just . . . pay attention. And if anything looks . . . weird, ya know . . . *inconsistent* in some way, let me know right away."

"Tha-a-a-t's why the scene in the department office, then? Instead of a nice quiet talk—say in her office or at her home? I *knew* something was fishy about that! You were trying to *shake the trees* in case Jane isn't guilty."

He shrugged and reached for another cookie. "Well, I gotta admit, I'd like us to be wrong on this one. We talked to Ms. Birdwort for a long time today—and then we had to release her. For now."

Whew! I wasn't certain why I cared so much. Maybe it was because of Jane's poetry. Her work voiced such a strong woman's spirit. It would be *wrong* for Jane to be silenced before she'd finished writing whatever was in her to write. Too many women poets had been prematurely stifled, either by death or by social circumstances. I thought of Sylvia Plath, Anne Sexton—and Emmeline Foster. We'd lost a lot. I didn't want that to happen again.

Piotrowski took a third molasses cookie. "Ms. Birdwort may be a little nuts, but she just doesn't . . . well . . . The whole thing just doesn't smell right. But I hafta tell ya—the evidence is damn solid—" He chomped; half the cookie vanished.

"Fingerprints?"

"Well—no. That's the sticking point. The handle was wiped clean after the blade was folded over. It was one a them big Swiss Army knives—"

A chill frosted my spine. "Monica!" I blurted.

"What?" Like a bird dog on a hot trail, he became hyperalert, cookie paused halfway to his lips, eyes focused and still.

"Monica's missing Swiss Army knife!"

"Ms. Cassale? . . . Hmm." The lieutenant stuffed the remainder of the cookie in his mouth, plopped his mug down on the side table, sat abruptly upright, and, still chewing, reached in his suit jacket pocket for his notebook. "Tell me about it, Dr. Pelletier. Tell me all about it."

I got to Smith's Bookshop just as the store was closing. The sidewalk trees in downtown Enfield were twisted with white fairy lights, the lampposts swagged in green pine garlands so almost-natural I almost thought they were almost-real. At five-thirty on a December evening, dinnertime shoppers rushed into Enright's Market for last-minute fresh pasta and homemade pesto sauce. Two students taking a break from college food-service meals slipped into Scalzo's for sausage wedges just like the kind their mothers used to buy. As I was about to turn into Smith's, a tall woman in a bulky, lined jean jacket pushed through the doors of Bread and Roses with a dozen baguettes in a brown paper bag. It was Harriet Person. She brushed past me without acknowledgment or apology. *Gorgonzola,* she muttered as I stepped back to let her by. *Gorgonzola. Gorgonzola.*

Smith's was a hardwood-floor and pressed-tin-ceiling bookstore, small, with narrow aisles, and floor-to-ceiling shelves. Aside from Amber Nichols, browsing through the Biography section, I was the only last-minute customer, and the elderly owner, Whit Meyers, jangled his keys, clearly anxious to close. Jane Birdwort's new volume of poetry—the one she'd read from at the public library— was featured in the Local Authors section by the front counter, and I snagged a copy. While Whit rang up the sale, I flipped through pages until I found the poem that had so gripped my imagination at Jane's library reading. "Doing Violence." Now, after Elliot's death, the poem's title resonated gratingly. Was Jane's usurpation of the language of violence merely a powerful metaphoric tool? Or did it reflect a decades-long desire for personal revenge?

19.

T HAT NIGHT I TOOK JANE'S book to bed and read "Doing Violence." The literary critic in me understood that these were the words of a poet musing on the situation of the modern artist. The midnight reader found it far more sinister than that.

Night and day to cruise
the streets in my high red boots
screwing all the sullen gang,
cigarette hanging from my lip,
like another fang, this is the silent me.
This one knows death,
reads the paper, thrives on rape.
But she is apocryphal . . .

Jane's images gave me the creeps—just as they were
meant to. But the lieutenant had asked for my help, and
if these unsettling verses could yield any clues to the mystery of Elliot's death, I was the one qualified to find
them.

> . . . *Folks, this is a vicious century.*
> *The horrendous possibility lurks in the corridor,*
> *picking its teeth and whistling.*
> *Are you prepared?*

In the night wind, the house gave a sudden, loud,
ominous creak. I half leapt out of bed, then caught myself
with an embarrassed giggle. The old house *always* creaked
in the night wind. I turned back to Jane's poem.

> *The plump matron in the pink Sunday dress*
> *is ogling the Picassos. If she could see*
> *what I see, she would come out of here in pieces.*
> *Like me, she would come out of here with one eye.*
> *Blue-lipped. A hag.*

Had I locked the doors? *All* of them? And the windows too? I jumped up and padded into the kitchen in
my thick wool socks. Back door double-locked? Windows? In the living room a muted thump made me stiffen
with apprehension, as logs shifted and fell in the woodstove. A flame flared up briefly behind the glass. Front
door locked? Deadbolt engaged? Amanda had made me
purchase the deadbolt when she'd started reading up on
Criminal Science as a possible career choice. I'd always
felt perfectly safe way out here in the country—until my
daughter started entertaining me with serial-killer stories.
Let's see now? Living room windows? Locked solid. I

padded through the bathroom, the study, Amanda's room. No one was going to get in this house tonight without a battering ram.

Somehow that didn't make me feel any safer. The kind of terrors Jane wrote about don't need a battering ram.

Back under the covers I picked up the book again.

The other one, she is afraid.
She pours her coffee in a glass,
she shakes it, studies it, gives it to me to test.
She takes no risks, sipping slowly, sitting with her
    back
to no doors. But never mind. She is not safe.
She still has dreams. Around her she gathers
her scraps of comfort. Mozart and Donne. The
    green trees
that grow tall and strong. That live for years and
    years.
The re-occurring sun. White wine in an amber
    glass.
Peace. Solitude.

Peace? Solitude? Mozart and Donne? This was more like it. The fist around my heart unclenched. I began to breathe evenly. My eyelids grew heavy. I forced them open again so I could finish the poem.

Oh? I see. *Forget* peace and solitude. Forget *sleep.*

But never mind. Here I come again
with my stiletto
heels, my third breast,
the snake that coils on my own split tongue.
She is not safe. Her face splinters and turns
green. There is a small lump in her neck.

Already her feet hurt.
Where will they take her now? Dancing?
These red and vicious shoes?

And the police hadn't locked this woman up? I slapped the book shut. *Sweet dreams*, I whispered to myself, and turned out the light. I lay awake in the dark for a long time. I'd been wrong: A Ph.D. in English is *not* the credential required to determine innocence or guilt.

The Blue Dolphin was quiet when I met Sophia there after a frantic early-morning phone call. The diner's breakfast rush was over, and the smell of chili wafting from the kitchen foretold a hearty meal for the lunchtime crowd. Shiny metallic holiday swags in red, green, and gold decorated the laminated walls of the diner, and Alvin and the Chipmunks sang "Jingle Bells," accompanied *sotto voce* by the pink-uniformed waitress who showed up instantly with a pot of coffee. *Jingle Bells?* I thought. *Christmas is almost here. I've got to get started on my shopping.*

Sophia had chosen a booth in the back, and was writing intently on a yellow pad when I joined her. The instant I rounded the curved end of the chrome-trimmed counter, the pad vanished into the backpack sitting next to her on the red vinyl bench.

"Thanks for coming, Karen," Sophia began. She'd twisted her lank hair into a bun at the nape of her neck, and her tired blue eyes were rimmed with shadows. "I called you because you're the only one I could think of who might be able to help Ms. Birdwort . . . Jane. I'm so worried about her, I didn't sleep at all last night."

"She seems to have that effect on people," I said, dryly, and took a slurp from the mug of coffee. The woman in the booth across from us was wearing knee-high red leather boots, and I couldn't keep my eyes off them.

"Jane didn't have anything to do with Professor Corbin's death," Sophia insisted. "She couldn't have. Poetry is her life—her entire existence. She wouldn't hurt a . . . a . . ."—Sophia fell back on cliché, decidedly the last resort for a fledgling poet—"a *flea!*" she concluded haplessly.

"Sophia, I know you care about Jane, but you've got to relax. She hasn't been arrested. She hasn't even been charged with anything."

"But why would they take her in if they didn't think they had evidence? Why would they hold her so long? She was there for hours! I called her last night, and she said the police just kept on and on about whether or not she had an alibi for Thanksgiving Day. But she doesn't. She was home alone all day, writing—and she didn't go anywhere for a holiday meal. She just had a frozen turkey dinner for supper. Isn't that sad? Frozen turkey! On Thanksgiving! Isn't that totally *tragic?*" Every once in a while I was jolted into remembering just how young Sophia was. "And . . . why I thought you could help? I know you have connections with the police—that big lieutenant, you know, from when . . ."

"Yeah," I said, "I know."

"Anyhow, I . . . I want to talk to him." Sophia drew herself up and squared her narrow shoulders. "Jane couldn't have killed Professor Corbin on Thanksgiving Day, and I can prove it!"

Sophia wouldn't tell me anything more, no matter how hard I pressed her. I gave her Piotrowski's phone number, and walked her out to her car. I was worried about Sophia; she was genuinely distraught about Jane, and I feared she was on the verge of doing something rash.

20.

Ah! Woman still
Must veil the shrine,
Where feeling feeds the fire divine,
Nor sing at will,
Untaught by art,
The music prison'd in her heart!

—FRANCES SARGENT OSGOOD

W HEN I ENTERED THE CLASSROOM at five minutes before the FroshHum exam's scheduled nine
A.M. start, my students were sitting in the early-morning
gloom with no lights on, as if they anticipated a two-hour
snooze instead of a two-hour exam. I flicked the switch,
and twenty sets of eyes narrowed against the light. I
hadn't seen Freddie Whitby since the day Piotrowski had
spooked her in my office, but now she swaggered into the
classroom behind me, pulled out her chair with a screech,
and plunked herself down. I sighed. If I'd thought about
Freddie at all, I'd entertained the sweet fantasy that
she'd simply decided to drop out of my course—and out
of my life. But no such luck. Here she was in her size-four
jeans and bleached-red Ralph Lauren sweatshirt. A cold
rain tapped monotonously against the large, multi-paned

windows that constituted one wall of the room. Even with the fluorescent overheads, this test was going to be administered in the semidarkness. I looked out over my anxious students, counting heads. *Nineteen?* Who was missing?

"Has anyone seen Mike Vitale?" I asked. Students glanced nervously at each other; they wanted to get on with the exam. I checked my watch: 9:05. Conscientious Mike was the last student I would ever have expected to be late for a final.

Tom Lundgren raised his hand. "Mike's roommate thinks he went home."

"Went home?"

"He hasn't seen him in a few days."

"He *thinks* he went home?"

Tom shrugged. Amy Bloomberg tapped her pen against her teeth. Nina McBride rattled the pages of her bluebook. Jeff Wilen scrawled his name over and over on the cover of his. I checked my watch again—9:07—and handed out the exams.

Where the hell was Mike?

As if synchronized, student heads bent over exam papers, student breaths deepened. In the small classroom, the oxygen level seemed to drop perceptibly. Freddie hunched over her little blue exam book, face scrunched with concentration, most likely scribbling, *"J. Alfred Prufrock" is alot like life.* When she handed in her exam, I intended to schedule a conference with her about the plagiarized Poe paper. Tom Lundgren, his plump, fair face flushed, worked methodically, making outlines of his answers on the inside cover of the exam book, then writing the essays out in a careful rounded hand. I knew this, because he'd shown me the outlines while I was answering the first of his several questions about the exam. Most likely Tom would remain till the bitter end, and beyond, as if five extra minutes would make the difference between an A-minus and (horrid thought) a B-plus.

Then, while I was in the middle of answering Tom's anguished query about just exactly what I wanted him to say in essay number two, Freddie dropped her bluebook on my desk and skittered out of the classroom so fast I couldn't stop her without leaving the room—a definite no-no during a final exam. I checked my watch again; only Freddie Whitby could possibly have the arrogance to leave the exam room after a mere forty minutes. Maybe I didn't need to do further library research on Edgar Allan Poe scholarship. I was tempted simply to let Freddie's plagiarism slide; I could flunk her for the course based on the number of classes she'd missed and the perfunctory exam she'd just turned in.

In the roller coaster of my current personal and professional life, Freddie Whitby and her plagiarized essay had taken a back seat: a murdered colleague; a poet under suspicion of his death; a detective who hounded me relentlessly for information about my associates; a daughter who asked uncomfortable questions about family members I firmly intended never to see again; the weird sense I kept having on campus that someone was watching me; a student in excellent standing—okay, a teacher's pet—unaccountably missing from the final exam. Final papers; final exams; final grades.

Leaving the classroom at 11:10, I dropped my bag with the exam bluebooks in my office and headed across campus to the Dean of Students' office in Emerson Hall. I'd made a date with Earlene for an early lunch at Rudolph's. I wanted to follow up on comments she'd made at Thanksgiving about Jane and Elliot, and now I needed to consult with her about Mike Vitale. I was worried about Mike: His tearful visit to my office, his uncharacteristic absences from class, and his failure to show up for the final exam—it all gnawed at me like a dull toothache.

The rain had stopped, and a pallid sun struggled resolutely through the lightening cloud cover. On the quad, the shower had reduced to grimy hillocks the majestic mounds of snow that had lined the walkways for the past week. I watched my booted feet carefully as I navigated the paths; the temperature was dropping fast and puddles of slush were on the verge of turning into treacherous slicks of ice. Two women students in bulky down jackets brushed past me, deep in conversation. "It wasn't as if I actually let him *do* anything," the bundled-up blonde said to her shorter, darker friend.

"They're all so fucking arrogant," the other girl replied. She was at least nineteen; she knew everything there was to know about men.

"And now he thinks he *owns* me," the blonde continued. Neither student wore gloves or a hat. Their outrage at the male sex was keeping them warm.

As I entered Emerson Hall from the quad, the administration building's central corridor was dim. Until my eyes adjusted, I could see only the half-moons of radiance glowing from brass sconces positioned at ten-foot intervals on either side of the hallway. At the far end of the corridor, the enormous peacock-tail fanlight above the massive eighteen-foot-high front doors radiated kaleidoscopic blues, greens, and golds across the dark wainscoting, thick burgundy carpeting, heavy paneled doors. Luminous peacock spots brightened the maroons, browns, and blacks of the gilt-framed, near-life-size portraits of Enfield's past presidents. Surprisingly, the usually empty corridor was bustling today with custodians and suit-clad men. Stepladders and extension ladders clustered around a huge rectangular shape presently leaning lengthwise against the oak wainscoting: Another gilt-framed portrait was about to be hung on the high ecru wall across from the President's office. I bypassed the burgundy-carpeted stairs leading directly to Earlene's second-floor office in favor of the more circuitous route that would allow me to meander oh-so-casually past this picture-hanging event.

As custodians shifted ladders back and forth under the officious direction of various minor administrators, I paused to gape at the new addition to the gallery of presidential portraits that lined the corridor: a three-quarter-length oil painting of Avery Mitchell in his Harvard doctoral robes. Framed for posterity, our president sat ensconced in the elaborate nineteenth-century ebony-wood Enfield College ceremonial chair, his elegant pale hands with their long, slender fingers resting easily on the winged dragons carved into the armrest. The painted blue eyes gazed pensively somewhere just beyond my left shoulder. The angular face, with its long nose and thin, sensitive lips was composed, and the square jaw was set. This was a portrait of a man born to mastery.

"Well, Karen, what do you think?"

The real Avery touched me lightly on the arm to announce his presence. He must have been lurking in his office doorway watching the preparations for his induction into the rogues' gallery of presidential portraits.

I gazed at the painting for perhaps a millisecond longer than strictly required. "I like it," I replied. It was only the truth; last summer's impulsive kiss had erased any tenuous objectivity I'd ever felt about Avery Mitchell.

He paused for a second or two. Was he also recalling that damn kiss? If so, he hid it well. His voice was exceedingly level as he continued, "A little pretentious, perhaps, but the trustees insisted on the robes and the chair."

"Well . . . they become you."

The portrait's original stood silent for another brief second, then unexpectedly gestured toward his office. "Karen, do you have a minute?" I was late for my date with Earlene, but at Enfield a summons from our president, no matter how impromptu or hesitantly phrased, means a command appearance.

Especially for me.

"Sure." I followed Avery past the secretaries' desks and into an office beautifully furnished with Persian rugs in jewel tones, leather chairs, and nineteenth-century landscapes. The unseasonal scent of roses directed my attention to a ceramic bowl overflowing with a tasteful cluster of plump ivory blooms in artistic disarray. Did the President's office have a standing order with a local florist? Or was this floral display the loving work of Avery's wife, Liz?

It really didn't matter, I scolded myself, as I accepted Avery's offer of a seat on one of the maroon chairs. No relationship with my elegant boss, aside from the sanctioned one of employer-employee, had ever really been in the cards, not at this small, decorum-shackled school, even long before Liz had taken a whim in her pretty head to return to Avery.

"So, Karen," Avery leaned against the fireplace mantel, "about Elliot? What a terrible, terrible thing."

I nodded, and he went on, "Security tells me the . . . ah . . . investigating officers have been . . . ah . . . consulting with you?"

So, this was a fishing expedition. I gave him what I hoped would be interpreted as a knowledgeable but enigmatic gaze.

"I've talked with Lieutenant Piotrowski, yes. If that's what you mean by *consulting?*" Even my own ears could hear the tone of challenge: *Is there a problem? Sir?* I thought I saw Avery wince. Maybe I'd overdone it.

"Of course," he said, hastily. "We all have our civic duty. I simply wondered if there was anything you could tell me about how the police investigation is proceeding? As President, I—"

I spread my hands, the weight of their emptiness heavy upon them, and Earlene came striding into the room. "There you are, Karen! I just called your office—I thought maybe you'd forgotten our lunch date. But the guys in the hallway said you were in here."

"Hello, Earlene. How *are* you?" Avery's relief at her arrival was almost palpable. "Well, ladies, don't let me keep you." He escorted us to the door.

Earlene stopped in front of the portrait, tilted her head. Turning to Avery, she raised a knowledgeable eyebrow. "Very nice," she said. "Very nice, indeed." I wasn't certain whether she was speaking as a connoisseur of art or a connoisseur of men, but at that very second, as if in some sort of mystical epiphany, radiant pinpoints of blue, green, and gold suddenly illuminated the painted image of our president's handsome head.

Earlene scowled at the menu through oval glasses with red wire frames. "Get this," she said, "Special of the Day, Trout Soup with Carrots and Barley. Yuck!"

"What's the matter, Earlene? You don't have a taste for kitchen scrapings?"

She laughed. "The menu here is so damn outré, I never know what I'm going to end up with. Pesto on my hamburger? Pumpkin seeds on my pasta?"

I ordered a burger, medium rare, hold the boursin, and Earlene chose a Caesar salad and pea soup. "What's in the salad?" she asked. "No cheese or ham, right? No bacon bits?" The ponytailed waiter shook his head. The diamond stud in his left eyebrow winked. "What about trout?" She cut her eyes at me. "There's no trout in it, is there?"

"Trout?" he echoed. "In the salad? Nooo . . ."

Our meal was delivered with unusual promptness. Earlene's salad was top-heavy with anchovies. I bit into my burger. It was loaded with cracked pepper and Worcestershire sauce. We'd need a quart or so of ice water to get us through the meal.

"Earlene," I asked, "do you know a student named Mike Vitale?"

"I've met him. Tall kid with a ponytail, right? Why do you ask? Is there a problem?"

I told her about Mike's absence from the final, the missed classes, the crying jag in my office. "And now it seems that he's been gone from campus for the past few days. Even his roommate doesn't know where he is. This is a good kid, Earlene. I'm seriously concerned about him."

"I'll look into it." Earlene fiddled with the earpieces of her red-rimmed glasses. "But sometimes freshmen just freak out at exam time."

"Mike's not that type," I protested. I knew Earlene would use all the resources of the Dean's Office to find out what she could about my student.

Earlene plucked an anchovy from her salad, deposited it on the rim of her plate as she changed the subject. "So, I was really surprised to hear that the police were seriously questioning Jane Birdwort about Elliot's death."

"Me, too." Before he'd left my house Tuesday afternoon, the lieutenant had asked me to keep my doubts to myself. "But I do recall that at Thanksgiving dinner you said you'd heard something interesting about the two of them. Was it that they'd once been married?" I didn't think I was betraying any secrets; if the case went to trial this would be public knowledge.

Earlene's brown eyes widened. "That's it! Harriet

Person told me that last spring, when the English Department hired Jane. Harriet thought it was hilarious that the department was confronting Elliot with his ex-wife.''

"So Harriet knew all along about their marriage?"

Earlene plucked another anchovy off the romaine, examined it, this time popped it in her mouth. "I guess. To tell you the truth, Karen, when I heard Elliot had been killed, I immediately suspected Harriet, not Jane. She wants that Palaver Chair thing so bad. . . ." Earlene let her words trail off, a cue for me to share any possible suspicions of my own.

"Harriet *is* quite ambitious. . . ." I let it hang. We had our conversational code; the ball was in her court again.

"You don't know the half of it," she replied. "Did you know she once sued the school for promotion? Oh, about ten years ago, now; just after I first got here."

"Really? . . ." This I *didn't* know about. Miles Jewell walked by our table on his way to a solitary lunch in the bar. I nodded at him. Earlene watched him pass, then lowered her voice.

"Yeah. And it had something to do with Elliot. Harriet had applied for a full professorship, and the department turned her down, ostensibly on the basis of insufficient publication, although she'd published almost as much as a number of the men who were fulls. She got a hot-shot lawyer, charged the school with gender discrimination—and won."

"Really? . . ."

"So she became the first female full professor ever in the Enfield College English Department. It was about time, but—my God—it escalated into such a nasty situation. And Elliot was her chief adversary."

"Really? . . ." Hmm. I wondered if Piotrowski knew

about this ancient departmental skirmish. I also wondered if my vocabulary had permanently shrunk to that
one titillated word: *really*.

"And, then, I also wondered about . . ." Earlene
pushed her half-eaten salad away, ignored the soup,
stirred a dollop of milk into her Earl Grey tea, and went
on about Elliot Corbin's nasty squabbles over the years
with Miles Jewell, Avery Mitchell, countless students.
Earlene knew everything that went on at Enfield; I had
tapped into the gossip mother lode.

"Earlene," I asked as we dodged fica trees on our way
out through Rudolph's foyer, "is it okay with you if I tell
this stuff to Lieutenant Piotrowski?"

"Sure." She lowered her red-framed glasses and regarded me owlishly over the top. "You're seeing him,
huh?"

"I'm not *seeing* him! I'm simply talking to him about
the homicide."

"Hmm," she murmured, nudging the glasses back up
to the bridge of her nose and tying a cherry-red scarf
around the collar of her sweeping black coat. "I always
did like a big man."

"Then give him a call, Earlene," I said evilly. "I'm
sure he'd be happy to hear from you."

"If you don't do it, Karen, I just might." She winked
at me and led the way down the restaurant's salt-strewn
steps.

One of Emmeline Foster's black copybooks slid out of the
manila file folder containing the semester's backlog of
notes for my Emily Dickinson seminar. Where the hell
had that come from?

Returning from lunch at Rudolph's, I'd taken advantage of the few hours left in the afternoon—miraculously

with no meetings or student conferences scheduled—to get myself organized for the end-of-semester grading crunch. This was Wednesday and final grades were due on Friday. I knew myself well enough to anticipate that I would engage in all sorts of codified procrastination rituals before I actually sat down and *graded* these exams. First I had to alphabetize the bluebooks. Then, I had to turn back the covers so I wouldn't actually know whose exam I was reading until I'd already graded it. Then I had to sort the tests into piles of five, which I stacked crisscross on each other in preparation for grading at home. During the next few days I wouldn't get through more than five exams or papers at a time without giving myself some kind of reward. Read five: have a cookie. Read another five: watch fifteen minutes of CNN. Yet another five, and take a brisk walk on the wooded road that runs past my little house. Another five: run a bath. It was the only way to survive grading student papers without incurring permanent brain cramp.

Finally, surrounded by the orderly piles of bluebooks, I'd pulled the semester's mess of file folders out of my book bag. I needed to organize my class notes in case I had to check them while grading. When the ancient black notebook slipped out of the folder, I stared at it in astonishment. And then I remembered that on the day we opened the Foster box, I'd been so enthralled with its contents I'd forgotten all about my afternoon seminar meeting. When Shamega Gilfoyle showed up to remind me, I'd hastened off to class, slipping the volume into my book bag. Whoever had stolen the other journals from my office over the long holiday weekend hadn't gotten this one. I'd been carting it around all this time in my overloaded bag!

Placing Emmeline Foster's recovered copybook in

the center of my green desk pad, I reached immediately
for the phone; since part of his commission to me had
been to search for the lost Foster material, my first impulse was to call Lieutenant Piotrowski. But I let my
hand drop before it touched the receiver. I'd already
called Piotrowski today to tell him about Harriet's long-
term grudge against Elliot. What else did I have to report? Nothing but my own forgetfulness.

Reverently, I opened the journal, then—half-
embarrassed at my paranoia—closed it, rose and crossed
the room to shut and lock my office door. Who knew?
Some nefarious killer might just be skulking around out
there in the busy hallway looking for this one remaining
volume.

Settled comfortably again, this time in the green
vinyl armchair, I turned to the first page of Emmeline
Foster's journal and began to read.

10 January 1842

Dear Friend:
A gratifying notice in Mrs. Hale's magazine. She says,
"Miss Foster's **The Nightingale** *sings of everything that is*
delightful in woman's nature, with much that is strong and
beautiful, and much more that is quiet and courageous." If
she only knew how courageous! Mr. Cummins says the
book has been selling briskly, and that the **Godey's** *notice*
will increase the sales. If only my mother's husband would
allow her to visit me here in the city, I think I would be
the happiest woman in the world! I know I could make her
comfortable. But, as I have been forbidden Tarrytown, and
I am certain Mr. Lawrence reads my letters before passing
them on to her, I have little hope of that happiness. Would
that I could be certain she has received the little volume I
sent by the hand of Mrs. Thrall. Mr. Poe has written

today, asking me for verses for Mr. Graham's magazine.
Shall I venture the new poem?—

The entry ended there, without an answer to its concluding question. This was fascinating! Edgar Allan Poe had actually solicited poems from Emmeline Foster. Was this how she'd met him? And what did she mean by mentioning her "mother's husband"? Emmeline's father must have died, and her mother remarried. I remembered the young girl's warm relationship with the Papa who had given her "a story by Miss Austen" for her birthday, and felt for her a twinge of loss, even after all these years. From this entry it seemed that there had been a falling-out in the family, and Foster's stepfather had forbidden Emmeline to visit with—or even correspond with—her mother. What, I wondered, had brought that cruel proscription about? And what did she mean by referring to her "courage"?

And, then, there was that intriguing mention of "Mr. Poe." Foster was obviously contemplating letting him publish one of her poems. I glanced up to the entry's date—January 1842. In 1842, if I recalled correctly, Poe was editing *Graham's,* a well-regarded literary magazine published in Philadelphia. If Poe had been soliciting Foster's work for *Graham's,* her poetic career must really have been hot. I wondered if she'd ever actually let him have a poem. The next time I went to the American Antiquarian Society to do research, I'd request the 1842 run of *Graham's* and check it out, see if he'd published any of Foster's work there.

Outside the casement window, the late-afternoon darkness had gathered, and I could hear the twilight cawing of the crows. I reached for the desk lamp switch, illuminating my desk and a small island of shiny oak flooring, and banishing the far corners of the room into darkness. It was time to go home. I packed the Foster notebook carefully with the exams and papers I'd be grading over the next few days and slipped into my coat.

Unexpectedly hearing a child's voice as I passed the department office, I poked my head in curiously. Joey Cassale sat at Monica's computer. With a gazillion enemy warships hovering in the sights of his Stealth Bomber's precision guns, the boy deployed the computer mouse with valor and panache. Once again I was seized by a sense of Joey's familiarity. Then, like a lightning bolt out of a clear noontime sky, it hit me. The dark curls, the close-set ears: Joey Cassale looked exactly like Elliot Corbin! Joey Cassale was Elliot Corbin's child!

21.

"Tears are our birth-right . . ."

—LYDIA HUNTLEY SIGOURNEY

A T AMAZING CHINESE, LIEUTENANT PIOTROWSKI sat at a table near the door, deploying chopsticks with grace and skill on a heaping platter of General Tso's Chicken. He rose from his seat as I stopped in at the restaurant to pick up a carton of Mu Shu Pork. "Dr. Pelletier. Glad I ran into you. Now I don't have to bother you at home." He motioned me to a chair. "You weren't going anywhere important, were you?"

"Home," I said, wistfully.

"Well. Then." His meaty hand flapped dismissively. "Why don't you join me?" It wasn't really a question. "You like General Tso's?" Without waiting for a response, Piotrowski beckoned the waiter. "Another order of the chicken, please. And bring the professor a cup of wonton and a spring roll while she's waiting."

"Piotrowski, you're shanghaiing me!" I picked up a fork, reached over to the platter, and speared a chunk of chicken.

He grunted and gestured around the room with a chopstick. "Well, this is the right place for it."

Some inhabitants of Enfield would have considered that to be a derisive ethnic slur. I laughed. Piotrowski could be good company. I might as well relax and enjoy myself; I wasn't going anywhere for a while.

A thin waiter in a white shirt and a black vest embroidered with green metallic thread brought the soup, and, while I scooped up a wonton, the lieutenant got to his questions. "Doctor—"

"Piotrowski," I interrupted, "you don't have to call me *Doctor* all the time. Why don't you call me *Karen?* Everyone else does—even some of my students."

He gave me his most inscrutable look. With no more than a second's contemplation, he replied, "No, I don't think so. Now, what I wanted to ask you, Doctor, is—how well do you know Ms. Cassale?"

"Monica?" An image of little Joey sporting Elliot's curls flashed into my mind. Did Piotrowski know the truth about Joey's parentage? Should I tell him? "Not well at all, Lieutenant. Monica's been with the department for, let's see, maybe four months, but she's not exactly the friendly kind. Why do you ask? Because of the knife?"

"Hmm." That wasn't really a response, but what did I expect from the man? He was expert at asking questions—and at evading answers. "Do you know anything about Ms. Cassale's beliefs?"

"Beliefs? You mean . . . as in politics, or as in what church she belongs to?"

"Well, not exactly a church. . . ."

"Huh?"

The lieutenant lowered his chopsticks. I picked up the crisp spring roll the waiter had set in front of me and was about to chomp into it, when Piotrowski asked, "What do you know about Wicca?"

I paused, spring roll halfway to my lips. "Wicca?"

"Ms. Cassale claims to be a follower of a . . . religion . . . called Wicca."

The spring roll thudded onto my plate. "Monica is a *witch?*"

"She prefers the term *neopagan.*"

"*Neopagan!* Monica?"

"I said so, didn't I?" He was beginning to sound irritated.

Then I recalled the pendant Monica had been wearing the night I ran into her at the supermarket: a five-pointed star enclosed in a circle. I'd seen it again in her purse the morning she was rooting around in there, looking for her knife.

"The pentagram! She was wearing a pentagram! I should have recognized it." The pentagram is a symbol of Wicca. I knew, because Jill Greenberg—trend-hopper that she is—had worn a pentagram devoutly when she'd first come to Enfield. Devoutly, that is, for about two weeks.

"The pentagram supposedly represents the perfected human," Piotrowski informed me through tightened lips. No one is more leery of occult religions than a lapsed Polish Catholic.

"Oh? Then you know something about Wiccan beliefs?"

"Schultz has done a little research," he replied cryptically.

Undercover, I translated mentally, and grinned at the image of the hardheaded sergeant sitting around a consecrated coven circle sharing experiences with astral powers.

The lieutenant filled my porcelain cup with jasmine tea from the bamboo-handled pot, then topped off his own. "But tell me, Doctor, what I wanna know is . . . well, you seem to be up on everything kinda strange that goes on around here—"

"Thanks."

"—what do *you* think about this . . . *witch-craft* . . . stuff?"

I consulted my vast stores of ignorance on the subject. "It seems pretty benign. Witches have a bad rep, of course, because of all the fairy tales and—you know—centuries of patriarchal persecution, and all—but, really, for the most part Wicca is a type of . . . ah . . . alternative spirituality stemming—I think—from a belief in the beneficent powers of nature. My sense is that there's a good bit of Wiccan activity around here, especially out in the hill country—both covens and solitary practitioners."

"A neopagan subculture, huh?"

"Well, all the colleges and the hippie holdovers lend themselves to a certain kind of back-to-nature feminist spirituality—you know, herbal-based health practices, alternative religions . . ."

"I never ran into any of these people in my investigations."

"That in itself should tell you Wiccans are a fairly benign bunch." I didn't remember eating the spring roll, but it had vanished from my plate. "Listen, Piotrowski," I pointed my chicken-laden fork at him before I popped the morsel in my mouth. "Why are you asking me questions about Monica, and her . . . ah . . . spiritual inclinations? Do you really suspect she might have something to do with Elliot's death?"

"It's just that, well . . . this witchcraft stuff seems pretty wacko. Ms. Cassale might of been using her . . .

er . . . 'powers,' ya think, to get revenge on Corbin for . . . well . . . whatever?"

"*Joey,*" I blurted. "Maybe she—" Then I caught myself. "Well, Jeez, Lieutenant, don't go persecuting Monica just because she practices an . . . an alternative religion!"

"Yeah, yeah, I know: Pagans have rites, too." I laughed, but the big cop regarded me soberly. "Ms. Cassale has denied to us all along that Corbin was her son's father. Has she confided otherwise in you?"

"No! It's just, you know, the dark curly hair . . . and his *ears!*"

"Yep," he said, aligning the chopsticks across his empty plate, "I think so, too. But she won't admit it, and there's no father's name on the birth certificate." He made a spinsterly *tsk*ing sound strangely at odds with his tough-guy appearance and shook his head. "What a jerk that Corbin guy must have been."

Leaving the restaurant, I turned back toward campus— the Jetta was still in the college lot. As I passed Bread and Roses a glimpse at the display of fancy breads in the darkened window reminded me of Sophia Warzek, and set me pivoting on my boot heel. Lieutenant Piotrowski was already out of sight. Damn! I'd wanted to ask him about Sophia, if she'd ever contacted him about Jane Birdwort. What was it she had said? Jane couldn't have killed Elliot on Thanksgiving? And she could prove it? But it was too late; Piotrowski was gone.

The red VW Rabbit was parked by the kitchen door when I pulled into the driveway. "Yessss!" I exclaimed, and gleefully smacked the steering wheel with the flat of my hand. I hadn't expected Amanda for at least another two days.

"Mom!" My daughter threw the door open and enveloped me in a bear hug. "My Statistics exam got canceled, so I thought I'd surprise you. Where've you been? Is there anything to eat?"

I held up the bag with the untouched carton of Mu Shu Pork, and she grabbed it from me. "Chinese. Yum!" She headed for the table.

"Hi, Sweetie," I said, grinning. "I'm so glad to see you. I love you so very much."

"Yeah," she replied, spreading the little Chinese pancake with plum sauce, "me, too. All of that." She heaped the shredded pork and vegetables on the pancake, rolled it up deftly and ate it cold. It looked good, and, really, it had been a while since my General Tso's. I grabbed a plate and peeled a pancake from the stack, spread plum sauce, caught up on all the news.

Forty-five minutes later, as I cleared the table, Amanda abruptly became serious. "You know, Mom, we haven't talked about my visit to Lowell."

"Oh?" The cold Mu Shu sat in my stomach like a lead baseball. I pushed the faucet handle to its hottest setting, and plunged a plate under the scalding stream.

Amanda picked up a dish towel. "I know you're still furious at your family, but I didn't think they were so bad. I saw Aunt Connie and her kids—I have cousins, you know—and . . . Grandma."

I sat down at the round oak table with the dish towel still in my hands. "How is . . . Grandma?"

"Well, she's sort of a sad old lady."

Old lady? My plump, energetic mother had become an *old lady?* For years I've sent monthly checks to help out with her support, but I haven't seen my mother since my father's funeral. In a letter to a friend Emily Dickinson had written *I never had a mother,* and when I'd first seen those haunting words, they were as familiar as if I'd penned them myself. Like my own mother, Dickinson's had been a shadow presence in a family dominated by an overbearing man. Like my mother, she had left her daughter with a powerful sense of having been . . . unmothered.

"You know, Mom," Amanda continued, "there's always only just been you and me. And then Tony, of course. I never had any other family. But all of a sudden there's aunts and cousins—and a grandmother. You really should have told me about them."

I handed her the second dripping plate. She didn't seem to notice that I hadn't responded.

"When I was in Lowell, I was really angry that you'd kept all this family from me. I was . . . well . . . gonna give you hell about it—depriving me like that. But then you told me your story, and I didn't know what to think. What they did to you, they did to me, too, right?"

I nodded. *Sure did, Baby.*

"But that was so long ago, and it was all your father's fault and now he's dead. And you, you've made it. You've survived. Do you think maybe we could give them another chance?" When I opened my mouth to protest, she raised a hand to stop me. "I'm not just being sentimental, you know. After all, it's our . . . well . . . gene pool we're talking about here. That's important. My cousin Courtney looks enough like me to be my sister."

Another Amanda walking around in the world without me knowing her. The thought gave me pause—but not for long. "Honey, of course I understand. And if you want to go back to Lowell, it's fine with me. But don't expect me to go with you. I *know* my origins, and I've worked damn hard to get away from them. I have absolutely no desire to go back." Was it heartburn, that hard little knot in my chest?

She shook her head. *The mother's feet of clay.* "Mom,

can't you forgive them? Just a little? You know, Christmas is coming. Couldn't we—"

Christmas! Our Christmas! "No! Nothing doing! Absolutely not!"

I might as well have snarled, *bah humbug.* Amanda raised both hands, palms out. "Okay! Okay! Just thought I'd ask."

At a few minutes before ten, Amanda left for a club date with Sophia. I knew she'd be gone for hours; the music scene around Enfield was hot. The night, however, was cold, the kind of dry New England cold that continues to radiate from objects in a room long after the air has been warmed. I needed to stop brooding about my daughter and her importunate demands. I built up the fire in the woodstove, pulled a rocking chair close so I could take full advantage of the heat crackling from the open doors, and began to page through the recovered volume of Emmeline Foster's journal. Maybe the nineteenth-century would offer a much-needed respite from the anxieties of my own very-late-twentieth-century life.

22.

*"The death . . . of a beautiful woman is,
unquestionably, the most
poetical topic in the world—"*

—EDGAR ALLAN POE

A LTHOUGH EMMELINE FOSTER DID NOT write in it
every day, her journal was nonetheless closely
penned and densely detailed about many aspects of her
life, both momentous and mundane. A full reading would
have to wait for sometime when I was fully conscious.
Tonight, I decided, I would just skim the pages, pausing
wherever her story particularly caught my interest. Given
the rumors about her perhaps fatal infatuation with Edgar Allan Poe, I was, of course, most intrigued by any
mention of the famous poet. I skipped the initial entry—
the one where she'd pondered Poe's solicitation of a poem
for *Graham's*—and began with the second.

18 February 1842

Dear Friend,
My Mother has sent me a line by Mrs. Thrall. Her
headaches are worse and she sometimes suffers strange
holes in her eyesight, and the physicians can do little to
help. If only Mr. Lawrence would allow me to be of some
Comfort to her! My dear Father knew just what little
cossettings and attentions helped her through the sicknesses,
and many were the dainties from the kitchen and roses
from the conservatory that eased her days. I never shall
forget the afternoon he wrapped Mother in the big India
shawl and carried her to her bedroom balcony so she could
view an Eagle as it took Flight above the river, sunlight
glinting off its majestic wings. She so loved the Birds then,
and my own dear Father made certain her infirmities did
not deny her them. I fear that under her new husband's
care, she sees little of our Avian Friends. Oh—I must not
think further on this! "That way lies madness," as the
Bard so astutely wrote. I have not yet heard from Mr. Poe
about my Poem. I am too impatient, I know. He is a busy
man. If **Graham's** *does not want "The Bird of the*
Dream," I know Mrs. Hale will print it.

This old journal had plunged me into the middle of a
tragic family tale: Emmeline's father dead, and she forbidden—or so it seemed—to see her mother. But at least,
I assured myself, before pity ran away with me, at least
she had her poetry. From this entry, it sounded as if she'd
sent a poem to *Graham's*. I wondered again whether or
not Poe ever published it. Would the journal tell me? I'd
brewed my evening cup of chamomile in a gold-rimmed
fluted teacup I'd picked up at an antique shop in the
Berkshires, and, as I sipped the tea and continued to read
Foster's prim handwriting, I felt myself tugged into the
mysteries of the past.

1 March 1842

Dear Friend,
I spent a pleasant afternoon with little Mrs. Osgood in her
rooms. She is a true Poet and sympathizes with my
passion for the incandescent Life of Words. She asked why
I write so often of Birds. I did not tell her this, but I
think it is because they are so fleet—like our lives. Here in
full beauteous Plume and Song, and then—gone, to where
no one can truly say, in spite of all the warbling from the
Pulpit! I said to Mrs. Osgood that for me the creatures of
the Sky capture the nature of the Eternal as it lives in the
manifestations of the natural world. And that, also, is true.
We talked about our poetic aspirations and about the
Literature of this new Country. She thinks, as do I, that a
new day is dawning in which American writing will
provide the standard for the World. What that writing will
look like is still a Mystery to us—to me and to Mrs.
Osgood, that is. Will it be all savages and forests like Mr.
Cooper? Or will the softer influences of our Ladies such as
Miss Sedgwick and Mrs. Sigourney have also a place?
Will Home and Family and quiet domesticated Nature
serve as national emblems equal to the bloody head and
bones of life at the frontier? Perhaps not. But the life of the
Spirit in the parlor and the park is what I know best, and
what I needs must write. It would be immodest of me to
admit that I have hopes of being someday listed among the
names of our national Poets, and I would never say as
much to my dear Fanny, with her so very feminine
Modesty. But still, it is most pleasant to have a friend who
understands the inkstained fingers and the odd
preoccupations of my days!

In-ter-est-ing! At least to a scholar of women's literature like myself. Fanny Osgood was an unjustly forgotten
poet whose witty verses and poignant poems of children

and lost love had won her much acclaim and many friends among the New York literati of the 1840's. Now, here was a record that these two women poets had carried on serious conversations about the nature and future of American literature—and at the precise moment when such a national literature was first being consciously crafted.

And here, too, was yet another link to Edgar Allan Poe! Osgood had carried on a much-talked-about flirtation with Poe in the pages of the *Broadway Journal,* of which he was editor in 1845. But that little romance would have been somewhat after the period of this journal, wouldn't it? Foster had died in . . . let's see. I flung the heavy afghan off my knees, and headed for the study and my copy of the *Oxford Companion to Women's Writing in the United States.* Hmm, they just listed the year of Foster's death—1845—not the month and day. I pulled the afghan around my shoulders again and stared into the flames. That cranial data bank of miscellaneous knowledge that constitutes my brain went into overdrive. Then —bingo!: *February first.* That's right. Emmeline Foster's body had been found floating in the Hudson River on February first, 1845. Osgood and Poe didn't meet until later that spring, so there would be nothing new about *them* in this record. Too bad. But it should tell me about the love that Emmeline was rumored to have felt for the famous, tortured, Poe. I dropped my gaze again to the brownish ink inscription on the closely written page in front of me.

15 March 1842

Dear Friend,
My Mother is gone. I have had today a stiff little note from Mr. Lawrence to that effect. She was taken by a fever of the Brain last evening at about eight o'clock, and Passed

almost at once. She is now at Peace—would it be
unnatural to say I am glad? Without my father to guide
her, she had no evening star and Mr. Lawrence found her
a burden at the last—although he did not find her Fortune
so! Had my father not willed his estate as he did, with
such foresight as to my Mother's weaknesses, I fear I
would this day be among the penniless women who ply
their thankless trades in the manufactories and—yes—on
the cruel streets of this Heartless City. To spend my days
as I do in a comfortable home with little anxiety about the
satisfaction of my modest daily wants is Bliss. Were I
forced to scribble for my food and lodging as do so many
literary Ladies in this city of literary Men, I would not
write a word in which I could take any pride. I must
prepare now for the trip to Tarrytown. Even Mr. Lawrence
would not deny me attendance at my Mother's final
services. It would not look well to his elegant friends!

The phone rang. The unanticipated shrill in the silent
house startled me, and the journal jerked out of my hand,
landing upside down on the braided hearth rug. I
snatched a look at my watch: 11:22 P.M. Who could be
calling at this hour? Then my ever vigilant parental soul
went into overdrive: *Amanda! Ohmigod. She's had an acci-*
dent! I snatched up the receiver. "Yeah?" The caller was
Amber Nichols. My pulse rate slowed. I glanced at my
watch again. Still 11:22. What the hell did Amber want
with me at this hour of the night?

"Karen," Amber said, in her precise, high voice.
"How are you?"

"Fine." I stretched the phone cord out as far as it
would go so I could retrieve Emmeline Foster's journal
from the hearth rug.

"I hope I didn't wake you, Karen, but I wanted to
ask you about the Christmas party."

"Oh?" I smoothed out the crinkled pages where the old copybook had hit the floor. "The President's party, you mean?" I flipped through to find my place.

"No. The English Department party on Wednesday."

I wanted this mundane call to be over so I could get back to the personal tragedies unfolding in the pages in front of me. "That's no big deal. Just cookies and punch in the lounge."

"Oh," she said. "Oh. I see. And—will you be there?"

Okay, I'd found my place: . . . *would not look well to his elegant friends!* . . . "Yes, I will."

"And—does everyone come?"

"Sure. It's kind of obligatory. But, don't worry if you're going away . . ."

"No, that's not it!" Amber's words speeded up, as if suddenly she was in a hurry to get off the phone. "I'll be there. I do hope I didn't wake you." But she'd hung up before I could respond, and I stood with the phone in one hand and the ancient notebook in the other. What the hell was that all about? I shook my head to clear it, then turned back to the journal.

Let's see, where was I? Oh, yes. . . . *would not look well to his elegant friends!* Emmeline Foster's family situation just got sadder and sadder. And there was no further mention of her mother's funeral, simply a cross-hatched page where she had written something, then obliterated it in a bold and angry hand, as if determined that even she would never be able to read it again. In spite of the aura of anger created by the furious obliteration, the following entry was as cool and collected as usual. And it was about Poe.

April the second, 1842

Dear Friend,
After several Missives querying the fate of my little poem,

Mr. Poe today replies that he must have "Mislaid my Verse," for he can find it nowhere. Well, he shall not have another from my hand! Mr. Griswold who is just up from Philadelphia tells me that Mr. Graham's editor is not always a Reliable man. There have been scenes of public Drunkenness in the City of Brotherly Love, and even accusations of Plagiarism! Now I do not believe everything I hear, but it is too bad American Letters should be sullied by such charges!

At this moment through my casement I see the first Robin of the year flitting through the Park. Now she has perched on the scrollwork of the gate and is rousing the Universe with her Song—or at the very least is rousing the Gramercy neighborhood! And so, Spring still comes, even with my Dear Mother gone! Why, when I am happy for her Escape from constant pain and oppression, do I feel this dead hand on my Heart each time I think of her? My Verses are my only Relief, for otherwise I share this Grief with no one.

The fire was dying down, and the embers burned with a deeper, hotter glow than had the flames. A memory of my own mother superimposed itself on the smoldering coals. She was sitting at the dented enamel kitchen table peeling apples for a pie. And then the door opened and my father came in from work—

I jerked my thoughts back from my own past; it was easier to deal with Emmeline's. She seemed so little interested in Poe that I was intrigued. These did not seem to be the writings of a lovelorn woman. I skimmed pages for the next mention of the famous poet.

30 June 1842

*Miss Lynch, in whom I have confided about Mr. Poe's
loss of my little Poem, tells me the latest disturbing news of
this benighted man. Having differences with Mr. Graham
as to his editing of the Magazine, Mr. Poe has abruptly
resigned his position. This was two months ago, and now
his poor little wife and her mother find themselves destitute.
Even worse, Mr. Poe came earlier this week to New-York
seeking work and in an intoxicated condition visited Mr.
Langley of the* Democratic Review *and Mr. Hamilton of
the* Ladies Companion, *distressing them both. Then he
vanished from his friends and was found several days later
wandering like one Demented in the woods near Jersey
City. It is generally conceded that Mr. Poe is a Genius of
American letters, but, oh, must Genius end inevitably in
Madness?*

The fire crackled hypnotically in the stove, and in
spite of the compelling tale unfolding in front of me, my
eyelids were drooping. I skipped several entries that
seemed to focus largely on household details.

22 February 1843

*Dear Friend,
I live too much in the Past. The Present flies before my
reach as do the Redbreasts in the park. My Mother is not
gone a full year, and Mr. Lawrence has married again.
Rumor has it that his new young wife was* enceinte *before
her wedding day. He has sold the river house at
Tarrytown, and is at present engaged in building a house
in town. A mansion, I suspect, as he has situated it in
that section of Fifth Avenue near 34th Street where Mr.
Stewart the Merchant has so recently located. So go the
proceeds of all my Father's endeavors. That I find myself*

*situated so comfortably in this City has naught to do with
Mr. Lawrence's paternal care, or with the misguided laws
of a Nation that puts all property in husbands' hands.
Rather it is that my Father saw beyond his own masculine
advantages to the needs of a daughter whom he loved as a
Person in herself—rather than as a mere Appendage to
some yet unknown man.*

I checked the date of the entry: 1843. Five years before New York State passed the Married Woman's Property Act. Until 1848, in New York, a husband had legal
ownership of all his wife's money and belongings, whether
they were inherited or earned. At her marriage to Mr.
Lawrence, Emmeline's mother would have lost any right
to determine how her money was allocated. Emmeline
had indeed been lucky that her father had made separate
provisions for her: Her stepfather was beginning to look
like a cad.

29 June 1843

*Dear Friend,
A hot day today. I walked up Fifth Avenue to see Mr.
Lawrence's house. Truly it is an imposing Pile. How does
my mother's widower afford such Luxury? Although
appearing very much the Gentleman, he comes himself
from less than extravagant means, and surely my Mother's
fortune does not extend so far as this brownstone mansion
would suggest. Perhaps the new Mrs. Lawrence brings
wealth to the marriage? I should not mind, I know, but
anger gnaws like a Rodent. My dear Mother was easy prey
for such a fortune hunter as he. There! I have said it at
last! But I will confide it in you alone, dear Friend, and
will say it nowhere else, for I have no Recourse, and would
not engage in public wrangling in any case. I am*

comfortable as I am, if not luxurious, and have my
Writing and my friends for satisfaction. And that is—
must be—*enough!*

Poor Emmeline. In spite of her passionate disclaimer,
she seems to have been a lonely soul. I skimmed more
entries. Visits, writing habits, health, household concerns:
Life. Then my eye was snagged by yet another mention of
Poe's name.

12 October 1843

Dear Friend,
Mrs. Barhyte tells of meeting Mr. Poe at Saratoga this
past summer. She was much flattered by his asking her
advice on a new Poem he is writing. He says it will be his
Masterpiece. I saw her at Miss Lynch's, where I visit
most Saturday evenings. I meet many persons of interest
there, and some of note, and the conversationes *are most*
stimulating. Mr. Greeley asked me for a poem for the
Tribune, but I declined. I have decided to save my new
Verses, and to present them fresh to the world in a Book
compilation. There would seem to me to be more Power in
that manner of publication than in printing them
scattershot throughout the Magazines. And I am fortunate
to be able to live without the income from the Verse—as
others cannot. Dear Fanny Osgood tells an amusing story
of riding down Broadway with Miss Lynch on a shopping
expedition and realizing she had no Money on hand. On
the spot she wrote a two-stanza Poem, took it into a
Magazine office, and came out with ten dollars! She laughs
at her own facility, but I know what it costs her in
Artistry. I would not for the world barter my Talent for all
the yards of satin ribbon ever made. I say this knowing
my good Fortune—that I have never had to, and, God
willing, never shall.

This journal was proving to be a historical treasure trove. Anne Lynch's soirees were famous in New York City literary history for bringing together notables of the literary and cultural worlds. But, as fascinating as this material was, the time was now well after midnight, and my exhausted eyes were winning the battle over my scholarly willpower. I skimmed faster, looking for two keywords—*Poe*—and, having been totally appalled by what Foster had said so far about her stepfather—*Lawrence*. The next relevant entry came a few months later.

23 February 1844

Dear Friend,
Mr. Poe is in New York. I met him at Miss Lynch's soiree, and to me he seems not to be the Reprobate of whom they speak. Rather he was circumspect in his manner and careful in his dress—and extremely courteous in the Southern way. He is not a handsome man, but Romantic in his aspect, with dark hair curling over the most prominent forehead I have ever seen, heavily shadowed eyes like sad, dark pools, an unhappy mouth and chin. I have read some of Mr. Poe's tales in the press and, as I said to Mrs. Oakes Smith, he appears in person as Fantastic as many of the disturbed Souls of whom he writes.

A shiver ran through me, whether at this firsthand image of the uncanny Edgar Allan Poe, or at the increasing chilliness of the room, and I wrapped the afghan more tightly around my shoulders. Was this the fateful moment in which Emmeline Foster's doom was sealed? If I were reading fiction instead of fact, it certainly would be. But Emmeline's cool account of the meeting did not sound anything like a record of passionate love at first sight. And the following entry seemed to confirm her lack of interest.

3 May 1844

Dear Friend,
Friends ask why I have not printed Verses recently. I smile, and they infer that the Muse comes not so readily these days, but the truth is that more and more I am determined to put together a Book of Poems that will read as an extended sequence, or perhaps as something of a Novel in Verse. It will be unique, I think, in American Letters, less than an Epic but more than a simple gathering of disparate Verses. The Poems will speak to each other in accretion, and the length of the Volume will allow me a deeper Reflection, and some play with the pleasures of language. I am so pleased in the long run that Mr. Poe did not publish "The Bird of the Dream," for I shall base all the poems on the images and themes there initiated—the sense of unholy loss, the haunting refrain. I work every day at my escritoire by the window overlooking the Park and inscribe the finished Verses in a little leather book. I am in no haste to conclude the volume; this shall be a work for the Ages.

Little leather book? Had I seen it? The blue leather notebook that had been passed around among my colleagues the day we'd opened the box? Free from the necessity to write for the popular market, Emmeline Foster had devoted herself to a far more ambitious project than anyone had previously known about.

Was there someone among my colleagues who wanted to make certain that no one ever did?

As I approached the end of this journal, the entries were few and far between. I read through them at top

speed, not pausing at all for reflection. Then I hit the
following, which stopped me cold.

23 August 1844

*I have had a most distressing visit from Mr. Lawrence,
who tells me I have misappropriated his rightful Property,
and has demanded the immediate return of various
Keepsakes given me by my Mother! She had no right, he
said, as all her jewelry and little knickknacks by Law
belonged to him. I am shattered by his claims! These
Tokens are all I have of her. I have consulted with Mr.
Cummins, always so helpful in business matters, and he
says Mr. Lawrence is in the legal right—if not the moral.
My heart sinks when I contemplate the return to him of
even such trivial but deeply felt Gifts as her little ormolu
clock and the cameo I wear always at my throat. How can
one man be so sunk in Cruelty? First he stole my Mother
from me; now he steals all my Remembrances of her. I am
distraught! If it were not for my Verses I fear what I
might do. . . .*

Poor Emmeline. The man was a monster, and yet the
laws of the land were on his side. I sped through the final
entries.

November 1844

*Dear Friend,
Mr. Poe was at Miss Lynch's converzatione, and
strangely excited. He comes seldom to the Soirees, as he
lives out of the City now and is much engaged, or so I
hear, in exercising his Muse to feed his family. But this
evening he drew me aside in the window seat and, all
unsolicited, confided in me his concerns about his
impecunious state, his poor wife's ill health, and his
difficulty at the moment in writing anything at all. He was*

overly confidential, and I made several excuses to leave our sequestered nook, but he would not allow it. Then, incredibly, he praised my "facility" in verse and asked if I would write for him a Poem he could publish as his own! I all but sputtered in refusal, and then he was on to another confidant—or, shall I say—victim. What a strange and pathetic man! Genius wedded to a dark Demon gnawing at its own Soul. Little does Mr. Poe know it, but my battle with Mr. Lawrence leaves me—as well—in peril of Destitution. Mr. Cummins fears that my father's provisions for me were too hastily penned, and that the wording of a clause or two may open the way for Mr. Lawrence to reclaim that portion of my father's Estate settled on me. Mr. Cummins has obtained for me a lawyer who makes large claims of saving me from the evil Laws that invest the baser sex with all power over women. I have no choice but to trust in my Attorney and my Publisher, who is an experienced Man of Business, but I do not sleep well at nights thinking on my precarious State—

Her voice was so vivid and seemed so very present that my anxiety for Emmeline Foster increased, as if she were still alive and still in danger of destitution. A woman of her time, I knew, had far fewer options than even I had had in similar circumstances, although mine had certainly been limited enough. In addition to my empathy with Foster's situation, I was increasingly puzzled about the tone she took when talking about Poe. Her irritated response to his fatuous behavior convinced me beyond a doubt that Foster had never been in love with the famous poet. But, in that case, where had the rumor come from that she had committed suicide because of his indifference? As I turned back to the page in front of me, it was with the sense of participating in an increasingly knotty mystery.

29 January 1845
I had this morning a visit from Fanny, who says that Mr.
Poe has published in this issue of the Mirror *a most*
unique poem called the "Raven." She is all afire, she says,
to meet the man who could pen such exciting verses. I
cannot get out today for the Mirror *for I feel most unwell,*
but must acknowledge that I myself am anxious to see the
poem that could cause such a stir.

31 January 1845
He has stolen my poem! The treacherous Man! He has
taken my "Bird of the Dream" and rewritten it as a
ghastly vision of a Raven, retaining the somber Bird, the
unhallowed Love—even the refrain of "Nevermore"! But
he has twisted them, and darkened them—and given them
his name. Oh, what shall I do? I am surrounded by
perfidy! I must see him! I must plead with him to retract
the Poem! All my work depends on it! I hear he has
relocated to a house not far from the Washington Square. I
shall seek him out— Bridie tells me Mr. Lawrence is at
the door. What does he want now? The last pitiful remnant
of my Father's estate? I shall rid myself of him directly
and take a cab to Mr. Poe's. And I will get
acknowledgment of my Poem, or I will expose his theft to
the World!

And here the entries ended. I lifted my eyes from the
half-completed page, checked the date, just to make certain—January 31, 1845—and stared into the dying embers of the stove. On February first, 1845—the very next
morning—Emmeline Foster's dead body had been found
floating among the ice floes around the filthy New York
City docks.

23.

"I heard a voice that said,
Death was among us."

—LYDIA HUNTLEY SIGOURNEY

L ET ME GET THIS STRAIGHT, Dr. Pelletier. You're
calling me—at home, on a Saturday morning—to report a death that maybe was a homicide and maybe it
wasn't, and even if it was, it occurred more than a hundred fifty years ago?" You couldn't have fit dental floss
between Piotrowski's words, his voice was so tight. It was
seven-thirty A.M.; I'd been waiting hours for the first possible non-boorish moment to call. It looked as if I hadn't
found it.

"But . . . don't you see, Lieutenant? This may well
have been a precipitating factor in Elliot Corbin's
murder!"

"A precipitating factor?"

"That means—"

"I *know* what it means, Doctor. But just tell me *how.*

That's all I wanna know. How could a hundred-and-fifty-year-old homicide suddenly become a *precipitating factor* in a last-month's murder? Give me the benefit of your scholarly speculations, Doctor."

"Don't be snide, Piotrowski! You asked me to bring my literary expertise to bear on this crime, and I'm doing my best."

"I'm not being snide. I really wanna know. A good imagination is part of being a good investigator, but I need some fodder for my imagination; I do appreciate any . . . er . . . expert hypothesizing you bring to the case. If I sound bummed about your call, it's just that it's . . . *what* time?"

"Early. And you haven't had your coffee yet. I'm sorry." I tried to sound contrite, but I'd been brooding all night over the possible implications of Emmeline Foster's story, and was dying to get this off my chest.

"I'm pouring the first cup now. So, okay, I'm gonna get comfortable here, and you're gonna tell me how you think a homicide from the 1800's might impact enough on a . . . er . . . modern individual to incite them to murder."

"I said, a *possible* homicide, remember. It might have been suicide. I suppose it might even have been an accident—but I don't see how. She wasn't exactly the type of woman who hung out around the docks." And I told the lieutenant about Emmeline Foster's plight—the stolen inheritance, the purloined poem. "The odd thing is, Piotrowski, that everyone always thought Foster's death was a suicide, committed out of unrequited love for Poe. But the journal makes it very clear that love didn't have anything to do with it. She died either for money or for poetry. Her stepfather was a greedy bastard: Maybe he killed her to get the last of her fortune. Or, on the other hand—if Poe refused to acknowledge he'd used her poem as the basis for 'The Raven'—maybe she became despondent and jumped in the river. Or—maybe—and here is where it gets really shaky—just maybe Edgar Allan Poe was so terrified by her threats to expose him as a plagiarist that he . . . that he—"

"That he pushed her in the Hudson." His words were totally without inflection.

"Don't mock me!" I yanked the old plaid bathrobe closed over my gray thermal pj's, then had a sudden—and totally irrelevant—twinge of gratitude that videoconferencing hadn't yet come to the home phone.

"Don't be so defensive-like, Doctor; I'm not mocking you. It's just that . . . I don't know what you want from me. How is this information relevant? You expect me to solve this crime, maybe? And after . . . let's see, you said 1845, so it would be—"

"Almost one hundred and fifty-five years. Yeah, yeah, I know. The statute of limitations would've run out by now."

Maybe the caffeine was beginning to stimulate his neural synapses; he picked up on my little joke. "There *is* no statute of limitations on capital crimes, but finding witnesses is gonna be iffy. And trying the perp in a court of law? . . . Forget about it!" I heard him slurp deliciously from his cup.

"Yeah." Now I craved coffee, too; I should have called him from the phone in the kitchen.

"But, seriously, Doctor, maybe you're right. Maybe we gotta concentrate on possible implications of these . . . er . . . historical findings, for Elliot Corbin and his killer. Tell me where ya wanna go with this. I'm listening." On his end of the line, I could hear more slurping.

Suddenly the smell of coffee was so strong in my living room, I actually thought the aroma of his brew was seeping through the wires. Then Amanda plopped an overfull mug of black Colombian on the table by my elbow. Hallelujah! I mouthed my thanks at her. She mouthed, guppy-like, back at me, mocking my spaced-out condition; I'd been concentrating so hard on my conversation with the police officer that I hadn't even noticed my sleep-tousled daughter pass by on the way from her bedroom to the kitchen.

I hoisted my cup; now I could slurp back at Piotrowski. Where *did* I want to go with this? I thought about Elliot and his work on Poe. I thought about Elliot and his professional ambitions. I thought about Elliot and his unconscionable exploitation of other people. A damp and feeble idea was beginning to peck its way out of the shell of my ignorance.

"Honey," I asked, over my second coffee, as I sat at the kitchen table and watched Amanda down a bowl of oatmeal with brown sugar and milk, "last night, when you were out with Sophia, did she say anything to you about the poet Jane Birdwort?" I was still concerned that Sophia may have done something impulsive and rash, like, maybe, *lie* to Piotrowski to provide an alibi for Jane. The right moment had not yet arisen to ask the lieutenant about what Sophia had told him—or even if Sophia had spoken to him at all.

Amanda tilted her head in inquiry. "Why do you want to know?"

"I'm worried about her—Sophia, I mean. She seems so . . . well, wrought up . . . when it comes to Jane. I don't understand it. I know she admires Jane's poems, but last time I talked to her, I was concerned she was somehow . . . overinvested in Jane. I mean, as a person."

"Hmm." Amanda rose from her chair and refilled her bowl from the pot on the stove. "You want some?" I shook my head, and she dumped the remaining oatmeal in the bowl, crumbled sugar between her fingers, topped it all off with milk, and sat down again. "She *does* seem really worried—about something. The only thing she said, though, was that Jane Birdwort had submitted a group of her . . . Sophia's . . . poems to an editor she knew at some alternative press. He publishes those little books of poems . . . What d'ya call them? . . ."

"Chapbooks?"

"Yeah. Sophia's never had a poem published—outside of a college magazine. She's all wound up about seeing her name in print. You know—lurks around, waiting for the mailman."

"I used to do that." I chortled, remembering. "When I first sent essays out to scholarly journals. I was convinced that once my name was in print, my life would take on a whole different character, would have a whole different *substance*. The very *air* I breathed would be more rarefied. That I would somehow be more *real*. . . ." I peered at the coffee remaining in my mug; it had passed the point of palatability. I drank it anyhow. "It was all a delusion, of course; everything stayed just the same."

"But you've got your *job* because of that, and your scholarly reputation."

"Yeah, I know. But the *air* is the same, and the touch of the breeze on my *skin,* and the—"

"The taste of the coffee."

"Yeah, that, too." *How badly,* I mused, *did Sophia want to be published, need to be published? Badly enough that she'd* lie *for her mentor?*

Earlene called that day at noon, as I was mushing canned tuna into a mixture of minced onion and mayonnaise. "I've talked to Mike's roommate and three of his friends, Karen, and no one seems to have any idea where Mike has gone. Scott Duhan, the roommate, says that Mike left the dorm with a backpack last Saturday. Scott thought he was going home for the weekend, but he hasn't seen him or heard from him since."

"Oh." The niggling little Mike Vitale worryache started up again.

"When I asked Scott why he didn't let the R.A. know Mike was missing, he claims he didn't want to butt into Mike's business."

"Kids!"

"Then I called his home, but his mother hasn't seen him since Thanksgiving. Now I've got her freaked out; she says he's never done anything like this before."

"What are you going to do now, Earlene? Call the police?"

"I've talked to Security, and they're going to ask around among the students. If they don't turn him up, they'll call the Enfield police. It has, after all, been a week since anyone's seen Mike. And . . ." Her voice faltered. ". . . if the worst *has* happened, the police would be the ones to know."

Walking into the English Department lounge Wednesday afternoon was like walking into the heart of an iceberg. In actual temperature, the room was warm, but the decor was so austere that it always felt frigid: ice-blue walls, ice-gray carpeting, ice-green draperies. On the pale ash table against the wall, a huge, multifaceted crystal vase refracted the watery beams of the winter sun. With their greeny-white flowers, even the seasonal plants chosen for the windowsills were pale—etiolated poinsettias utterly alien to the vivid tropical longings at the heart of the Christmas holidays.

As I entered the room, Amber Nichols grabbed me by the arm. Evidently we were buddies now, after our little talk in the library and our recent midnight chat on the phone. "Karen, do you know anyone at Duke?" I'd never seen Amber quite so lively. On the shawl collar of her fawn-brown cashmere sweater she wore a plastic Rudolph pin. *Rudolph the Nose*, my daughter used to call him when she was three, and we were living in half of a ramshackle farmhouse in the woods. At twilight she'd stand on the couch and watch reverently for Rudolph to emerge from the trees. Of course I knew Amber was sporting the pin with a huge dose of ironic postmodernist self-mockery, but to me it brought back festive holiday memories.

"Duke?" I replied to her question. "No. Why?"

"Well, listen. The department chair there called me. They're interested in some, ah, new developments in my work, and they want to talk to me about a job. I've got an interview at MLA."

"Great," I said. The Modern Language Association Convention, heartlessly scheduled each year for the week between Christmas and New Year's, is where most initial hiring interviews for college English teachers are held. Given the brutal job market for Ph.D.'s in English, Amber was fortunate indeed to have snagged even one interview. I racked my brain, trying to remember what her dissertation was about. Something in the nineteenth century, wasn't it . . . Gothic conventions? . . . sensation literature? . . . or was it one of those trendy death-of-the-author things? I couldn't recall. But before I could ask, Jane Birdwort showed up at her side, and Amber's brown eyes unexpectedly grew wide and spooked, like those of a startled palomino pony. With a twisted smile, Jane watched Amber sidle hastily away, "to, ah, talk to Miles about my syllabus for next semester."

"So she doesn't want to be seen with a suspected murderer?" In her pink brocade dress and satin shoes, chewing on a cherry pecan meringue, Jane couldn't have looked any less like a violent killer. "That makes three so-called colleagues who've skittered away from me so far at this feeble excuse for a party. You're not going to suddenly remember an urgent appointment, are you, Karen?"

My covert investigation into Elliot's death demanded, among other things, a good long conversation with Jane. "Don't worry, Jane, I'm here for the duration. And, by the way, this isn't the *real* Enfield Christmas party. Avery gives that next week—at the President's House—and it's a blowout: champagne, caviar, petits fours—a string quartet. This is just Miles's little cookies-and-punch bow to Tradition. Do you think there's anything in that punch besides punch?"

My plan was to inform each of the colleagues who'd been in my office for the opening of the Foster box that I'd found Emmeline Foster's last journal. From the start, someone in that room had had a particular interest in the contents of the box. The little blue book of poems had been swiped immediately, and then the thief had come back for the journal copybooks. Did these thefts have anything to do with Elliot's death? Could I "shake someone's tree," to borrow Piotrowski's apt phrase, by casually admitting to possession of the final copybook? The department party provided the perfect opportunity to chat with the surviving members of the Emmeline Foster Box-Opening-Club: Amber Nichols, Harriet Person, Jane Birdwort, and Monica Cassale. I'd drop the information about my discovery of the journal volume and see if anyone's tree had gotten shook. Shaken? Shaked? Then maybe I'd have some solid information for the lieutenant.

In green wool slacks and a festive red silk shirt, Monica—presiding at the punch bowl—was the brightest seasonal note in the pallid room. As she poured the lurid cranberry beverage into my plastic glass and refilled Jane's, she suddenly scowled and blurted out, "Dammit!"

I laughed. "Why don't you just say 'Bah, humbug,' Monica?"

"I forgot the mistletoe." Monica frowned as she handed me the cup of punch. Then she glanced around the room and lowered her voice. "Not that there's anyone here worth kissing. It's just that Miles'll have my butt."

"Yeah," I said, recalling last year's party: Miles *did* appreciate the opportunity for a little smooch. I glanced around at my colleagues, surveying them for the first time with their kissability in mind. Miles, with his perpetually tight, disapproving lips, seemed deep in conversation with Harriet, who, for some reason, had slathered her lips with a '50's fire-engine-red lipstick. Ned Hilton's depressed frown rendered his already thin lips almost invisible as he lectured Amber Nichols on the evils of the post-Colonialist literary mentality. Amber's lips were set in their customary smug pout. Joe Gagliardi, visiting from Comp Lit, had a gold stud adorning his pendulous lower lip. Ouch! Michael Dunkerling— Oh, it was too discouraging to go on.

"If Monica had anything to do with making this punch," Jane muttered as I handed her the second glass, "it could have something a wee bit more exotic in it than the usual Christmas rum." She raised a snarky brow. "Like maybe eye of newt, or—if newts are scarce on the ground around Enfield, then at least some powdered toe of frog."

I carefully set my unsipped-from punch glass on the acrylic end table next to the ice-blue chair and wiped my hands on the mistletoe-patterned paper cocktail napkin: Wasn't mistletoe some kind of ancient druidic poison? "Tell me, Jane, am I the only one around here who wasn't aware of Monica's Wiccan affiliation?"

"I wouldn't know about that. But my first day on campus I noticed that pentagram she wears around her neck, and I knew right away what it was. I used to be into that stuff." She shuddered. "But that was a long time ago—in a different life."

I thought I knew *which* life, and decided on impulse to push her a bit. "Really? Is that where the red shoes come from?"

"The red shoes?" She glanced hastily down at her feet, as if maybe bloody sandals had somehow magically replaced her staid pink pumps.

"I've been reading your poems."

"Oh, *those* red shoes." She looked relieved.

"I just wondered about them, that's all. How does the poem go? *Here I come again, with my stiletto heels, my third breast, the snake that coils on my own split tongue.* . . . Sounds pretty witchy to me." I softened my words with a smile.

"Well, yes, of course," Jane said impatiently, as if to a particularly dense freshman, "that's the whole point of the poem, isn't it? The incongruous—even violent—elements of every woman's life." *Every* woman? I immediately flashed on my early marriage to Amanda's father, then pushed the memory away. What had Jane's experience with Elliot been like?

"Umm. Speaking of poetry, Jane. I just found something extremely interesting. Remember the poet Emmeline Foster and the stuff in that box we opened? . . ."

But to my disappointment, nothing in Jane's expression suggested anything more than polite interest in my find.

"I can't begin to tell you how excited I am about this job interview." And indeed, Amber was so animated that for a moment I found myself almost able to tolerate her. We were seated in the blue chairs by the window, and I was on my second cherry meringue. "These're good," Amber said, picking up her own meringue. "Monica made them."

I set the unfinished confection next to the unsipped-from punch glass. The half-chewed sweetness in my mouth had turned to powdered newt eye. I swallowed hastily. "Yeah. Well, it's really great that you got an interview—with the job market the way it is."

"Being an English professor is the most important thing in the world to me." The punch was definitely spiked with something: Amber was downright chatty. "What more noble career could a learned person want?"

"Umm." I could think of at least a dozen.

"You know," she leaned toward me confidingly, "I grew up in a house with no books."

"Umm." I could relate to that.

She took a gulp from her glass. "They called me a loser—I read all the time. I'd have to go sit on the toilet with my book, because the bathroom was the only place in the house where you couldn't hear the TV blaring."

"Umm." I'd had a rough childhood, too, but hadn't drunk nearly enough tonight to begin confiding my youthful deprivations to Amber.

"As soon as I could, I got out of there, and I've paid my own way ever since—through college and grad school. It's been damn hard." She narrowed her eyes at me, assessingly. "But then, of course, *you* wouldn't under-stand about that."

"Umm." Just exactly what was *in* that punch?

"But I'll show *them* who the losers are." Amber yanked down the sleeves of her fawn-colored pullover. "I'll show them all." Something in the ferocity of her expression diffused any empathy I might otherwise have felt.

"So, Amber," I said, more than ready to change the

subject. "You know that box we opened? The one with the Emmeline Foster papers? . . ."

But her condescending manner had returned, and Amber showed little interest in the journal's recovery.

I snagged Harriet as the party was beginning to break up. "About the Palaver Chair," I asked, for lack of any other credible topic for an opener, "I wondered—have you heard how the search is going?"

Harriet frowned. In spite of her bright red lips, there was no holiday spirit in her expression. "Miles refuses to talk about the search until after MLA. And Monica keeps those damned applications locked up tighter than Walpole Correctional Facility. I don't know a thing."

I walked down the stairs with her to the first floor. As she glanced at the closed door of the department office, I saw something flicker in Harriet's eyes—something like a comic-strip lightbulb. Both Monica and Miles were busy upstairs, and—she turned the brass knob—the office door was unlocked. She stood there with her hand nonchalantly on the knob while I told her about the recovered Emmeline Foster copybook. She, too, didn't seem the least bit interested.

"Monica," I said, as I helped the secretary pick up crumbled napkins and sticky punch glasses, "do you remember that box? The one with all the old papers and books?" And I informed her of the reappearance of the final journal copybook.

Monica slam-dunked a fistful of soggy cocktail napkins into a tall trash basket the custodian had dragged into the lounge. "Well, whoop-di-doo," she said.

24.

"He looked within his very soul,
Its hidden chamber saw,
Inscribed with records dark and deep
Of many a broken law."

—ELIZABETH OAKES SMITH

MOM?'' I WALKED INTO A house made cheerful by Amanda's presence, a fire flickering in the stove, Willie Nelson singing "Silent Night," the cinnamon smell of snickerdoodles baking in the oven, and a small, multicolored mountain of brightly wrapped Christmas gifts heaped on the coffee table. "Mom, I'm a little nervous," my daughter said. "Have you been getting weird calls lately? The phone rang three times in the last hour, but when I answered, the caller always hung up."

"Probably a student." I dropped my briefcase on the floor, shrugged out of my coat and hung it on the rack by the door. "Grades are due Friday, and the barbarians have been pounding on the gates to find out how they did."

She laughed. "Sometimes you talk about students as if they were some kind of hostile aliens."

"Toward the end of the semester it begins to feel that way. *Oh, Professor, I know you assigned the paper six weeks ago, but I re-e-e-ally need an extension. Oh, Professor, I know the exam was only this morning, but have you got it graded yet? Oh, Professor—*"

She punched me lightly on the arm. "Don't forget *I'm* one of those alien creatures."

I grabbed her in an affectionate headlock. "Yeah, but *you*, you're perfect. You're my *kid.*"

The next morning I graded papers and exams in my office, and left the door ajar on the off-chance that someone might want to chat with me about Emmeline Foster's journal. The deadline for submitting grades wasn't until the next day at five P.M., but I was determined to get my grades in to the Registrar *today*. Christmas was just a week away and I hadn't even begun to think about it yet, let alone done any actual, down-and-dirty shopping. The weather was ominous, murky and cold, but not cold enough to snow. Most students had already departed for the holidays, and Dickinson Hall was hushed. My phone rang only once, and that was a hang-up. I sipped cold coffee from the Bread and Roses environmentally-sensitive recycled-paper cup and checked my bluebook piles: The stack I'd already graded was beginning to gain on the yet-to-be-looked-at stack. Good. Then I heard a rustling noise at my partially open door, and something came slithering across the floor. I peered at the object from my vantage point at the desk: another paper. Must be from one of the students to whom I'd given an extension. But why hadn't the kid simply knocked on the door and come in with the paper? Odd. But, then, everyone was a little bit squirrelly this time of semester.

Squirrelly: That was a word I'd picked up from Lieutenant Piotrowski. Hanging around with cops tends to add some kick to the academic's vocabulary.

I let the paper lie where it had slid to a halt—I'd retrieve the essay when I went out for lunch.

At 12:09, when I rose from my desk and stretched, only five papers remained to be graded—two hours' work. Then: final grade compilation. Then: dropping the grade sheets off at the Registrar. Then . . . freedom. I felt pretty smug: For once, I'd get my grades in early. I slipped into my jacket and scooped up the paper from the floor: Make that *six* papers remaining to be graded. Tugging at the industrial-strength zipper on my puffy new storm jacket, I glanced down at the paper in my hand. Across the top of the typed first page was scrawled in black ink: *Michael Vitale. Final Exam, Freshman Humanities.* PLEASE ACCEPT IT, PROFESSOR PELLETIER. PLEASE!!!

I had to clutch at the essay to keep from dropping it: *Mike Vitale!* Mike had been outside my office door? If I'd gotten up right away to retrieve the paper, I might have been able to waylay him in the hall! I yanked the door open, as if I expected Mike to be lurking there still. No one was in the hall but Monica and Amber. The secretary was just emerging from the main office with a file folder in her hand, and the adjunct professor stood at the photocopier with a stack of books, their colorful spines neatly aligned. I shut the door, unzipped my jacket, lowered myself into the green chair, and stared at the paper. Mike Vitale's final exam! I grabbed the Enfield College directory from the shelf behind my desk; if Mike was back on campus, maybe I could catch him in his room. The phone rang fifteen times in the empty dorm before I hung up and went back to my chair.

Turning back to the essay's scrawled-over first page, I read: *My father died this month.*

Oh, Mike, I thought. The poor kid! He'd lost his father. *That's* why he'd been so upset when he visited my office that last time. But why hadn't he told me? And why hadn't he informed the Dean of Students' Office? I shook my head, and lowered my gaze back to the paper.

His name was Elliot Corbin . . .

"Whaaa!" It came out as a squeak. My head shot up. *Elliot Corbin* was Mike's father? Oh, my God! I read on at warp speed.

. . . and I have no memory of him. I grew up with my mother and stepfather and four younger siblings. It was okay, I guess. It's just that people always did a double take; I don't look like anyone else in my family.

My mother was Elliot Corbin's student at City College. He got her pregnant when she was eighteen—my age! I was born five months after their wedding. I haven't seen him since I was two years old—except from a distance since I've been on campus, but he's the reason I'm here at Enfield. As the child of a faculty member, I'm eligible for a tuition waiver. My father traded that waiver for all the child support the cheapskate never sent my mother anyhow. He was a jerk. I hated him. I shouldn't even be thinking about him. But since his horrible death—I can't help it. I never knew my father, but suddenly I'm obsessed with him. I can't study; I can't write; I can't even take exams. (This last phrase was underlined twice, once on the computer, once in black ink.) *I think I'm going out of my mind. Elliot Corbin's face is in my head from the minute I wake up till the minute my brain finally clicks off at night. I can't forget it: His face is my face. Sometimes I'm afraid I'm* becoming *Elliot Corbin!* The personal preface ended there with an emphatic series of exclamation points. Following was an essay on "The Love Song of J. Alfred Prufrock."

Reaching over to the shelf again, I pulled out the freshman "face book," found Mike's picture, and studied his image on the page. Elliot's cutting-edge, intellectual-male beard had obscured the resemblance, but with Mike's crisp curls pulled back in a ponytail, his sharply angled jawline, and close-set ears, he looked so much like Elliot, I was amazed I hadn't pinpointed the likeness immediately. Then I flashed on a memory of my student standing by my classroom desk with an essay draft in his hand, imploring me to go over it then and there because he didn't want to come to Dickinson Hall. So *that's* why Mike wouldn't consult with me in my office: He was terrified of bumping into his estranged father!

Earlene wasn't in, and wouldn't be back until morning, the perky work-study student who answered her phone informed me. Did I wish to speak to Dean Johnson's Administrative Assistant? No, I didn't. I wished to speak to Dean Johnson. Now. I called Earlene at home and left a message on the machine. Then I dialed Mike's dorm number again. No answer. I sat there with my hand on the phone, letting my distracted mind float over the myriad possibilities. What if? . . . *His face is my face.* . . . What if? . . . *Sometimes I'm afraid I'm becoming Elliot Corbin.* . . . Here I began to think like a literary critic: What was it I always taught my students about Gothic literary conventions when we studied Poe's tales? The Doppelganger—that was it! The eerie mythic creature who assumed the shape and likeness of his doomed victim. *His face is my face.* . . . What if? . . . *And* the convention of the decrepit Gothic mansion, fated to destroy and be destroyed. What if? . . . I stared at the silent phone for hours and hours—maybe two minutes in all. Then I picked up the college directory and riffled slowly through its pages till I found Elliot Corbin's home phone number. *Pelletier, you have flipped for sure,* I admonished myself. *Calling a dead man on the telephone!* The phone rang and rang in Elliot's abandoned house. And then, on the twentieth ring, Mike Vitale answered.

• • •

Mike peered around the back door of his father's house as I entered—almost as if he feared he was under some kind of surveillance. Then he pushed the door shut, and it closed with a resounding slam. He winced. "It does that all the time," he said.

In the days since I'd last seen him, Mike had gotten perceptibly thinner, and—obviously attempting to emulate Elliot's trendy beard—he'd grown a scraggly goatee that barely extended beyond the cleft that defined his chin. A haphazard tower of beer cans on the kitchen counter probably accounted for his bloodshot eyes and pale, shaky appearance.

I stamped my feet on the green-and-yellow daisy-print mat inside the kitchen door. My boots had accumulated a thick coating of muddy slush during the trek from the ramshackle wooden garage behind the house where Mike had insisted I hide my car. "Mike, what the hell are you doing here?"

"Did you bring sandwiches?" If he wasn't such a well-brought-up kid, Mike would have snatched the plastic deli bag from my hand. When I'd informed him on the phone that I was coming right over, his only words were, "Bring something to eat—I'm starving."

I handed my student the bulging bag, and he ripped open the paper wrapping on the ham-and-cheese closest to the top. I remembered from Amanda just how much teenagers eat: I'd picked up four sandwiches and a six-pack of Coke.

Wholly involved in scarfing down the sandwich, Mike didn't immediately answer my question. I sat with him at the kitchen table and unwrapped my turkey on rye. The caraway-studded bread was so dry it curled at the edges, but the smoked turkey was edible. I tore the meat into long strips, picked up a strip with my fingers, and looked around me. Except for the accumulation of beer cans, nothing had changed in Elliot Corbin's kitchen since I'd been there with the police two weeks earlier. The appliances were still avocado green, the light fixture was still brass and frosted glass, the cluttered, cat-shaped bulletin board still guarded the phone, the light from the windows over the sink was as storm-bleak as ever.

Maybe a skilled psychotherapist could have told me what Mike was doing here, soused, in the home of the man who had fathered, then abandoned, him, but Mike himself didn't seem to have a clue.

As he finished the first sandwich, he gestured around at the outdated room. "This is my legacy."

"Really?" I responded, giving the pile of beer cans a deliberate glare. "You plan on being *wasted* for the rest of your life?"

He winced. "I stopped drinking two days ago. I wanted to write the paper for you."

"Mike," I said. "Oh, Mi-i-i-ke." Thank God I'd never had an alcohol problem with Amanda.

"Yeah, I know—it was dumb. We had a keg in the dorm, and it felt so good to stop thinking about . . . him . . . for a few hours, so I thought I'd just come here and keep on going. Then I really got *polluted*." His expression grew reminiscent. "God, do I *hate* barfing."

Thanks for sharing, I thought. Aloud, I *tsk-tsk*ed like a Victorian maiden-aunt.

"It's over, all right? It's *over!* I don't know how I could have been so stupid! I spent one entire night hugging the porcelain babe."

It took half a minute, but I got the metaphor. "Yuck!"

"Yeah. But—when I said that about my legacy, I didn't mean the booze. I meant the *house*."

"This house belongs to *you?*"

He shrugged. "I think so. My mother didn't talk much about him . . . my father . . . Corbin, the jerk, I mean. But when she heard he was dead, she said I was the only one left. He didn't have other children—or any living relatives. So—I figure it's all mine, right? That's why I came here." He paused, then announced, mock-melodramatically, "to claim my heritage." The pickle slice dangling from his thumb and forefinger vanished in one crunchy chomp. He retrieved the second ham-and-cheese and popped the top on another can of soda.

I glanced around, taking in the dingy harvest-gold fiberglass curtains and the worn linoleum floor. Some heritage. "How'd you get in?"

"The window locks suck."

"Mike, don't you realize how worried people have been about you?"

"Really?" He regarded me blankly. "Why?"

"Why? What do you mean, *why?*" The flimsy deli napkin disintegrated under the touch of my moist fingertips. Could this otherwise intelligent young man be as oblivious to the consequences of his disappearance as he seemed? "Nobody knew where you were!"

"I'm an adult now. It's nobody's business where I go." His response was as close to sullen as this nice boy could get.

I bit back my impulsive first comment: *Adult? You kidding?* "Mike . . . ," I said—I really couldn't seem to shake off the maiden-aunt role—"*adults* let their friends and family know where they are. That's basic *adult* consideration."

"I tried to call you a few times—about the exam— but someone else kept answering your phone."

"My daughter," I replied. "And you scared the heck out of her when you kept hanging up."

"Sorry." His pout made him look like a preschooler.

"And your mother is worried sick," I added.

"My mother?" The resentment at being scolded vanished from his eyes. "Someone called my *mother?*"

"Of course. You've been gone over a week. What do you think? The college is going to let you disappear without any inquiry?"

"Ohmigod!" he exclaimed. "I gotta call home. My poor mom'll be out of her tree!"

While Mike was upstairs on the phone, I wandered around the house. The blue recycling bin in the butler's pantry between the kitchen and dining room contained more beer cans, plus a goodly number of red-and-white cans of Campbell's soup. No wonder the poor kid was famished: He'd been living on watered-down soup.

Aside from the kitchen, the house was exactly as Elliot—and the police—had left it, dingy, dusty, and outdated, and no one had turned off the electricity, water, or phone. Who would take care of that, I wondered, if there was no surviving family? A lawyer, perhaps? Maybe the housekeeper? Was Monica still responsible for this house? I remembered Piotrowski saying Monica didn't work for Elliot anymore. But did someone else clean the house once in a while? Elliot wasn't the type to do it himself. Did someone else have a key?

"I think this house is haunted."

I jumped a good three inches as Mike came up behind me in the shadow-filled entry hall. *"Haunted?* Oh, come on, Mike!" But I immediately switched on the light; the few bulbs still working in the ornate chandelier overhead chased the ghostly murk to the corners of the room.

Mike pulled on his purple-and-white Enfield football jacket and hefted his backpack. He must have decided to come back to campus with me; he'd gathered up his

things in a hurry. From a half-zipped backpack pocket
dangled a pair of jockey shorts imprinted with fat pink
pigs. "I mean it," he said. "I've never believed in ghosts,
but I've been staying here, what?—a week now? ten
days?—and there've been . . . *noises*. It freaked me
out." He paused, then snickered self-consciously. "Of
course, I was pretty wasted at the time."

"I bet." But given the circumstances—that a man
had been murdered here—I couldn't completely discount
Mike's story. "You really heard noises?"

"Yeah. Creakings. Rustlings. In the night. It gave me
the cold creepies. And a couple of times I came downstairs in the morning and found . . . and found things
that had . . . had been . . . interfered with during the
night!"

"Interfered with? How?" Now *my* skin crawled with
the cold creepies.

"Come here," he commanded, and led me into Elliot's
study. "You see . . . that . . . thing . . . on the
desk?" He pointed, grimacing. "You see it? With the
dark stain on the edges?"

Reluctantly I looked. The blood-soaked blotter that
Sergeant Schultz had removed from Elliot's desk at my
request had been returned, but the topmost layer of thick
green paper had been ripped off, and the remaining sheets
were pulled awry. "Yeah? I see it."

"Well, that stain? I figured it was . . . his . . . you
know . . . his *blood*. And when I heard the noise in the
night, I was . . . scared to come down. In the morning
this is how it was. I figured he'd come back—"

"Come back?"

"Yeah, you know, to haunt his house." Mike looked
drawn, his young face tight and pale. "*You* know . . .
his restless spirit, searching for revenge. Maybe," he whispered, "maybe trying to get his blood back."

"Jeez, Mike," I blurted. "Didn't you say you'd quit the booze?"

"Yeah, but I read a lot of vampire novels." He grinned at me, that sudden, irrepressible and utterly contagious young-kid grin.

I laughed. "Let's get out of here," I said, and led him back through the entry hall into the dining room. Suddenly, from the kitchen came the resounding slam of the back door.

Mike opened his eyes even wider than I did. The whites were bloodshot clear to the rims.

"Mike," I murmured, "you shut that door behind me, didn't you?"

"Shut it and locked it," he replied, *sotto voce*. We stared at each other, then turned simultaneously toward the kitchen door, as heavy footsteps traversed the floor.

"Who's there?" I called, shakily, motioning to Mike to get behind the heavy butler's-pantry door. He glared at me, his young masculinity offended. "Do it," I hissed. I was still the teacher, and he scampered behind the door.

Monica Cassale burst into the room, a Louisville Slugger baseball bat clutched menacingly in one hand. She stopped dead when she saw me.

"Karen Pelletier!" she exclaimed. "What the fuck're *you* doing here?"

25.

A Word dropped careless on a Page

—EMILY DICKINSON

M E?'' I SPUTTERED. "WHAT AM *I* doing here? What about *you?*"

Monica lowered the bat, and granted me a narrow stare. "I drove by and saw the tire tracks in the driveway."

"Oh."

"No one's supposed to be here, so I thought I'd check it out. I got a little nervous when the tracks went into that old garage, so . . ." She swung the bat loosely, then strode toward me. In her baggy wool Red Sox jacket and thick leather gloves, she looked well prepared to wield her weapon. I took three instinctive steps backward and narrowly missed being clobbered by the dining-room door as Mike slammed it open . . . right into Monica's face.

"*I* told her to put the car in the garage," he said,

stepping into sight. "Give me the bat." He held out his hand.

"Who the fuck are *you?*" was Monica's startled response. Then she took a good look at Mike, paled, and stared, aghast. In the dimly lit dining room, with his assured manner, Mike resembled Elliot so strongly it took even me aback. Monica's remaining challenge—"and what the fuck are you doing here?"—trailed off from something resembling the bark of a patrolling rottweiler to a kittenlike whimper.

"This is my house." Mike's suddenly proprietary attitude added years to his age. "Give me the bat," he repeated. He flexed his fingers, as if commanding it in his direction.

"*Your* house?" Monica floundered. Then her eyes widened, she whispered, "Elliot?" and I realized that the broad-shouldered, tough-talking secretary literally thought she was seeing a ghost. Without hesitation she passed Mike the bat. Then her shaking hand flew to the silver pentagram at her throat, and she clutched the amulet convulsively. "How in hell? . . ."

For a long silent moment in the gloomy chamber, *hell* must have seemed all too terribly real to Monica Cassale. Then the back door crashed open again, and we all jumped. Young Joey materialized in the doorway. He was brandishing a Little League softball bat.

"Leave my mother alone!" Joey's wide-legged stance and belligerent expression mirrored Monica's at her most menacing, but his face with its neat features was an immature replica of Elliot Corbin's. He saw Mike, and his jaw dropped. Mike seemed equally startled, as if he suspected the universe of matter had somehow hiccuped out a clone.

Belatedly, I remembered my manners. "Mike," I interposed. "Meet your little brother Joey. Joey, this is

Mike. You guys are going to want to get to know each other."

"Brother!" Monica's sharp exclamation was a knife hurled straight at Elliot Corbin's cold, dead heart.

As I lay in bed that night, something I'd seen at Elliot's house clamored for my attention, but, stressed by the events of the day, I couldn't identify exactly what it was. The weather was borderline freezing. A slushy rain threatened to turn into an early winter ice storm. Before I'd gotten into bed, I'd made certain I had a flashlight and candles in reach, in the all-too-likely event of a power outage.

I was alone. Amanda had deserted me to spend a couple of precious pre-Christmas vacation days in Lowell with her newly discovered grandmother, aunt, and cousin. Was I pissed? Damn right, I was pissed. The family that had abandoned us in our hour of need twenty years earlier was now luring my daughter away from me—and at Christmas time, too. Amanda had invited me to come to Lowell with her, but I'd pleaded overwork. She'd looked at me with the narrow-eyed, untested sagacity of the twenty-year-old. "Why do I have a feeling you'll *always* be too busy to go to Lowell?" she'd asked. I'd shrugged. I was having a hard enough time with my own feelings; I didn't intend to conjecture about hers.

So, it was now eleven P.M., and I lay in bed, alone except for Emmeline Foster's final journal. I wanted to reread the journal, but tonight the poignant entries didn't engage my attention. I couldn't erase from my mind the encounters with Mike and Monica at Elliot's dilapidated mansion. For one mad moment when Monica had stood there in the doorway hefting her lethal-looking bat, I'd thought the mystery of Elliot Corbin's murder was solved at last—that Monica Cassale, furious over El-

liot's cavalier treatment of her and Joey, had knifed him
to death at his desk after she'd dished up his turkey and
gravy. I'd also half-hysterically concluded that Monica—
Bad Witch Monica—had followed me from my office to
the Corbin house, and that I was fated to die a hideous
death in a Poesque Gothic mansion at the hands of a
villainess straight out of the pages of Stephen King, if not
precisely of Edgar Allan Poe. But Mike's phantasmagoric
appearance and my identification of him as Elliot's son—
and Joey's brother—had melted the murderous Monica
into a puddle of resentful tears. Then I had a gloopy
marshmallow witch to deal with as well as the hung-over
putative heir to the house of Corbin. *The evil that men do*,
I mused, contemplating Elliot's selfish, careless life, *may
long live after them*. I couldn't think of any good that
might have been interred with my departed colleague's
bones.

Sorting everyone out involved brewing strong coffee
for Monica in Elliot's dismal kitchen, then making numerous phone calls from the kitchen phone. Mike's mother
hadn't been home when he called, and for reasons known
only to himself, he hadn't left the poor woman a message.
That task was left to me as Mike got to know his new
brother over a computer game Joey had retrieved from
Monica's Ford. I scratched Mike's mother's phone number on the back of an old Chinese-food menu I'd pulled off
the cluttered little bulletin board by the Princess wall
phone and started making calls: to Earlene, to the dorm
R.A., to Piotrowski, and to Mike's mother, the former
Angela Vitale—now Angela McDonald—arranging for her
to pick up her wayward son at my home. I wasn't about
to let Mike out of my sight until I'd personally given him
over to the custody of his mother. While I made the calls,
Monica huddled at the kitchen table drinking endless
cups of black coffee and muttering to herself about false

spiritual guides and pernicious earth-plane deceivers, and the boys bonded noisily over their game. "Die, you wicked sorcerer!" I heard Joey shriek as I climbed the back stairs to tell them it was time to leave. In the waning light, the house seemed to take on an ageless quality. It was as if those sidelit, brooding balustrades, arches, and cornices had preexisted time and would long outlast it.

Now, I was safe at home in my own cozy bungalow, snug under a down comforter. I let Emmeline Foster's old copybook fall shut, and clicked off the light. It was dark, I was alone, and wet snow slithered down the windowpanes with a monotonous, unrelenting *shush*. My overburdened brain drifted into a sleepy fugue where Poesque images of beautiful revenants and hideous, hissing black felines ushered me into a dreamless abyss.

The flickering light of a long black candle alerted me to a presence in the room. I opened my eyes to see shadows dancing eerily across Harriet Person's face as she loomed over my bed. In a thin white hand with tapered black-painted nails, she gripped a needle-sharp stiletto. The knife was pointed directly at my breast. "Where is it?" she demanded.

I was dreaming. I knew it. This was too bizarre to be real. I closed my eyes again, craving the peaceful, sleepy oblivion that usually constituted my midnight repose.

"Where *is* it?" Harriet's voice persisted.

I forced my eyelids open. Oh, God! Harriet was still there! She was wearing cat-burglar clothing: black jeans, a sleek black jacket and a black knit watch cap. Her winter-pale face was streaked with something dark—she'd obviously seen the same movies I had, the ones where charcoal-smeared crooks break into heavily guarded palaces in search of the Orient's most fabulous treasures. But what was she doing *here?* There was no treasure anywhere in my functional little house.

"Where *is* it?"

I sat up cautiously, clutching the comforter to my chest. "Where is *what?*"

"You know. The notebook."

"Notebook?"

"The Emmeline Foster diary. You were obliging enough to inform me you'd found it again. Now hand it over." Harriet had placed the pewter candlestick on the nightstand, and her face with its beak of a nose was lit flickeringly from below. *Oh, God,* I thought. *Oh, God.* I'd tried to shake someone's tree, and look what had flown out: a vulture!

I'd never before noticed how raptorlike Harriet's features were: narrow skull, long thin nose, practically lipless mouth, heavy brows over dark, fathomless eyes. And that livid white streak peeking out from under the skull-tight cap!

"Get up. Now!" she commanded, motioning with the long knife. She wanted me out of bed. I obliged, swinging my flannel-covered legs from under the blankets with a great show of alacrity.

"I don't have it, Harriet," I said, feeling with my sock-covered feet for the fleecy slippers I'd left beside the bed. "I . . . I took Emmeline Foster's books and papers to the Special Collections librarian. You can find the notebook in the college archives."

Harriet's eyes narrowed. "You are a liar, Karen Pelletier, and an unwitting tool of the patriarchy!"

Huh? Tool of the— "No, Harriet," I pled, abjectly. "I'm a *good* feminist!"

But my colleague wasn't paying attention. From out of some fathomless corner of my bedroom, a black cat leapt and landed on her head with a hellish screech. Harriet, blinded, flailed at the needle-clawed beast. The vicious knife—or was it a pen?—or a knitting needle?—clattered to the floor. I kicked it away and bodyslammed Harriet into the book-lined alcove that had somehow inexplicably appeared behind my bed. She grunted at the impact, smashed into a nine-foot-high library shelf, crumpled to the floor, and lay there, momentarily stunned by the weight of the falling books. Without a second's hesitation, I brained Harriet with a variorum edition of *Paradise Lost*, and followed the concussive attack with an American Library hardcover of *Moby Dick*. A massive edition of the Riverside Shakespeare followed, and then I was flinging book after book at her recumbent body: *The Adventures of Huckleberry Finn, The Portrait of a Lady, Sister Carrie, Rasselas, The Rape of the Lock, The Old Man and the Sea, The Faerie Queene.* When Harriet finally lay immobile under the fatal load of texts, I came to my senses, appalled at the bloody carnage. Or was it . . . *verbiage?* I wasn't certain. The black cat eyed me with its evil yellow glare from the penultimate shelf of this vast, never-before-noticed library of massive tomes hidden away behind my bedroom wall. Ever so deliberately, I retrieved a Penguin paperback edition of *The Scarlet Letter* from the wheelbarrow of books placed so conveniently close to hand, laid my hand on a convenient trowel, slid it into the mortar, and began to brick up the archway, book by book by book.

When I woke, I was exhausted. Early sunlight peeked through my window, illuminating every corner of the small, bare room. Except for the copy of Emmeline Foster's journal tangled in the bedclothes, there wasn't a book in sight.

Evergreen swags and white fairy lights captivated me as I drove through the shopping district that morning on my way to school. Instead of heading right to my office, I parked in the college lot closest to Field Street and strolled toward the stores.

It was seven days and counting to Christmas, and the town of Enfield was in full festal mode. The night's storm had left just enough ice on bare branches to create an otherworldly sparkle above the heads of harried shoppers. As Harriet Person passed me on the street, toting a plastic bag from Smith's Bookshop, I felt a twinge of unease, but couldn't put my finger on its source. I shrugged; it hadn't been a peaceful night and I was too tired to deal with either paranoia or my colleagues. A force field of negative psychic energy was keeping me away from my office and the papers remaining to be graded. I hoped a sixteen-ounce infusion of caffeine would get me in gear for the final push. Just outside Bread and Roses, I ran into Greg Samoorian. Tucked under each of Greg's arms was a miniature Canadian fir—one for each of his twin daughters, I supposed. With his thick beard and burly build, he resembled a youthful Santa Claus.

"Hey, Karen." Greg greeted me by waggling each tree in turn. "Think Jane and Sally will like these?"

"You bet," I replied. "What are they? Three months old now? Deck the boughs with a few strands of those trendy citrus-colored blinking lights, and they'll be totally awed. How about a cup of coffee, Greg? I haven't seen you in . . . millennia."

Dark circles of sleep deprivation shadowed Greg's eyes, but he had the relaxed appearance of a very satisfied man. "I didn't realize being a good daddy would take up every second, but I guess that's what parental leave is for. Yeah, sure, I could use coffee. I could also use a chat with someone who's already cut her eyeteeth."

Sophia was behind the counter at Bread and Roses, serving eggnog and fruitcake to a couple of indeterminate sex who wore green and red jingle bells in their earlobes. The air was redolent with cinnamon. The notion of such rich fare so early in the morning gagged me.

"Karen," Sophia said, as I ordered my breakfast coffee and scone, "have you heard anything from Professor Birdwort?"

"Jane? No. . . ."

"She was in here earlier. She said she tried to find you on campus yesterday afternoon, but you weren't around. I'm really worried about her; she seems a little . . . irrational. She said she wanted to talk to you about the *shoes*. Does that make any sense to you?"

"No." Then I thought about my conversation with Jane at the Christmas party. I'd asked her about the red shoes in her poem. "Well, maybe."

"She said she'd look for you in your office today."

"Great," I said, then hoped I didn't sound sarcastic. But, really, that's all I needed, a conversation with an irrational poet about red shoes. Maybe I should just abandon the office and hide in the library to finish grading my papers.

Greg and I carried our cups to a table by the window. "So," he asked, "what're you doing for Christmas?" For Greg, Christmas involves weeks and weeks of gleeful preparations.

"Just the usual. Me and Amanda at home. What about you?"

"We've got *big* plans. Christmas Eve we're going to my folks' house. It'll be the first Christmas with the babies, and it'll be a mob scene: Everyone wants to see them. Then for Christmas dinner we're going to Greenwich—"

"You are? Things are better with Irena's family, then?"

"We've produced grandchildren. 'Nuff said?"

We both laughed.

"But what about you, Karen? Don't you have family to go to for the holiday? You never talk about them, but you and Amanda must have someone . . ."

"You're right, Greg, I don't talk about them. And I have my reasons." Suddenly the memory of my mother in a flowered apron baking the Christmas *tourtière* flooded me with a longing so unexpected and intense, I could all but smell the meat and spices sizzling in the iron skillet on the old gas-burning stove in the overheated kitchen. What *was* it with these flashbacks? Now they had my eyes watering.

"Karen?" Greg leaned forward and took my hand. "Karen, are you okay?"

"Uh-huh," I replied, swallowing the last of my coffee. "Hey, listen, Greg, I've got to go. I've got work to do."

The library was almost deserted as I placed my little pile—papers, grade book, grade sheets, red pencil—on the dark oak top of my favorite third-floor corner desk. I often came here, to this secluded nook in the American Literature section, when I needed some quiet time alone. No sooner had I set pencil to paper, however, than Jane Birdwort rounded the corner. She wore the regulation New England winter uniform of heavy jacket and heavy boots, and carried her battered leather book bag.

"Monica told me you'd be here," Jane said without preamble. "She said you always hide out in the PS section when you don't want anyone to find you." She must have hustled from Dickinson Hall, she was so out of breath.

"Right," I replied, pointedly, "I do. I'm trying to finish these papers. Grades are due today."

"Oh, *that.*" She waved a slender hand dismissively. "I hear they don't really bother you for the grade sheets until after New Year's."

Her cavalier attitude annoyed me. After all, what did Jane have to grade? A few poems? How hard could that be? And how did you grade a poem anyhow? A-plus for Emily Dickinson and her pre-modernist experimentation with oblique referentiality? C-minus for e. e. cummings and his lack of proper capitalization?

"For regular faculty," I snapped, "the grades have to be in on time." I immediately regretted my irritable retort, but it was too late.

Jane gave me a cool stare. "Oh," she said, "I'm *sorry*. I just thought you wanted to know about Elliot and the red shoes." Her expression was oddly intent. "But if you're too *busy* . . ."

She turned abruptly on the chunky heel of her drab brown boot and huffed away.

"Jane . . ." I called apologetically, but either she didn't hear me, or she was terminally offended, because she didn't look back.

Frederica Whitby's FroshHum final exam was the last essay I graded, and it was barely passable. My red pencil hovered over the bluebook's front cover: D? Or F? I sat in my dim library nook with the pencil gone suddenly limp in my hand, unexpectedly overwhelmed by the cloud of gloom that seemed to have shadowed my life ever since Elliot Corbin's death. Someone had killed my colleague, a man whose reverberant voice had been a neighboring presence—irritating, but undeniably alive and vibrant—in my daily interactions with students. The rituals of academic life seemed inane. D? Or F? F? Or D? What was the point? What difference did it really make? While I pondered Elliot Corbin's murder and the broader mysteries of life, I doodled aimlessly on the cover of Freddie's exam book. Elliot was a lopsided circle in the middle of the page and Jane and Monica appeared as ovals. As an

afterthought I added a third oval: Mike's mother, Angela
Vitale McDonald. Mike and Joey took the form of second-
generation triangles. Elliot's long history of twisted, exploitative relationships with people like Monica and Jane
inscribed itself on the robin's-egg-hued paper as an indeci-
pherable tangle of crimson pencil marks. I moistened the
tip of my pencil with my tongue while I contemplated
further, then added Harriet Person. Harriet was inscribed
as a circle, to the bottom of which I whimsically added a
little penciled cross. Then I sat back and studied my jottings: Poor Elliot. The man seemed to have outraged or
alienated almost every woman he'd ever come across. I
idly doodled another oval and penned in another name.
Then the pencil dropped from my fingers, and I stared in
stunned revelation at the suddenly meaningful scribbles
on the bluebook cover. Heart racing, I scooped up Freddie's ungraded essay, and packed it away with the others
in my canvas book bag. Jane was right; I could get away
with turning my grades in late. What were they going to
do? Shoot me? Right now I wanted lunch and a talk, and
I wanted them both with the sometimes irritating but
always insightful investigator Lieutenant Piotrowski.

The lieutenant was busy until supper time, he told me
over the phone. My disappointment brought me up short.
But, then, who did I think I was, anyhow? A woman who
snaps her fingers and police detectives jump? Piotrowski
would meet me at Amazing Chinese at six P.M., or as soon
thereafter as he could make it. I would have to be satisfied with that.

Back in my office, I pulled out my grade sheet, about
to mark a D as Freddie Whitby's course grade in the one
remaining blank space. What good would it do to give her
an F and fail her in the course? I picked up the black pen
I use for recording grades, and it hovered over the grade

sheet's marking grid. Then I let it drop and sat back in my chair. *Had* I exhausted all avenues of research for the source of Freddie's obviously plagiarized paper? No, I hadn't. I hadn't even found time to check out the university's library. That was something I could do this afternoon, before I met Piotrowski. I sighed with frustration; the last thing I needed was a twenty-minute drive to Amherst, endless circling to find a parking space on the vast campus, a search through the shelves of the PS section, decimated at this time of semester by students writing research papers. It would surely be a futile effort, but I simply couldn't not do it. I couldn't bring myself to pass Freddie Whitby if I hadn't done absolutely everything I could to find the source from which she had cribbed her paper.

I loaded my book bag, making certain Freddie's paper was there, buttoned my long black wool coat, pulled the burgundy knitted cap down over my ears, slipped on my gloves, closed the office door behind me. From Monica's office I could hear little Joey's voice. *"Vroom,"* he vroomed. *"Vrrooomm.* Red Baron at three o'clock!" He was playing games on Monica's computer again.

I stood with my gloved hand on the doorknob. Computer. *Computer? Computer!* The key slid back into the keyhole automatically, with no conscious direction on my part. I dropped the book bag inside the door, peeled off my gloves, and plopped down at the computer without removing my coat. Once online, I called up the net browser, pulled out Freddie's paper one last time and set it on my lap, looked over the suspect language, and keyed in: " *'The Raven' functions as surreal trope for a pre-modernist unknowing"* making certain to include the quotation marks that would tell the Internet I was searching for an identical phrase. Instantly, up popped a familiar paragraph on the screen, part of a long essay:

> *"As a case in point, the infamous bird in Poe's
> 'The Raven' functions as surreal trope for a pre-
> modernist unknowing, as emblem of an existen-
> tialist angst prescient of post-Freudian, post-
> Christian poesis, as enigmatic metaphor for a po-
> etics of the abyss."*

I sat back in my chair, almost weak with victory.
Gotcha, you brat! Gotcha!

After I'd called to inform Earlene of my discovery, written the formal plagiarism report—with documentation—
then submitted my completed grade sheet to the Registrar, I left campus on foot, heading for Jill's. I needed to
see little Eloise and get myself a redeeming fix of sweetness and light. After all, isn't Christmas all about children? As I rounded the corner, a green Volvo pulled up to
the big Victorian house. A short, balding man and a tall,
red-haired woman, both in Abercrombie country wear,
strode eagerly down the walk toward Jill and Eloise, sil-
houetted in the doorway. Kenny stood to one side, as if
he wasn't quite certain of his role in this family scene.
Neither was I.

I walked back to campus, fired up the Jetta, and
spent the afternoon at the mall, Christmas shopping.
Aside from three big cloth dolls for the three infants in
my life, it was a bust. The feeling of accomplishment I'd
had in my office had faded almost immediately: finding
Freddie's source had left me, ultimately, with nothing
but a bad taste in my mouth. And, I had to admit it: I
was lonely. Aside from Amanda, I had only the family I'd
made for myself here in Enfield, and they all seemed to be
preoccupied with families of their own. Added to this
sense of isolation there were, of course, my disquieting
speculations about Elliot's violent death. I was too rest-

less to begin any scholarly projects, too morose to do any holiday shopping, and too nervous to go home.

It was dark when I left the mall at five-thirty. The snow had melted, and the cold sky was choked with gray scrub-mop clouds through which neither moon nor stars could be discerned. A week before Christmas, and it still seemed more like Poe's "drear November" than the holly-jolly festive season.

When I pushed open the big glass door at Amazing Chinese, Piotrowski was already settled in a booth at the rear of the restaurant. His short hair was slicked back, as if he'd just run a damp comb through it, and his gray cable-knit sweater retained ghosts of department-store folds, as if only that afternoon it had resided with its clones on the Extra Large shelf in Filene's men's department. His broad Slavic face with its high cheekbones shone, perhaps from the recent application of a damp towel. In other words, the lieutenant looked as if he'd prepped for this meeting. He looked good.

I, on the other hand, had done nothing to alter my countenance, hair, or black turtleneck and jeans since I'd left home that morning. Plus, I suffered from a hideous case of mall-face, the disfiguring ailment in which everything I'd ever thought even the least bit attractive about myself had been systematically obliterated by hours of relentless fluorescent-light comparison with the flawless features of department-store mannequins and makeup consultants.

I slid into the booth, thanked the lieutenant for meeting me, ordered the restaurant's irresistible General Tso's Chicken, then pulled out Freddie Whitby's exam book with its crimson-scrawled blue cover. "Now, Lieutenant, I may be way off the wall here, but let me tell you what I think."

26.

She dealt her pretty words like Blades—
How glittering they shone——
And every One unbared a Nerve
Or wantoned with a Bone——

AN HOUR LATER I WAS riding shotgun when Piotrowski's Jeep pulled into the long driveway of Elliot Corbin's house, maneuvering the icy ruts as smoothly as if it were on steel tracks. The day before, I'd watched Monica replace the back-door key under a fake rock by the steps, and, by the light of the lieutenant's high-intensity flashlight, I retrieved that key, offering it to him with a flourish. The door opened with its usual grating creak, and I stood once again in Elliot's gloomy kitchen.

As we traversed the house from the kitchen to the study, I switched on one light after another. I knew exactly where I was going and exactly what I was looking for. The folder of graduate-student papers was right where I remembered, in a hanging file in the lower drawer of Elliot's bloodstained desk. I pulled the folder out and leafed through it until I found the essay I sought. It was entitled "Poe in a Dress: Deconstructing Sex and Gender in the Verse of Edgar Allan Poe."

"Eureka!"

"You found it?" Piotrowski peered over my shoulder at the typed essay. Elliot's bold blue comments adorned the first page. "An A-plus, huh? Must be real smart."

"I'm sure of that," I replied. "No one who wasn't smart could write quite so badly." I leafed through the essay to the end, grimacing at the convoluted, jargon-laden prose. At the bottom of the final page was a blue-ink note in Elliot's blocky handwriting: *Cutting-edge work, if seriously underdeveloped. Please see me after class about possibilities that might work to your advantage.*

"You know what's odd about this?" I demanded of Piotrowski.

"The whole thing is odd," he responded, taking the essay by its edges and turning back to the opening page. "I mean, listen, I went to college, ya know. I never got to finish—but I went. But, ya know, I don't understand a word of this thing. What the hell is . . . er . . . 'post-semiotic deconstructive epistemology'?"

I flipped a hand at him. "You're not supposed to understand it. That's the whole point. But, look, all the other grad essays here are photocopies. This is the original. What do you suppose that means?"

"You tell me. You're the expert here. And you're the one who knows Amber Nichols."

Amber Nichols. If I was right in my speculations, the Enfield College adjunct instructor had committed a heinous crime in this disordered study. I glanced around and shuddered when my gaze paused at the soaked-in blood-stain now permanently marring Elliot's oak desk. "Can we go somewhere else? This room gives me the creeps."

"How about the kitchen?"

"That's not a hell of a lot better," I replied, "but at least there won't be blood on the Formica."

Overgrown branches tapped and scratched on the kitchen window panes, as if they were malevolent limbs from the ghastly decaying trees of the House of Usher itself. The lieutenant pulled out a chair and lowered his bulky body into it, then he reached into the pocket of his heavy gray jacket for a tissue to wipe his glasses. "So—what're ya thinking, Doctor?" Along with one of his ubiquitous Kleenex packets, Piotrowski retrieved the two cellophane-wrapped fortune cookies we'd been too rushed to open before we'd left the restaurant. He eyed the cookies contemplatively, then shoved one in my direction and began to strip the wrapper from the other.

I sat across from Piotrowski and rubbed my eyes; it wasn't late, maybe seven-thirty, but it seemed like midnight. Despite my warm jacket, I shivered in the cold. Then I jumped up from the table and twisted the corroded thermostat by the door to the butler's pantry. Something snagged my attention as I glanced around the kitchen, something that was . . . missing. That was it— something that was supposed to be here, something I was used to seeing in this room, was gone, but what?

In the depths of the house, the furnace kicked on with a thunk and a groan. I jumped wildly, and Piotrowski let loose with a seemingly involuntary guffaw. I glared. He was smiling at me, almost . . . affectionately. I instantly assumed my most authoritative pedagogical manner; no cop was going to patronize me and get away with it. "As I said at dinner, Lieutenant, I think you can add Amber Nichols to your list of serious suspects in the murder of Elliot Corbin. And this"—I tapped the cover sheet of the essay manuscript with a tutorial forefinger— "is why." I sat down again, leaned back in my chair, and raised an eyebrow. He met my gaze and waited, lips tight in an effort to suppress a grin. So, it was going to be like that, was it? I picked up the fortune cookie, broke it open, took a careless glance at the fortune, popped the crisp cookie half in my mouth, and crunched down. The words on the narrow paper strip meant nothing. Just another generic Chinese restaurant fortune: *Happiness is close by. Reach out and grab it.*

I let the weightless scrap of paper flutter to the floor, and considered the man across the table. Ragged eyebrows furrowed in a crooked V; his fleeting amusement had been replaced by impatience. Well, okay—maybe I'd made him wait long enough. "You see, Lieutenant, I think Elliot Corbin used this essay of Amber's as the basis for the book on Poe that made him famous. The title of her paper is 'Poe in a Dress.' It's dated four years ago. Elliot's book was called *The Transvestite Poe*. It was published . . . oh, maybe . . . eighteen months ago. Plenty of time for him to rewrite—"

"Transvestite, huh?" Piotrowski interrupted. "Edgar Allan Poe was into that kinky cross-dressing stuff? Or . . . you think Corbin was?"

I grinned at the notion of my goateed colleague in Victoria's Secret panties and bra. "Well, no, not really. This would be more . . . ah, semiotic than sexual."

"Ah." Piotrowski's coffee-brown eyes didn't flicker; you'd have thought he had at least a full semester of grad school in literary theory.

"You see, what I think is that . . . well . . . you know, Elliot's career had been flagging for years—decades, really. Then, suddenly, out of a cloudless empyrean comes this wildly successful little book on Poe. I think when he read Amber's essay, he saw its potential and somehow coerced her into letting him claim her work as his own. I mean, look, he still has the original paper here. Teachers usually give papers back to students after grading them. Maybe he bribed Amber, offered to mentor her in exchange for her ideas—you know, get her on conference panels, introduce her to influential scholars, write letters of recommendation. Or maybe he simply paid her for the paper. Grad students really struggle to get by. A few thousand bucks would go a long way."

"Wouldn't that be plagiarism?"

I thought for a minute. "Legally, I'm not certain if it is—not if it was done with Amber's permission. But in terms of intellectual integrity . . . Well, let's just say if word got out, it would pulverize Elliot's reputation as a scholar."

But Piotrowski had taken my conjectures far beyond their professional ramifications. "Would having your ideas . . . er . . . *taken* be a strong enough motive to kill for?" He looked skeptical.

"Who knows, Lieutenant? I'm just speculating here."

"I dunno, Doctor. You say this woulda happened three, four years ago. So why wait till *now* to kill him? That just doesn't fly as a motive."

It made so much sense to me, I couldn't believe he didn't see it. "Amber was desperate, Piotrowski. She's trying to finish her dissertation and she's also teaching five courses a semester at three different schools just to make ends meet. Can you imagine?"

He shrugged.

"And—let's say, she was struggling with her dissertation, and the job prospects were looking dimmer and dimmer, and there's Elliot, junketing off around the world, getting all the acclaim for *her* ideas. . . . Suddenly she'd had enough."

Piotrowski said nothing.

"You know," I persisted, "either Amber or Elliot could have taken Monica's knife from my office. Think of it this way, Amber gets one more turndown on a job application, she freaks out, goes to his house, threatens him with the knife, or . . ."

"Or, *what*, Doctor?"

"Or . . . maybe . . . Elliot threatened *her*—"

"Ugh." It was an eloquent *ugh;* I glanced at him. "That sounds more like it," he said. "In my opinion, anyhow. Nichols threatens to expose him, humiliate him in front of the other profs, maybe she even tries to blackmail him. He goes into a rage, knows he has to get rid of her, strikes out at her with the knife he'd swiped from your office. They struggle, she gets the knife—she's a tall, strong young woman—and . . . bam, she kills him."

The scene was so vivid, the way he put it, that I shuddered again. "Blackmail . . . You know, Piotrowski, I wouldn't put it past her. How much character could a woman have who would agree to a scam like his in the first place?"

"So, ya think it was all about blackmail?"

I spread my hands: *Who knows?* "As I said, Lieutenant, I'm simply theorizing from the data. I'm not making any accusations."

"Well, Doctor . . ." The lieutenant's words trailed off, and he fell into deep thought, his forefinger tapping his lips. With his broad features and monochrome coloring, Piotrowski wasn't a classically handsome man, but he did have the *nicest* lips. . . .

The house was noisy. Walls creaked in the wind. Barren branches clawed at the windows. Clanks and clunks announced the rising of heat in the old steam pipes. My restless gaze wandered around the kitchen. Something was . . . *missing;* what *was* it? I frowned in concentration. Then a livid bolt of lightning threw the gnarled limbs outside the window into momentary high relief, the power went out, the house was plunged into sudden dark-

ness, and all at once things became weirdly phantasmagoric. Bony fingers clattered against the windows. The
furnace groaned piteously, then died. The image of the
bare kitchen walls lingered like a spectral imprint on my
brain. And in that ghostly afterimage I saw what I hadn't
been able to discern in full light. As Piotrowski groped for
his flashlight, I jumped up from the table. "Where's that
black cat?"

"Huh?" He flicked the switch and swung the beam of
concentrated light toward me.

"Jeez, Lieutenant! Get that thing out of my face!" I
yelped, blinded.

He lowered the high-intensity beam; light puddled at
our feet. "Sorry, Doctor. What d'ya mean, *black cat?*
What black cat? I haven't seen any cats here."

I didn't respond; my attention was elsewhere. "Give
me the light!" I grabbed for the flashlight, and Piotrowski
instinctively stepped back twisting it from my grasp. The
poor man probably thought I'd taken leave of my senses.
The wind howled.

"What the hell?" he exclaimed. The luminous circle
danced crazily around the room like a demented will o'
the wisp. My wrist ached, and I reminded myself: *Never,
ever, ever make sudden, unexplained moves around a cop.*

"Shine that flashlight over there," I ordered. After a
second, he obeyed. The beam illuminated the corroded
thermostat by the door, then a hanging ivy, long dead.
"No! There! There to the left!" The light abruptly picked
out the avocado Princess phone mounted in lonely splen-
dor on the otherwise empty wall.

"It's gone!" I exclaimed triumphantly.

"What's gone?" The light was shining on me again.

I bumped it away from my eyes. "The black cat! You
know, Elliot's bulletin board—the one in the shape of
a cat."

Starkly limned at the perimeter of the flashlight's beam, Piotrowski's broad features were wrinkled in puzzlement. "So?"

Before I could answer, the lieutenant's pager beeped, and, without warning, the lights came back on. For a second or two it seemed like cause and effect, as if some external force had beeped the lights back on. The detective plucked the pager from his belt, squinted at the readout, then grabbed the receiver from the phone. He'd pressed two buttons before he removed the phone from his ear and frowned at it. "Huh?" He jiggled the hook, then listened again. "No dial tone. Must of turned the phone service off."

"It was on yesterday. I made several calls." My thoughts were racing. Where could that bulletin board have gone? I knew it was still hanging there when Monica, Mike, and I had left the house the afternoon before. But the detective was focused on his little gray beeper; he wasn't interested in any pussycat bulletin board.

"Listen, Doctor, I gotta get this page *toot sweet*. I'm gonna call from the car. We done here?" Icy rain suddenly launched an assault on the window panes. It was going to be a hell of a night.

"Give me a couple of minutes, Lieutenant."

"Okay. Ya need me, I'll be in the Jeep."

"Right," I replied absently. A wild gust of frigid wind whipped through the room as Piotrowski headed out the back door to his Jeep. Rain pounded the windows. I searched the cluttered kitchen counters for the memo-and-coupon-laden black cat. Next I drifted toward the butler's pantry. No bulletin board there, either. In the dining room, dust and a residue of black fingerprint powder filmed the disheveled piles of scholarly books with which the table was laden.

I checked the chair seats and the sideboard: no bulletin board. Nothing but scholarly detritus: notepads, printouts, xeroxes. Who would eventually inherit this mess, I wondered? *Would* it be Mike Vitale, as my student himself seemed to think? But probably not—not solely, anyhow. Now little Joey was on the scene, and Monica would make very certain *her* son by Elliot also got his share.

The back door screeched, and the sound of the storm intensified. Piotrowski called from the kitchen, "Doctor, I gotta go take care of something right away. You wanna come, or are you okay here for . . . oh, maybe twenty minutes?"

Sometimes my scholarly training renders me a bit myopic when I'm tracking an intriguing piece of information. "I'll be fine," I yelled back, impulsively. "Don't worry about me. I'm just giving the place one last look-see."

"Ya sure? It might be a half hour."

"A half hour's fine. Go do what you've got to do."

Wind howled, then the back door slammed with its usual ear-splitting bang. I was alone in the house.

In the central hall, I peered into dim corners and scrutinized the wide staircase as far as the first landing, where the steps abruptly turned left and vanished from sight. I'd search the downstairs rooms first, I decided, before I headed up those stairs into the dreary second-floor chambers. I crossed the threshold into Elliot's study. Except for the body of Amber Nichols sprawled across the blood-soaked desk in the far corner, the room looked exactly as it had when Piotrowski and I had riffled the file cabinets earlier.

The body of Amber Nichols sprawled across the blood-soaked desk! I did a quick double take, and a croak uncannily like a raven's caw caught in my throat. I closed my eyes, then opened them. No. This was no stress-induced phantasm. Amber Nichols, her long, honey-hued hair obscuring her face, was sprawled across Elliot Corbin's fatal desk. I bolted across the room to see if there was anything I could do to help her, then croaked again as I touched the body: still warm. Well—of course it was; scarcely twenty minutes ago I'd sat at that very desk and gone through those very cabinets with Piotrowski. One of us would have noticed a corpse.

Piotrowski! Pivoting, I sped to the hallway to summon him, then snapped my mouth shut before the yell could emerge from my throat. Piotrowski wasn't here, of course. He'd gone off on a call. Those were his storm-streaked taillights vanishing down the drive. I was alone in this creepy house with this dead—or dying—woman. Any help for Amber Nichols would have to come from me.

I turned back to the body at the desk, and slid my hand under the mass of Amber's hair to feel for a pulse at the carotid artery. Thank God! She was still alive! But what should I do now? Piotrowski was unreachable, the phone line was disconnected, and Amber didn't seem to be breathing; it was up to me to take some action. Tony had made me take a CPR course once—years ago. Surely I could still remember the moves. First—get Amber out of that chair and onto the floor. A clap of thunder shook the house, as I grabbed the body by the upper arms, and pulled. Just as I tensed my shoulder muscles, anticipating Amber's full weight, the body suddenly gave a powerful twist, leapt up, and grabbed me back. I let out a screech. The next instant, very much alive, Amber Nichols had me in a cruel grasp from behind, with my left arm bent, and a cold, thin blade pressing at my throat.

In my ear I heard her high, pedantic voice. "Sorry, Karen, but you really seem to have backed me into a corner here. I've been trying to get out of this damn house without being seen ever since you came in with that boneheaded cop. I almost made it, but no, you—you just had to keep snooping around."

"My God, Amber! What's going on? What are you doing here?"

I struggled. Her grip on my neck tightened cruelly. "Oh, I was looking for something—and I found it." This close, I could smell alcohol on her breath: gin. "And, no one's going to take it away from me." I was pressed so close to Amber's body, I could feel her tension in my own. Every muscle, mine as well as hers, was as taut as a length of steel cable.

"Believe me, Amber, I don't want anything you have." *I just want to get out of here alive.*

"Oh, you'd want *this.*" She was silent then, as if in deep contemplation. "You know I murdered Elliot, don't you?" Her hand on my arm trembled slightly; the blade of the knife nudged my windpipe. I was so shocked by her admission that I couldn't respond, and Amber continued, in her precise voice, strained now with anxiety. "I don't think it's going to be possible for me to allow you to leave here, Karen."

"Gaaah," I choked. Hail hit the windows and Amber started. Then she shook off her alarm.

"I didn't really mean to kill him. It just . . . happened. But you? You're a different story. Given the circumstances, I don't see that I have a choice. If only you hadn't been so damn persistent. . . ."

"Amber, I don't understand anything about this. Just let me go, and I'll forget I ever—"

"It's too bad I can't. When I heard the cop say he had to leave, I thought for certain you'd go with him, and I'd be home-free. There wouldn't have to be more violence." The growing edge of hysteria in Amber's voice told me this was no cold-blooded killer, but a woman who, for some unknown reason, had been driven beyond endurance. "But you kept on snooping around, and there was no place left to hide, so on the spur of the moment I thought up the dead-woman ruse. It was the only way I could catch you off-balance." She laughed. "Quite Poesque, huh? The dead woman returns to life?" She shuddered, then she intoned, " *'We have put her living in the tomb!'* " A bolt of lightning emphasized her words. I'd never heard Edgar Allan Poe quoted to such devastating effect. Was Amber living in a fantasy world where real people stalked the boards of her own mad psychic drama? Around me, the books on Elliot's haphazardly stacked library shelves seemed to come to life, the shelves themselves to press more closely around me. A devastating clap of thunder followed the lightning.

Get a grip, Pelletier! I admonished myself. *Here's the story: You're trapped in an old house with a madwoman. You're not the first girl to find herself in a situation like this.*

I had to think about this. I had no idea what had driven Amber over the edge—unless, of course, it was the job market. Hmm? An off-the-wall hunch, but what if I went with it? Could Amber's murderous desperation have something to do with her tortured dreams of a job in academe?

I recalled Piotrowski's assessment that desperate people feel compelled to tell their stories. As an English professor, I knew the power of stories. And she *was* talking. Piotrowski had said: *Gotta keep 'em talking; gotta form a bond.* "Amber," I said, and heard the wobble in my voice. "First of all, you're hurting me."

"Sorry." With the automatic surface civility of academic culture, she slackened her hold, but not enough to allow me any real movement. She might have to kill me, but God forbid she should inconvenience me in any other way.

"And I'm really sorry you're feeling so . . . desper—ah, stressed," I amended. "Tell me, Amber, what's going on? I'd like to know. I'd like to understand. What did you find? Why is it so important?"

"You'd like to know, huh?" The irony in her voice was as thick as the clotted prose in the essay I'd just shown Piotrowski.

"Yes," I croaked, a tad desperate myself, "I would. I really, really would." More lightning.

"Ha." The syllable expressed more sarcasm than humor. "Well, all right, then, Karen. You might as well know it all before I . . . before I . . . dispose of you." More thunder.

What fiendish plan was she conceiving? My imagination went into hyper-drive again, projecting horror after horror. *Would she knife me? Garrote me? Bury me alive—brick me up forever in some hideous vault far beneath this hideous house?* Face it: we had read the same books. Whatever abomination I could imagine, Amber could come up with, too.

"You see, Karen, when you were in the kitchen with that cop, I was in the dining room, and I heard you talking. You were wrong, you know." For a second, Amber pressed the blade so hard into my throat, I knew she must have drawn blood. *I'm in such a state of shock,* I thought, *that I can't even feel the slicing of my own throat.*

The furnace clanked. Another crack of thunder sounded, and the old house creaked as the storm shook it. Amber didn't seem to notice. "I didn't kill Elliot because of my essay. He died because of . . . Emmeline's poem."

"What? Emmeline Foster? Elliot had an Emmeline Foster poem?"

"You remember that day everyone was in your office? The day we opened the box?" The pressure on my throat lessened enough for me to nod. I swallowed for the first time in at least a light-year.

"I was leafing through that little notebook of her poems. . . . You remember a little blue leather notebook?"

I nodded again. Very carefully.

"And I came across a poem that . . . that . . . well . . . Let's just say the discovery of *that* particular old poem would make . . . *will* make"—I felt her breath steady with resolution—"my scholarly career. But Elliot was nosing over my shoulder. One look and he knew what I had there. He snatched the notebook out of my hand, and, five minutes later he waltzed out of your office with it. How could I protest? I didn't want to alert anyone else to my find. And then he wouldn't answer my calls. By the time I saw Elliot again, the night of the study-group meeting, he had squirreled that damn poem away somewhere."

Out of the corner of my eye, I spied the object I'd been searching for, the black-cat bulletin board that had gotten me into this deadly confrontation in the first place. Stripped of its notes and coupons, the empty board tilted crazily, half in and half out of the big wire wastebasket next to the desk. "Amber, what's the—?"

She yanked my attention back from the discarded bulletin board. "I told Elliot to give me back the poem or I'd let everyone know I was the one who'd written the Poe monograph. He laughed at me—said I wouldn't dare, said I was pathetic. He said I'd never find the manuscript. Said Poe himself had told him where to hide it. Then he said that I was ineffectual. That I'd never make it in the academic literary profession. That I didn't have the right cutthroat instincts . . ."

With her blade at my throat, I hoped to hell Elliot had been right.

I had some dim fantasy that if I kept Amber talking she wouldn't kill me—at least not until she was done telling her tale. And, face it, I was genuinely curious. "What was it, Amber? What was the poem Elliot hid from you?"

"It was—'The Raven,' " she said. And, as if in some bad melodrama, lightning flashed, thunder crashed, and, once again, the lights went out.

Instantly the knife was so tight against my windpipe I whimpered. "Don't try anything, Karen. I don't need to be able to see you in order to slit your throat."

An errant breeze wafted against my cheek, as if a door or window had suddenly been opened somewhere, and just as swiftly shut. The darkness took on texture and shadow and motion. Death was no longer some far-fetched Poesque fantasy; suddenly it had become all too real. I thought of Amanda, and how I would miss her. Tony flittered through my mind, how we had loved each other. Every minute of my past life became a . . . a treasure chest of memories. I thought of the music I would never hear again, the laughs I would never laugh, the books I would never read. Nevermore would I know love. Nevermore would I feel joy. Nevermore . . . I thought of Lieutenant Piotrowski and his very nice lips. Nevermore would I— *Piotrowski? Whaaa? I'm on the cusp of eternal oblivion; why the hell am I thinking about—*

Then—out of the thick darkness—came an unearthly rushing sound, followed by a solid impact and a grunt. *Umffph!* Amber and I slammed to the floor. I heard something—the knife?—skitter across hardwood, and I twisted swiftly away, out of Amber's grip. I had no idea what supernatural force had just intervened, but whatever it was, at least now Amber was disarmed, and it was a fair fight between us. But before I could scramble to my feet, an imperious voice from somewhere in the darkness of the room intoned: *For chrissake, gimme some light!* Powerful beams instantly glared in from the direction of the French doors, illuminating that beautiful, beautiful, beautiful policeman, Lieutenant Piotrowski. While a uniformed state trooper materialized from out of the same blessed nowhere as the lieutenant, Amber Nichols struggled in Piotrowski's relentless headlock, and the trooper clamped handcuffs on Amber's suddenly impotent hands.

27.

"Ah! what to us where foolish talk or wise?
Were persons, places, books, desires or aims,
Without the deeper sense that underlies,
The sweet encircling thought that neither names?"

—SOPHIE JEWETT

WITHIN FIVE MINUTES, THE ELECTRICITY was back on, and Elliot Corbin's house for the second time in a month was crawling with police. Upon pulling away from the dilapidated mansion on his errand, Lieutenant Piotrowski had become curious about an old Toyota with a UMass parking decal pulled over half a mile down on the otherwise deserted road. He'd called in the plate number, learned that the car belonged to Amber Nichols, and, with my speculations vivid in his mind, summoned help and sped back to the scene. A quick glimpse through the library window had shown him my plight, and he'd immediately organized a silent entry, the dousing of the lights, and the apprehension of Amber Nichols.

I recalled the chill touch of steel against my throat.

As soon as I recovered my breath and stopped trembling, I asked the lieutenant, "Weren't you worried that when you tackled Amber like that, she might actually cut my throat? Accidentally or otherwise?"

Piotrowski bent, casually, and retrieved a heavy, gem-encrusted Victorian letter opener from the corner by the door, where it had halted in its skittering voyage across the floor. "With *this?*"

My eyes widened.

"The only way you'd been in any real danger from this particular deadly instrument, Doctor, was if you'd been a nine-by-twelve heavy-duty manila envelope."

"Oh." I swallowed hard. So I hadn't been on the verge of death after all. "But how'd you know it wasn't a real knife?" I protested. "You were way the hell outside the window."

"An ostentatious thing like this? Any serious knife is sleek and deadly. And, besides, this useless doodad's been sitting on Corbin's desk since the murder. How could I forget it? Nichols must have grabbed it at the last minute, when she realized you were about to discover her presence in the house."

"*Ostentatious?*" Sometimes Piotrowski surprised me.

"Too big a word for you, Doctor? It means—"

"God damn it, Piotrowski, I know what it means!"

Amber Nichols was under guard in the kitchen, waiting for transport to State Police headquarters. A preliminary body search for weapons had found none, but it had located a curious, bedraggled sheet of paper in the inside pocket of Amber's caramel-colored blazer. Piotrowski took one look at the scrap, then slid it across the table toward me. "This what she told you about, Doctor?"

I glanced at it, puzzled: heavy, unlined paper, ripped ragged along one side, with a thumbtack hole in its center

and a phone number and name scrawled across it in pencil: *555-9792——Guido's Pizza*. I looked up at Amber.
Her gaze was fixed on the paper in my hand, and she was
crying, silently. Pensively, I considered her words: *Poe
himself told him where to hide it.* Somewhere in my cranial
case, a chemical transformation occurred and neurons
connected. *Poe. Told. Him. Where. To. Hide. It.* Oh. My.
God. "The Purloined Letter!" As the Minister D. had
done in Poe's story, Elliot had disguised the poem as
something ordinary, then had hidden it in plain sight—on
his black-cat bulletin board! I flipped the tattered scrap
of paper over and stared. There, in Emmeline Foster's
handwriting, was inscribed a brooding sonnet. A verse
about a mysterious black bird that haunts a grieving,
lovelorn poet and drives him irrevocably to madness. A
sonnet whose every quatrain and the final couplet ended
with the word *nevermore!* Was it possible? . . . Could it
be? . . . Had Edgar Allan Poe done some "purloining"
of his own, as Foster had charged in her diary? Had he
shamelessly adapted the poem that made him famous
from the sonnet Emmeline had submitted to him for publication in *Graham's* magazine?

I was just about to put this question to Amber, when
a red-headed trooper announced the arrival of the transport car. Piotrowski explained to Amber where she was
being taken, but she paid no attention to him. She was
staring at me. "I suppose . . . ," she murmured patheti-
cally, "I suppose this means that now I'll *never* find a job
in the profession. . . ."

In the wee hours, after having interrogated Amber and
taken, in excruciating detail, my statement about her
confession to me, Lieutenant Piotrowski drove me back
to Enfield through a rain-washed night and treated me to
breakfast at the Blue Dolphin, the only place open at

that hour of the morning. Above the counter, the luminous hands of a large round clock encircled in a slim tube
of blue neon read 4:23, and I could swear the counterman
groaned when he saw us walk in. He must have expected
at least another hour of dead time in which to read his
copy of *The Political Unconscious* before he had to fire up
the grill.

"I don't get it," the lieutenant said, having inhaled
half a carafe of coffee. "Who actually did write 'The
Raven'?"

I retrieved the photocopy of Emmeline Foster's sonnet that Piotrowski had allowed me to make. My mind
was still reeling: Mere hours ago I'd thought for certain I
was nose to nose with the Grim Reaper; in the interests of
her own professional advancement, one of my colleagues
had callously murdered another; the classic poem I'd
been teaching for years as Edgar Allan Poe's actually had
a far more complicated authorship.

With its address to a raven, and its repeated refrain
of "Nevermore," Emmeline Foster's modest little sonnet
was obviously the direct source of Poe's "Raven," but it
was nothing at all *like* the troubled poet's extravagant,
hysterical poem.

"They both did, Lieutenant," I replied, and words
I'd read the day I'd gone through Elliot Corbin's letters
came back to mind. *There can be no such phenomenon as
"plagiarism,"* Elliot had written to a well-known colleague. *All texts circulate within a prior textual matrix . . .
who can "own" ideas or hold "property" in language?*

I glanced down at the verses in my hand.

THE BIRD OF THE DREAM

One midnight dreary at my windowpane,
I sobbed, "Ah, love," and did the night implore,

"Bring back lost heart whose life I pled in vain."
But darkness fluttered, croaking,
   "Nevermore". . . . .

"Maybe she didn't own the concept, Lieutenant, but I do think Emmeline Foster ought to have gotten credit for her contribution to Poe's poem."

"Well," Piotrowski ladled sugar generously into his coffee. "I got a feeling you'll be making sure that happens."

"Yeah, I guess. . . ." I was too weary even to think about it.

"Ms. Nichols admitted to everything, ya know. You were right that she'd sold him her essay, and I was right that she tried to blackmail him with it. They had a . . . disagreement, right there in his office—"

"So that's what I heard."

"But she didn't kill him because of that. Like she told you, it was over that poem you got there." He tapped the photocopy with his forefinger. "She called it a 'source poem,' figured it was gonna make her real rich. She went to see Corbin, and they got into another altercation. She'd swiped Ms. Cassale's knife from your office, and she threatened him with it, trying to make him give the poem back. He laughed and taunted her. Told her finding the poem was going to be the 'capstone of his illustrious career.' So she stabbed him. She was so out of control with rage she hardly knew what she was doing. It's my feeling it was manslaughter more than homicide. Thank God I don't have to make that decision! But she was fully cognizant what she was doing when she planted that knife at Ms. Birdwort's house. No question that was premeditated. Professor Person had told her about the Corbin-Birdwort marriage—seemed to think it was a big joke—so Nichols figured that Ms. Birdwort was the perfect person to throw suspicion on. And she knew what she was up to when she kept coming back to Corbin's and prowling around during the night looking for that poem."

"Mike *told* me he heard things in the night. He thought the house was haunted."

"Well, it was," the lieutenant said. "By the worst kind of ghost—a real murderer."

"But did Amber say anything about those journals of Emmeline Foster's? I assume she's the one who took them."

"I asked her about that. She said they were useless; they didn't say a thing about 'The Raven.' So . . ." He hesitated, then plunged ahead. "So, she burned them."

"Arrggh," I shrieked.

The counterman looked at me askance as he delivered eggs over and hash browns.

"I knew you'd feel that way," Piotrowski said, shaking Tabasco sauce over his eggs. "But at least you got *one* of them. . . ."

We ate in silence. Amber's confession had brought me no sense of relief or closure—and, now, the loss of the journals. I was enveloped in a fog of depression and exhaustion, but Piotrowski had the contented air of a man who knows he's done a good, professional, job, and he wanted to mull it all over.

"Ya know, it was the oddest thing, Doctor. I knew she'd break in Corbin's kitchen when she looked over at you and asked if you thought she'd ever find a job in the profession. You just stood there like you do, with that look of yours, and it was all over for her. This is one a the weirdest stories I ever heard. She offed that man because she wanted to be an English professor. Tell me, Doctor, what's so great about your profession that makes people go through such ordeals? I mean—you did it."

"I didn't *kill* anybody, Piotrowski!"

"No, a'course not, but all those years in grad school, and all those, what d'ya call 'em, adjunct jobs, and I know you get paid a hell of a lot less than you're worth, with all your education—a lot less than I do, ferrinstance. I just don't understand the appeal."

"Oh, it's kind of a vocation," I said vaguely. But I was still feeling Amber's blade prick my skin. "What did she intend to *do* with me? She'd convinced me she had a knife, but she couldn't have fooled me forever. Eventually I would have figured it out and gotten away from her."

"I dunno, Doctor. I don't think she thought it through that far."

Suddenly, I wanted—needed—a piece of chocolate cake—dark, dense, moist, chocolate cake, with thick chocolate icing.

"You eat that stuff for *breakfast?*" Piotrowski asked.

"It's therapy," I responded, minutes later, picking the final crumbs off the plate with a damp forefinger. I hadn't forgotten the lieutenant's earlier remark. "*What* look of mine?" I frowned at him. "What are you talking about—*that look of yours?*"

He chuckled. "That look you get. A certain kinda look I don't see on too many people. Like you're thinking in a complicated kind of way . . . intelligence that hasn't had all the human feeling drained out of it."

"Give me a break, Lieutenant!"

"No, I mean it. It's kind of . . . oh, I dunno . . . kinda *poetic.*"

"Jeez!" My face was hot.

"It's not just like *head* knowledge. It's got depth to it, and contradictions, and . . . and . . . *compassion.*"

I couldn't take any more. "I saw your face when she made that pathetic statement, Piotrowski. You were no deadpan."

"Yeah, but, then . . . I don't have a Ph.D."

"You make the Ph.D. sound like some sort of a developmental handicap, for Godsake!"

"Yeah? Well . . . ," he said, and shook his head as he poured another cup of coffee.

The sun was rising as we left the diner. As we turned onto Route 138, I asked Piotrowski if Sophia Warzek had ever actually approached him with an alibi for Jane, as she'd told me she intended to.

"Alibi?" He laughed. "Is *that* what that was? More like an ali-*pie*, if ya ask me!"

"What?"

"Yeah, Sophie called me. Sweet kid! She had this theory that Ms. Birdwort couldna done the murder that day because she was 'in the middle of writing a poem and was . . . *too abstracted,*' Ms. Warzek said, to stab anyone. She'd stopped by on her way home from baking Thanksgiving morning at Bread and Roses to surprise Ms. Birdwort with a holiday pumpkin pie, and Ms. Birdwort didn't even say *thank you,* she was so out of it. Ya ask me, sounds more like the professor was under the influence of some illicit substance—"

"The Muse isn't illicit, Lieutenant. At least not as far as I know. At least not *yet.*"

"Yeah, you're right. But there's stuff I know. . . ." He let it trail off. I wouldn't be surprised if Jane Birdwort wasn't in for some further visits from our boys in blue.

My car was still in the college lot. Lights flickered on in houses as we drove the few blocks toward town to pick it up. We turned past the Corbin house, a flight of crows started from a bare-branched oak tree, and a few tumblers turned in my memory.

"You know, Lieutenant, for about a month now, every time I'd drop in at my office before class, I'd have this feeling, like someone was watching me. Or in the library. Or the coffee shop. Sometimes even downtown. Just an odd sensation that someone's eyes were on me. And it just hit me, do you think maybe it was Amber?"

The policeman started to laugh, rich, deep, very amused chuckles. I turned and stared at him. "Oh, that," he said, between chortles. "Dr. Pelletier, I think you got yourself an admirer. Pudgy kid? Glasses? Follows you everywhere?"

"Tom Lundgren! Oh, no!" I hid my face in my hands.

Piotrowski signaled the turn onto the Enfield campus. "You know . . ." He cleared his throat. "You know, seriously . . . you should be more careful. Good-looking woman like you on her own . . ." He pulled his Jeep in next to the Jetta, and gazed at me consideringly. I was suddenly acutely aware of the depths of . . . what? . . . intelligence? feeling? knowledge? . . . layered in his brown eyes. Consciousness! That's what it was. A consciousness so deep a woman could . . . could . . . A momentary chill caused the fine hair on my arms to shiver. What the hell? I tore my gaze away from Piotrowski's speculative brown eyes. His intense expression most likely signified nothing more than a professional contemplation of public-safety policy.

"Don't worry about me, Lieutenant. I know how to take care of myself."

"I know ya do. It's just that you shouldn't always hafta."

I had the door open and one foot out of the Jeep, when he reached over and squeezed my arm gently. "Take it easy, Dr. Pelletier . . . Karen."

Karen! He called me *Karen!* This was the most personal the big cop had ever gotten with me. I was so shocked, I nearly fell out of the car.

"Be seeing ya," he said. He had such a nice smile.

He waited until I had the Jetta warmed up and followed me as far as the campus gate. I turned right, and Piotrowski turned left, toward wherever it was he was headed next. As usual, I hadn't bothered to ask, but all at once I was extremely curious.

Epilogue

Life is real—life is earnest—
And the grave is not its goal:

—HENRY WADSWORTH LONGFELLOW

A N UNFAMILIAR CAR WAS PARKED next to Amanda's Rabbit in my driveway, a brown Dodge Dart of some unknown vintage. *Amanda!* My God! I hadn't expected her, and she must have been worried sick when she didn't find me at home. But whose was the second car? I slammed the Jetta's door. In the early-morning silence, the sound was as startling as a shotgun's blast. The house looked serene enough, the curtains closed against the early light, smoke spiraling from the woodstove's chimney.

Suddenly the front door banged open and two Amandas stood grinning in the door frame. *Two Amandas!* Doppelgangers once again invaded my all-too-receptive imagination. Then my daughter's well-known voice caroled out, "Oh, Mom, I'm so glad to see you. Where've you been? I brought Courtney home with me." One Amanda ran up and flung her arms around me. The other Amanda smiled at me, shyly. "You know, Courtney?" my Amanda continued. "My cousin? Your niece? And, look— look who else is here!" The girls moved aside to reveal the dumpy form of an elderly-looking woman in a yellow cotton bathrobe. I stopped dead in my tracks, struck mute by the sight of this long-unseen but indelibly familiar figure. Then I took the deepest breath of which I was capable. "M . . . M . . . ?" I stuttered. "Mommy? Is that you?"

Hours later, we sat around the kitchen table with the doughnuts Amanda had insisted on making. I told the story of the "Raven" murder—or murders, if you count Emmeline Foster. My mother gave me a diffident look. It had taken Amanda three days to persuade her to come to Greenfield, and she was still skittish. So was I. "Karen . . . Karen, what I don't understand is—who killed Emmeline Foster?"

I smiled at her tentatively; I didn't remember her being so small. "Who do *you* think did it?"

"It was the stepfather." The chunk of doughnut crumpled between her fingers, and she hastily swept the crumbs into a neat pile and covered them with her napkin.

Impulsively I reached out and squeezed her hand. Then I turned to my newfound niece. She didn't look so *very* much like Amanda, after all. Just the thick brown hair, the slim, rangy body, and—well, yes, the long thin nose, and delicate mouth. Her eyes were different, though—blue to Amanda's hazel. No one in the world has Amanda's beautiful eyes. "Courtney, who do you think did it?"

"It was definitely Edgar Allan Poe. He sounds like such a loser." She had Amanda's clear, precise voice.

"And you, Amanda?"

My daughter frowned as she fished three doughnuts from the bubbling oil in the cast-iron Dutch oven. With her metal tongs she dropped each into a sugar-filled paper bag. "It was suicide. Had to be. Emmeline's poetry was all she lived for, and it had been stolen from her." Amanda shook the bag, then held it open in front of me. "What do you think, Mom? You're the literary detective here. In your informed opinion, who do you think murdered the poet Emmeline Foster?"

I raised my shoulders, spread my hands. "Who knows?" I replied. I peered in the bag and plucked out the largest doughnut. "It's all a mystery to me."

Afterword

The historical circumstances reflected in the journals of the fictional Emmeline Foster are based on research into the New York City literary milieu of the 1840's. Although the poet Emmeline Foster herself exists only in the pages of this novel, other writers mentioned in her journal—Frances Sargent Osgood, Horace Greeley, Anne Lynch—actually lived, and socialized at the same Manhattan literary salons Emmeline attends. Edgar Allan Poe also frequented these salon gatherings, and, except for his dealings with the imaginary Emmeline, all other tales of his life recounted in *The Raven and the Nightingale* are based on sound biographical and historical evidence—even a preoccupation with the issue of plagiarism. I have taken the title of Emmeline Foster's poem "The Bird of the Dream" from a letter published in the *Broadway Journal* when Poe was editor of that publication. According to Kenneth Silverman, author of *Edgar A. Poe: Mournful and Never-ending Remembrance*, an anonymous letter published on 1 March, 1845, explicitly raised the issue of "The Raven" and plagiarism, comparing:

> "The Raven" with an anonymous poem called "The Bird of the Dream." [The writer] pointed out fifteen distinct "identities," such as the existence in both poems of a broken-hearted lover

and of a bird at the poet's window. He made it
clear at the same time that no "imitation" by
Poe was involved. (251)

Silverman goes on to suggest that "the great likelihood"
is that Poe himself, with the aid of a friend, concocted the
letter in the first place, thus simultaneously raising the
possibility of plagiarism and denying that it ever took
place. One can only speculate why Poe might have felt
such a ploy was necessary. The verse from Emmeline Foster's "The Bird of the Dream" is my own creation; it is
not based on the *Broadway Journal* poem.

The chapter epigraphs in *The Raven and the Nightingale* are taken from the work of eighteenth- and nineteenth-century American poets.

About the Author

JOANNE DOBSON, an associate professor of English at Fordham University, lives in Westchester, New York. She is the author of two previous Karen Pelletier mysteries, Agatha Award–nominated *Quieter than Sleep*, and *The Northbury Papers*, and she has just completed her fourth, *Cold & Pure & Very Dead*.

If you enjoyed Joanne Dobson's
The Raven and the Nightingale, you
won't want to miss any of her academic
mysteries featuring Professor Karen
Pelletier. Look for *Quieter than Sleep*
and *The Northbury Papers* at your
favorite bookseller's.

And you won't want to miss
Joanne Dobson's newest hardcover,
Cold & Pure & Very Dead, coming
from Doubleday in October 2000.